ECHOES FROM THE EDGE

ETERNITY'S EDGE

Other books by Bryan Davis:

Echoes from the Edge series:
Beyond the Reflection's Edge (Book One)

Dragons in Our Midst® series:
Raising Dragons
The Candlestone
Circles of Seven
Tears of a Dragon

Oracles of Fire® series:
Eye of the Oracle
Enoch's Ghost

Pronunciation Guide:
Mictar—Mis-tawr'
Patar—Paw-tar'

ECHOES FROM THE EDGE

ETERNITY'S EDGE

BRYAN DAVIS

ZONDERVAN®

ZONDERVAN.com/
AUTHORTRACKER
follow your favorite authors

We want to hear from you. Please send your comments about this book to us in care of zreview@zondervan.com. Thank you.

Eternity's Edge
Copyright © 2008 by Bryan Davis

Requests for information should be addressed to:

Zondervan, *Grand Rapids, Michigan* 49530

Library of Congress Cataloging-in-Publication Data: Applied for
ISBN 978-0-310-71555-9

Internet addresses (websites, blogs, etc.) and telephone numbers printed in this book are offered as a resource to you. These are not intended in any way to be or imply an endorsement on the part of Zondervan, nor do we vouch for the content of these sites and numbers for the life of this book.

All rights reserved. No part of this publication may be reproduced, stored in a retrieval system, or transmitted in any form or by any means — electronic, mechanical, photocopy, recording, or any other — except for brief quotations in printed reviews, without the prior permission of the publisher.

"Dragons in our Midst" and "Oracles of Fire" are registered trademarks of AMG Publishers.

Interior design by Christine Orejuela-Winkelman

Art direction by Michelle Lenger

Printed in the United States of America

08 09 10 11 12 • 23 22 21 20 19 18 17 16 15 14 13 12 11 10 9 8 7 6 5 4 3 2 1

ECHOES FROM THE EDGE

ETERNITY'S EDGE

1
A STALKER

Nathan strode down the hospital hallway, his brain focused on a single thought—finding his parents. Once mutilated and dead in matching coffins, now they were alive. He had touched his father's chain-bound arms through the dimensional mirror and felt his loving strength. He had heard his mother's voice and once again bathed in the majesty of her matchless violin.

Yet, the beautiful duet they had played at the funeral had once again become a solo. He had failed. The dimensional portal collapsed, and there was no word from Earth Blue as to whether or not his parents might still be in the bedroom where they had sought rescue from their captivity.

He sat down on a coffee-stained sofa in the waiting area and clenched his fist. His parents were real. They were alive. And now he had to move heaven and earth, maybe even three earths, to find them.

Staring into the hall, he mentally reentered Kelly's room and saw her lying on the bed, beaten and bruised from their ordeal, her shoulder lacerated and her eyes half blind. The words he spoke to her just moments ago came back to him. *We'll search for them together.* But how could she help? With all the dangers ahead, how could a blinded, wounded girl help him find his parents?

A sharp, matronly voice shook him from his meditative trance. "Ah! There you are!"

Nathan shot to his feet. Clara marched toward him, her heels clacking on the tile floor as she pushed back her wind-blown gray hair. Walking stride for stride next to the tall lady, Dr. Gordon stared at a cell phone, his face as grim as ever.

As they entered the waiting area, Nathan nodded toward the hallway. "Tony's with Kelly. Thought I'd let them have some daddy-daughter time."

While Dr. Gordon punched his cell phone keys, apparently typing out a text message, Clara lowered her voice. "Dr. Gordon received a cryptic email from Simon Blue. Solomon and Francesca aren't there in your Earth Blue bedroom, but apparently some-thing very unusual is going on, and we're trying to get details."

"So that's our next destination," Nathan said.

"Yes. We have already alerted my counterpart on Earth Blue. She and Daryl will be ready to pick you up at the observatory and take you to Kelly Blue's house."

"Good. Even if Mom and Dad aren't there, it's the logical place to start looking for them."

"Are you going to break the news to Kelly?"

"I guess I'll have to. She's in no shape to come with me, but convincing her of that won't be easy."

Dr. Gordon closed his phone and slid it into his pocket. Turning toward Nathan, he spoke in his usual formal manner. "There are no further details available. We should proceed to the observatory at once. With Mictar's associates gone, there should be no trouble gaining access. I have dismissed the guards, with the exception of one whom I trust, so we should not run into any unexpected company."

"Okay," Nathan said. "Let me talk to Kelly. I'll be right back."

As he walked down the hall, he wondered about Dr. Gordon's words. It was true that Mictar's goons were gone, giving him free access to the dimensional transport mirror on the observatory ceiling, but what about Mictar himself? He had disappeared into the mirror with Jack riding on top of him, but where could he have gone? And what could have become of Jack? Even if he escaped, he would be lost, especially after his recent brush with death in the Earth Yellow airline disaster and his subsequent discovery of his own burial site. Since Jack's dimension lagged Earth Red's by about thirty years, he would feel like a time-traveling visitor from the past.

A man in scrubs caught up with and passed Nathan, pushing a lab tray stuffed with glass bottles and tubes. With lanky pale arms protruding from his short green sleeves, he kept his head low as he hurried. He slowed down in front of Kelly's door, but when it opened, he resumed his pace and turned into a side corridor, his head still low.

Nathan could barely breathe. Could that have been Mictar? Would he be bold enough to come into the hospital? And why would he be so persistent in trying to get to Kelly? What value was she to him?

As Nathan neared the room, Tony came out. Bending his tall frame, he released the latch gently and walked away on tiptoes. When he spied Nathan, he jerked up and smiled, his booming voice contradicting his earlier attempts to be quiet. "Hey! What brings you back so soon?"

Nathan kept his eyes on the side hallway. No sign of the technician. "Some news for Kelly. I have to head back to the scene of the crime."

Tony shook his finger. "Better not. She was so tired, she fell asleep in mid-bite. And if she's too tired for pizza, she's too tired for company."

"You let her eat it? She's only supposed to have—"

"Hey," Tony said, pointing at himself, "I didn't know about her diet until after I brought the pizza. But if you want to tell her what she should and shouldn't eat, be my guest."

"I know what you mean." Nathan glanced between the

door and the other hallway. "Okay if I sneak in and leave her a note?"

He grinned, his eyes bugging out even more than usual. "Just don't get any ideas, Romeo."

Nathan returned the smile, though he chaffed at the comment. Tony was joking, of course, but sometimes he blurted out the dumbest things. He wouldn't dream of touching her inappropriately, not in a million years. His father had drilled that into his head a long time ago—never intimately touch a woman who is not your wife.

"I'll behave myself." He reached for the knob and nodded toward the other hallway. "Mind checking something out for me? I saw someone suspicious, a guy in scrubs, head that way. It looked like he was going into Kelly's room, but when you came out, he took off."

"You got it." Tony crept toward the other hall, pointing. "That way?"

"Yeah. Just a few seconds ago."

"I'm on it." When he reached the corridor, he looked back, his muscular arms flexing. "Time to take out the trash."

Nathan opened the door a crack, eased in, and closed it behind him. Walking slowly as his eyes adjusted, he quietly drew the partitioning curtain to the side and focused on Kelly's head resting on a pillow, her shoulder-length brown hair splashed across the white linen. He stopped at her bedside, unable to draw his stare away from her lovely face.

Black scorch marks on her brow and cheeks and a thick bandage on her shoulder bore witness to her recent battle with Mictar. Her closed lids concealed wounded eyes, maybe the worst of all her injuries, the result of Mictar's efforts to burn through to her brain and steal her life. So far, no corrective lenses seemed to help at all. If anything, they made her vision worse. Still, even in such a battle-torn condition, she was beautiful to behold, a true warrior wrapped in the sleeping shell of a petite, yet athletic, young lady.

He searched her side table for a pen and paper. A portable radio next to a flower vase played soft music, a piano concerto—elegant, but unfamiliar. He spotted a pen and pad and pushed the radio out of the way, but it knocked against the vase, making a clinking noise. He cringed and swiveled toward Kelly.

Her chest heaved. Her hands clenched the side rails. She scanned the room with glassy eyes, panting as she cried out. "Who's there?"

Nathan grasped her wrist. "It's just me," he said softly.

Her eyes locked on his, wide and terrified. "Mictar is here!"

Making a shushing sound, he lowered the bed rail and pried her fingers loose. "You were just dreaming."

"No!" She wagged her head hard. "I saw him! In the hospital!"

"Do you know where?"

She turned her head slowly toward the door. As a shaft of light split the darkness, her voice lowered to a whisper. "He's here."

A shadowy form stretched an arm into the room, then a body, movement so painstakingly deliberate, the intruder obviously didn't want anyone to hear him.

Nathan grabbed the vase and dumped the flowers into a basin. Wielding it like a club, he crept toward the door, glancing between Kelly and the emerging figure. She yanked out her IV tube, swung her bare legs to the side, and dropped to the floor, blood dripping behind her.

The shadow, now fully in the room, halted. Nathan clenched his teeth. Kelly scooted to his side, tying her hospital gown closed in the back.

As the door swung shut, darkening the room, a low voice emanated from the black figure. "If it is a fight you seek, son of

Solomon, I am more than capable of delivering it. In my current form, a glass vase will be a pitifully inadequate weapon. I suggest you give me what I want, and I will leave you in peace."

Nathan tightened his grip on the vase. Should he ask what he wanted? Even replying to a simple remark seemed like giving in. Mictar was baiting him, and he didn't want to bite. "Just get out, Mictar. It's two against one. It only took a violin upside your head to beat you before, and you couldn't even take on Jack by yourself at the funeral."

Mictar's voice rose in a mock lament. "Alas! Poor Jack. He was a formidable foe ... may he rest in peace." His tone lowered to a growl. "You can't take me by surprise this time, you fool. Your base use of that instrument proves that you have no respect for its true power. And now you have neither a violin nor a Quattro mirror to provide a coward's escape."

Nathan peered at Mictar's glowing eyes. The scarlet beacons seemed powerful and filled with malice. Yet, if he had as much power as he boasted, why hadn't he attacked? Nathan set his feet and lifted the vase higher. Maybe it would be okay to find out what this demon wanted. "Why are you here?"

"To finish my meal. I have enough energy left to fight for what I want, but I would prefer not to expend it. If you will turn the girl over to me freely, I will consume what I merely tasted at the funeral and be on my way. In exchange, I will leave you with two precious gifts. I will tell you how to find your parents, and I will relieve you of that handicapped little harlot."

Nathan flinched. Kelly gasped and backed away a step.

"Ah, yes," Mictar continued, his dark shape slowly expanding. "That word is profane in your ears, yet I wager that it rings true in your mind. Kelly Clark is not the paragon of virtue your father would want for your bride. She clings to you like a leech, because she is soiled by—"

"Just shut up!" Nathan shouted. "I don't want to hear it!"

The humanlike shadow swelled to twice its original size.

"Oh, yes, you do. You want to know every lurid detail. She is your dark shadow, and you will never find your parents while you entertain a harlot at your side."

"No!" Nathan slung the vase at Mictar. When it came within inches of his dark head, it stopped in midair. Nathan tried to reach for Kelly, but his arm locked in place. His head wouldn't even swivel. Everything in the room had frozen ... except for Mictar.

The shadow continued to grow. His dark hands drew closer and closer. "I saved the last bit of my energy," Mictar said, "to perform one of my brother's favorite tricks, motor suspension of everything within my sight. Now I will take yours and the harlot's eyes, and I will need no more to fill Lucifer's engine."

A knock sounded at the door. "Nathan? Is everything okay?"

Tony's voice! Nathan tried to answer, but his jaw wouldn't move. His tongue cleaved to the roof of his mouth. A dark hand wrapped around his neck and clamped down, throttling his windpipe.

Another knock sounded, louder this time. "Nathan, the nurse says it's time for vitals."

Another hand draped his face. Sparks of electricity shot out, stinging his eyes.

"I'm coming in!" Light flashed around Mictar's hand, but Nathan still couldn't budge. Pain jolted his senses. His legs shook wildly as if he had been lifted off the floor and rattled like a baby's toy.

Suddenly, the darkness flew away. Mictar's body, a black human form with no face or clothes, zoomed past the nurse and crashed against the back wall. "Stay right there," Tony shouted, "or I'll introduce your face to the other wall."

Like a streaking shadow, Mictar pounced on Tony, wrenched his arm behind him until it snapped, and slung him against the wall. Tony staggered for a moment, then slumped to the floor, dazed.

Mictar grabbed the nurse from behind. As she kicked and screamed, he laid a fingerless hand over her eyes and pressed down. Sparks flew, and Mictar's body lightened to a dark gray, details tracing across his gaunt pale face and bony hands. His white hair materialized, slick and tied back in a ponytail. The lines of a silk shirt and denim trousers etched across the edges of his frame, completing the full-body portrait of the evil stalker.

Nathan tried to help, but his feet seemed stuck in clay. He slid one ahead, but the other stayed planted. Kelly hobbled toward the melee and helped her father to his feet. While she cradled his broken arm, Mictar's body continued to clarify. The nurse sagged in his clutches, but he held on, light still pouring into his body from hers.

His legs finally loosening, Nathan stumbled ahead and thrust his arms forward. He rammed into Mictar, but, as if repelled by a force field, he bounced back and slammed against the floor. New jolts sizzled across his skin, painful, but short-lived. He looked up at the stalker's pulsing form, now complete and radiant.

Mictar dropped the nurse into a heap of limp arms and legs and kicked her body to the side. Tony crouched as if ready to pounce again, but his movements had slowed. Wincing, he picked up an IV stand and drew it back, ready to strike.

Mictar tilted his head up and opened his mouth, but instead of speaking, he began to sing. His voice, a brilliant tenor, grew in volume, crooning a single note that seemed to thicken the air.

Dropping the IV stand, Tony fell to his knees. Kelly stumbled back and pressed her body against the wall. A vase exploded, sending sharp bits of glass flying, and a long crack etched its way from one corner of the outer window to the other.

Fighting the piercing agony, Nathan rolled up to his knees and climbed to his feet, but the latest shock had stiffened his legs, and the noise seemed to be cracking his bones in half. He could barely move at all.

Mictar took a breath and sang again. This time, he belted out what seemed to be a tune, but it carried no real melody, just a hodgepodge of unrelated notes that further thickened the air. Red mist formed along the floor, an inch deep and swirling. As Mictar sang on, the fog rose to Nathan's shins, churning like a cauldron of blood. With the door partially open, the dense mist poured out, but it wasn't enough to keep the flood from rising.

A security guard yanked the door wide open. With a pistol drawn, he waded into the knee-high wall of red. Dr. Gordon and Clara followed, but when the sonic waves blasted across their bodies, the guard dropped his gun, and all three covered their ears, their faces wrinkling in pain.

The window shattered. Mist crawled up the wall and streamed through the jagged opening. The floor trembled. Cracking sounds popped all around. The entire room seemed to spin in a slow rotation, like the beginning of a carousel ride.

"Nathan!" Dr. Gordon shouted. "He's creating a dimensional hole! He'll take us all to his domain!"

"How can he? There's no mirror!"

"He can stretch one of the wounds that already exists."

The spin accelerated, drawing Nathan toward the window. "How do we stop him? He's electrified!"

Dr. Gordon staggered toward Nathan, fighting the centrifugal force, but he managed only two steps. "Neutralize his song!"

Nathan leaned toward the center of the room but kept sliding away. "I don't have my violin!"

The outer wall collapsed. Fog rolled out and tumbled into the expanse, six stories above the ground. The floor buckled and pitched, knocking everyone to their seats. While Nathan pushed to keep from being spun out of the room, the nurse's body slid across the tile and plunged over the edge with the river of red mist.

Too weak to fight, Nathan slipped toward the precipice. He latched on to the partitioning curtain and hung on with all his strength.

Mictar took a quick breath and sang on.

The bed's side table bumped against Nathan's body. The pen fell, bounced off his shoulder, and disappeared in the fog. Still hanging on to the curtain with one hand, he looked up at the wobbling table. The radio! With his free hand, he shook the supporting leg and caught the radio as it fell. With a quick twist, he turned the volume to maximum.

Now playing a Dvořák symphony, the radio blasted measure after measure of deep cellos and kettle drums. Trumpets blared. Cymbals crashed. Violins joined in and created a tsunami of music that swept through the room.

As if squeezed toward him, the mist swirled around Mictar's body. His song weakened. He coughed and gasped, but he managed to spew a string of obscenities before finally shouting, "You haven't seen the last of me, son of Solomon!"

The mist covered his head and continued to coil around him until he looked like a tightly wound scarlet cocoon. The room's spin slowed, and the cocoon seemed to absorb the momentum. Mictar transformed into a red tornado and shrank as if slurped into an invisible void.

Seconds later, he vanished. Everything stopped shaking. Nathan turned off the radio and crawled up the sloping floor to where everyone else crouched. Dr. Gordon latched on to Nathan's wrist and heaved him up the rest of the way. His voice stayed calm and low. "Well done, Nathan."

Kelly threw her arms around Nathan from one side and Clara did the same from the other. "Don't ever leave me alone again," Kelly said, "not for a single minute."

Sirens wailed. An amplified voice barked from somewhere

below, but Nathan paid no attention to the words. He just pulled his friends closer and enjoyed their embraces.

Tony, sitting on his haunches in front of Nathan, clenched his fist. "Now that's what I call taking out the trash!"

2

GHOSTS IN THE VORTEX

Nathan slid into the backseat of Dr. Gordon's Town Car and collapsed his umbrella, shaking it for a moment before pulling it in and closing the door. "Whew! It's really pouring. Earth Yellow must be having a monsoon."

"That would be my guess," Dr. Gordon said from the driver's seat. "I apologize for the lack of curb service. The police wouldn't let me drive under the portico."

"No wonder." Nathan used his sleeve to clear the side window. From the parking lot, the elephant-sized hole in the sixth floor made the hospital look like the victim of a missile attack. Kelly's room and the entire wing had been evacuated to secure that part of the building. One casualty was already too many. But only a day after the disaster, the rest of the hospital seemed back to normal.

"Did you get her new room number?" Clara asked from the front passenger's seat. She sat with a pencil poised over a notepad.

"Three fourteen. There's a guard at the door, so she should be okay."

Clara printed the number in neat block numerals. "How was she when you left?"

"She was pretty upset. She didn't want to be alone. Her dad's there, but he had already conked out. After they put his arm in a cast and gave him some painkillers, he refused any more treatment and sacked out in her room. They were both sawing logs when I finally left."

Dr. Gordon started the engine and flipped on the windshield wipers. "Your description of Kelly's interpretive skills is quite remarkable. She is a valuable asset to our cause, but with her handicap, she would become a liability if she were to accompany you, and that's to say nothing about her wounds."

Nathan banged the heel of his hand against the window. "Don't say that word."

"What word?" Dr. Gordon looked at him in the rearview mirror. "Wounds?"

"Never mind." Nathan slumped back in his seat. Dr. Gordon's mention of "handicapped" was innocent, of course, but it called to mind the slur Mictar had used as a dagger.

Dr. Gordon shifted the car into reverse and rolled it out of the parking space. "I will try to remember this peculiar aversion."

"Don't worry about it." Nathan scanned the backseat area. "Did you bring Mom's violin?"

"Yes." Clara motioned toward the rear. "In the trunk. It's—"

Something slapped the back of the car. Dr. Gordon slammed the brakes. "What was that?"

Nathan spun in his seat. A person hobbled to the door and pulled the handle, but the lock had engaged. He opened the door, revealing Kelly standing in the pouring rain, still in her hospital gown and clutching a small duffle bag.

"Slide over!" she barked.

He bounced to the other side, while Kelly, soaked to the skin and her hair dripping, stepped in, plopped down on the seat, and slammed the door.

"Oh, my goodness!" Clara said. "Dear child!"

While Nathan stared at Kelly's pain-streaked face, Dr. Gordon stripped off his jacket and handed it to her. "I will raise the temperature," he said, reaching for a button on the dashboard.

Nathan swallowed down a lump. As Kelly put on the jacket, the deep furrow in her forehead told him his first words had better be a stroke of genius.

"Uh . . . I guess your plan worked," he said.

She buttoned the jacket, her frown easing. "My plan?"

"Right. Wait until your father's asleep and I'm convinced that you're asleep, too. I leave to find Dr. Gordon's car. You sneak past the nurses, catch sight of me when you get outside, and get here just in the nick of time. That was a . . ." He paused, reaching for the right words. "A stroke of genius!" He settled back and let out a long breath, watching her with a sideways glance. "Good thing we took our time," he added. "I'm glad I don't have to go on this adventure without you."

At first her furrows deepened. Then her expression transformed from skepticism, to anger, and finally to resignation. She let out a sigh and stared at him through her glazed-over eyes. "I told you never to leave me again, Nathan Shepherd, not for one minute."

Nathan reached for her hand, now resting on the seat. It slid away, but only a few inches. He reached farther and grasped her fingers. "I'm sorry," he whispered. "I didn't want you to get hurt any worse."

As Dr. Gordon drove out of the parking lot, Clara made a "tsk, tsk" sound and shook her head. "You poor, pitiful, hard-headed girl. I admire your spunk, but you do realize we will have to notify your father."

She drooped her head and nodded. "I really *was* asleep. I saw Mictar in my dreams again, and when I woke up, I was scared. I didn't want to wake up Daddy, and Nathan was gone. I told the guard about my dream and asked him to check the other hallway. I assumed Daddy would be safer if I left, since Mictar's after me and not him, so I sneaked past the nurses. I knew no one would believe that Mictar was still around, so I had to find the only people who would." She looked at Nathan, her wet eyebrows arching. "That is, I hope they still believe in me."

Nathan opened his mouth to reply, but Dr. Gordon spoke up first. "My belief in you is actually enhanced by your tenacity. Virtue shines through our outer layers by means of our deeds."

Gesturing with his thumb toward Dr. Gordon, Nathan whispered, "What he said." He enclosed her hand with his. "I believe in you."

She winced and rotated her shoulder. "My bandage is going to need changing. I brought some fresh ones in my bag."

Dr. Gordon nodded ahead. "My lodging is on the way. We can stop there."

A few minutes later, they pulled into a Holiday Inn Express and parked under the motel's portico. Dr. Gordon held up a key card. "I suggest that Clara escort Kelly into my room to take care of her needs while Nathan and I stay out here to go over our strategy."

Clara took the card and helped Kelly get out. A few seconds later, Nathan sat alone in the backseat with Dr. Gordon staring at him from the front. Nathan tried to settle back, but his muscles tensed. The two dark eyes peering out from under two darker eyebrows made him feel like the next victim of a diving eagle.

Dr. Gordon's stare eased, and he rested his arm on the top of the seat. "Daryl is staying with friends of mine outside of town. She will meet us at the observatory in order to assist me, or, alternatively, she may accompany you on your journey to Earth Blue. Although Kelly's determination is admirable, and her interpretive skills are extremely important, her wounds ... excuse me ... her injuries are very real. I would never allow her to go unless her father approves and you are willing to shoulder the risk of taking on this extra burden."

22

Nathan let his muscles relax. Dr. Gordon's gentle tone worked wonders, and his mention of Daryl brought memories of her unique humor to mind. Since she was an academic genius and had studied under Dr. Gordon, her technological prowess had made her indispensable, but her knack for funny, oblique movie references seemed even more valuable at times. She was always able to break the tension. "Kelly's not a burden at all. I wouldn't want to go without her. Besides, won't Clara and Daryl Blue be there? They can help, too, can't they?"

"Yes, of course. Daryl Blue is already waiting at the Earth Blue observatory to secure your arrival there, and Clara has the surviving camera and mirror piece. They also have Nathan Blue's cell phone, which might come in handy."

Nathan pulled out his own cell phone and looked at the display. Since his old one sat at the bottom of the river in Chicago, this newer one wouldn't be any good on Earth Blue, since his replacement number wouldn't be activated there. The other Nathan never had to experience that cold, dirty swim, so he got to keep his original phone.

He punched in a number. "I'll see what Tony has to say. I hope he doesn't mind me waking him up."

"I think not. He would want to know where his daughter is."

The ringer sang out twice, then a roar blasted through the earpiece, the sound of a cheering crowd.

"Yeah!" Tony yelled over the racket. "What's up?"

"It's Nathan." He raised his voice to compete with the noise. "Kelly decided to leave the hospital early. Is that okay with you?"

"The leaves are hostile early? What are you talking about? Wait!" The roar grew deafening. Tony's voice piped over the others. "Touchdown! All right!"

After a few seconds, Tony's voice returned, calmer. "Say it again, buddy. I turned down the volume."

"You're watching a game on TV?"

"Yeah, I'm still in Kelly's room. She just called me a couple of minutes ago and told me that she skipped out. Figured I'd watch the game while I'm gathering the stuff she left behind."

Nathan took in a breath and let it all out in one long sentence. "Kelly wants to go with me to the Earth Blue dimension to look for my parents, and I need her, because she's the music interpreter, and my parents might die if we don't work together to find them, so we're asking your permission to go, even though she hurt her shoulder and her eyes aren't working right, but since Clara is taking care of her, she should be fine, and I'll take good care of her, too, I promise."

He drew in another breath and held it while waiting for Tony's reply. He'd say no at first, of course, but maybe he could be persuaded to —

"Yeah." Tony's voice echoed. "Sure. That's fine. Just be careful."

Nathan caught Dr. Gordon's eye. "It's okay?"

"That's what I said. She's a tough girl. Comes from good stock. Just let me know when you get back."

"Uh ... okay. Sure. We'll let you know." Nathan closed the phone and slid it back into his pocket. "That was easy. He said it was fine."

"Very well. Now we can rest while we wait." Dr. Gordon reached for the car stereo. "I have a CD in my player that you might find interesting — Haydn's String Quartet Opus 77 in G Major — performed by my own group."

"You play an instrument?"

"Yes. Viola. You are not the only accomplished musician in this car."

"Cool." Nathan settled back again. "Let's hear it."

He closed his eyes and listened to the quartet, a highly skilled group, but the amateurish recording made them sound a bit distant. Still, it was a great rendition, enhanced by a lively style that the piece required. Before it was over, the opening of

24

the car door interrupted his reverie. Kelly hopped in, her hair clean and brushed and her clothes dry. She sported fresh blue jeans, blue Nikes, and a gray Newton High School sweatshirt. A thick white bandage protruded at the neckline and made a lump over her shoulder.

Kelly touched the cardinal logo on the front of her sweatshirt. "I thought a red bird would be good for traveling to Earth Blue, sort of like a passport saying where I'm from."

"Good idea," Nathan said. "I called your father, and he—"

"*You* called my father?" she asked, pointing at him.

"Yeah, just a couple of minutes ago. He said—"

"But *I* called him as soon as we got into the motel lobby. I told him that I left the hospital and asked him if he'd let me go with you to Earth Blue."

"What did he say?"

"At first he said no, that he wasn't about to risk losing me, but I talked him into it."

"Really? How?"

"I told him how proud I was of him when he attacked Mictar and that I wanted to learn to be a hero, just like he was."

Nathan raised a thumb. "Good for you!"

"What did he say to you?"

"Just that you're tough enough to handle it." Nathan looked past Kelly. "Where's Clara?"

"She's getting something for me at the coffee shop. My pizza kind of took a nose dive yesterday, and I checked out before dinner came today."

The hospital room scene flashed in Nathan's mind—the poor nurse getting her eyes burned out and her body sliding over the edge. Nausea churned his stomach as he pressed a hand against his abdomen. "I was hungry, but not anymore."

When Clara arrived with a steaming cup of soup, they headed for the observatory, an hour-long drive into a rural zone northwest of Chicago. After Kelly drank the soup, she settled back and rested.

Watching the countryside through bleary eyes, Nathan pondered the scene of their next adventure—Interfinity Labs, the company that built the cross-dimensional travel platforms. Every time he thought about the huge curved mirror on Interfinity's observatory ceiling, the word *Quattro* came to mind, his father's code name for the technology that allowed the use of certain mirrors for seeing into and traveling to distant places or even other dimensions. And now he was about to use that mirror again to make a quantum leap.

Since Gordon Blue was in jail, and his henchmen were either dead or no longer in the picture, the Interfinity Labs' observatories in both worlds would probably be safe. The two Daryls had changed all the security codes, so only Gordon Red, and whomever else he trusted, could get in. Still, Mictar posed the most obvious threat. Who could tell when he might show up again?

Nathan looked over at Kelly leaning against the window, sound asleep. That was good. With the dangers that lay ahead, she needed all the rest she could get. She had been pounded physically and emotionally, and the latest assault must have been a drain.

Letting his gaze drift, he surveyed her thick sweatshirt and loose-fitting jeans—warm, secure, and modest. He took a mental snapshot. This was how it should be. This was the portrait of Kelly Clark he wanted ingrained in his mind, not the one that was stamped there when she wore that thin hospital gown and Mictar called her a—

He jerked his head away. No more thoughts like that. They were hurtful, vulgar, and ... He sighed. And troubling.

After Dr. Gordon parked next to the main door, Nathan retrieved his violin case from the trunk, and all four made their way through the observatory. Since only two people could fit

into the service elevator, Nathan and Kelly rode up to the telescope level first. When the doors opened, Daryl jumped up
from the computer desk at the left edge of the enormous domed
room. "Well, if it isn't Beauty and the beast!"

Laying a hand on Kelly's back, Nathan led her out onto the
tiled floor. With her eyesight still blurry, this dim room would
be almost impossible for her to navigate. "I guess you're right,"
he said. "Beauty and the beast fits."

Daryl jogged toward them, passing through the shadow of
a huge telescope that stood on a pedestal at the center of the
floor. Her red hair still bouncing when she stopped, she spread
out her arms, and a wide grin stretched her freckled face. "But
which one is the beast?"

"That would be me," Kelly said, raising her hand. "I feel
pretty beastly."

Daryl gave Kelly a gentle hug, then peeled back her sweatshirt
at the shoulder, cringing as she exposed more of the bandage,
now tinged with blood. "Forget the beast. Are you auditioning
for a zombie movie?"

Kelly shrugged. "If they need a victim, I'm their girl. I feel
like I have a bull's-eye painted on my forehead."

"Not good, Kelly-kins, not good at all." As the elevator door
closed, Daryl's grin contracted, giving her an uncharacteristically serious aspect. "I was searching for signals on the radio
telescope," she said, nodding toward the computer desk, "and I
picked up some weird stuff."

Kelly pulled her sweatshirt back in place, covering her bandage. "Define *weird*. After what we've been through, I might
not ever call anything 'weird' again."

Daryl spun and headed back to her station. "C'mon and take
a look."

Nathan took Kelly's hand and guided her to the desk where
Daryl was already tapping at the keyboard. "With all the wounds
in the celestial fabric," Daryl explained, "it's pretty easy to grab

some cross-dimensional traffic. I found one traffic stream in particular that's really strong, and it has cadence and structure, sort of like a language. While the other signals kind of come and go, this one stays steady."

"Can you translate it and show it on the screen?" Nathan asked.

Daryl looked up at the curved mirror that coated the observatory's ceiling. "Not without the music, and Francesca's not here to decode it for us."

"Go ahead and put it on the speakers." Nathan set down the violin case and popped the latches open. "Maybe Kelly and I can pick something up."

As Daryl slid her finger up a laptop's touchpad, random musical notes began to pour from unseen speakers. The mirrored ceiling flashed to life, displaying hundreds of irregular shapes — some red, some blue, some yellow — and many with swirls of blended colors. They bounced against each other, excited globules beating in time with the noise.

Nathan raised the violin and angled his head to listen, but when the elevator door opened again, Clara's booming voice interrupted his concentration. She stepped into the room and marched toward the desk. "And I am his tutor, the executor of his father's will, and the trustee of his estate. I will make that decision, thank you very much."

Dr. Gordon trailed her, his face stern, apparently not intimidated by Clara's forceful ways. "You have no idea how dangerous travel is now," he said, holding up his cell phone. "We cannot ignore Dr. Simon's warnings."

She spun and pointed at the phone's display. "I am not going to rely on a message that has come quite literally out of the blue. Can you verify the message's sender or its accuracy?"

"No ..." Dr. Gordon clapped the phone shut. "But it is a reasonable conclusion. I am familiar enough with Dr. Simon's normal communications to identify one of his messages."

Nathan lowered the violin and shook his head. The static coming from the verbal combatants was stronger than the static from the skies. "What's going on?" he asked.

Dr. Gordon straightened and focused on Nathan. "I received a forwarded text message from Dr. Simon. He says that recent cross-dimensional activity has weakened the cosmic structure to the point that all transport is now extremely hazardous. There are holes within the holes, or embedded wounds, if you don't mind me using that word. You could think you are going one place and end up in another, or, worse yet, fall into a timeless vortex."

"A vortex?" Nathan repeated.

"Yes. It is only a theory of mine, but data suggests the existence of places that are not physically within any of the three worlds. The signals match nothing else I have seen, and echoes I receive from the pulses I send out have an intelligent cadence but lack consistency in a time framework. The only conclusion I can draw is that the inhabitants have enough intellect to recognize they are being called by an outside entity, yet they are inconsistent in presentation."

"Put it in English, please," Kelly said. "We're not all geniuses like Daryl."

Dr. Gordon spread out his hands. "The beings are spaceless … timeless. You might call them phantasms, or perhaps even ghosts."

Nathan pondered the new data. The mention of Dr. Simon and phantasms brought back to mind the day when Mictar killed the Earth Red version of Dr. Simon, the head of the security corporation Interfinity had employed to help recover stolen technology. In order to protect Nathan's parents from Mictar, Dr. Simon had switched the bodies of the already murdered couple from Earth Blue. He sent the living couple from Earth Red into the blue dimension to try to find a solution to the coming crisis of interfinity—the imminent merging of the three worlds. Although he succeeded in deceiving Mictar for a while, Dr. Simon died in the grip of that monster's life-absorbing hand. Now it seemed that the Dr. Simon from Earth Blue had contacted Dr. Gordon with a new warning. "So," Nathan said, "you don't want us to risk it."

"There is no sense in sending you to a likely death. As far as we know, your parents are now free. I have great confidence that your father will be able to devise a solution to the interfinity collapse or signal us if he needs our help."

"Speaking of signals ..." Nathan nodded toward the ceiling. "Daryl's picked up something. We're trying to decipher it."

Dr. Gordon looked up at the dome and slid his phone into his pocket. "I apologize. Please continue."

Nathan concentrated again on the random notes, glancing at Kelly from time to time. She closed her eyes, while Daryl, Clara, and Dr. Gordon looked on.

The noise eased for a moment, then started again, beginning a series of pulses that sounded familiar. Nathan closed his eyes, too. Was it cycling? What could be embedded in all that turmoil? How did Francesca figure it out when she listened to these impossibly mixed-up sounds? And if he and she were both gifted, shouldn't he be able to duplicate what she could do at the age of ten?

He pictured the young prodigy playing her violin in the midst of a shower of chaotic noise. Her eyes began to glow, reminding him of the shining light that seemed to emanate from her matchless spirit, the same spirit he always saw and loved in his mother. She had the gift of insight, the ability to recognize and comprehend what no one else could see. Phony masks would melt in her piercing gaze. Liars held their tongues. Cryptic puzzles gave up their secrets. They were no contest for her spiritually penetrating vision.

Obviously, listening with his physical ears wouldn't be enough. He had to probe with invisible receptors, antennae of heart and mind that would melt the mask of confusion and piece together the scattered sounds.

Keeping his eyes closed, he imagined a musical staff floating in the middle of a black void, blank except for the lines and clef mark. In his mind, he stood in front of the sheet with his violin poised to play. As each note popped into his ear, his image played that note. A black spider flew from his strings and formed itself into a musical quarter note in midair. It then landed on the middle of the staff and positioned itself on the proper line.

With the second sound, another spider flew toward the page, transformed into an eighth note, and stuck to the staff on the second line near the end. Spider after spider glided to the page, and whenever they landed near one another, they shot out black webbing that tied them together until they created a perfectly arranged musical piece.

Nathan copied his imaginary stance and played the notes he saw on the visionary staff in order. After the first measure, the sounds from the speakers seemed to arrange themselves, as if the cosmos now played the sheet he had created in his mind. He opened his eyes and played along, copying each note he heard.

Daryl pointed at him and whispered in Kelly's ear. Kelly made a harsh shushing sound, while Clara gazed at the ceiling and Dr. Gordon studied the computer screen.

Above, the colors had blended together and were stretching out into a recognizable scene. A man and a woman sat in the midst of darkness, as though neither moon nor stars could break the black nightscape. Even their resting place was nothing more than a shapeless black lump.

After a few seconds, their faces clarified, but they were still too fuzzy to recognize. Nathan poured his heart into his playing until his mother's violin sounded like it sizzled with flaming passion. Every stroke of his bow brought the couple more clearly into focus until each face blazed into Nathan's mind.

He wanted to scream out, "Mom! Dad!" but he had to keep his concentration steady and hold this vision of the other world on the screen as long as he could.

While his mother played a violin, his father rose and paced, staying within a short range, as if blocked by invisible walls on each side. With his hand to his chin, he seemed to be deep in thought. Soon, the violin's sweet tones became audible, one of his mother's own pieces, a soothing tune to which she had also composed lyrics, a ballad about a long-lost son who found his way home after many years of toil and torture at the hands of a wicked king in a faraway land.

His father stopped and raised a finger. He spoke, but his words didn't come through. Nathan concentrated on his playing. He had to bring in their conversation. Their lives might depend on it.

Lowering her violin, his mother replied, but she, too, seemed like a player in a silent movie. After a few seconds of conversation, she rose from her seat, and the two embraced tenderly. Then, tears flowing, she waved as he walked away. He stepped gingerly, as if treading on thin ice, and disappeared from view.

As his mother reseated herself and raised her violin, Nathan's arms weakened, feeling limp and numb. How long could he go on? And why did this effort drain his energy so easily? Would continuing to play do any good? He had already given it all he had, and he couldn't hear a word they said.

He sidestepped toward the center of the chamber. There really was only one option. Knowing he couldn't speak and play at the same time, he tried to signal Kelly with his eyes. But would she see him with her foggy vision? Had she been able to watch the scene unfolding in the mirror above? Still, she had read his mind before, so maybe ...

"Get ready to flash the lights!" Kelly yelled as she ran to join him. "We're taking off!"

Daryl jumped up and dashed over to the switches. "On your signal!"

"No!" Dr. Gordon raised his hand. "The data stream suggests exactly what I described. This is likely a vortex. It's too dangerous!"

Nathan, now breathing rapidly, played with all his might. Of course he wanted to be with his parents, but falling into a timeless vortex along the way would end their journey forever. Still, this might be their only chance to find them. Didn't they have to try? He heaved a loud grunt. If only someone else would make this decision!

Holding the violin case in one hand, Kelly put her other hand on Nathan's back. "Clara! It's your call! What do you say?"

Clara stood next to Dr. Gordon, who typed madly at the keyboard. "Are you both willing to take the risk?" she asked.

"I am!" Kelly pressed Nathan's back. "You?"

He gave a quick nod and played on.

Clara pointed at Daryl. "Hit it!"

"No!" Dr. Gordon screamed, red-faced and still typing. "This is not your observatory, nor your equipment! I will not allow you to die on my watch!"

Daryl flipped the switch. The perimeter lights flashed on.

Dr. Gordon hit a final key with a commanding stroke. A chaotic array of colors splashed across the ceiling mirror, and the music shifted to Dvořák's *New World Symphony*.

White beams shot out from the trumpet-shaped lamps and collected at the apex of the dome. Dozens of shafts of light rebounded toward the floor and surrounded Nathan and Kelly with a glowing picket fence.

The scene in the mirrored ceiling reshaped into a reflection of the observatory room floor, a reflection that showed Clara and Daryl, but not Dr. Gordon, Nathan, or Kelly. The image melted and slid down the picket fence's vertical shafts until everything outside of their laser prison vanished.

Within a few seconds, their surroundings reappeared—the same floor, the same telescope, though tilted at a slightly different angle, and the same Clara and Daryl. Nathan slowed his playing and squinted at them. Or were they the same?

His arms feeling like rags, he lowered his violin and let his shoulders droop. "We're on Earth Blue, aren't we?"

Daryl sashayed toward them, flipping her hair back in mock offense. "Well! Don't act so disappointed!"

Nathan dropped to the floor and sat, his face buried in his hands. "We were close! So close!"

A voice came down from above. "No, you were not close."

Nathan looked up at the ceiling. Dr. Gordon, appearing upside-down in the reflection and standing near the telescope in the Earth Red observatory, stared down at him. "The signal emanating through the cosmic wound dissipated just as I was switching you over to Earth Blue. You and Kelly would have been thrown into a vacuum, where you would have died instantly."

Nathan probed Daryl Blue's eyes. He could no longer speak. If he tried, he would cry for sure. So he asked the question with his gaze, hoping Daryl would figure it out. Was Dr. Gordon telling the truth?

Daryl stooped and looked Nathan in the eye. "I watched the whole thing from my computer. You and Kelly would be sparkling space dust by now, and I don't think anyone would name a star after you."

Nathan glanced up at Dr. Gordon again, but he was walking toward the desk, shaking his head.

Daryl reached down her hand. "Looks like you could use a lift."

"In more ways than one." Nathan took her hand and rode her hefty pull to his feet.

Kelly raised the violin case. "I got this at the last minute. Want to pack up?"

While Nathan put the violin away, Daryl Blue hugged Kelly briefly, then pulled back. "Take a good look, Kelly-kins," she said, tugging on her collar. "My shirt is blue, through and through. Daryl Red and I decided to be color coded."

"I can see that," Kelly said, squinting. "Barely."

"Oh, yeah. Forgot about your run-in with the evil eye snatcher."

"Daryl!" Clara Blue marched up behind her, wagging her finger. "Watch your tongue, young lady. Kelly's vision is not a joking matter."

"Don't worry about it, Ms. Jackson," Kelly said. "I've put up with Daryl Red for years. I once broke my wrist in a basketball game, and she accused me of sticking my hand too far in the toilet to get Steven's promise ri—" She jerked her fist up to her mouth and bit it. "I think I'd better shut up for a while." Without even offering Nathan a glance, she hurried to the computer desk. Daryl followed.

Clara handed Nathan a six-inch-by-six-inch square mirror, now protected by a rubberized frame. "Here's the Quattro mirror. I know you're disappointed about the strange turn of events, but can you get up enough gumption to go to Tony Blue's house?"

Nathan took the mirror and gave her a half-hearted nod. He wanted to stay quiet, but he would have to get over his funk soon. His parents needed him.

Daryl's voice piped up again, this time from the Earth Red observatory above. "We'll watch the fort from here. Keep Nathan Blue's cell phone on, so we can text you if necessary."

"Oh, yeah." Nathan leaned toward the desk and scanned its surface. "Where is it?"

Daryl Blue held up the phone and a Nikon on a strap. "Got you covered. And we have the other camera. Let's get moving."

3

THE MISTY VEIL

Clara drove Tony's Camry off the interstate ramp and into Newton, Iowa. A cold, steady drizzle dampened the road, just enough to slicken the pavement and make the tires swish.

As they passed by the local Wal-Mart, Nathan watched an old man with a cane hobble toward a beat-up station wagon, one of the few cars in the parking lot. A scarf wrapped his neck, and gloves covered his hands, but his shivering body showed that his winter garb wasn't quite adequate.

Nathan shivered with the poor old guy. With the heater barely pumping out enough warm air to melt ice, he had to rub his hands together briskly in front of the vent to keep them from stiffening. He might soon have to play the violin, so keeping everything limber was crucial.

He checked on Kelly sitting in the backseat behind Clara. With her oversized sweatshirt now rumpled, she looked bulky as she leaned against the door, her eyes closed and her mouth partially open. She hadn't uttered a word the entire trip. Of course, Daryl's effervescent chatter helped pass the time, but occasional periods of silence allowed Kelly to nod off and then sleep through some of Daryl's stories about their antics in elementary school. Kelly had probably heard them before, so her exhaustion held sway.

Although the bandage was completely hidden, Nathan let his gaze linger on her shoulder. Clara had changed her bandage again at a rest stop and announced that the stitches had sealed the wound, and the oozing blood had almost stopped. That was good. Kelly had only two bandages left in her bag. Maybe they wouldn't have to change it again.

Images of Kelly's ordeal reentered his mind—Gordon Blue's stabbing dagger, Mictar's blinding grip, and even her potential death—a vision granted by Patar, Mictar's less-malevolent twin, that showed Nathan what would have happened if he had chosen to save his parents. Her scorched face and vacant eye sockets stared up at him from her quivering body, a fatal victim of Mictar's cruel torture.

Nathan clenched his fist and lightly smacked his palm. If only he had another chance at that creep, he would—

"Getting ready for a fight?" Clara asked.

He looked at his fist and loosened his fingers. "I guess so. If Mictar can stretch dimensional wounds and go through them, he could pop into a room when you least expect it."

"It's probably not so simple. If he were able to come and go as he pleased, we would all have sooty eye sockets by now."

"Good point." As they drove between two browning corn-fields on the final road leading to the Clarks' Earth Blue home, Nathan scanned the area for any movement. With sleet pellets now mixing with the spattering raindrops in the midst of thickening fog, no one in his right mind would be out in the open air, but this was Mictar they were talking about, so he didn't qualify.

When the Clarks' house came into sight, memories of his first view of the beautiful old mansion came to mind, recalling the morning after he thought his parents had been killed. Clara had driven him here, trying to hide him from the murderers. Tony, his father's college buddy, had agreed to take him in, thus beginning Nathan's adventures with Kelly. Even though the thousand acres of rolling cornfields and the huge shade trees surrounding the house painted a regal landscape, with thoughts of death and danger creeping in, it seemed more melancholy than majestic.

When they stopped in the driveway, Nathan reached for the door. "Everyone stay here while I check it out."

"Not on your life," Clara said as she whipped off her seat belt. "There is safety in numbers."

Daryl leaned forward. "Yeah, Nathan. This house has ambush written all over it."

He pulled the mirror from the glove box. "This will let me know if there's any trouble ahead. If everything checks out, I'll give the all-clear signal. No use risking anyone else's life."

"I'm going!" Kelly yawned and shook her head as if casting off a fog. "You're stuck with me until this is over. Besides, you might need an interpreter."

Nathan pointed at her. "Okay Just you. Everyone else stay put. If something happens and we don't come back, go to the observatory. If we're alive, we'll try to contact you there somehow."

Clara set her finger on the trunk release button. "Do you want your mother's violin?"

"Not yet, but pop it anyway so I can get an umbrella." Still holding the mirror, Nathan got out and hurried around to the trunk. He grabbed an umbrella and opened it over Kelly's head as she stepped out of the car. Together, they splashed through the driveway's puddles, puffing clouds of white on their way to the front door.

Nathan jiggled the knob. Locked. Kelly dug into her jeans and withdrew a key ring. She chose a short silver key from a collection of four and inserted it into the deadbolt lock. It disengaged easily. And why not? The Clarks' Earth Blue and Earth Red houses were identical, so Kelly Red's key was bound to fit in the lock.

With a turn of the knob and a push on the hardwood panel, Nathan opened the door and leaned inside. As he took a few skulking steps into the spacious foyer, white vapor continued to stream from his mouth. Obviously the furnace was off.

He flipped the light switch, but the room stayed dim, illuminated only by inadequate daylight coming from a nearby picture window behind a dusty grand piano. They had seen sagging power lines along the way, ice weighing them down and knocking out electricity for every house in the area. No wonder all the roads had been deserted.

The bizarre September weather had probably frozen people's hearts in fear. It seemed that everyone had chosen to hibernate for a while, hoping they would wake up and find everything back to normal. But that wouldn't happen, at least not until they solved the interfinity problem. With Earths Blue and Red getting Earth Yellow's weather, and with Earth Yellow's time racing along at an unpredictable rate, "normal" would have to wait.

Nathan tucked the mirror under his arm and sneaked along the dim hallway, taking one slow step at a time. He shivered in the cold, drafty air. Something felt wrong, terribly wrong—not just the chill, but a sense of danger that seemed to increase with every step.

Ahead on the right lay his bedroom, yet, not really his. It had belonged to his Earth Blue twin, a victim of Mictar's fiery hand. Nathan tried to shake away the memory. The poor guy's face and his burned-out eye sockets had been stamped indelibly in his mind.

He searched for any sign of the murderer. The mental image of Mictar's fiendish eyes, ghostly pale complexion, and slick white hair sent shivers across his skin, especially now that he had watched the monster feed off yet another victim, the unsuspecting nurse back at the hospital. Since the celestial wounds were probably huge in this house, Mictar could easily be lurking nearby.

As he continued his furtive march, Kelly followed a mere

step behind, her rapid breaths the only sound in the hallway. Apparently she also felt the strange sensation, the stillness that belies the brewing storm. As she clutched the back of his sweatshirt, her trembling hand sent another shiver across his skin.

"Are you going to use the mirror?" she whispered.

"In a second." When they came within a foot or so of the bedroom, he stopped and reached his mirror across the doorway, angling it so he could see inside. So many times before, this mirror had provided a way to escape danger, either by showing him a threat in advance or creating a scenario that saved his skin, such as the time it displayed police officers arresting the gunman on the bridge even as he continued shooting while Nathan and Clara floundered in the Chicago River.

This time, the mirror reflected a thin white mist swirling at the center of the room, a slowly twisting eddy that stretched from the floor to near the ceiling. It looked like a skinny, stationary tornado, yet slower, more mysterious. As it spun, tiny pinpoints of light pulsed on its perimeter, glowing and fading, as if generated by the misty turbine but unable to draw enough energy from the sluggish engine to stay illuminated.

Nathan eased his head toward the opening. Dr. Simon had said that something unusual was going on here, and a swirl of mist hovering over the floor wasn't exactly normal, but with all they had been through, it seemed no more than another oddity in a long string of oddities. Still, Mictar had disappeared in a spinning mist of red. Could this be something similar, a visible manifestation of one of the cosmic wounds?

Tucking his mirror again, he stepped in. A much bigger mirror covered the wall to his left, reflecting his worried face and dampened, wind-tousled hair. This matrix of smaller mirror squares matched the one in his Earth Red bedroom, including the missing square in the lower left-hand corner. So many times before, this mirror had acted in the same way his portable mirror had, showing things that weren't really there and creating alternate realities that allowed for cross-dimensional transport, at least when accompanied by music and a flash of light. But now it just showed the room and the twisting mist, nothing unexpected.

Behind his image, a queen-size poster bed abutted the opposite wall, and the misty funnel spun near the bed's footboard. The mattress, covered with only a bare white pad, leaned precariously against the wall, its shell torn by a long gash and its inner stuffing scattered across the carpet. The old trunk, the mysterious wooden box that had once hidden treasures in its impenetrable casing, sat against the wall, unopened, as usual.

A frigid breeze blew in through the window at the far side of the room, flapping the drapes and blowing a clump of mattress padding over a toppled desk and lamp that had once stood to the right of the window. Yet, the gusts seemed to have no effect on the funnel. It continued to spin unabated.

"Something weird's going on," Nathan whispered.

"That's nothing new." Kelly tugged on his shirt. "Go in farther. I can't see a thing with you blocking the way."

Now walking on tiptoes, as if to sneak by the swirl without drawing its attention, he crossed the room and closed the window. He rubbed a fingertip across two deep scratches in the painted sash. Could Patar have dug these ruts with his pointed nails? Or Mictar?

Nathan tried to twist the lock into place. The brass piece slipped and fell to the carpet, obviously already broken before he touched it. Forced open, no doubt.

Kelly leaned against the doorjamb, the Nikon camera dangling over her sweatshirt's cardinal logo. She blinked her glassy eyes. "Something's moving."

Nathan edged closer to the swirl but stayed just outside of its misty funnel. "It's like a little dust devil made out of fog, and it has tiny sparks around it, like miniature fireflies. Seems harmless, but I'm not taking any chances."

"Better get Daryl in here. She can send a photo back to Earth Red and get Dr. Gordon's opinion."

"Good thought." Nathan looked out the window at the Camry. Barely visible through the mist-covered glass, Clara flexed her fingers in front of the air vents. He caught her eye, and she lifted her hands in an "is it okay for us to come in now?" kind of pose.

He pulled Nathan Blue's cell phone from his pocket and punched in Clara's number.

She raised the phone to her ear. "Yes, Nathan."

"All clear so far. Can you send Daryl in? We need her to transmit a photo. You might as well stay out there. It's freezing in here."

"Will do. Be careful."

"Always." He stuffed the phone back in his pocket and kept his eye on the car. Daryl leaped out and hustled toward the front porch, her eyes darting in every direction. While blowing fog whipped her hair into a frenzy, she puffed short bursts of white into the wind as she rubbed her hands up and down her arms.

Nathan turned back to Kelly. "She's on her way."

A door slammed. "It's just me!" Daryl called. Light footsteps padded their way down the hall, then her smiling face appeared at the door, eyebrows scrunching down. "What a mess! Either someone had the worst nightmare in history, or the bed frame just vomited the mattress."

Kelly grimaced. "Thanks for the lovely imagery."

"No problem." Pointing at the swirl, Daryl shuffled in. "What's this all about?"

Nathan shrugged. "Can you send a photo? Get Gordon's take?"

"Sure thing." Daryl lifted her cell phone, pointed it at the funnel, and clicked a button. Then, while her thumbs flew across the keypad, she chattered rapid-fire. "I got a message from Daryl Red. She says Gordon got another email from Simon Blue. They finished analyzing the Earth Red Nikon. It's like you thought. It has a Quattro lens, and when you pointed it at a Quattro mirror and took a flash picture, you did a *Ghost Busters* no-no."

Nathan rolled his eyes. Daryl had dropped a cryptic movie reference on them again. "Okay," he said with a sigh. "I give. What's a *Ghost Busters* no-no?"

A satisfied grin spreading across her face, Daryl acted out her explanation, using her cell phone as a ray gun as she rattled off her words. "Egon told Peter not to cross the energy streams with their ghost-capturing guns or all life as they knew it would end. It was sort of the same thing the two Dr. Gordons did when they sent a flash through their observatory mirrors at each other. It created a ginormous dimensional hole that allowed Mictar and Patar to sneak out of who-knows-where and show up in our worlds."

When Daryl took a breath, Nathan held up his hand. "Give me a minute to think." He studied the swirl. Could it have materialized because of the recent photo Kelly took at the funeral? Was it some kind of cosmic hole? Could this be the path his parents took to that black vortex he had seen earlier? If so, why was the hole only in this dimension and not on Earth Red? And how could it last so long?

As Kelly drew closer, she kicked aside a pile of mattress padding. Something clinked near her feet. "What was that?"

Stooping, Nathan picked up a short chain. A broken manacle dangled at the end. Where the band was broken, the metal seemed malformed, as if it had been melted. "Dad's chains came off. Maybe a blowtorch?"

"No way," Kelly said, touching one of the links. "I've watched my father use his. It would've broiled your dad's wrists."

Staying low, Nathan dropped the chain and peeked under the bed's wooden frame. A violin case lay on the carpet next to more of the ripped-out mattress padding. He slid it out and snapped it open. Inside, he found his old violin, the one he had smashed against Mictar's face in the performance hall's prop room just a few days ago. Apparently, Nathan Blue had never experienced that adventure, so his violin remained intact.

He handed Kelly his mirror. "Let's see what the big picture looks like."

She slid open the frame's fastener, pulled the glass free, and set the square in the wall mirror's empty space. It seemed to jump from her fingers and snap into place. A burst of energy swept across the reflection like a rippling wave of light, ending at the upper corner with a quiet popping sound.

Daryl's jaw dropped open. "Coolness!"

Staring at his reflection, Nathan lifted the violin and bow. What should he play this time? Interfinity's mirrored observatory ceiling needed specific melodies to create dimensional portals, but this Quattro-enhanced mirror had responded to almost any kind of music. Yet, it worked only when it wanted to, as if it had a mind of its own.

After giving the violin a quick tuning, he pressed the bow against the strings. With the ridiculous weather outside, a Christmas song seemed appropriate. As he played Mendelssohn's tune for "Hark! The Herald Angels Sing," Kelly closed her eyes. Her brow furrowed, accentuating the gash across her forehead, the wound the mirror's edge had gouged into her skin during their recent plunge toward the Mississippi River.

Nathan tried to read her expression. Was she hearing words this time? Since she was the music interpreter, maybe she was getting another message from his mother that would help them figure out where she and his father went.

As he continued the melody, the swirl in the reflection expanded. The tiny lights on the funnel's perimeter brightened, pulsing like miniature strobes. The misty edges drew closer to the reflections of the trio. Although the real swirl stayed small,

Nathan and Daryl backed away from it, giving their mirror images some space between them and the mysterious funnel.

Her eyes still glassy, Kelly stared again at the mirror. Moving her feet in time with the music, she inched toward the reflection. She lifted her hand and eased her palm close to the glass, murmuring, "There's something inside the swirl."

Nathan squinted at the swirl in the mirror—nothing but fog and lights, thicker and brighter, yes, but nothing else.

Daryl touched the outer edge of the funnel. "I don't see anything."

"It's a human figure." Kelly drew a picture in the air with her finger. "Like a ghost ... shapeless ... floating with the spin."

"Do you hear any words?" Daryl asked.

Kelly nodded. "A female voice. Singing. The words fit Nathan's music perfectly."

"Then belt it out, sister. What are you waiting for?"

"I'm waiting for a new verse to start. It'll be hard to listen at the same time." Kelly cleared her throat and sang, weakly at first, but her strength grew as the verse poured out.

Called to courage, called to rescue,
Called to join the precious few;
Given strength to rise from earth,
Reach for light and give it birth.
Plucked from earth and rising sunward,
Plunge within and journey onward,
Never fear the cries of men,
Rise above their mortal ken.
Take the reigns of freedom's light;
Help the weak escape the night.

Kelly let out a long breath. "Now she's repeating that verse."

Still playing, Nathan eyed the funnel in the mirror as it expanded toward their images. Was the reflection showing the future? Did it need a flash of some kind to come true? With the electricity out and no time to hunt for a battery-operated light, the only option they had was the flash on the camera from Earth Blue, but that would be, as Daryl had said, "crossing the streams." It always created a huge explosion of light that came back to zap them. Should they just jump into the vortex and hope for the best?

While Kelly kept her gaze locked on the mirror, Daryl turned to Nathan. "So, Amadeus, what's the verdict?"

"Just wait," Nathan said, lifting his bow for a brief second to answer. Maybe the mirror would tell them what to do.

Daryl backed away from the reflection and spoke in elongated sing-song. "We've got company!"

In the mirror, the room's window to the front yard slid open, forced upward by a hand with sharp fingernails. A white-haired man climbed through. Tall and lanky, he was dressed in black boots, loose trousers made out of some kind of shimmering white fabric with royal blue stripes running up each leg, and a darker blue shirt, silky, with three-quarter-length sleeves and a V-neck that revealed a snowy plume of chest hairs.

Nathan caught a glimpse of the back of his head. No ponytail. Unless Mictar had cut his off, this had to be Patar.

The newcomer approached the foreground of the mirror, though he was absent from the bedroom itself. The reflected images of Nathan, Kelly, and Daryl froze in place, staring at the now stationary funnel of mist.

Nathan looked back at the real Kelly and Daryl. They, too, stood petrified, their arms and legs stiff and their expressions locked as if time had stopped.

Patar set his hands on his hips, a frown dressing his face with scorn. "What are you doing here, son of Solomon?"

Nathan fumed. Patar wasn't exactly Mr. Congeniality, but Nathan knew he had to pay attention. His father had said this vision stalker would guide him in the right direction, but he emanated the charm of a headless horseman. He had more riddles than answers. "I'm looking for my parents. What was I supposed to do?"

"Are you so dull of senses? You saw for yourself how your father was trying to help your mother play the great violin. Have you forgotten his wisdom?"

Balling a hand into a fist, Nathan took a step toward the mirror. "Spit it out, Patar. Cut the questions and just tell it to me straight."

Patar's eyes flamed red, but his voice stayed calm. "I tell it straight, as you say, to those with enough wisdom to understand the mysteries of the cosmos. You, child that you are, must learn wisdom as you proceed through the maze of unknowns. Otherwise, you would never be able to choose the right path when no one with wisdom is there to guide you."

Nathan let out an exasperated sigh. What choice did he have? He would have to play along. "Okay. So, I'm a child. Just give me something to go on."

"Very well." Patar's brow lifted. "Finding your parents is an act that most would declare noble, but it is the selfish vision of an unlearned boy."

"Selfish!" Nathan slapped the mirror with his palm. "They're trapped in some kind of black vortex. Releasing them from their prison isn't selfish."

Patar thrust out his hands. As if blown by a hurricane gust, Nathan staggered backwards and fell on his bottom.

Holding up two fingers, Patar roared. "Two humans! Only two! You search the universe for the ones you think you love, while the lives of over fifteen billion others hang in the balance! You try to save two *Homo sapiens* who give you comfort and status, while billions of souls you care nothing about teeter on the brink of destruction." He pointed a rigid finger at Nathan. "That, young traveler, is selfish."

Nathan scrambled to his feet and matched Patar's pointing

finger with one of his own. "If you would get off your high horse and tell me what to do, I wouldn't be searching for two needles in a galaxy-sized haystack. My father probably knows how to save the universe, so tell me where to find him, and we'll do it together."

A wry smile crossed Patar's face. "Your father is in no position to help, and even if you found him, you would become as incapacitated as he is. Just carry out what he began. Play the violin, and all will be made right." He backed away and set his hand near the misty funnel, still frozen within the reflection. "Use the camera. It will cut through to a place you have never been, the realm that houses Sarah's Womb. There you will find the violin, the healing instrument. Once you do, follow the wisdom you gain each step along the way."

"Sarah's Womb? What's that?"

"Allow words and places to define themselves, son of Solomon. All in good time."

As Patar touched the funnel, it jumped back into motion, spinning as before. He vaporized, and his own misty form joined the slowly turning cyclone.

Kelly shook her head, blinking. "Did something weird happen? I just had a big-time déjà vu."

"Yeah," Nathan said, "super weird." He nodded at the camera hanging at her chest. "Go ahead and use it. It'll be all right."

"Who was the creepy cotton-top character?" Daryl asked. "He just disappeared."

"Patar. Don't worry about him. He's *my* problem."

The Nathan in the mirror packed the violin in its case while Kelly's reflected image lifted the camera to her eye and aimed it at the trio in the real bedroom.

"Uh-oh," Daryl said, reaching for Kelly. "Your twin's way ahead of us."

Nathan shoved the violin into its case. "It's showing what we're supposed to do. Let's just follow along."

As the real Kelly lifted the camera and pointed it at her duplicate, the funnel in the mirror enfolded their reflections in its cyclonic swirl. The mist veiled their bodies, and they slowly faded away.

Nathan pulled them into a tight group. "Now, Kelly!"

She pushed the shutter button. The camera flashed. A jagged bolt of light bounced off the mirror, but it bent away from the camera and knifed into the swirl. The lights on the perimeter brightened, seemingly absorbing the energy. As the vortex expanded toward them, Nathan kept one arm around Kelly and the other clutching the violin. Daryl latched on to his elbow and squeezed until it hurt.

Within seconds, thick fog and sparkling lights drifted across their eyes. A floating sensation—weightlessness, or maybe air pushing them upward—gave Nathan an awkward, unbalanced feeling. Unable to see anything, he lost all sense of position. Were they flying? Upside-down? Zooming at a million miles per hour? The mist, swirling around them far more quickly now, gave him an awareness of motion, like a bullet spinning toward its target.

Kelly and Daryl stayed quiet, their eyes wide and their bodies stiff. Daryl's grip tightened even more, but Nathan just endured the pain.

Finally, the mist slowed its spin and thinned out, evaporating as if burned away by the sun. Yet, there was no sun. When the fog disappeared, only darkness met their eyes—complete, utter darkness.

Nathan pressed his toes down. Whatever they were standing on seemed firm enough, but without even a hint of light, could they go anywhere? Might a single step plunge them into a void? Music filled the air, sweet and gentle. Was it a voice? Just the wind? It resembled no instrument he had ever heard. It was more like a thousand instruments blending their tones into a sound so perfectly balanced, they seemed to play as one.

He breathed a sigh. Such richness! Such clarity! He could listen for hours and still beg for more.

The sound of Daryl's wheezing breaths broke through the music. "You two sure know how to travel!" she said. "That made the bus in *Speed* look like a kiddie ride!"

"Yeah," he replied, "but it looks like the bus station needs better lighting. I can't see a thing."

Kelly's voice drifted by. "You can't? I see fine. Better than ever."

Nathan searched for the source of the voice. Two bright spots pierced the darkness— Kelly's eyes, shining through a black canopy. The glow spilled across her face and illuminated her cheeks and forehead. He let out a breathy whistle. "It's like there's a ten megawatt light bulb inside your head!"

"Check it out!" Daryl said, laughing. "Kelly's got headlights!"

Kelly blinked several times, casting their new world into blackness with each stroke of her lids. "That's not cool. You mean I have to lead you two around like a guide dog?"

"Let's hope it's just temporary," Nathan said. "What does this place look like?"

As Kelly's eyes drifted back and forth, the beams followed her movements. "We're standing on an elevated walkway of some kind. It looks like it's made of glass. I can see through it, but there isn't anything holding it up, at least nothing I can see."

"What's down below, and how far?"

"Just a blanket of colorful mist moving parallel to the walkway on both sides, kind of slow, slower than a walking pace. Some swirls are caught up in the flow, like whirlpools of fog, sort of like that thing in your bedroom."

"Where does the walkway go?"

Kelly paused for a moment, blinking as her eyebeams penetrated a transparent floor. "Hard to tell. It's like we're out in the middle of a catwalk over a foggy swamp. We can go either way, but we'd just walk into another fog bank."

"Do you see any good reason to stay where we are?" Nathan asked.

Her eyebeams waved back and forth. "Nothing but rainbow-colored fog up, down, and all around."

Nathan reached toward Kelly's glowing eyes. "Give me your sleeve, and we'll make a train."

"Here you go."

Her sleeve pushed into his palm. As soon as he tightened his grip on it, a tug pulled back his sweatshirt. "I'll be the caboose," Daryl said. "Lead the way, Kelly-kins."

"But which way?" Again, Kelly's beams moved from side to side. "There are two ways to walk."

"You said the mist is moving," Daryl said. "Let's just go with the flow."

"Makes sense to me." Nathan tucked the violin case against his side. "I'm ready."

Kelly turned her head, blocking the twin lights. The sleeve pulled. Nathan hung on and shuffled his shoes against the smooth surface as he followed. Daryl added just a little weight to his slow progress, her body warmth and gentle breaths indicating her presence very close behind. She whispered, "It feels like we should chant, 'Lions and tigers and bears, oh my.'"

"If you do," Nathan said, "you're going over the side."

"I see. That's a horse of a different color. No chanting."

"When I get close to the fog bank," Kelly said, "it seems to get farther away. But when it does, I don't see anything except more walkway."

Nathan pulled back on her sleeve. "Maybe we should—"

"Wait!" Kelly halted. "I hear something. Voices."

Nathan held his breath, hoping his silence would help her figure out what was going on. Daryl's breaths also fell to a barely perceptible buzz. Still, the ever-present symphony in the air played on, more beautiful than ever.

"The voices are coming from those swirls I told you about." The sleeve jerked out of Nathan's hand. "Wait here," she said, her voice fading. "Don't move a muscle."

Nathan froze in place. "Don't worry. We won't."

After a few seconds, Daryl whispered, "Can you see her eyes?"

He scanned the darkness. "No sign of them."

The darkness felt heavy, as if the black air weighed down his shoulders and seeped into his mind. Yet, the beautiful sounds eased any fear that tried to bubble up. This was a place of stark contrasts—a symphony of angels in the midst of a black void.

After almost a full minute, Daryl's hand began to tremble. "Okay, Captain Cool," she said, "I'm losing *my* cool. Say something to make me feel better."

"Uh ... this sure beats falling into a bottomless pit?"

"Wrong answer. Try again."

"How about—"

"I'm coming!" Kelly's voice pierced the dark curtain. Seconds later, her eyes appeared, brighter than ever. A strong tug pulled Nathan's hand. "I think I figured something out. Come on!"

Nathan followed, shuffling his feet far more rapidly than his nerves would have allowed. Daryl stayed close, but her breaths came faster and heavier. As they walked, the music grew in volume, and the blended instruments seemed to break apart into distinct tones.

Finally slowing down, Kelly patted Nathan's hand. "We're walking alongside one of the swirls. I hear lots of voices coming out of the top, like a bunch of people talking at the same time."

Nathan tried to penetrate the blackness with his vision, but it was no use. The music in the air continued to flood his ears. He could hear little else. "What are they saying?"

"It's so jumbled, it's hard to tell. I just pick up some of the louder words." Kelly tightened her grip on his hand. "But get this. The swirls have different colors—one red, one blue, and one yellow. They kind of pop up out of rivers of color, like the colors are heading somewhere, and something boils from underneath, and words spew out through a swirl."

Daryl released Nathan's shirt. "The three dimensions?"

"Maybe. There are other swirls, and they're all red, blue, or yellow. Maybe a swirl represents something in its dimension, like a city or a family."

"Did voices come out of the other ones?" Nathan asked.

Kelly's bright eyes bobbed up and down. "Most of them."

Nathan let go of her hand and drummed his fingers on the violin case. This hall of darkness was proving to be the weirdest place they had been yet. What could it all mean? Did those swirls really have something to do with the Earth dimensions they had visited? If so, the people at Interfinity Labs must have named them based on the colors here, but that would mean one of them had been to this misty world before.

As he thought, a new sound merged into the musical air. A feminine voice? An alto? Maybe. But it was too perfect, too precise to be human. Yet, something was missing. The voice was like a question without an answer, an expression of love unrequited. It needed ... something.

Nathan set down the case and fumbled with the fasteners until they snapped open. When he raised the violin and bow, he looked into Kelly's blinking eyes. "I'm going to try something."

Listening carefully to the simple aria, he waited for a phrase to end. Then, brushing his bow lightly across the strings, he answered in the same key, C Major, but altered the notes, composing an appropriate counterpoint.

The music in the air shifted to F Major, and the tempo slowed, still a wordless tune that seemed to beg for another answer. Closing his eyes, Nathan replied again, following the singer's key and timing, yet with his own composition. He played a mellow harmony that seemed to capture and bring back echoes of the first musician's song. Then, the two played together—a perfect blend of melody and harmony—singer and musician in a rhapsodic ensemble that filled the air with a flowery scent. Roses, maybe? As he inhaled, something coated his throat and the back of his tongue with a sweet flavor, yet with a bitter aftertaste, like vanilla with a bite.

"Nathan," Kelly said. "What's happening?"

He opened his eyes. A stream of lively sparks flowed from his violin and through the darkness, eating away the black field and leaving light in its wake. When the stream swept past Nathan's ear, the music suddenly increased in volume, then faded again as the sparks painted the canopy with an ever-expanding brush of radiance. Music became light, as if someone had sung the words of old, "Let there be light," and continued the refrain until the singer's eloquent vocal strokes finished his masterpiece—a world of vision and revelation.

When every spot of blackness had vanished, Nathan lowered his violin, but his brain continued constructing harmonizing notes. The surrounding fog pushed away, as if blown by the musical wind. Another voice joined the chorus, a contralto that picked up Nathan's harmony and added new measures the moment Nathan thought them.

He stood on a transparent walkway about two strides in width and looked all around—nothing but clear white sky above and a soupy blanket of multicolored mist surrounded the path. The glassy trail extended into emptiness in both directions—a long walk into a wall of fog.

Kelly's eyes, as clear as crystals, twinkled with pleasure, like two drops of starlight decorating the face of a radiant angel. "You can see now, can't you?" she asked.

He nodded but said nothing. What could he say? This new realm seemed to beg for silence, if only to allow for hearing the blessed voice that graced the air. And hearing it made everything seem as beautiful as a master's painting—Kelly, the portrait of heavenly majesty; Daryl, an ivory-skinned icon; and the misty world, a palace of rainbows.

Daryl stuffed her hands into her sweatshirt's front pocket and inched toward the edge of the walkway, her knees shaking as she peered into the mist. Wide-eyed and mouth agape, she also seemed uncharacteristically mute.

As Nathan stared at the mesmerizing scene, the music slowly grew louder, adding to the hypnotic spell. An urgent tap on his shoulder broke him away. Kelly, her eyebrows arching up, pointed down the path with her thumb.

Far in the distance, a solitary figure walked toward them. With his eyes focused on a book, he seemed in no hurry, nor did he seem aware of their presence. Either that, or he simply didn't care.

Still feeling the need to stay quiet, Nathan silently repacked his violin, left it on the walkway, and stepped in front of the two girls. As the man continued his approach, the material in his loose-fitting trousers swished together, the same blue-trimmed pants Patar had worn in the mirror. Muscles in his forearms, extending from his flowing navy blue shirt, flexed as he turned a page, and tufts of white hair blew across his forehead, staying just out of his eyes. His clean-shaven face seemed without wrinkle or blemish, a youthful contrast to his hoary head, and his pale complexion gave him a ghostly pallor, raising memories of Mictar and Patar, though this man was clearly neither of them.

Nathan cleared his throat. The man looked up, his sparkling eyes widening as he slowed to a halt and scanned the trio. With white eyebrows lifting and mouth slowly opening, he seemed ready to speak, but he just kept staring, his expression giving away only surprise, no hint of pleasure or anger.

Extending his hand, Nathan took a step forward. Feeling a

need to honor the sanctity of this place, he kept his voice low. "I'm Nathan Shepherd."

The man shifted his gaze to Nathan's hand, but he didn't grasp it. Instead, he took in a deep breath and, scanning them one by one, began to sing, yet, not with words, but with vowel sounds, long and short forms as well as diphthongs that rose and fell with the changing notes.

Kelly tapped Nathan's elbow. "He says, 'Greetings, young supplicants from the misty mire. It has been a very long time since our land has been graced by the presence of new arrivals. Yet, no one notified me that replacements were coming.'"

4
SCARLET

The man paused his song, allowing Kelly to take a breath. He smiled as if realizing she was interpreting and needed him to slow down. After another brief second, he continued at a more deliberate pace, and Kelly resumed her echo.

"As you have likely been told by whoever sent for you, this is the land above the worlds. I am Tsayad, one of the guardians, the chosen priests who watch over this realm and those beneath it. Since your interpreter is here, I assume that you have been fully informed and are ready to tell me what your mission is, though it seems clear, given your number and genders, that you have come to replace our supplicants."

Pausing again, he pressed his thumb into his book, marking his page, and gave them a gentle smile. His snowy eyebrows arched as though he expected a reply.

Nathan glanced at Kelly, then at Daryl. Daryl gave him an "I have no idea" kind of look, while Kelly bobbed her head, glancing between him and the camera dangling at her chest.

Nathan squinted at her. What was she signaling? Was she asking if she should take a picture of this guy? He gave her a firm shake of his head. This was no time to guess what that camera might do.

Turning back to Tsayad, Nathan opened his mouth to speak, then closed it again. Should he try to talk? His words had no effect before. Everything about this place seemed geared toward communicating with music. The violin might work. But how could he translate his thoughts into notes?

He shrugged. Why not give it a try? He seemed able to compose something that cleared the darkness. Maybe he could communicate that way again.

Keeping his eye on Tsayad, Nathan stooped, pulled out the violin, and gave the empty case to Daryl. The guardian's eyes brightened, and his smile stretched wider.

As Nathan lifted his bow over the strings, the guardian drew close, angling his ear toward the violin. Excited expectation lit up his face, like a child surveying a room of wrapped presents on Christmas morning.

Nathan paused. What should he play? Classical? Baroque? Modern? He shook his head. No, none of those seemed right. Would any piece created by someone else really work to communicate his thoughts? Wouldn't the music have to be something new, something he composed based on the passions and moods running through his mind?

Taking a deep breath, Nathan concentrated on his thoughts and set his composing spirit in line with his emotions. Then, leading with a long A note and moving into a series of arpeggios, he recalled their story and poured out his feelings—his anguish over his parents' loss, his flight from Dr. Gordon of Earth Blue, his joy over finding a friend like Kelly—into his musical score. As he played, the story flowed from his hands more freely and fully than words could ever express. It seemed as though speech should always have been this way, so expressive, so pure, so pulsing with life.

When he finally reached the end, he let his arms dangle limply, exhausted by the effort.

Tsayad stared at him, his mouth agape. Then, ever so slowly, the white-haired man's lips spread out again into a wide smile. He clapped his hands twice, intertwining his fingers after the second clap. Then, swiveling toward Kelly, he sang again, this time in rapid bursts.

Kelly interpreted. "I am pleased to see that you are a virtuoso with my master's chosen instrument. This bodes well for your qualifications. And I am saddened over your losses, but I cannot help you find your loved ones. Perhaps your tragedies explain why you have been sent here. Our current supplicants always bear heart-wrenching sorrows, but that is their purpose, is it not?"

For a moment, he stopped singing. He raised one hand to his chin while the other held the book at his thigh with the pages facing out, his thumb still marking his place. Nathan peeked at the black marks within — a complex musical score, too far away to read.

After a few more seconds, Tsayad's eyes flashed with light. He sang once more, this time with even greater enthusiasm.

Kelly's voice spiked with energy, as if echoing the man's emotion. "It is clear from your musical gift that you are a qualified supplicant, so we should take you to your station immediately. With the brewing crisis in the triad, it is fitting that the travelers sent you to us."

When he stopped singing again, he turned and gestured for them to follow, his smile warm and inviting.

Nathan glanced at Kelly and Daryl in turn. "Any clue what he's talking about?"

Both girls shook their heads. "I guess we can follow," Kelly said. "What choice do we have?"

"I can't argue with that." As Nathan advanced with Kelly and Daryl following close behind, the guardian nodded, opened his book, and marched away slowly, singing once again.

Kelly whispered the meaning, her words barely audible as their shoes squeaked on the glassy path.

To conquer wisdom's doom,
We lift the holy tower
With darkness fed by gloom
Absorbed by torment's power.

Nathan grimaced. So dark and dismal. And this certainly wasn't the voice that had filled his mind with beauty, a beauty so rich he could smell it in the air. Even the tune seemed warped, dissonant, twisted.

As they continued, the fog bank enveloped them, leaving only the bare outline of the guardian visible in front. The vapor muffled his song and Kelly's translation, yet not enough to make them inaudible.

> *Travailing songs they raise*
> *In desperation's throes.*
> *Their sacrifice we praise*
> *In cantabile prose.*
>
> *O let the worlds below,*
> *Forever locked in dread,*
> *Send anguished cries of woe,*
> *Our sustenance, our bread.*

A sense of cold filtered through the air. Nathan shivered. Every verse sounded more and more ominous, matching the foreboding gloom that weighed him down with each step into the thickening mist. Yet, what could they do but follow? He had no idea how to go home.

Fortunately, Tsayad ended his song. A more textured surface below had silenced their shoes, leaving their uneasy breathing as the only discernible sounds. Kelly clutched his elbow from behind but said nothing. She didn't have to speak. Her fears came through her trembling fingers loud and clear.

After another minute or so, the mist thinned out, allowing a vague white light to shine through from above. The path widened until the edges disappeared from sight, the surface now a terrazzo floor with sparkling flecks of copper and silver blended into the polished stones.

When they finally broke into a clearing, Nathan blinked at the brighter light. The floor had become a vast circle of glittering gemstones, so wide he could barely see the rainbow mist that lapped against the outer edges. Curved walls bordered the circle, sloping up to an apex that arched high overhead. Thousands of glass squares covered the surface, creating a huge dome of polished crystal.

On three of the surrounding walls, separated by equal distances, an image of an enormous rotating Earth seemed to float on the transparent mosaic—one with thin red mist swirling all around, another with blue mist, and the third with yellow. The mist that poured in from the walkway crept along the base of the boundary wall, making a river all the way around. When the multicolored stream passed one of the earth images, the mist of that earth's color crawled upward on the wall and joined the foggy portrait, as if feeding the planet's misty veil.

A loud crack sounded from one of the earth images. Tsayad spun toward it. A jagged line crawled along the wall. It stretched from the earth veiled in red toward the one in blue and struck its surface with a sizzling splash. Mist followed the crack from each side—red from one and blue from the other—and met in the middle, mixing together and turning purple. The purple mist bled into the crooked trail back toward each earth and began to spread slowly over the surface of the planets.

Nathan scanned the rest of the wall. Other lines carved jagged paths between the earths, some arching over the ceiling to reach their targets. Orange, green, and purple mist traversed the crooked highways and created islands of blended colors that spread slowly across the respective Earths.

The guardian turned back to the trio, a stoic countenance dressing his face. He sang a few quick vowels toward the center of the circular floor, where, maybe a hundred feet away, a group of twelve people stood. Dressed in garb similar to his own, they huddled around a glass dome, the apex of which rose a foot or so higher than their heads.

Kelly whispered the translation. "Another breach. Widen it while it is fresh."

The twelve joined hands and sang toward the dome, a tune that carried a sharp cadence and a blend of tones: male and female; tenors, basses, sopranos, and altos; lovely, yet harsh; hypnotic, yet troubling.

Kelly's grip deepened. "Nathan. That song creeps me out."

He turned toward her. "What are they saying?"

"Awful things." Kelly gave him a quick "Shh!" and nodded ahead.

When Nathan swung back around, Tsayad stood only a couple of feet away, reaching out a hand as he began a new song.

"Come and see," Kelly translated. "You are at the threshold of the altar where you will soon take your station."

The guardian strode toward the center of the room, now quickening his pace. Nathan glanced back at Kelly again. "Maybe you'd better stay here."

She tightened her grip on his elbow. "Not on your life. I'm not leaving you for a minute."

"Me neither," Daryl said. "This place makes *The Village* look friendly."

Nathan gave them a nod and followed Tsayad, closing the gap as they neared the strange gathering. When the guardian came within several paces of the group, he sang a short burst of vowels that sounded more like an "ahem" than words.

The group turned toward them. The seven men and five women, all with short white hair, flashed eerie smiles that gave Nathan a new shiver. Three of them shifted to the right, leaving a gap that provided a view of the glass dome. As they parted, they revealed the rest of the chamber's central area. Two other domes abutted this one, making a triangle of domes, each one with white-haired people gazing into it.

Nathan took a step toward the closest dome. Resembling

the top half of a transparent sphere, the glass edges had been anchored to the floor with foot-long clasps and fist-sized bolts. Within the dim interior, a girl no more than fifteen years old sat at the center, shivering. With her head tucked between her knees, she pulled at the hem of her simple cloth skirt, trying unsuccessfully to cover her legs.

Kelly gasped. "Oh, Nathan!"

His heart pounding, Nathan crept closer. The girl looked so pitiful ... so frightened. Why would she be in there?

Suddenly, the girl swiped at her shoulder, as if swatting a bug away. Her face stretched by terror, she slid on her bottom toward the outer wall, pumping her legs furiously. When she reached the glass, she pressed a hand against her chest, panting and swinging her head back and forth as if searching for something on the floor.

"Could she be having a nightmare?" Nathan asked Kelly. "I don't see anything in there with her."

Then, closing her eyes, the girl raised her head and moved her lips, apparently in song, but as Nathan leaned toward her to listen, the men and women raised their hands and sang a warbling phrase that drowned out her voice.

Their song jolted Nathan's senses. This was nothing like the heavenly aria he had heard when he first arrived. It was an operatic train wreck. Every note clashed with the others, as if battling to see which one could most effectively sabotage the choir. Still, it seemed that the individual singers hit each note perfectly, as though twelve master artists had chosen to paint a different portrait on the same canvas.

As the singing continued, clouds of black mist rose to the top of the room and disappeared into a purplish haze above, as if there were a chimney drawing out and dispersing this solidified music.

A cracking sound returned. The purple breach stretching from the red planet to the blue widened, slowly, yet noticeably.

As the song continued, the girl inside the dome shook. Still singing, she wrapped her arms around herself, but she seemed unable to quell her shivers.

Nathan rushed to the dome and laid his palms on the glass. "She's terrified! Let her out of there!" He swung toward the other domes. They also enclosed human figures, but the interiors were too dim to discern any details.

Turning back, he gazed at the forlorn girl behind the crystal wall. Her features were all too clear—tear-streaked face, frazzled braids of red hair, and wringing hands. Her terror shook him to the bone. Suddenly, she looked straight at him. With her eyes wide again, she mouthed two silent words. *Help me.*

A firm tug on his sweatshirt sent Nathan flying backwards. Holding his violin aloft, he fell on his side and slid at least twenty yards across the polished floor. He jumped to his feet and whirled back toward the dome. Tsayad scowled at him and sang a string of vowel sounds that resembled a strident scolding.

Kelly ran to Nathan's side. "He says it is forbidden to aid the supplicants. You will soon learn the rules that govern this sacred temple."

As Daryl slowly backed toward them, she stretched out her words. "I think we should be going now."

Nathan searched for an escape route. Two white-haired men guarded the sides of the narrow doorway they had entered.

Tsayad walked slowly toward them, extending his hand, his song now gentle and coaxing.

Kelly pressed close to Nathan. "He says, 'Your fear is most exhilarating. You will make fine supplicants. Come and we will prepare you for your office.'"

Nathan swung the violin up and played a frenzied series of dissonant notes. When he stopped, the guardian's scowl returned, only deeper ... perplexed.

Leaning next to his ear, Kelly whispered, "Uh-oh!"

"What?" Nathan asked. "What did I say?"

Daryl hugged the violin case close to her chest. "I think you cursed in the language of the lyrically limited."

Kelly pulled Nathan backwards. "You told him to release the supplicants or else."

"Or else, what?"

"You didn't say."

Tsayad stalked toward him. As he stretched out his arms, his eyes seemed to burst into flames.

Nathan raised his violin, ready to swing. "Let's see if he understands this composition!"

A loud, shrieking note pierced the air. Tsayad halted and pivoted toward the source. From the gathering around the dome, a white-haired woman rushed their way, shouting in a melodic trill.

Kelly translated. "Allow me to dispose of these dissemblers. They cannot be true supplicants."

The woman pulled down the neckline of Nathan's sweatshirt, exposing his chest. She sang two quick notes.

"You see?" Kelly echoed.

The woman released Nathan and scowled. As she sang a mocking phrase, she seemed to laugh.

Kelly shuddered. "The grinding stone is too good for them."

Tsayad's eyes lit up again. "The abyss?" Kelly said, giving words to his musical response.

The woman replied with a single low note. Kelly didn't bother to translate. Apparently the abyss would be their next stop.

"Take this," Nathan said, pushing the violin into Kelly's hands. "You and Daryl get ready to run."

The woman snapped her fingers. The two men at the door marched toward them, each one brandishing a transparent rod, like a policeman's nightstick made out of glass.

"Go!" Nathan rushed toward the guards. He dropped low and swept his leg under one of the men, toppling him to the ground. The other guard lunged, his glass rod now pulsing with light. A shrill noise spewed from his weapon, so high-pitched Nathan had to cover his ears to keep his brain from exploding.

With a quick roll, he dodged the guard, but just as he tried to jump to his feet, a burning pain stabbed his back. His limbs stiffened. His teeth clenched. A bone-rattling jolt surged up and down his spine and shot out to his fingers and toes. He tried to gasp for breath, but his lungs felt like stones.

Darkness seeped across his vision, streams of black bleeding through a scene of Kelly and Daryl being led toward him by the white-haired woman. Finally, everything went black. He could still sense his surroundings—smells, pressure on his skin, and sounds—but a harsh ringing in his ears made the garbled notes of the jabbering guardians sound far away.

Strong arms lifted him into the air. Finally able to breathe without pain, he floated comfortably. The familiar feeling of approaching sleep crept in. He tried to shake it away. He had to get down! He had to escape with Kelly and Daryl! But his limbs wouldn't obey. They hung limply, unable to move.

The encroaching sleep flooded his senses. Yet, it seemed to last for only a few seconds. Something prodded his shoulder.

"Wake up, Nathan."

He blinked until his eyes opened fully. His vision had returned, still dim, but clear enough. Sitting next to him, the girl in the dome smoothed her skirt of crimson cloth over her crossed legs. "Are you hurt?" she asked.

Still lying on his back, Nathan arched and stretched out his arms before propping himself on his elbows to look at her. Wide and worn by tears, her eyes reflected a weariness that cried out for relief. Yet, the furrows etching her brow spelled out a deep compassion that overwhelmed her sorrows.

"No," he replied. "I think I'm okay." He looked around at the dome. The inner glass reflected their bodies, shielding their view of the outside world.

"You are okay now, my beloved." She laid a hand on his arm. Her face, though as youthful as her petite body, radiated wisdom far beyond her years. "But if you do not awaken soon, you will not be okay. Your rescuer will need your aid."

"Awaken? What do you mean?"

"You are dreaming, and you need to arouse yourself so that you may help your friends."

He sat up and blinked again. "Dreaming? But this is so real."

With thin fingers, she twirled a button at the front of her dress, a tiny white button that fastened a high neckline. "I am real, and this prison is real, but you are not really here. I saw what they did to you. Since we made eye contact, I was able to enter your dream as soon as you lost consciousness."

Nathan glanced at the mirrored walls. "How could you see me?"

"I am Scarlet. I see many things." She looked up at the low ceiling. "Behold, the tragedy of lost lives."

In the curved mirror above, an airliner flying at a ninety-degree angle dropped slowly from the sky. The tip of its wing scraped the ground, sending it into a cartwheel tumble. Finally, it flipped, smashed into a field, and exploded in a huge fireball.

As memory of the searing heat raised prickles along his skin, Nathan shuddered. "I was on that plane ... at least for a while. I got off just in time."

She folded her hands and sighed. "I know. I helped you get off."

"You helped me? How?"

"You have asked for my help many times, and I, in turn, take your supplications to your ultimate helper. My songs are the prayers you were unable to utter. The answers came in many ways—a gunman arrested on a bridge; your body shifted to another world just before a bullet pierced your chest while your clothes miraculously changed into a hunter's raiment; you and your friends transported out of a falling car while at another time the entire car went with you; and any number of escapes in the midst of chases, unknown paths, and even violent winds. Such are the miracles of answered supplications."

"But how does it work? How can you know what's going on all the time?"

She slid closer to him and gazed into his eyes. "It is not wise to waste precious moments explaining the complexities of my ministration while you are dreaming. Soon after you awaken, you will not remember the details, only images ... images of me, my habitat, my sorrow. Just remember that you must come back and rescue us, the three seers in the domes. Since you are an Earth Red dweller, you have only a little time. Interfinity is coming, and the fools here have no idea that it will destroy them along with the three Earths."

She took his hand and caressed his knuckles. "Yet, there is still hope. You, my love, are one of the gifted, and another is searching for you in her dreams. Perhaps we can guide her to a convenient place to meet you. If it is possible to heal the wounds through music rather than through sacrifice, the two of you will have to work together and play the violin in Sarah's Womb. On this possibility rests the future of all the supplicants."

"Patar mentioned Sarah's Womb. What—"

She pressed a finger against his lips. "No, Nathan. Save your questions." As she withdrew her finger, her whispered voice took on a sense of urgency. "Arouse yourself now, or you will perish, and the hope of the Earth triad will perish with you. One truth you must remember as you make this journey—the stalkers feed on fear and the dissonance fear creates. If you run from the shadows that haunt your mind, all will be lost."

"But how will I remember all these things? Like you said, dreams just kind of fade away."

"I will do what I can to revive your memory." As she kissed him tenderly on the cheek, her lips trembled. "Someday I hope to anoint your cheek in person, but for now a dream will have to do."

Her vibrating voice tickled his skin, and the fragrance of roses wafted into his nose. He drank in the sweet sensations. This seemed far too real to be a dream, but he had no choice but to believe. If she said he had to wake up, he had better get to work.

Closing his eyes and clenching his fists, he tried to refocus his mind on reality and strain his senses to tune into his surroundings. After a few seconds, Kelly's voice drizzled into his ears. "He's twitching. Look, he's making a fist."

Something poked him in the side. "Nathan! Wake up!"

He blinked. This time reality flashed in his eyes. The girl and the domed prison had vanished, leaving only fog and the worried faces of Kelly and Daryl.

Kelly grasped his hand. "Can you get up?"

Nathan surveyed his body. The pain had returned, a hundred aches stabbing him from head to toe. "I'll try." He pulled on her hand and rose to his feet, teetering for a moment while Kelly and Daryl kept him from falling.

He took in his surroundings, the glassy path and swirls of colored mist all around. A musical note, friendly but firm, made him turn his head. The white-haired woman stood behind them, a serious aspect bending her face downward as she glanced nervously both ways along the path.

Kelly held the camera to keep it from swaying at her chest. "She says we have to hurry. She's really on our side."

"Our side?"

"Yes, she—"

The woman sang again, rushing through her notes. Kelly

translated with a rapid chatter. "My name is Abodah. If you are truly the healer, I have much to do."

Nathan reached for the violin and bow tucked at Kelly's side. "I need to ask some questions, like, what is this place? How do I get to the violin in Sarah's Womb? When can I come back and rescue those prisoners?"

The woman laid a firm hand on his arm. She sang again, this time more slowly.

"No need to play music to ask your questions," Kelly translated. "My mate and I have learned to understand your language, though I cannot yet speak it. He knows the ways of your people, so I suggest that you heed his counsel as he leads you to the places you must go. While you are gone, I will work with the supplicants to ensure that you have a clear path to the instrument, but if playing the healing music fails, rescuing them could well be impossible. Yet, I will see what I can do. Let us have no more questions. It is time for you to go."

Abodah knelt on the walkway and dipped her hands into the mist. Then, cupping a cloud of all three colors, she straightened and held out her hands. A stream of red mist drifted toward Kelly, while a blue one rose up and floated Daryl's way. Finally, a second red stream lifted from her hands and caressed Nathan's cheek. Soon, all three streams evaporated, leaving only yellow mist in Abodah's hands.

With a quizzical look in her eyes, she sang a brief tune.

"You are not from the same worlds," Kelly said. "To which one shall I send you?"

Nathan laid a hand against his pounding head. Earth Blue seemed the obvious choice. That's where Clara was waiting for them, and they left the mirror there. They needed that if they were to go anywhere else. "I guess we should go to Earth Blue," he finally said. "Is that okay?"

Abodah gave him a pleasant smile. She sang once more, and Kelly interpreted, this time speaking the words in song, following her tune. "That is the easiest option. I will send you back through the door you entered."

She reached again into the mist and scooped out a handful of blue vapor. Then, singing again, she anointed each of their foreheads with her moistened finger.

"I am marking you for travel," Kelly said. "The ancient legend has never been tested, but I believe this sign will lead you home."

She turned toward the opposite side, spread out her arms, and sang a shrill note. The multicolored mist instantly parted, piling up on each edge of the divide. In the gap, a deep gulf plunged into a black void.

Daryl gulped. "Holy Moses!"

Abodah extended her hand toward the chasm as if inviting them to jump. Nathan looked at Kelly, then Daryl, and read fear in their eyes. He stooped and peered into the darkness. "So is it safe to just jump right in?"

Kelly sang Abodah's reply. "It is a leap of faith, to be sure. My mate pursued Mictar through this rift in the cosmos, and one of the supplicants told me that he arrived safely. I assume that you, too, will land without harm."

"I guess we have no choice." Nathan retrieved the case from Daryl, repacked the violin, and lined up his toes with the very edge. After what he had been through, leaping into a void seemed like no big deal. And, besides, the quicker he got home, the quicker he could try to solve all the mysteries and figure out a way to rescue Scarlet and the other supplicants.

Kelly took his hand, her eyes as bright as ever as she leaned close and whispered, "I rode on a doomed jet. I can do this."

Nathan twisted toward Daryl. Wringing her hands against her chest, she slid her feet away from the edge.

"Come on." He set the violin down and reached for her. "It'll be fine. Kelly and I have been through worse stuff than this."

She stopped, her eyes wide. "Ever see *Vertigo?*"

He took a step toward her. "Alfred Hitchcock, right?"

"Yep." Her voice trembled as she leaned away from his reach. "That's me. Crazy scared of heights."

With a quick lunge, he snatched her wrist. "Then keep your eyes closed and hang on."

"No!" She jerked away. "I can't. I . . . I just can't."

Nathan huffed. Even though Scarlet's words were already fading, her warning about giving in to fear still echoed. He gritted his teeth to keep from shouting. "We can't leave you here, and there's no other way home." He reached for her again. "This is no time to lose your cool!"

She leaped away and teetered on the opposite edge, her arms flailing. In a flash, Abodah was at her side and pushed her upright with a gentle hand.

As Daryl lowered herself to a shivering crouch, Abodah sang.

"She must go with you," Kelly translated. "There is little time to lose." She then whispered to Nathan, "What should we do?"

"We'll have to force her," he whispered back. "We can't stay. Her going phobic might get us all killed."

Kelly's voice sharpened. "Give her a break. Isn't there anything that scares you like that?"

"Not that I can think of." Nathan frowned at his own words. They sounded merciless. Actually, lots of things scared him, but nothing made him lose his nerve like this. And, merciless or not, he had to be tough to get them out of this jam. He lowered his whisper even further. "We can't stand around and wait. You get on one side of her, and I'll get on the other. We'll take her kicking and screaming if we have to."

"Are you sure?"

"You have another idea?"

She shrugged.

"Then, c'mon."

While Daryl kept her head tucked low, Nathan crept to her

side. As soon as Kelly stooped at her other side, he grasped Daryl's upper arm and pulled her upright. Daryl tried to twist free, but Kelly held her in place. Tears streaming and her whole body shaking, Daryl looked back and forth at her captors. "Oh, please. Please don't make me go."

"We don't have any choice." Nathan pulled, and Daryl hobbled along, though with her legs buckling, he practically dragged her across the path.

When they reached the edge, Kelly spoke in a smooth, quiet tone. "It's okay, Daryl. Trust us. Like Nathan said, we've been through scarier stuff than this, and he hasn't let me down yet."

"Yet?" Daryl squeaked.

Nathan tried to hide a painful swallow. How could he be sure? Maybe this Abodah lady had no clue. Maybe she was lying and thought it some kind of macabre joke to get them to jump in on their own. But he had to believe the best, and he had to give Daryl reason to believe. Softening his tone, he loosened his grip. "Daryl, we're going, and you can't stay here. Are you with us?"

As her trembling eased, Daryl gazed into the void. "It's ... so dark."

Kelly looped her arm around Daryl's. "C'mon. We'll stay together no matter what happens."

Daryl squeezed Kelly's arm and closed her eyes. "Tell me when it's over!"

Abodah jerked her head to the side. Far along the pathway another white-haired figure approached. Nathan snatched up the violin, gave her a nod, and whispered, "Now!" The three bent their knees and jumped into the void.

5

FOUNDATION'S KEY

As soon as they fell into the chasm, a stream of blue rushed out from the surrounding walls of mist, wrapped around their bodies, and guided them down a dizzying corkscrew path into the darkness. Above, the edges of the chasm seemed to merge, like a giant animal's jaws closing to trap its prey. The sense of utter helplessness, falling without knowing when or if the plunge would end, jerked the breath right out of Nathan's lungs. Daryl screamed, but the rushing wind snuffed out her cry. Kelly's eyes dimmed until her inner light completely vanished.

After what seemed like a full minute of free falling, a sense of wetness brushed Nathan's cheeks. The darkness began to fade, revealing a familiar swirling mist surrounding their bodies. Seconds later, their descent slowed. The mist thinned out. The mirror, jagged and misshapen at first, materialized in front of them, slowly regaining its square form and reflective clarity as the fog swept away.

Nathan pried Daryl's fingers from his arm. "It's okay. We're back."

She crouched and laid her palms on the carpet. "Terra firma! Am I glad to see you!"

"So," Nathan said as he walked toward the mirror, "we have to find Abodah's mate if we want to know what to do next. I'm guessing it's Patar, but how do we get him to come back?"

Kelly, her eyes glassy once again, lifted the camera. "In the meantime, do you want to develop the film? I took quite a few pictures while we were up there, especially the girl in the dome. Maybe—"

"You did? That's great! I was trying to tell you not to."

"I know," she said with a wink. "That's why I left the flash off." She angled the camera's photo counter toward him. "Only a couple of pictures left, but it won't hurt to go ahead and process the film."

Nathan glanced at the mirror. For a second he thought he caught a glimpse of Patar, but nothing unusual appeared in the reflection. Patar's words, however, continued to haunt his mind. *Play the violin, and all will be made right ... Sarah's Womb ... follow the wisdom you gain each step along the way.*

He touched the top of the camera. Could the photos be part of that wisdom? He couldn't risk missing out on such a potentially important clue. "They might help," he said. "I'll call Wal-Mart and see if they're open. The roads are dicey, but we should be able to make it."

"Only if you walk," Daryl said as she looked out the window.

Nathan set the violin on the floor and strode toward her. "What do you mean?"

As she backed away, she pulled a curtain to the side. "The car's gone. No sign of Clara."

Nathan pressed his nose against the glass. Although wind-blown fog still saturated the area, he could see the entire yard. "She just left without us?"

"Or something made her leave." Kelly peeked over his shoulder. "Maybe she had to escape."

Nathan checked his watch. Five till noon. Only about a half hour had passed. Backing away from the mirror, he searched the walls. "Is there a clock around here? Something that doesn't run on electricity?"

"I get your drift," Daryl said. "A time warp kind of thing. Maybe she got tired of waiting."

Kelly pointed toward the hall. "My father has a clock in his den with a battery backup. Kelly Blue's father probably had one, too."

"I'll look." Nathan jogged to Tony Clark's den at the opposite end of the house and halted at the doorway. A wide-screen plasma TV dangled on the wall by one of its corners. A half-size refrigerator lay open on its side with at least ten bottles of beer lying next to the door. Three long gashes marred a plush recliner, and clumps of padding lay scattered across the carpet. Jagged slices ripped through basketball posters that lined the perimeter. What was once a sports fan's paradise was now the victim of a malevolent vandal, or worse.

A digital clock sat on top of a trophy case. The numerals read 3:36. Nathan checked his watch again. They had been gone for four hours! No wonder Clara took off.

He walked in and pushed the trophy case's door closed, using his foot to move a toppled basketball statuette out of the way. Shards of glass lay on the carpet and inside the case. Obviously a hefty kick made an entry key unnecessary. Someone must have been desperate to find something.

Inside the case, a folded sheet of paper under one of the trophies caught his eye. He pulled it out and read a scribbled note on top, "Foundation's Key." The lettering was clearly his own. He unfolded the sheet and found musical notes hastily written on a hand-drawn staff. He recognized the style—the way the quarter notes weren't completely filled in and how the numerals in the time signature didn't quite align. Again, this was his own notation. Nathan Blue must have squirreled this music away in the trophy case for safekeeping.

After tucking the sheet in his back pocket, he hustled across the house again. When he breezed into the bedroom, Daryl lifted her cell phone. "I had a signal for a minute, but Clara didn't answer."

Kelly cocked her head toward the garage side of the house. "If the motorcycles are here, we have wheels."

Nathan laid his hand on his back pocket. Telling them about the music could wait. It might be nothing. Best to develop the photos and try to call Clara later. "Daryl, can you operate a motorcycle?"

"I've seen *Ghost Rider* six times," Daryl said. "Looks easy enough."

Kelly rolled her eyes. "Oh, sure. In fog, on icy roads, with high winds." She pressed her finger against Daryl's shoulder. "You ride with Nathan. I can see well enough to stick to your trail."

Nathan touched his shoulder. "Do you need to change your bandage first?"

"No. The bleeding's stopped. I'll be fine."

After prying the Quattro mirror loose and packing it, the camera, and Nathan Blue's violin in a waterproof saddle pack, the three mounted the twin motorcycles and navigated the icy roads toward Wal-Mart.

While Nathan watched Kelly in the rearview mirror, Daryl kept a death grip around his ribcage as she sat in the saddle behind him. With every icy skid and blind journey through a dense fog bank, her arms tightened around his torso. Kelly seemed to have no trouble. With her head tilted downward, she kept her front tire planted in his rear tire's groove.

Nathan slowed down in front of an Arby's restaurant at the entrance to the Wal-Mart parking lot. At least twenty cars roared out of the main lot, ignoring the traffic light. Tires squealed. Horns blared. Most of the drivers displayed sheer terror — wide eyes, gritting teeth, and fingers strangling the steering wheels.

When the last car cleared the intersection, as if summoned by the wake of the frenzied exodus, a fresh breeze from the north swept the fog away and left a clear, sunny sky. But the wind brought with it a sharp chill, like the coldest day in January.

The frigid air beat against Nathan's dampened sweatshirt, making him shiver hard. Earth Blue's reflection of Earth Yellow's weather felt like a climatic roller-coaster ride. But what effects was interfinity having on Yellow? Was the nightmare epidemic he had witnessed there still going strong? Had their prophetic dreams spread to Earth Blue? *Something* had sent the Wal-Mart customers scampering away like frightened mice.

They parked the motorcycles in the nearly empty lot. Nathan dismounted, pulled off his helmet, and tried to call Clara again. After several rings, her voice mail picked up. He left a message, then fished out the mirror and camera.

Kelly set her cycle's stand and slid up her visor. "You going in?"

"Yeah, but I'll try to stay in sight. You two hang here till I signal you."

Hugging herself, Daryl shivered. "Glad to. Just make sure the signal doesn't include burned-out eyeballs."

He hustled to the door and peered through the glass. Only the barest of lights illuminated the aisles, leaving the shopping area almost completely dark. He pulled the door open a crack. Obviously the store wasn't closed

Raising a finger to signal "hang on a minute" to the girls, he squeezed through the opening and eased inside. Taking small, quiet steps, he scanned the massive store. Dim light from the windows revealed long lines of shelving with shadowed merchandise, but little else. The aroma of burnt popcorn blended with a cleaning fluid of some kind, and a low hum sounded in the background—a good sign that electrical power was available somewhere in the building.

An odd crackling sound mixed into the hum, like garbled music played on blended radio stations. It seemed to carry a cadence, a musical rhythm searching for a matching melody.

He returned to the door and held it open, waving at the girls. After a few seconds, they walked in, shivering as they pulled off their helmets and shook out their hair.

"There's not a soul in the store," Daryl said, her voice echoing.

"I'll run the photo machine myself if I have to." Nathan pointed at the ceiling. "But if the store's on generator power, these hazard lights might be the only thing drawing electricity."

Kelly turned toward the registers. "Are those lights over there?"

Nathan set his helmet in an empty space on a clearance shelf and walked toward the vacant checkout lanes. Indeed, two of the registers in the self-serve aisle were turned on and seemed ready to operate. He glanced out the window. Snow. Heavy snow. Whatever reason the employees had for jumping ship, with this weather, they wouldn't likely be returning soon.

He stripped off his wet sweatshirt and gestured with his thumb toward the merchandise area. "Daryl, Kelly, I'll find the photo lab. You two get some warmer clothes. I'll need a coat ... large, maybe with a lining."

Daryl set the other helmets beside Nathan's and took Kelly's elbow. "You got it, boss." The two walked into the dimness and disappeared from sight.

After finding the lab at the front of the store, Nathan turned on a desk lamp and aimed it at the film processor. He draped the camera strap around his neck and scanned the controls. Good. It was similar to a machine his father often used when he was in a hurry and couldn't process the film at his home lab. Since his photos were frequently top secret, a drugstore owner would let him come in after hours and develop them himself, and Nathan often helped.

He flipped on the switch. If it had been shut down only recently, the chemistry wouldn't take too long to warm up, and there was no need to turn on the printer. He could just burn them all to a CD and print them later.

A dull thud sounded from the main store area. He jerked his head toward the noise. Nothing but motionless shadows in the dimness. A new chill raised goose bumps all over his arms. Were the girls safe? Should he have let them wander into the darkness without him?

He grabbed his mirror and jogged toward the women's department. As he closed in on the racks of clothing, he slowed, trying to make sure his shoes didn't squeak. A heavy foreboding of danger throbbed in his mind. Yet, no one was in sight—no hint of Daryl's usual chatter or the sound of footsteps. Everything was deathly quiet.

Still pressing his feet softly, he turned and walked backwards, using his mirror to see what lay behind him. Nothing. Only circular racks of ladies' sweatshirts and jeans.

He stared at the shadowy, feminine clothes. No sign of movement. Could they be in the men's department looking for his coat? He hurried along the dim aisle and again slowed and soft-stepped backwards, guided by his mirror. After passing the underwear and sock aisles, a rack of coats came into view, dark and indistinct.

A shadow darted from one rack to another—small, fast, fleeting. He jerked around. Nothing there. Walking on tiptoes, he approached the rack where the shadow had hidden, reaching his hand toward the thick coats hanging from the circular turnstile.

He snatched a coat and shoved it to the side. Still nothing.

Leaning over, he peered into the dark gap. Something touched his shoulder. He jumped and swung his fist but pulled back just in time to miss Kelly's chin. He shook his head hard. "Don't scare me like that!"

"Sorry. I wasn't sure it was you till I got close. It took me a while to grope my way over here."

He searched the dark aisle. "Where's Daryl?"

"In the restroom. We found one of the customers hiding there, shaking like a leaf. Her name's Carlita. Daryl knows her, so she stayed behind to settle her down. I heard you walking around, so I knew I could find you."

"Did Daryl's friend say why the place is deserted?"

Kelly leaned close and whispered, "Ghosts."

"Ghosts?" Nathan glanced back at the coat rack. Still no sign of the shadow.

She nodded and pulled on his sleeve. "Come on. You can hear her story for yourself."

"Not the ladies' room again," he said, rolling his eyes.

She pushed him into the aisle. "Lead the way. You should be good at finding it by now."

After taking a last look at the coat rack, Nathan hustled with Kelly to the restroom. Inside, they found a petite Hispanic woman leaning back in a lounge chair. Daryl, wearing a new coat with a tag still hanging over the collar, knelt at the middle-aged woman's side. She fanned her with a newspaper, blowing back her mussed black hair and open white collar. When the lady looked up at Nathan, her eyes widened. Sweat glistened on her brow as she raised two fingers. "*¡Fantasmas!... ¡Vi fantasmas negros!*"

Nathan translated in his mind. *Ghosts! I saw black ghosts!* Through all of his travels, he had learned enough Spanish to figure out what some people were saying, but he didn't dare try to speak it. He'd botch it for sure. "What did they look like?" Nathan asked. "Could you see their faces?"

The lady shook her head. "*No sé cómo responder.*"

Daryl dabbed the lady's forehead with a paper towel. "Kelly, can you be her interpreter? She understands some English, but she's pretty spooked. Besides, my Spanish stinks."

"Sure." Kelly set her hands on her knees and leaned toward Carlita. "*¿Pudiste ver las caras?*"

"¡*Sí!*" Her eyes widened again. "*Una joven y un hombre.*"

Kelly turned toward Nathan. "She saw a girl and a man."

"Yeah, I picked that up." Nathan read the sincerity in Kelly's glazed eyes. Barely able to see, she'd do anything to help. And now he had learned another one of her many talents. "One more question," he said. "Did the ghosts speak?"

As Kelly leaned over again, she touched her lips. "*¿Te hablaron los fantasmas?*"

Carlita nodded vigorously. "*La muchacha dijo que ella desea tocar el violín.*"

"*¿El violín?*" Kelly repeated.

"*Sí. Pero ella era muy amable.*"

Kelly murmured, "I see," then rejoined Nathan. "She says the girl wanted to play the violin, and she was very polite."

Daryl rose to her feet and joined their huddle. "What should we do?"

"I think I saw one of the ghosts," Nathan whispered. "Probably the girl. I'm going to see if I can catch her on film." He pulled a wadded five-dollar bill from his pocket and gave it to Daryl. "Kelly and I'll stay here and hunt for the ghosts while you get Carlita over to Arby's for some coffee."

Daryl took the five and unfolded it. "And some curly fries." She yanked the tag from her coat and handed it to Nathan, pointing at the UPC code. "Just in case you figure out how to pay for it."

He nodded, grabbed Kelly's hand, and led her out of the restroom. "If you'll take the mirror, I'll take the camera on this ghost hunt."

"We should be wearing those safari outfits," she said, squeezing his hand playfully.

Nathan handed her the mirror. "Save those for the next nightmare."

With the camera poised in front of him, he led the way back to the men's department. When they approached the coat rack, he slowed his pace and tiptoed, searching the darkness for an animated shadow. The garbled radio music grew louder and faster, as if echoing his thumping heart. As he reached for the coat rack, a hint of movement guided his eyes toward an end cap stuffed with gym socks. A small human-shaped figure, as dark and shapeless as a shadow, stood at the edge of the aisle, facing him.

He raised the camera to his eye, turned on the flash, and focused on the diminutive ghost. Hair flowed past her shoulders, and feminine contours lined her frame, revealing her gender. Yet, with vague blackness veiling any details, she seemed like a bodiless soul.

As he reached for the shutter button, the background noise heightened to a frenzy, buzzing, beating, sizzling in his ears and sending a tingle through his body. His finger trembled as it hovered over the button.

"Nathan," Kelly said, backing away, "maybe you'd better not."

The ghost walked slowly toward them, reaching out her dark hand.

"Don't you want to know what's going on?" Nathan asked.

The noise grew so loud, Kelly had to raise her voice. "Yeah ... kind of. But ..."

Another shadow stepped up behind the smaller one, taller, thicker, obviously masculine. The static thumped in Nathan's ears like an audio jackhammer, threatening to break his eardrums. Both shadows now approached. In the camera's viewfinder, the girl's face grew clearer. A glimmer of light glowed in her eyes. Lips emerged, thin and delicate.

Suddenly, the noise fell silent. The girl's lips moved. "Nathan," she said. "I finally found you. I need your help to play the violin."

Nathan gasped. He hit the shutter button and staggered back. The camera flashed. Light shot out in a shimmering conic wave and spilled over the ghosts, illuminating every detail. Although the flash lasted only a split second, the light seemed to linger in the air, like glittering dust that spread the glow from one particle to the next.

As if blown by the wind, the girl's hair streamed behind her. Blues and reds painted her dress and smock. Her face blushed with pink, accenting her familiar high cheekbones. Although she was taller now, her identity was unmistakable.

Nathan could only form the words with his lips. *Francesca!* But no sound came out.

Behind her, the man's face took shape—clearly Dr. Nikolai Malenkov, Francesca's adoptive father. His face carried a confused look, though not unpleasant. In his hands he cradled something long and thin, but with the flash still pulsing in his vision, Nathan couldn't tell what it was.

Like the embers of a dying campfire, the glitters faded, and the surrounding darkness swallowed their glow. Within seconds, the ghosts dimmed to black, then disappeared.

Standing in the middle of the shadowed aisle, Nathan lowered the camera and stared. His feet seemed anchored to the floor.

Kelly laid a hand on his back, her voice quavering. "Was that Francesca?"

He could only nod, hoping she could see his head bob up and down. His throat had clamped shut. What had he done? Did he send Francesca off into another dimension? What were she and Dr. Malenkov doing at Wal-Mart in the first place? Why were they ghostly shadows? And what was he carrying?

A whisper, or maybe an echo of a whisper, drifted through his mind. *You, my love, are one of the gifted, and another is searching for you in her dreams. Perhaps we can guide her to a convenient place to meet you.* And there was something else, something about a violin, but the dream seemed like wisps of vapor, transparent and impossible to grab.

Nathan shook his head. Could Francesca's phantasmic appearance in Earth Blue have been a manifestation of a dream? Francesca's dream? That would be truly bizarre.

He listened to the silence. The buzzing noise didn't return, only the gentle hum of a distant motor. Maybe the static had been a sign of Francesca's presence, a cacophony that needed to be decoded as they had done for the chaotic music at the observatory. If so, the silence proved that she and Nikolai were gone. Not a trace of moving shadow or hint of static remained.

Finally, Nathan forced out a few high-pitched words. "Let's get out of here."

After finding a coat for himself and Kelly, he hustled back to the development lab, leaving Kelly at the adjacent vision center to try on glasses. The photo processor hummed, but the ready light, the indicator that the chemicals had come up to operating temperature, was still dark. He glared at the bulb. How long would it take? They had to hurry.

He found a plastic leader card and attached the end of the film with splice tape. No time to test a blank. It would have to work on the first try. Finally, the ready light flashed on. Perfect. Time to get busy.

Nathan loaded the card on the feeder sprockets, closed the cover, and listened to the chorus of noises. The film reeled out of the cartridge, then a snick sounded from inside, and the empty cartridge clattered into a recycle bin. The first step was underway.

"You all right over there?" Nathan called.

"Fine," Kelly replied. "I can't find any glasses that help, though."

"Hang on. This shouldn't take too long."

As the machine hummed, images of evenings he and his father spent developing photos in a lab at home came to mind—a darkroom light, the odor of chemicals, a line for hanging the photos, and his father's tedious, yet thoughtful way of caring for every detail. By comparison, this machine was ten times easier.

After a few minutes, the last frame slid out the other end, and he sliced the roll free from the card with a pair of scissors. He then loaded the film into the scanner, pulled up the thumbnail images on the monitor, and clicked the mouse on an icon to burn the pictures to a CD.

When the process completed, he pulled the first photo up on the screen. A tremble shook Nathan's hand. Since this camera had belonged to Nathan Blue's father, who could tell what might be on the film? This picture showed Dr. Simon and Dr. Gordon standing together next to the telescope in the observatory. Near the top border the mirrored ceiling reflected the scene below it—a copy of the telescope and the two men.

Nathan zoomed in on the image. There was something in the mirror, something that reminded him of ... Yes. That was it. A misty funnel spinning between Simon and Gordon. Could this be the arrival of Mictar?

He shook away his stare. No more time. He grabbed the CD, stuffed it in a protective envelope, and snatched up a new roll of film from the store's stock. He found Kelly sliding a pair of old-lady spectacles into its case and took her hand. "Let's hit the road!"

After figuring out how to pay for everything at the self-checkout lane, they ran outside with their valuables—mirror, camera, photos, CD, and helmets. Although the snow had stopped, the blistering wind continued. Bundling up, they shuffled to the motorcycles through a two-inch layer of snow. Nathan pulled out his cell phone and punched Clara's speed dial. A few seconds later, he let out a huff. Voice mail again.

They packed their load in the saddlebags, mounted the bikes, and plowed across the parking lot to the Arby's where they found Daryl coming out the door. Nathan handed her a helmet.

Flashing a thumbs-up, she yelled over the motorcycles' rumble, "Carlita's husband is coming to get her."

"That's good. Thanks for doing that." Nathan cut his engine and gazed at the snowy highway, now devoid of cars. At least Carlita was going to be okay, but what about Clara? Where could she have gone? The observatory? And where might Francesca be now? If she needed his help, he had to find her right away. Yet, Patar's warnings were all too clear. He had to play the violin, but should he get Francesca's help? If she couldn't play it by herself, how could he hope to?

He glanced at each of the girls in turn. Kelly shivered under her new coat, and Daryl's lips had turned blue. They couldn't go to the observatory, not in this weather. It was much too far away.

A ray of sunlight caught Nathan's eye. He looked up. The clouds streamed away far more quickly than normal, leaving behind a brilliant blue sky. And something else seemed strange. Sparkles coated the blue canopy, as if an artist had used glitter paint to spruce up the heavens. What could it mean? Another sign of interfinity?

After a tortuous ride through high winds that brushed them back and forth on the snow-covered roads, they arrived at the house. With the electricity still off, Nathan had to run inside and open the garage manually.

When they filed into the bedroom, they tossed their new coats on top of the trunk against the wall. The three sat cross-legged in a circle on the floor with the camera, the mirror section, and the photo CD in the center. With no laptop available, all they could do was stare at the CD's white paper envelope. The hidden photos would remain a mystery for a while longer.

Nathan reached into his back pocket and pulled out the music sheet he had found in the trophy case. "Almost forgot about this." He spread it out close to Kelly's eyes. "Any clue? The only words said, 'Foundation's Key.'"

She leaned to within a few inches of the sheet and squinted. "C Major?"

"Yeah. It's really simple. I could've played it when I was four."

Daryl poked his thigh. "Don't just sit there, Mozart. Play it and get the mirror stoked for action."

While Nathan applied the mirror to its place in the wall and tuned his violin, Daryl chattered. "When Carlita and I went into the Arby's, there was only one guy working, and he was zoned out, couldn't figure out how to use the register, didn't know the prices, you name it. Some guy in the corner was playing a little radio, cradling it like it was his pet hamster or something, and holding it so close I thought he was going to kiss it. Turns out, he was listening to the news, so Carlita and I slid into the booth next to his and eavesdropped. Good thing she didn't understand a lot of it, or she would've started shrieking *fantasmas* again."

Daryl took a breath. "Apparently, a couple of those people you saved on Earth Yellow showed up here on Earth Blue. That author you told me about —Jack, was it?"

Still adjusting his violin, Nathan shook himself out of a trance. Although he had listened to every word, the image of Scarlet and her desperate *Help me!* kept flashing in his mind. "No. Jack was another guy from the plane crash. He showed up on Earth Red."

"Right. Anyway, this author went up to his old house in Chicago and rang the doorbell. Seems his key didn't work anymore. His daughter answered and screamed so loud, the neighbors called the cops. So, when the guy explained his story, the media picked it up and went into a free-for-all frenzy. Then, a woman survivor showed up at her place of business after thirty years of being dead. You can imagine what happened. When that piece of gossip joined the media circus, every freakazoid end-of-the-worlder came out from under their respective rocks and announced the apocalypse. The whole world is scared spitless."

Nathan lifted his bow to the strings. Those weren't the only scary happenings. Should he mention the weird sky? Probably not. No use getting anyone more phobic than they already were. "Are you ready?"

Kelly stood and faced the mirror while holding the music sheet in front of him. "I'm not ready. But go ahead."

"Rarin' to go!" Daryl jumped up and hooked her arm around Kelly's. "That is ... if there aren't any bottomless pits to jump into."

Concentrating on giving the simple tune the best rendering possible, Nathan played it through flawlessly. As soon as he finished and the final note faded, the upper-left square of the mirror flashed like a camera and released a faint popping sound. Then, less than a second later, the square to its right flashed and popped. One by one, moving horizontally to the end and beginning again on the next row, each mirrored square flashed with a burst of light.

Before the series of flashes reached the third row, the image in the first square transformed. Instead of reflecting the room, it showed a snowy field dotted with small shrubs. The second square gave a side view of a gray-haired woman bending over the open hood of a car as if trying to do something to the engine. And on it went, square after square showing different scenes, popping up so fast, Nathan couldn't fully take in one before he shifted to the next.

Finally, four-hundred images—each one showing a different, live-action scene—spanned the wall before them.

Daryl pointed at the second square. "Isn't that Clara?"

Nathan scooted close and peered up at the woman. Although black grease smeared her cheek, there was no mistaking his tutor. "She's stuck somewhere with engine problems."

Squinting as she joined Nathan, Kelly touched one of the

squares. "Does that mean we can go to any of these places if we flash a light?"

"Who knows?" He stepped back and tried to take in the hundreds of images. Could his mother and father be in one of them? That would be the first place he'd want to go, but in some of the scenes, people moved in and out of the square, so even if one of the mirrors represented his parents' location, they might not show up in the image to let him know.

He took a deep breath. It was time to concentrate, do this logically. "Daryl," he said in a gentle tone, "you start in the lower-right corner and work your way to the left and up. I'll work from the top-left corner down. You know what my parents look like, right?"

"Yeah, you showed me their pictures. Well, not you. Nathan Blue did. I think I could spot them."

Nathan raised three fingers, one at a time. "Try to find my parents, Francesca, or that girl in the dome."

"What about Clara?" Daryl asked, looking up at him. "Won't she freeze?"

Nathan gazed at his tutor's image as she stood next to the car's open hood, searching the snow-covered highway for help. No one was in sight. With the bone-chilling wind whipping against her inadequate coat, she wouldn't last long out there. He had to help her right away. But should he go? What about Patar's warnings? Could he afford the time it would take to save one old lady?

After a few seconds, he nodded. Of course he had to go. Patar would just have to deal with it. "Okay. I'll go."

"Me, too." Kelly pressed her thumb against her chest. "I'm the mechanic. Clara can be my eyes."

Again watching the mirror, Nathan bobbed his head. Kelly was right. She was the best option. But how would it work? Should he pry that square off and have her hold it while flashing a light? Would that shut the rest of the mirror down? Not only that, wouldn't this display mean that every square was really a Quattro mirror with power equal to the one in the corner, and equal danger if it fell into the wrong hands?

Nathan headed for the bedroom door. "Gotta get a flashlight and a screwdriver."

After a few minutes of fumbling around in the dark garage, he returned with his items. Daryl, now wearing the camera strap around her neck, nodded toward the hall. "We heard something out there, like someone hitting the floor."

"I didn't see anyone. Probably just the pipes. That's what my father always used to say when I heard noises." Nathan pushed the trunk in front of the mirror, stood on it, and pried Clara's square loose. As soon as it came off, the rest of the squares flashed brightly, then returned to normal.

He looked at the mirror in his hand. Clara was still there, now shivering in the car's driver seat with the door closed.

When he slid the mirror back, it snapped into place. It, too, blinked off and then displayed a six-inch-square reflection of the room. In the image, Kelly and Daryl stared at him, but they said nothing.

Nathan studied the mosaic. He could probably play the music and resurrect the four-hundred images without a problem. But what would happen if they tried traveling to one of the places the mirrors displayed without removing a square? Wouldn't that leave the entire mirror and its abilities available to a thief while they were gone? Not only that, they would be without a mirror themselves, and it had always helped them get around before.

A creaking noise sounded from somewhere in the house, then another. Nathan stiffened. Could it be footsteps? He pried the square loose again, jumped down from the trunk, and, finding the detachable frame on the floor, he snapped it back around the mirror, whisper-shouting, "Huddle up!" He pulled the lower-left-hand square from the wall and moved it to the empty space on the top row. The mirror jumped into place.

He grabbed the coats and passed them around. As soon as everyone had pushed their arms through the sleeves, another floor board creaked, much closer. He handed the "Clara mirror" to Kelly, lifted his violin, and played the key. The square in her hands flashed to life, again showing Clara in her car, while the other mirrors still displayed a reflection of the room.

Nathan scanned the floor. "Where's the flashlight?"

Holding the photo CD in one hand, Daryl pointed the flashlight at the mirror with the other. "On your command, Captain!"

Just outside the doorway, the floor creaked again. Something thumped against the wall. Nathan stared at the bedroom entrance, every limb stiff. Was it Mictar? Dr. Simon? Who would be stalking the house without announcing himself? Certainly not a friend.

He whispered at Daryl. "Let's do it."

6

BACK TO YELLOW

Just as Daryl flashed the light, a series of thumps sounded inside the room, as if someone had repeatedly struck the floor with a rubber mallet, but no one was there.

Kelly gasped. "Nathan! Do you see him?"

"See who?" Nathan shouted, but his voice stretched out and flew apart. The image of the bedroom pixelized and broke into a million pieces. A snowy highway scene took shape, and a blustery wind slapped his face, biting his cheeks with a frigid blast.

The Toyota sat on the side of the road only two paces away. Clara threw open the door and stumbled out, laughing. "Leave it to you to appear out of nowhere!"

Daryl pushed the flashlight into her coat pocket and raised the camera to her eye. "We're cross-dimensional paparazzi. We show up when you least expect it."

Nathan helped Kelly fasten her coat. "What did you see back there?"

Her lips already turning blue, she chattered, "I ... I'm not sure. It looked like the guy who helped us at the funeral. He had a beard, but his face was so bloodied and swollen, I couldn't tell. He just fell to his hands and knees on the floor."

"Sounds like Jack. If I couldn't see him, how could you?"

"I've been seeing other things." She hugged the coat closer to her body. "If we can get someplace warm, I'll tell you about it."

He turned toward Clara. "How far back to the house?"

"Under normal driving conditions, about four hours." Streams of white puffed from Clara's nose. "With these conditions? Who can tell?"

Nathan kicked a snow drift, scattering crystals into the wind. "Four hours!" He fumed inside. Patar had warned him about getting sidetracked, and now here he was, risking the entire universe to save Clara's life while precious minutes ticked away.

She patted Nathan on the arm. "Where have you been?"

"Too much to tell right now. How long did you wait for us?"

"I went in to check on you after a half hour or so, but the house was empty." Clara gave him a scolding stare. "You literally left me out in the cold, so what else could I do? You said to meet you at the observatory, so I headed that way."

"Sorry. I couldn't help it." He looked at the mirror—back to normal. "Let's see if this thing will take us home."

While Kelly held the mirror, Nathan played the violin. He tried "Foundation's Key" again as well as a few other tunes that had worked to animate the mirror images before, but the reflection never changed. After several minutes, with the frigid wind stiffening his fingers, he could barely play a decent note.

Letting out a deep sigh, he nodded at the car. "Let's see if we can get this thing started."

"Not likely," Clara said. "I think it's just out of gas, and the service stations either have no power, or they're shut down because no one's minding the store. No cell service, either."

He searched both ways on the four-lane interstate highway—nothing but snow-covered trees and grass along with a couple of farm houses dotting the white landscape, certainly no cars to flag down for help. A few vehicles sat stranded at the side of the road. About a hundred yards away, at the end of a spinning trail in the snow, an old station wagon pointed in the wrong direction.

"Have you seen anyone at all?" he asked.

Clara stuffed her hands into her coat pockets and nodded at

a two-story house on a distant hill. Although no lights shone in any of its front windows, smoke poured through brick chimneys, one on each end of the roof. "Two people hiked up there. I was about to join them."

Nathan touched Kelly's arm and nodded toward the station wagon. "Ever siphoned?"

"No, but I've seen my dad do it."

"Maybe that'll be enough. What did he use?"

"Just a hose and a gas can." As she replied, her ragged puffs of white seemed to match her shivers. "We can probably ask up at that house."

Nathan squinted at the house atop the snow-covered hill. In the window, a yellow light moved from one side of the room to the other — probably a candle or lantern. Apparently electricity had gone out there, as well. "They should have a pen and paper, too."

"Pen and paper?" Daryl asked.

"To leave a note on the car. We'll owe that guy some gas."

Daryl shoved him on the shoulder. "You're such a Boy Scout!"

"Thanks ... I guess." Smiling, he handed Daryl the violin. Not long ago, a comment like that would've sent him into a self-doubting tailspin, but he was used to it now. "You guys try to stay warm in the car. I'll hoof it to the house."

Kelly looped her arm around Nathan's. "Not a chance. You're stuck with me, remember?"

While Daryl stayed with Clara, Nathan and Kelly hiked to the house. Although the bitter wind continued to claw through their coats, and snow seeped through their shoes, the fast pace up the hill kept them warm enough. He wanted to ask more about the things she had seen, but with her teeth chattering as they huffed and puffed through the climb, he thought better of it.

Her cheeks, rosy red now, expanded and contracted as she

blew through her mouth. Her eyes shifted his way, still glassy, but she had caught him looking.

"Is everything okay?" she asked.

"Besides being stuck out in the middle of nowhere?" He shrugged. "I guess so. Why?"

She refocused on the slope ahead as they trudged on. "You were watching me, so I thought maybe you wanted to talk."

"I was wondering about what you saw in the bedroom, but I didn't want to ask. You looked too cold."

She smiled and clutched his arm closer to her side. "You're always such a gentleman."

"Why wouldn't I be? That's what my father always taught me."

Her smile shriveled. "I don't know. I thought you were a gentleman because ..." She looked at him again. "Well ... because you like me."

He stopped and turned toward her. Her eyes, wide and pitifully glazed, locked on his. "Of course I like you," he said. "I've never had a better friend."

Her brow arched up. "A friend? Nothing more?"

Nathan read her facial expression — expectant, hopeful, longing. His answer could warm her heart or just as easily shatter it into pieces. But what could he say? That he wanted something more than friendship? He had always been taught that sixteen was too young for romance. And friendship always proved to be the best path to something more intimate later on. Still, his heart longed for hers, more now than ever, but it had to wait.

She pivoted and marched toward the house. "I can live with being friends."

With two quick strides, Nathan caught up and turned her around. "What's wrong?"

A tear tracked down her chapped skin. "You hesitated. That said it all."

Nathan drew her closer and pointed at his face. "Look at me. You used to be able to tell what was going on inside my head. I need you to help me figure it out now."

She gazed into his eyes. For a moment, a sparkle returned, clearing the foggy film. Nathan tried to let his emotions flow. Maybe since she was the interpreter, she could sense his true feelings. His words certainly weren't doing the job.

She drew back. "Your father is in the way?" She shook her head. "I'm sorry. I didn't mean it like that."

"It's okay. I knew what you meant." Letting out a sigh, he nodded. "Dad's never steered me wrong before."

She looked away. "Then you should do what he says."

With a gentle hand on her chin, he turned her face back toward him. "What are you going to do?"

A tear streamed down the other cheek. "I'll wait ... As long as it takes."

She turned again and plodded up the hill. This time, Nathan didn't stop her. He jogged up to her side, offered his elbow, and the two finished the journey to the house on the hill arm-in-arm.

The residents gladly let them cut a piece from an old hose and borrow an empty gas can, but they had no gas to offer. Instead, the lady of the house, a mother of three young daughters who pranced around the living room in snowsuits while singing Christmas songs, filled a thermos with hot soup and sent it back with them.

On the return trip, the wind slackened, and the sun grew warm, melting the snow. Kelly stayed quiet, her gaze far away as they scooted carefully down the now treacherous slope. By the time they returned, the temperature had climbed to at least eighty, and snow-melt rivulets created ankle-deep ponds at the roadside.

With some coaching from Kelly, Nathan managed to siphon enough gas to fill the two-gallon can, but a couple of mistakes along the way left him spitting, coughing, and gagging. The effort left a horrible coating on his tongue and lips, and washing with the remaining snow did little to wipe it away.

After transferring the gas to the Toyota, they settled into the car, Nathan at the wheel. Clara insisted on taking the backseat so Kelly could sit up front and "keep Nathan in line."

When he turned the key, the Camry roared to life. He glared at the fuel gauge. "Maybe the gas stations will open now that the snow's gone."

"We can't risk going back to your house," Clara said. "It's exactly thirty-two miles to the observatory. If we take it easy, we should make it."

"You're right. As usual." Nathan eased out onto the road. After explaining to Clara everything that happened in the strange misty world, all four settled into silence. Daryl reached into a backpack and pulled out a Sudoku book while Clara leaned her head against the side window and closed her eyes.

As he drove, the image of Scarlet filtered into his mind along with her haunting words. Although he recalled only a few, something in the way she said them seemed unearthly ... ghostly ... lyrics of a lullaby, some of the words lost in a dream world as if he were drifting in and out of sleep. *"Remember that you must come back and rescue us ... You have only a little time ... Interfinity is coming ... You, my love, are one of the gifted, and another is searching for you in her dreams ... The two of you will have to work together ... play the violin in Sarah's Womb."*

Nathan glanced at Kelly. Should he ask again about the things she had been seeing? Would another mystery add too much to the confusion? And should he let her in on the dream he had about Scarlet? Was it real? Could she help him interpret it? Francesca was obviously the other gifted one, but not much else made sense. How could she search for him in her dreams? Dreams weren't real. Yet, in Earth Yellow, at least, dreams seemed to be predicting the future, so maybe the world of dreams was beginning to blend with reality, or with the reality of another dimension.

He clutched the steering wheel tightly. He was being pulled in so many directions, he felt like he was being torn apart. Should he keep searching for his parents? Return to the house and help Jack? But maybe he wasn't really there at all. Should he try to get back to the misty world and rescue Scarlet? Go to Earth Yellow and find Francesca? Or should he heed Patar's warnings and concentrate on playing the big violin? But didn't he need Francesca for that task?

Kelly turned toward him. Something new sparkled in her eyes, something deep and searching. She seemed to want to say something but was unsure.

"What's up?" Nathan asked, his voice low, hoping not to disturb his backseat passengers.

Kelly copied his tone, keeping to a near whisper. "You've been wondering about the stuff I've been seeing."

He paused and cleared his throat quietly. "Sure. But you can take your time."

She gave him a weak but friendly smile. "You know how I hear voices when you're playing music and when those people sang?"

"Uh-huh."

"It's sort of like that, but it's visual. It's like I haven't really lost my eyesight. It's more like it's been replaced, like I'm seeing things that aren't there."

"How do you know they aren't there? I mean, if you can see them, how do you know other people can't see them?"

She opened and closed her hand twice. "They just sort of flash over the background for a second, then they disappear. Normally, everything's blurry, but the stuff that flashes is super clear."

"What did you see besides Jack?"

"Before that, while we were in the bedroom, I saw Francesca

pulling her music out of the trunk and packing it in a brief-case. Dr. Malenkov stood next to her, looking around kind of nervously. Then, they disappeared. I didn't want to tell you, because it was so crazy, but stuff like that keeps happening."

"Like what stuff?"

She nodded toward the windshield. "Cars on the road. The highway is deserted, but I see cars suddenly appearing and then vanishing. It feels like I'm dreaming while awake."

Nathan kept glancing back and forth between her and the road, but the occasional ice patch on the pavement made it impossible to keep his gaze on Kelly's intense brown eyes. He tried to imagine other cars whizzing around. What could it all mean? Was she seeing glimpses of Earth Yellow? Was Francesca back at her home, collecting her things while her new father stood guard? Did these visions confirm that they should go to Earth Yellow and find her?

Kelly stretched and yawned quietly, then looked back at him with bleary eyes.

He reached for her hand and gave it a gentle squeeze. "Maybe you should try to get a short nap."

"I guess it couldn't hurt." She settled back in her seat and closed her eyes. Within seconds, her breathing deepened into a rhythmic purr.

Daryl closed her puzzle book. "Is it all right that I heard everything you said?"

Nathan shrugged. "I guess so. No real secrets."

She paused for a moment. He caught a glimpse of her in the rearview mirror, biting her bottom lip. Finally, she looked up. A few wisps of red hair had fallen across her freckled forehead. "Are you mad at me for being afraid to jump?" Her voice was feeble, almost frail.

Nathan cringed but tried to hide it. How should he answer? Just be straightforward, or dance around the question? "Uh …

not really mad. We had to escape, and we couldn't wait around for you to get over your phobia."

She lowered her head. "I know. I'm sorry."

He angled the mirror to get a better view. She wrung her hands, intertwining her fingers. "My fear of heights started just a few days ago. You ... I mean, Nathan Blue before he died ... and Kelly Blue came over to my house. They said something crazy about Dr. Simon wanting them to stop an airliner crash in another dimension, and they wanted to learn more about how the big jets work. You see, my dad's a pilot, so they thought maybe he could help, but he only flies the regional routes, you know, like propeller planes that hop a few hundred miles. Nathan said it didn't matter. He wanted to take a flight and see if he could get the mirror to transport them while in the air. So he told my dad all about the Quattro mirror and even gave him a demonstration. Well, Dad got really excited about the whole thing, so he took us up in his private plane.

"Anyway, the mirror didn't work at first, so Nathan decided maybe it would only work if there was danger. Now, you have to understand that my dad is a real adventurer—you know, extreme sports, skydiving, whitewater kayaking—so he opened the back door and cut the engine. The plane kind of sailed for a while, and Nathan stood right next to the door playing his violin while Kelly held the mirror. Well, I didn't want to look like a coward, so I stood next to Kelly, but the plane took a sudden dip and I stumbled toward the door. Nathan caught me by my shirt, and I was hanging over the edge with just my toes touching the plane. Let me tell you, I was so scared, I ... well, never mind that. He pulled me back, Dad restarted the plane, and we went home. The mirror never did anything. Anyway, ever since then, I've been so scared of heights, I have a hard time just walking up the stairs."

She looked up at him in the rearview mirror, her eyes wide and wet.

"That must have been awful." He turned back to the road again. Should he say more? Try to give her comfort? It wouldn't be hard to say, "It's all right. Everyone's scared of something," but that would be a lie. It wasn't okay. Daryl's fear really was a handicap. A phobia was a phobia, no matter how it was caused. Their adventures had led them to a lot of precipices, and she'd probably freeze again the next time it happened. The mission was too important. The lives of billions of people were at stake. So, obviously he couldn't tell her everything was fine, but there had to be something he could do to make her feel better.

Finally, he reached a hand toward the backseat. She took it and wrapped it up in her clasped fingers. For a moment, he stayed silent, feeling the anguish in her painful grip. Then, beginning with a sigh, he said, "Since it just started a few days ago, maybe it's a temporary thing. You'll probably get over it eventually."

She lowered her head again. "I hope so."

When they arrived at the observatory, Nathan parked the car in front of the entrance. He surveyed the grounds, now green except for a few spots of snow in shady areas. With Gordon Blue in custody, the danger level seemed low, but who could tell where Mictar lurked? Also, the two Dr. Simons, the Blue and Yellow versions, hadn't made an appearance lately. Where could they be? With his father and mother?

He turned off the engine and jerked out the keys. He had to put his parents out of his mind for now and concentrate on the next step in the journey, finding Francesca.

Kelly popped her head up, blinking. "Are we here?"

"Yep," Daryl said, looking up at Nathan hopefully. "Time to start a new adventure."

After Nathan retrieved his mother's violin from the trunk, the foursome marched through the front door and used the numeric codes to enter the secure area of the facility and summon the elevator. Nathan and Kelly rode first, just in case trouble lay waiting for them at the telescope level.

As they traveled upward, he watched the exit door through the mirror. The reflection showed only their faces and the door behind them, no hint of any danger.

When the elevator opened and they entered the main chamber, Nathan scanned the area. Not a soul anywhere. He looked up. The mirrored ceiling showed a duplicate of the observatory room. Two females sat at the reflected computer desk, exact copies of Clara and Daryl, except that they were upside down in his perspective. Dr. Gordon looked over their shoulders at the computer screens. Soft music emanated from speakers embedded in the curved wall, Strauss's "Blue Danube."

Daryl Red stood and waved from the ceiling. Her voice broke through the lovely waltz. "Welcome back! We've been wondering what's been going on."

"We got sort of sidetracked," Nathan said.

Clara Red got up and stood at Daryl's side. "Another jump through dimensional portals?"

"Big time." Nathan glanced at the elevator's floor indicator. It had just arrived at the first floor to collect the others. As he looked up again, he fidgeted. "Uh ... Daryl? Are you afraid of heights?"

She walked closer to the center of the room. "Not especially. Why?"

"Daryl Blue is, so I was wondering."

Dr. Gordon raised his head. "Very interesting. A significant difference between parallel characters. The variance between my counterpart and myself was quite striking, as well."

"Anyway," Nathan continued, "we have to go back to Earth Yellow, and it's Daryl Red's turn for an adventure. Want to come along?"

She pumped her fist. "Yes! Adventure time!"

"Super. But just don't mention the fear of heights subject to Daryl Blue, okay?"

"Sure thing, boss. I'm just going along for the ride."

When the elevator door reopened, Daryl Blue bounced out and hustled to the laptop computers. She laid Nathan Blue's violin and camera on the desk and rubbed her hands together. With a big smile spreading across her face, her fingers flew between the keyboard and touch pad. "Setting course for Earth Yellow, Captain."

"No." Nathan set his mother's violin next to the other one. "Wait."

She paused and looked up at him. "A new course?"

"Uh ... Let's bring Daryl Red over. Don't you think it's her turn to go with us?"

The corners of Daryl's lips turned ever so slightly downward, and a hint of wetness made her eyes sparkle in the dim light. She cleared her throat and turned back to the computer. "Sure. Right. It *is* her turn."

Nathan looked at Kelly. She pursed her lips but said nothing. What was she thinking? She had seen Daryl Blue cower like a puppy. They couldn't afford to deal with that kind of phobia.

Holding back a sigh, he watched Daryl set up the transfer. Even after rearguing the points in his mind, pushing her out of the journey felt like slapping a baby for spilling milk. She couldn't help it. But the stalkers wouldn't care. They would exploit her fears.

As he thought about the strange white-haired race, Mictar's words from the performance hall's prop room came back to his mind. *The combination of fear and death is an aroma surpassing all others.* Nathan shivered. Obviously that monster enjoyed feeding on fear.

Nathan laid the photo CD envelope on the computer desk. "Maybe you and Dr. Gordon can analyze the pictures and let us know if you find anything important."

"Sure." Daryl inserted the CD into the laptop's drive but kept her head down. "I'll be glad to."

Kelly leaned close to Daryl and kissed her cheek. "You're a first-hand witness of that foggy world, so you can get Dr. Gordon up to speed while we're gone. No one else can do that."

"True. And I can give him the cell phone picture of the swirling mist." Daryl's focus didn't budge, but a weak smile wrinkled her face. "We're all set. Let's get that gorgeous redhead over here."

In the ceiling view, Daryl Red stood at the center of her chamber, her back within a foot or so of the observatory telescope. Lights flashed from all around. Beams of radiance knifed into the floor and surrounded her body. Within seconds she dissolved and vanished. Then, in the center of the Earth Blue observatory, an indistinct human shape materialized, slowly transforming into the familiar redheaded girl.

She shook her head hard and turned toward them. "Wow! That was a blast!"

"Yeah," Kelly said. "You never quite get used to it."

While Daryl Blue rose to her feet, Daryl Red ran over to the desk and stretched out her arms. "Daryl Blue!" she squealed.

As the two embraced warmly, a tear tracked down Daryl Blue's cheek. She drew back, stripped off her new coat, and helped Daryl Red put it on. "I'll bet it's a perfect fit," Daryl Blue said, wiping the tear away.

After buttoning up the downy, knee-length coat, Daryl Red held Daryl Blue's hand. "Thanks for letting me go. I'll tell you all about it."

Daryl Blue pulled free and spun back to the computer. "No use wasting time. I'll dial in Earth Yellow now."

She tapped in a few keystrokes. The Strauss waltz died away, and the ceiling view warped and twisted, then broke into thousands of irregularly shaped globs of color. As she turned up the sound, a new melody swept into the chamber.

Nathan trained his ear on the music. Subtle violins hummed a few simple notes, playing over a thrumming bass. Within seconds, the violins strengthened, blending with cellos and drums until they resounded in a brilliant crescendo. He closed his eyes and drank in the unmatchable glory of Beethoven's Ninth Symphony. The colors above splashed together with every pulse of vibrant music, as if called to order by the master's guiding baton.

Seconds later, the colors painted a devastated forest scene. New saplings dotted the grassy landscape, vibrating wildly, like a video run at ten times its normal speed. The larger trees were gone, snapped or uprooted by the tornado they had experienced here. Yet, someone had cleared the cones, leaves, and broken branches. Whoever did all the clearing work must have intentionally left the mirror standing. Otherwise, they wouldn't be able to see anything at all. Apparently, someone was expecting them, whether for good or bad.

Nathan checked his inventory—the camera, his mother's violin on the computer desk, and the mirror in his hand. Everything was here.

"Nathan?"

Dr. Gordon's voice. Nathan located the source—the laptop speaker. "Yes?"

"I have some advice. First, it is summer on Earth Yellow, or at least it will be for a little while. I suggest that you shed your coats so you can travel light. Once you are there, the seasonal changes will commence at a normal rate, but, since Earth Yellow's time passage compared to ours fluctuates so wildly, you won't know how time passes in either Earth Red or Earth Blue. Keep that in mind.

"Second, remember that we have no idea where Mictar is. If he is on Earth Yellow, since he is a stalker in a world of prophetic dreams, he will likely learn where you are. Third, my guess is that the two Dr. Simons are still there trying to meddle with coming events, so they might be able to help you locate your parents. Perhaps they will have thought ahead and provided transportation."

Nathan nodded at the speaker. "I hope so. It's a long walk from the observatory site to Kelly's house."

Nathan, Kelly, and Daryl stripped off their coats, leaving each one with sweatshirts and jeans. Daryl pulled her red shirt collar over her gray sweatshirt's neckline. "See?" she said, pointing at the collar. "I'm color coded."

Still seated at the desk, Daryl Blue did the same with her collar, revealing a sky-blue top. "Me too! A rhapsody in blue!"

Kelly shook her head and lifted the camera strap. "Let's get out of here. One Daryl is quite enough for me."

Nathan picked up his mother's violin and guided Kelly to the transport point. When the three had gathered near the telescope, Daryl Blue called from the computer desk. "Say hi to Francesca for me!"

As usual, lights flashed to life from trumpetlike fixtures around the base of the perimeter wall and shot toward the ceiling. Sizzling as they split apart, the beams zoomed toward the floor to create a cage of light around the trio.

The landscape in the mirror above seemed to reach down with a gaping maw and swallow them. As the new colors swept across Nathan's view, Clara and Daryl Blue waved, then disappeared in an undulating rainbow.

The forest scene sharpened, and the frenzied saplings slowed to a normal waving motion, blown by a fresh, warm breeze from the south. The sun, low over the eastern horizon, peeked through a thin bank of clouds.

Nathan turned around. A tri-fold mirror stood before him. New supporting boards anchored it to the ground, and a wood-frame portico stretched a half roof about five feet over the top. Ropes tied a flapping canvas tarp to the portico's frame, giving the mirror shade—probably to keep the sun from flashing a light and accidentally transporting an unsuspecting raccoon that happened to be wandering by.

"I can see!" Kelly grabbed Nathan's arm. "My vision is perfect!"

He gazed into her eyes. The glassy fog had faded away, leaving behind crystal clear brown irises. "That's fantastic!"

"Let's get this show on the road!" Daryl stripped off her sweatshirt, revealing a bright red polo, and tied the sleeves around her waist. "Uh ... where *is* the road?"

"Not far." Something behind the tarp caught Nathan's eye, a motorcycle tailpipe protruding beyond the mirror's support post.

He set down the violin case and hustled toward the pipe. The two motorcycles he and Kelly had used were parked between the mirror and the back of the makeshift portico. A helmet sat near each kickstand, red and blue, matching the trim of their corresponding bikes. "Simon Yellow's been busy," Nathan said as he wheeled the red-trimmed bike out into the open. "Want to bet they're gassed and ready to go?"

Daryl scooped up the helmets and handed one to Kelly. "Where to first?"

"Either of you hungry?" Kelly asked, laying a hand on her stomach. "All we've had lately is soup."

"Sure." Nathan packed the camera, mirror, and violin in the side bags. "But something fast."

Kelly put on the helmet, muffling her voice. "How are we going to find Francesca? Won't she and Dr. Malenkov be in hiding?"

"We don't have to find her." Nathan mounted the saddle, making room for Daryl behind him as she slid on the other helmet. "Just her guardian angel."

7

THE GUARDIAN ANGEL

Nathan cruised down the two-lane road, searching for a place to get a bite to eat. With the whistling wind brushing away all other sounds, his guardian angel comment echoed in his mind. Gunther Stoneman surely fit that label. The young delivery van driver had shown a true papa-bear spirit when they left him to watch over Francesca. If they could find Gunther, locating Nathan's Earth Yellow mother would be a snap.

After riding several miles, the three spotted a Burger King near the entrance to the interstate. They dismounted and hurried to the door, the two girls removing their helmets as they walked.

While Kelly and Daryl scanned the menu, Nathan kept his eye on the employees behind the service counter. They seemed slow, lethargic. The few customers seated at the tables were quiet ... deathly quiet. Even the young children said nothing as they pushed ketchup-coated french fries into their mouths and chewed without a sound. One pigtailed girl yawned and blinked weary eyes, barely able to hold her head up.

After the girls ordered and headed for the restroom, Nathan fished out the older dollar bills from his wallet, avoiding the new designs that would draw attention to the inscribed dates. He handed them to the cashier, a female teenager, short, with black hair pulled back into a bun. As he stretched and yawned, he read her name tag. "Rough night, huh, Paula?"

She stuffed the bills into her drawer and scooped coins out of change slots. "No worse than other nights."

As she counted the coins, Nathan studied her dark cheeks and the bags under her eyes. She looked like she hadn't slept for days. But why? Why did everyone look so tired? And why so quiet? Could the nightmare epidemic have infected everyone? How could he learn what was going on without giving himself away? He decided just to go for it. "So ... what did you dream about?"

Paula looked up and blinked at him. "You."

He pointed at himself. "Me? Really?"

"Well, not you, exactly." She laid the change in his hand. "I'm a next-day dreamer, so I've already seen all the customers who will come in today. I don't pay much attention, though. You've seen one, you've seen them all."

"Are you sure you saw me?"

As she narrowed her eyes at him, her brow bent low. "Maybe not. You'd think I'd remember a guy like ..." Her face suddenly turned ashen.

"What's wrong?"

Her eyes widening again, she took a half step back. "Are you a traveler?"

Nathan hesitated. Apparently he was supposed to know what a traveler was. "Uh ... what do you think?"

She studied his face again. "You don't look tired, so you have to be." She added a sigh as she continued. "It must be nice to walk freely outside of the dreamscape and see other places that no one else sees."

"I guess that's true," he replied. "Travelers do have an advantage."

She leaned over the counter and whispered. "Then you'd better get out of here. You know the rules."

"Oh, yeah. The rules." Nathan stared at the menu behind Paula. He really couldn't ask about the rules. Obviously everyone was already supposed to know them. He kept his focus on the menu, taking his time. Maybe her impatience would make her give away some information

She drummed her fingers on the counter, apparently to hide her whispers. "The other customers are looking at you. They're going to know you're a traveler."

He reached for his wallet. "If you get me a Whopper and a Coke, I'll get out of here as fast as I can."

She gave him a quick nod. "Just don't tell anyone, okay? I mean, you won't report me, will you?"

Leaning close, he whispered, "I won't tell. Everything will be fine."

"As if I could trust a traveler." She whirled around, snatched their sacks of food, and plopped them down on the counter. "The stalker won't make you suffer like I will tonight."

As Nathan paid for his order, he hid a nervous swallow. "White ponytail and ghoulish eyes, right?"

"So you *have* seen him." She tilted her head. "Are you sure you're a traveler?"

"I don't think I'm sure of anything." He gathered the food sacks and strode to the dining area where Kelly and Daryl waited at a booth. "Come on," he said, nodding at the exit. "We can't stay."

Daryl flicked her thumb toward the booth behind her. "Something weird's going on," she whispered. "Those people are talking about a murder that'll happen tonight. They say the police know about it, but they're not going to —"

"There you are!" A muscular young man strode in through the door, wearing jeans and a Chicago Bears T-shirt.

Nathan shot to his feet. "Gunther! I was just about to try to call you. How'd you know we'd be here?"

"Grab your food." Gunther leaned toward the door. "Let's get out of here. Too risky to explain in public."

All three followed Gunther out the exit. His Stoneman

Enterprises van, with a flatbed trailer in tow, was parked across several spaces at the back of the lot. A metal ramp spanned the gap between the trailer bed and the pavement.

"Load up your bikes," Gunther said, "and let's get moving."

Nathan pushed up his kickstand. "But how did you know we'd be riding—"

"Never mind that." Gunther grabbed Kelly's motorcycle handles. "Let's go!"

After securing the bikes with ropes, Gunther hustled to the driver's seat. Daryl sat up front with him while Nathan and Kelly climbed into the back where a comfortable new bench seat had been installed, much better than the hard floor they had used the last time.

Gunther slapped the van into drive and jerked the load into motion. He hurried through the parking lot and then into traffic with barely a glance at the other cars. Nathan bit into his hamburger and looked at Daryl, then at Kelly. While they munched their own sandwiches, their eyes seemed to ask the same questions he had on his own mind. When would Gunther explain what was going on? What was he so worried about?

As the van accelerated on the interstate, soft music played from all around, rich bass tones—a cellist performing a sacred hymn—combining with the mellow violins of an accompanying orchestra. Apparently Gunther had also installed a new stereo system, a timely addition. The soothing music seemed to calm everyone down.

Finally, when the van reached highway speed, Gunther let out a deep breath. "Have you figured out what's going on around here?"

After swallowing his mouthful, Nathan nodded. "Sort of." He glanced at a newspaper on the seat. The headline read, "New Dream Rules Now in Effect." He handed it to Kelly and leaned toward the front. "It looks like the nightmare epidemic we heard about when we were here before has spread to just about everyone. Some people are dreaming about their own future, and then it comes true. Even if it's a bad dream, they're afraid to do anything that might change it. If they try, they'll have a terrible nightmare the next night, usually about dying, and they can't stop it from happening."

"That's true for the next-day dreamers." Gunther pointed at himself. "I'm a traveler, and I saw you in my dream, even your motorcycles, so I knew to bring a trailer. It took me a while to figure out which Burger King it was. That's why I'm a little late."

Kelly passed the newspaper to the front seat. "Did you see yourself coming here?"

"No. Travelers don't always see the future. We see things that might happen anywhere in the world."

"Might happen?" Kelly repeated.

"Yeah, it's sort of an expectation, like what people want to happen. Sometimes it comes true, and sometimes it doesn't. Francesca's a traveler, and she saw you at the Burger King, too, so with both of us dreaming the same thing, I had to check it out."

"Have you been in contact with her a lot?" Nathan asked.

"Just about every day. She's been looking for you. She says the only way to stop this mess is for you to come with her in her dreams."

"I kind of figured that out. We saw her in the Earth Blue dimension while she was wandering around Wal-Mart in her dream." Nathan shook his head. That sounded too strange to be true. But what wasn't strange in this dawning of interfinity?

"Francesca didn't mention anything about Wal-Mart," Gunther said, "but you can ask her about it yourself. If you two don't put a stop to this dreaming business, the whole world is going to crack. The financial system almost collapsed when people started investing based on their dreams. That's the main reason the rules went into effect."

"But how can the government enforce them?" Nathan asked. "They can't control dreams."

Gunther looked back at him and wiggled his fingers as if casting a spell. He stretched out his reply, altering his voice to a creepy bass. "No, but Zelda can."

Nathan grinned at his antics. "Who's Zelda?"

"The only survivor from the flight one ninety-one crash three years ago."

"Three years?" Kelly said. "It's already been three years?"

"I'm afraid so." Gunther sighed. "Three very long years."

Kelly leaned forward and joined Nathan, copying his pose as he rested his chin on his hands against the front seat. "I met Zelda," she said. "I took some pictures of her, and she gave me her business card."

"Do you still have it?" Nathan asked.

"It's at home, but I remember her title said doctor, so she must be well educated."

Gunther laughed under his breath. "Well she's smart enough to cash in on her celebrity status. She claims to be a prophetess, that God saved her from the crash to prove her spiritual power. She started predicting major events perfectly and claimed that she could control the nightmare epidemic. When the dreams spread to almost half of the population, she had to set down rules. We're not allowed to try to change the future. She says it's predestined, and we shouldn't mess with God's plans. After that, when people tried to take advantage anyway, this ghostly guy would come and haunt their next nightmare. Lots of people died, either during the dream itself or because of a terrible accident the next day. She says she knows when people—as she says—'injure the fabric of predestined purpose.' And she knows who they are. So when she says the boogeyman's going to get you, she really means it."

"Mictar has to be the boogeyman." Nathan wondered at his own conclusion. Why would Mictar be working with Zelda, and how did that fit in with his agenda to merge the three earths? Maybe it had something to do with generating fear.

"So," Kelly said, "is Francesca thirteen now?"

"Yes, and a beautiful young lady. She has a great handle on what's going on, but her father is just confused by the whole thing. Fortunately, he trusts me completely, so I get to come over whenever I want to."

During the rest of the journey, Nathan explained to Gunther everything that had happened in the other dimensions, including Mictar's plunge into the mirror at the funeral, their encounter with Francesca at the Wal-Mart, and their experience with the stalkers and supplicants in the misty world. Since he filled in as many details as possible, and since Kelly added her color commentary in dozens of places, by the time he finished, they had passed Iowa City and were closing in on Newton.

Gunther pulled off the highway at the Newton exit. "We're meeting at Francesca's old house. It was sold at auction to a guy named Vernon Clark, but no one's moved in yet."

Kelly nudged Nathan's ribs but said nothing. It wasn't hard to figure out why. Tony, her father, had mentioned that his father had bought the house after Francesca's mother died. Vernon Clark was probably Kelly's grandfather.

"About a month ago," Gunther continued, "Dr. Malenkov asked Vernon for permission to come to the house to get the trunk Francesca left behind. Once he got a key, they started going there regularly. You'll see why in a few minutes."

After passing between the familiar cornfields, tall and fully tasseled, they pulled into the driveway next to the cottonwood tree now dressed in late summer greenery. Gunther got out and stretched as he looked up at the sky. "Cloudy. Maybe Iowa will sleep easy tonight."

Nathan joined him and gazed at the gray skies. Thick clouds streamed in from the west and covered the descending sun. "Do clouds keep Mictar from stalking dreams?"

"Not sure. The blanket effect might be psychological, but it seems to help. Maybe people feel kind of vulnerable when the weather's clear, like the ghosts can reach down from wherever they are and pierce our minds."

As they walked toward the front door, the sound of the garage opening made them halt. Dr. Malenkov, the younger Earth Yellow version, stepped out, his eyes darting all around. "Please park the van inside without delay."

While Gunther hustled back to his van, Nathan, Kelly, and Daryl quick-marched into the garage. Dr. Malenkov ushered them toward the inner doorway. "Welcome, friends. Francesca will be so glad to see you." He added a soft laugh. "And, of course, I am glad to see you, as well."

After Gunther drove the van into the garage, Nathan helped him detach the trailer and roll it next to the van. While the motorized door closed, he pulled the mirror and violin from the motorcycle pack. "Where is your car, Dr. Malenkov?"

"Hidden," the teacher replied. "I wanted to be sure we had enough room for you here." He waved his hand toward the open inner door. "Come, come. The time is approaching."

Nathan and Gunther joined the girls and followed the graying gentleman through the familiar laundry room, kitchen, and hallway. Sweet violin music filled the air, growing louder with each step. When they reached the bedroom door, Dr. Malenkov paused and peered inside. A white glow bathed his face as he turned to Nathan, smiling. "She is ready."

The music stopped. As the glow faded, Nathan and the others filed past Dr. Malenkov. Inside, Francesca sat on a solitary wooden chair with a music stand in front, her violin and bow on her lap. With her shoulders back and her head straight, her hair fell in ringlets of black down the sleeves of her flowing white dress. Although she was now a young lady, a familiar child-like mirth sparkled in her eyes.

She smiled as she rose to her feet. "I'm glad you finally came,

Son." Her soft voice carried across the empty room in lilting echoes. "I have been praying for your arrival for three years."

Nathan took a step closer. His throat narrowed painfully. She was more woman than girl now—too young to be his mother and too old for the playful banter they once shared. Shifting his weight nervously, he nodded. "I'm glad I could make it."

Kelly rushed forward and gave Francesca a warm hug. "It's so good to see you again!"

Francesca returned the embrace, her eyes staying focused on Nathan, as if probing his mind. Nathan cringed. His mother used to do the same thing, and a familiar sense of inescapability swept through his body. He would never be able to hide a thought from her, so he might as well give in.

She angled her bow toward him. "You've figured out the gift, haven't you?"

"I think so." Nathan lowered his head. Just looking at her scalded his soul. Somewhere in the cosmos his real mother needed help, and here he was, probably a billion miles away. Sure, being here was important, incredibly important, but his heart ached to find her.

Francesca glided forward, reached out a hand, and touched his cheek with her fingertips. As her smile weakened, a tear dressed her eye with wetness, and her voice returned to that of a little girl. "The gift is scary, Nathan. I'm not sure what to do with it."

Her touch felt cool and soft, just like his mother's. Trying to keep his voice from cracking, he reached for a lower tone. "Are you still on a mission to play the huge violin?"

She nodded. "But it's more complicated than that. When your mother described the violin, she only saw it in a vision. She wasn't really there. She and your father were trying to break through to another world, the Quattro world, I suppose, but they failed."

Nathan looked at the sheets of music on her stand, a variety of compositions from the classical and romantic periods. "I see you've been experimenting," he said.

"Different pieces have different effects, but ..." She pulled out a music book from behind the stack. "This one works the best. And it's the only baroque piece that works at all." She nodded at Dr. Malenkov, who stood next to Gunther near the door. "My father and I arranged it as a duet."

Nathan smiled at the title — Vivaldi's *Four Seasons*. Somehow it didn't seem so strange that his mother's Earth Yellow twin would come up with the same duet. "So you figured out how to get through to that world?"

"Only in one sense. I can walk through it like I'm in a dream."

"In a dream?" He bobbed his head slowly. "Something like that happened to me, too."

"Because you have the gift." Her bright smile widened. "But I learned something very important. I can take my father with me in the dream if we sleep while touching."

"Now that's really strange," Kelly said. "Touching can make people dream together?"

"If one of the sleepers is gifted. My father never remembers the dream when he wakes up, so I'm not sure if he's dreaming it, too, but it feels like he's really there, because he talks to me and gives me advice. I wish I could show you, but what we're about to do is a waking vision, not a sleeping dream." Francesca lifted the violin and set the bow over the strings. "Are you ready to join me, Son? It's always faster with two playing."

Nathan held up his mirror. "Don't we need this?"

She shook her head. "Not just to look. The interdimensional wound is so deep at this spot, we can pierce it visually with only music. We'll use the mirror for when we actually travel there. I want you to see what's going on while it's relatively safe."

"Sounds reasonable." He handed the mirror to Kelly and lifted his own violin. "Let's have a look."

"What do *we* do?" Daryl asked, nodding at Kelly. "Do the ungifted just stand here and play Old Maid?"

"You can stand with us," Francesca said. "But you won't be able to see what we see. Just listen carefully and you'll hear what's going on. You might pick up on something important."

"I guess that'll do," Kelly said.

Turning to Nathan, Francesca bowed her head. "Here we go. From the top." She played a long note, as crisp and clear as her older self ever played it. Yet, it rang out like a death knell, raising haunting memories of the recent funeral, the last place Nathan had attempted this piece. It would take all his strength to play without trembling.

He joined in, at first with an echo of her introduction, then with a blindingly fast run along the fingerboard, pausing at the high end with a series of eerily beautiful half notes. With each stroke of their bows, white mist erupted, as if brushing up thin dust from the strings of a violin long abandoned in an attic.

The streams of mist flowed together. Like two serpents slithering up a pole, they wrapped around each other, growing thicker with every note that sang from the enchanted strings. Soon, they created a funnel-like swirl, the same cyclonic fog that had sent Nathan and company to the misty world. The lower tip of the funnel hovered over the carpet next to his shoes, and the outer edges brushed against his bow arm as he continued playing.

He leaned forward to get a glimpse of Francesca on the other side of the swirl. Her eyes began to glow. Rays of white poured forth, like twin searchlights scanning the room. As the mist spread, two other spotlights intersected the first ones, creating a crisscross set of wandering headlamps. It seemed as though two cars were trying to find their way in a foggy parking lot.

Nathan blinked. Were those two other lights coming from him? He turned his head. The lights followed. He aimed them at the swirl. As his glowing vision penetrated the cyclone, images flowed through his senses—a long, glassy path; a dark chasm on one side, a foggy swamp on the other. It looked exactly like the misty world he had already visited.

"I think it's big enough." Francesca stopped playing and nodded toward the funnel, now at least five feet wide. "Everyone step in and huddle close."

Nathan lowered his violin and followed her into the funnel. The mist felt cool but not as wet as the funnel he had traveled in before. It felt more like dry ice vapor than fog. Kelly and Daryl joined them, but Dr. Malenkov stayed on the outside. "Gunther and I will keep watch," he said, patting Gunther on the shoulder. "You will be unaware of your physical surroundings while you are in there, so we will be your eyes in this world."

Francesca set her feet and raised her bow again. "We have to keep playing, or the viewing portal will collapse." She began the duet from the first measure. Nathan joined her again, trying to pour in the passion the piece deserved, but the overwhelmingly strange surroundings kept tugging at his concentration.

As the foursome stood within the swirl, the mist absorbed the eyebeams and spread the light throughout. Particle after particle of mist reflected the light with a pinpoint flash, each one a different color. As the number of flashing points grew, the reflections created a tapestry of tiny strobes that slowly eased their frantic pulses, finally staying lit in their chosen color.

Soon, the picture was complete, the living image of the misty world. Nathan and Francesca stood upon the glassy walk, safely away from the chasm on one side and the swamp on the other. This time, darkness didn't shroud their initial view. The long walkway, easily visible within the first fifty yards or so, led away in both directions, vanishing in cloudy curtains in the distance.

Nathan slid his shoe along the glass. It felt real enough, hard and smooth. As before, music filled the air, a sweet combination of perfectly blended, yet unidentifiable instruments. If all of this was just a vision, it had any virtual reality game beat by light years.

Gesturing with a curled finger, Francesca walked alongside the flowing mist. "This way."

Nathan hustled to stay at her side. "This leads to the vision stalkers," he said. "I've been here before."

"But you're not here now." She flashed a grin, that little grin he loved so much on the ten-year-old version of this young lady. "The stalkers won't give us any trouble as long as we stay quiet. They can't see us, so once we get to their domain, we will be able to go wherever we wish."

She marched quickly along the path, her violin and bow swinging with her gait. Nathan followed, glancing at his own violin as he rushed past the surrounding mist. It was so strange. Somehow he was still playing the Vivaldi duet in the Earth Yellow bedroom. He still felt the passion of the melody as he subconsciously stroked the vibrating strings, yet he carried that same violin now within a virtual reality world he had recently visited in concrete reality. But which reality was the *real* reality?

He shook his head and hurried to catch up. He had to push the weirdness out of his mind and concentrate on Francesca's instructions. She was a girl on a mission, and he had to figure out what this was all about.

After going through the bank of fog, they emerged into the enclosed mirrored circle with the images of earth emblazoned on the walls. At least one new jagged trail marred the crystal surface, a path of green that stretched between Earth Blue and Earth Yellow. The room seemed darker this time, as though the lights had been turned down for the evening. A gentle song played in the air, the now familiar nondescript vowel sounds, creating a soothing, repetitive chant. Nathan took in the lullaby-like melody. Maybe it was nighttime here, and most of the people had gone to bed, or whatever they did to rest.

Even in the dimness, most of the room's features were still visible. As before, the triangle of supplicant domes sat at the center of the terrazzo floor, but this time, no white-haired stalkers crowded the glass enclosures. One man walked around the periphery, but he neither paused to look within a dome, nor slowed his pace as he passed by.

As the man approached, Francesca took Nathan's hand and let out a quiet "Shhh." The stalker slowed for a moment and angled his head as if listening. Then, with a slight shrug, he continued his march until he reached an open door in one of the mirrored walls and disappeared inside.

Francesca whispered, "Remember, they can hear us."

"Have you seen the supplicants?" Nathan asked, pointing at the domes.

"Yes. I wasn't sure if they'd be dangerous, so I didn't try to contact them."

"They're not dangerous." Nathan strode up to the closest dome and gazed inside. Scarlet sat with her legs crossed and her head bowed. Her chest expanded and contracted in a steady rhythm. In her sleeping posture, eyes closed without a hint of tension or wrinkle, she seemed peaceful ... angelic.

Just as Nathan poised his knuckles on the glass to knock, Francesca tugged on his sleeve. "No time for afternoon tea. I have to show you the violin."

He paused and pulled back his hand. She was right. He'd have to visit Scarlet later. He glanced at the red-clad girl's lovely face again and sighed. *If there ever would be a "later."*

Francesca crept noiselessly around Scarlet's crystal prison until she reached the place where it abutted the next dome. She stepped over the point of intersection and into the small, curved triangle in the midst of the three abodes.

Nathan followed, peering into the other domes as he joined her. In the one to his left, another female sat in Scarlet's posture, a younger girl with long blonde hair that draped her pale yellow dress. To Nathan's right, a male teenager also slept, copying the pose of the other two.

Nathan slid closer. The boy, about his own age, seemed troubled, though he never opened his eyes. With dark hair in wild disarray, he cringed every few seconds, as if suffering through a nightmare.

Turning back toward Scarlet, Nathan let his gaze wander to the wall beyond her dome. The image of Earth Red towered above, blemished with shapeless clouds of orange and purple hovering over the points of injury inflicted by the other worlds. As he slowly turned to take in the entire vision, Earth Blue moved into view behind the boy's dome, and Earth Yellow behind the other girl's.

Francesca knelt and set her finger on a glass-panel inset in the terrazzo beneath their feet. The same size and shape of a door, the panel reflected the ceiling above as well as the top edges of the surrounding domes. Nathan swept his fingers over the mirror-like glass, but they didn't appear in the reflection, nor did their bodies. They were like ghosts in this place, able to haunt but unable to cast a shadow.

She moved her finger along a row of seven nickel-sized lights set in the glass, evenly spaced across the center. Looking up at him, she whispered, "Watch and listen."

As the misty world's background lullaby continued to play, the lights on the panel alternated between white and red, as if responding to each note of the song. He knelt with her and concentrated on the tones. There was a pattern, a definite code. When the third light from the left flashed red, he pointed at it. "Middle C." He then moved his finger to the first light. "That's an A, one octave down from middle A."

She grinned. "That's my son! I knew you'd figure it out."

"I figured out that it's a code, but that's about it."

"It's a musical combination to get through this door." Francesca touched each light in turn. "You have to produce a perfect A–B–C, and so on for each light, but the octaves change every time I come. I just have to listen until I pick them all out."

"Not very secure, is it?"

"It's not as easy as it sounds." She lifted her violin and bow. "I have to be fast and accurate."

"What happens if you get it wrong?"

"You don't want to know. Let's just say you'd hear enough dissonance to make Shostakovich proud."

Nathan frowned. "Very funny. I like Shostakovich. Mom and I always argued about his music."

She smiled and winked. "Just watch for approaching stalkers. When I play, anyone around will be able to hear me. We'll have to hurry, because the glass only stays open for a few seconds."

Nathan scanned the room. No one was coming. "Let's do it."

She lowered her gaze to the floor panel and played A through G at various octaves, so fast that her fingers seemed to blur. From left to right the lights flashed to red, then back to white. She played the string of notes again, and the lights flashed blue in the same order. Finally, on the third run, the lights flashed yellow, then faded to black.

The panel's reflective surface melted away. Now just a section of transparent glass, the doorway revealed a stairwell descending into darkness. Francesca stood and set her foot over the highest stair. Her gym shoe sank into the glass. "Let's go," she said as she descended into the clear gel. "We don't want to get stuck."

A movement in the distance caught Nathan's eye. The stalker they had seen earlier was heading their way. As he pushed his shoe into the goop, he tapped her shoulder. "Someone's coming."

Francesca quickened her pace, holding her nose as her face sank through. By the time Nathan had descended to waist level, she had submerged completely. As soon as he dropped below the surface and broke through into normal air, he looked up through the still-transparent door. The stalker climbed into the triangle area and stared quizzically at the glass panel. He laid a hand on the surface, his fingers splaying as he pressed down, but nothing passed through.

Walking on tiptoes to silence his shoes, Nathan held his breath. If the stalker couldn't see or hear them, maybe he would just go away.

The four-foot-wide staircase twisted in a steep spiral, eventually descending into complete darkness. After at least thirty more steps, Francesca whispered, "We're almost there. You still with me?"

"Right at your heels ... I think."

"Okay. Here it is." Her hand touched his chest, halting his progress. "It's another door," she said, "but it's upright and not transparent, and it always uses the same code as the other one. When it opens, just look. Don't step through or it'll be the longest step you ever took."

"Gotcha."

She played the seven notes again three times, pausing about a second between each run. A glow appeared around a rectangular shape, making the outline of the doorway easy to see, and the glow seemed to eat away at the edges, shrinking the door toward the center. Light filtered into the steep corridor, illuminating Francesca as she kept her violin poised in playing position.

"Take a look," she said, nodding at the doorway. "They call this place Sarah's Womb, but I haven't figured out why."

Touching the side of the opening to keep his balance, Nathan leaned out. An enormous chasm yawned below with rocky cliffs on each side, interrupted about a hundred feet down by a wide ledge that encircled the cylindrical chamber. That ledge seemed to be the lower level's floor, a floor that had collapsed in the center, leaving a circular pit. A single step would send them plunging through its jaws and into a black void.

He looked up. A jigsaw pattern of semi-transparent glass, the floor of the misty world, provided filtered light. A shadow crossed the glass, drifting slowly from one side of their ceiling to the other, a vision stalker on patrol.

Nathan grabbed a rocky protrusion at his side and held on. Danger lay below and above, and both directions looked like dead ends. Literally.

8
SARAH'S WOMB

Francesca pointed into the chasm with her bow. "The violin your mother mentioned in her vision is down there. The strings are stretched across this chasm. The only way down is a basket tied to a rope." She reached out with her bow and touched one of two ropes dangling in front of them. She then pointed at a pulley protruding from the rocky foundation above the outside of the doorway. The rope looped over it, and a large knot kept it in place. "I pull the basket up, get inside, and lower myself down, but there's only room for one of us."

"But we're right over the chasm," Nathan said. "What do you do, swing until you can get to the side?"

"Exactly. But it's pretty safe."

"Safe?" Nathan peered down again into the seemingly bottomless pit. "You gotta be kidding!"

She laughed. "It isn't easy, but it's safe. I slipped once and fell out of the basket. I kept falling for a long time but never hit bottom. I just snapped out of the vision. Since we're not really here, I guess we can't be harmed physically."

"Then why are we worried about the stalkers hearing us?"

She poked herself in the arm. "I said we can't be hurt *physically*. They have other ways of hurting us."

"When does the vision end? When we stop playing?"

She nodded. "But time passes a lot faster here. We're not even to your solo yet."

"Yeah. It's kind of weird, but I knew that. I still feel myself playing the piece." He looked down at the chasm once again, this time trying to focus on the shapes within the darkness. The violin strings, like four shimmering golden ropes, spanned the hole in the floor underneath their door. The basket swung lazily over the strings, as if pushed by a gentle draft. "I'll go first," he said. "Then I'll lower you down."

Nathan grabbed the rope just below the knot and pulled the basket to the top. Rectangular and made of dense wicker, it looked like a gondola from a hot air balloon, only smaller, barely enough room for one rider. The rope led into the passenger compartment and through a hole in its floor, apparently secured underneath with a knot big enough to keep it from popping out. He gave the base a nudge with his foot, making it sway. It seemed sturdy enough, but riding in it could prove to be a wobbly adventure.

Still hanging on to the rope on the knot side of the pulley, he climbed in, straddled the rope holding the basket, and descended, letting the rough, intertwined hemp slide bit by bit through his hands. Knowing he couldn't get hurt made the job easier. Still, friction warmed his skin, then burned, but not enough to make him let go. When the knot passed through his hands, the one that held the rope in place at the pulley, he knew he was about halfway down. It wouldn't be long now.

Finally, the basket stopped. The knot lodged in the pulley again, signaling that he had arrived at the right level. He pulled on the rope and gave the basket a shove with his body, then repeated the process until he swung back and forth several times. Again, pain burned his hands as the rope bit into his palms. He tried to blow on his skin, but it didn't help. Maybe Francesca was wrong. Maybe they could be hurt here. After all, she was a visitor, too. The mysteries of these visions had to be deeper than what appeared to the eye.

When the basket finally landed on the ledge, he jumped

out and began pulling the rope again to lift the basket back to Francesca. He let the excess rope add to a coil that already rested on the ground near his feet. Coming out from the bottom of the coil, the rope led to the wall where it was tied to a thick iron hook. The whole system seemed primitive, but it worked.

After Francesca climbed into the basket, Nathan lowered her, feeding the rope hand over hand. When the knot lodged at the pulley level, he dug his heels in to keep his balance. Then, pulling on the rope and letting it run through his hands, he made the basket swing. When it finally came close enough, he grabbed the side and pulled Francesca to safe ground. As soon as she disembarked, he noticed a long pole with a shepherd's crook on the end. Apparently that was how the stalkers reeled in the basket, but it was too late for that now.

Francesca pointed with her bow. "That way."

Just as she was about to march ahead, Nathan grabbed her elbow and pulled her back. "Wait a minute. Let me check this place out."

He gazed in the direction she had pointed. Just as it had appeared from above, the ledge curved into the dimness, creating a full ring around the void. The entire chamber was really a circular pit, with a rock-encapsulated stairway dangling over the middle like a stony finger reaching down to pluck the strings, their path downward from the stalkers' abode.

A glow emanated from narrow gaps at the edges of the ceiling. The ceiling and the walls didn't quite meet, allowing the gaps to reveal the lower arcs of three earths on the sides of the upper chamber. From this angle, the fissures between the planets seemed deeper, making the entire wall appear fragile.

A faint cracking sound echoed from above. A few shards of glass tumbled through the gap and down to the floor. As soon as the shards struck the stony surface, they melted into a crystal rivulet that coursed in a meandering path toward the dark pit. When the liquid spilled into the void, the entire chamber rumbled.

The ground quaked, shaking so hard, Francesca fell backwards. Nathan crouched at her side and hugged her close as the quake roared on. Fragments from the edge of the pit broke away and tumbled in. The basket tipped over the side and swung across the strings. With every jolt, the precipice inched closer, threatening to swallow them into its violent yawn. But they couldn't move, not without risking a tumble into the void. The basket suddenly plunged. Rope reeled off the coil until it tightened against the wall hook with a dull twang.

Soon, the last crystalline drop disappeared into the pit, and the trembling slowly eased. Nathan rose to his feet and helped Francesca to hers. Neither said a word. She ran her hand up and down his arm, her eyes wide. Her expression said it all. The danger was greater than she had thought, and the more wounds inflicted on the interdimensional fabric, the worse the danger would get.

"Okay," he said. "Let's go."

With the pit to her left, she walked near the edge and halted where the first golden string crossed their path at knee level. The other three strings lay beyond it, each separated by a gap of about six feet. Well to their right, the strings coiled around broomstick-sized dowels anchored to the stone floor. Underneath the strings, a polished black layer of wood acted as the fingerboard for this enormous violin.

She stepped over the first string and sat down on the second. It seemed to carry her weight without a problem.

Nathan ran his finger along the closest string of gold. As thick as rope, it pushed a tingling sensation through his still burning skin. So this was the place his mother described. During her visions, she tried to play a tune, obviously pizzicato since she didn't have a bow, but the strings were too far apart. She would have had to lunge from one string to the other, probably leaping over one or more strings between each plucked note, while still maintaining perfect rhythm.

No wonder Francesca needed his help. With two people it would be a lot easier, one person manning two strings, and no leaping required. But what was the point? She had said the strings spanned the celestial wound. Would playing the music repair it?

Gripping the string, he pulled it up an inch or so. Plucking it would be no problem, but would the sound alert the stalkers?

"Have you tried playing it?" he asked.

She nodded. "But I have no idea what I'm supposed to play." She bounced her weight up and down on the string. "And I can play only four notes, because I can't press a string down. Even if I were heavy enough, I couldn't pluck the string while I'm pushing on it. And every time I play a note, the ground shakes like it did a minute ago. It's impossible to keep your balance."

Nathan pushed all his weight on the string and pressed it firmly against the fingerboard. He was heavy enough, so Francesca could play while he pushed, but she'd still have to jump around from string to string like a maniac. Still, maybe only four notes were necessary. Mom didn't mention having to push the strings down during her vision.

He felt for the music sheet in his back pocket. "Foundation's Key" was a simple tune, but it had more than four basic notes. If that was the right piece to play, they would never manage it with only the two of them. Finally, he let out a sigh. "We'll need help."

"I know. I think if we come here for real with Kelly, Daryl, and my father, we could play almost anything."

Nathan gave her a slow nod. Kelly knew music, so she could help, and so could Dr. Malenkov, but what about Daryl Red? At least she wouldn't freeze when she saw the pit, like Daryl Blue would, and she could pluck a string when told to do it. "Okay, so if we use a flash from the camera to come here, how do we avoid being seen?"

"That's the tricky part. That's why I showed it to you first so you could see all the obstacles."

Nathan ran through the path in his mind, from the glassy walkway to the domes to the panel in the floor. Being invisible had made everything much easier, but they still had almost been caught.

He shook his head. "It's impossible. Once we're visible, we're dead meat."

"We have to try, don't we?" Francesca looked toward the void. "If we don't heal the wound, we'll all die anyway."

"I know that . . ." He paused. He had almost added "Mom" in response to the feminine voice that had nailed him with a good argument so many times before. Looking at the stairway above, he stooped low. From this angle, he could see more of the upper chamber through the gap near the wall. "Maybe I should go back upstairs and see if Scarlet can help somehow."

"The girl in the dome? The one in the red dress?"

"Uh-huh. She seems to know a lot about everything."

Francesca rose from the string, careful to keep it from sounding a note. "Well, it's time for your solo anyway. When I stop playing, I'll be pulled back into my bedroom. I'll tell everyone what's going on."

He rose to his full height. "So I guess I have to climb back up the rope to get to Scarlet."

"If you want to go that way. Like I said, if you fall, you'll just wake up in the bedroom. Then you could start over and come in through the foggy path."

"I'll climb. I want to test something."

She pointed her bow toward the stairwell. "Do you remember the notes to open the floor panel?"

"I think so."

"The door by the pulley stays open for a long time, but you'll have to play the key again if you want to go through the upper door." She angled her head as if listening to something in the air. "Okay. It's time for your solo. Play well, my son." Still clutching her violin, she blew him a kiss and faded away.

Nathan rubbed his eyes. Would he ever get used to all this appearing and disappearing?

He jogged back to where the basket had fallen, grabbed the rope, and reeled it up to his level. Apparently the knot had slipped through the pulley, and now he had to jerk it back over the wheel to pull the basket any higher. With a firm tug, he popped the knot through. Now the basket hung over a point near the center, swaying back over the violin strings and then toward him again in a rhythmic motion.

As if ringing a huge church bell in a tower, he pulled on the rope and released it, timing his pulls to increase the sway. He imagined the basket as a huge violin bow, stroking the strings with each pass, and composed music in his mind's ear to match the strokes.

He watched the surreal scene, the basket's hypnotic sway as it brushed over the strings again and again. Could that be the best way to play the gargantuan instrument? But with what? A bow the size of a vaulting pole?

When the basket finally swung close enough, he grabbed up the shepherd's crook and snagged the side, giving the rope slack as he fished in his prize. The knot now moved freely through the pulley. It would no longer work as a way to prevent a plunge.

After setting his violin inside and climbing aboard, he swung himself back over the center. As he passed by, he again imagined a bow stroking those beautiful golden strings and playing "Foundation's Key." With another slight pull, he adjusted the gap between the basket and the strings and pictured himself leaning over with a bow to reach them. Firming his chin, he nodded. It just might work.

He hoisted himself up, pulling hand over hand. His raw

skin burned, and his muscles ached, but he didn't want to test Francesca's claim that falling into a bottomless pit was nothing more than waking up from a nightmare. Even without Daryl Blue's phobia, that seemed like a scary way to snap out of this vision.

Soon, perspiration drenched his back and sleeves, but after a few minutes, he reached the doorway and leaped inside.

He retrieved his violin and released the basket, then hurried up the stairs. Again, his muscles ached. Even though he wasn't really here, the effort was grueling. No wonder his mother was exhausted after she explored this place in her own vision.

When he reached the glass panel, he peeked out. No one was around. He lifted his violin and bow, picturing Francesca doing the same when she unlocked this door from above. The notes flowed into his mind, and he played them through in a rapid echo. The lights in the panel, barely visible from below, flashed red. He played the notes again, and then a third time. The lights blinked yellow once and turned off.

He climbed the remaining stairs, pushing his body through the liquid glass, and emerged in the midst of the domes. Glancing all around for any sign of a stalker, he crept toward Scarlet's dome and peered through the transparent barrier. She still appeared to be asleep, sitting cross-legged with her head bowed low. But, with a sudden gasp, she jerked her head up and stared straight at Nathan. For a moment, she seemed ready to smile, but the sadness in her eyes spread to her lips, weighing the corners down.

As she spread her red dress over her legs as far as she could, her voice sounded through the glass loud and clear. "I am lonely, my beloved. Come in and talk with me for a while."

When Nathan set his hand on the dome, his fingers passed right through, followed by his hand and arm. As he leaned forward, his head and torso entered the dome as well.

This time, Scarlet allowed her smile to break through. "Fear not, Nathan. Wandering in the land of visions will bring you no harm, unless, of course, you awaken the stalkers."

Nathan pushed the rest of the way in and sat opposite her. Crossing his own legs to match hers, he laid the violin in his lap. "If I'm seeing a vision, how can you talk to me?"

"I am a supplicant," she said, touching her chest. "Entering visions is what I do. I entered your dream while you were unconscious, and now I have drawn you to myself in this new vision."

"But why? What is a supplicant?"

She smiled, though her brow furrowed. "I see that you have forgotten what I told you earlier."

"I remember some of it, but it's kind of foggy."

She spread out her hands, gesturing toward the walls lining her enclosure. "Through these mirrors, I see the outside worlds. Yet, I can see only whatever world you happen to be in, for I am assigned to protect you. You are the gifted one from Earth Red who carries the window to my world. When you have been in danger, you have asked for my help, and I have sung songs for you. You see, a supplicant is one who makes petitions on your behalf."

Nathan gazed into her reddish brown eyes. Something about her seemed very familiar. "So are you Quattro?"

She laughed gently. "Your father's name for me. It is pleasant, but I prefer Scarlet, for I am the supplicant for Earth Red."

He touched the floor, dirtier than the surface on the outside. Did they ever let her out to bathe? There was no noticeable odor. Her skin seemed clean and free of blemishes, and her auburn hair, though slightly tangled, showed no hint of oily residue.

"But why are you here?" he asked. "I mean, why are you trapped in this prison?"

"The prison is Mictar's work, but I will tell you no more about that." She reached across and took his hand, enfolding it in both of hers. "Although we are together only in a vision, you are the first assignment I have been able to meet. I am lonely and I have longed for your presence ever since I learned you were a gifted one. Let us talk of more pleasant things than my sufferings."

"Sure." Her touch sparked a surge of warmth, scrambling his thoughts. Not a single idea came to his mind. "Uh ... what do you want to talk about?"

Her voice perked up. "Your friend, Kelly. Tell me about her."

"Well ..." Nathan gazed again at her lovely face. Not a hint of jealousy spoiled the sincerity in her probing eyes. "She's really kind of amazing. I've never met anyone who is so ..." He searched for the right word, but it didn't seem to come. "So cool, I guess. I mean, she's brave, loyal, strong—"

"And lovely," Scarlet added, compressing his hand. "Don't tell me you haven't noticed."

Nathan lowered his head, trying to hide his uneasy smile. "Yeah ... She is."

Scarlet laid a hand on the side of his face. "Why, Nathan! Don't be embarrassed! God gave her beauty, just as he gave her strength, courage, and loyalty." As she stroked his cheek, she lowered her voice to a whisper. "And she has given you her most precious gift. Her heart."

He raised his head. Scarlet had scooted so close, their noses nearly touched, and her hands again wrapped around both of his. With breath like roses, she whispered, "I have also given you my heart, my beloved, but in a very different way. When you return in physical form, will you come for me? You have the power. Will you set me free before it's too late?"

He stared at her wide orbs. Everything felt so real—the warmth of her skin, the beat of her rapid pulse, the tingle from her thumb as it caressed his knuckles. How could this be a vision? Her eyes pleaded for an answer. Pure entreaty, intermingled with fear and love, poured forth.

He cleared his throat, trying to keep from squeaking. "I'll figure out a way to rescue you. I won't let you down."

Her head slowly drooped until it nearly rested on her chest. "I am thankful for your promise, though it is one you cannot keep without my help. When you return, I will—" She lifted her head suddenly, her eyes widening. "Go!" She slid away on her knees. "You must leave now!"

Nathan looked up at the dome's ceiling, but only his reflection stared back at him. Suddenly, a loud wail pierced the silence, like a panther squealing a high-pitched growl. He grabbed his violin, jumped up, and pressed his hand against the glass, but his fingers wouldn't pass through.

Scarlet leaped to her bare feet. "His song is binding the glass. Even a vision stalker cannot penetrate it."

Nathan searched for any sign of an exit. "Is there another way out? Can't I just stop playing my violin back where I really am?"

She shook her head. "The song cuts off your subconscious mind, so you can't communicate with your awake mind to tell it that you have to stop playing."

The song's pitch shot up in frequency. Excruciating pain tore across Nathan's skull, like an earthquake rolling inside his head. Still clutching his violin, he covered one ear and paced around the dome. "It's about to make my brain explode!"

Scarlet spread out her arms, her palms pointing upward. Raising her voice above the screeching din, she sang her words in a beautiful, fast-paced melody.

> O guiding hand of songs within the stars,
> You hear my cries from Red's accursed dome.
> O let the one who listens from afar
> Awake the gifted child and bring him home.

An invisible force snaked around Nathan's abdomen and squeezed his breath away. He could barely choke out his words. "What ... are they ... doing now?"

Scarlet smiled. "It is not a stalker who embraces you." Rising on tiptoes, she kissed his cheek. "Hurry back, my beloved. I will be waiting."

Nathan fell heavily onto his back. Something dropped on top of him, a body, but there was no red dress, only blue jeans and a sweatshirt. Whoever it was wrapped feminine arms tightly around his waist. He wriggled to loosen the strong grip, but his muscles were spent. Finally, his attacker sat up on his thighs and pushed her hair back.

He blinked. "Kelly?"

She rubbed her palms across the cardinal logo on her sweatshirt. "You're drenched."

He raised his perspiration-soaked sleeve and stared at the violin in his hand. As the misty funnel faded behind Kelly, Francesca and Daryl shuffled out of it and looked on.

"What happened?" he asked.

Sliding on her knees, Kelly moved to his side, keeping her eyes fixed on him. "I heard what was going on—you and Francesca with the big violin, you and Scarlet talking, that screeching noise, Scarlet's song, everything. I yelled at you to stop playing, but you wouldn't, so I just tackled you."

He stared at her. Some of his conversation with Scarlet replayed in his mind. "You heard ... everything?"

A hint of a smile bent her lips, but it quickly vanished. "Sure. What's the big deal?"

Nathan pushed against the carpet with his weary arms, too tired to string his words together. "We have to go there in physical form ... play the violin ... rescue Scarlet ... and the others."

Bracing his back as he rose, Kelly nodded. "And save the world. I got all that."

"We have to make sure we're ready," Francesca said. "If we keep breaking through dimensional walls, the celestial wound will swallow the very instrument that's supposed to heal it."

Still wobbly as he straightened, Nathan held out his hands as if playing his violin. "We need a bow ... a big one, maybe ten feet long. But it has to be real light, light enough to carry."

"Balsa wood?" Kelly asked. "And hollow it out?"

"Maybe. But even if it would be light enough, who could make it?" He turned to Gunther. "Could you?"

Gunther shrugged. "I don't know much about woodworking, much less about making a violin bow. Maybe Nikolai could help me."

Dr. Malenkov shook his head. "To make it so big while maintaining a light weight and proper balance would take an extraordinary craftsman. Perhaps we could employ a local instrument maker I know."

"If you mean Mr. Hancock," Gunther said. "No way. He'd be too scared to do anything besides what he sees in his dreams."

"My father could do it." Kelly touched Francesca's bow. "Just give him a normal-sized one and the proportions you want, and he'd make it work."

Nathan pressed his hands against the sides of his head. "Okay. Information overload. My brain's about to explode again." Closing his eyes, he ran through the confusing tangle of options. From Earth Yellow, they couldn't contact Kelly's father—no network connection to Earth Red. Back on Earth Blue, they still had four hundred mirrors to look through, any one of which might lead to his mother and father. Daryl Blue and both Claras have had time to study the photographs at the observatories. Should he go back and see if they'd learned anything? How could they minimize their interdimensional travels and still accomplish their tasks? And, finally, what could they do about the stranglehold Mictar held on the people of Earth Yellow?

Lowering his hands, he looked at Kelly. "How old would your father be on Earth Yellow now?"

Kelly looked up at the ceiling. "Let's see ... maybe sixteen or seventeen?"

"How young did he start woodworking?"

"Well, he used to brag about making a crossbow from a tree that lightning knocked down. He swore that the electric jolt made it the most accurate crossbow in the world." She raised a finger to her chin. "I think he was twelve, but I'm not sure, because every time he told the story, he seemed to get younger."

With his head pounding, Nathan cast his gaze on the wall mural, a musical staff with notes climbing up the lines. "So it's pretty likely that he's good at it now."

"I guess so, but how are you going to contact him? He won't have any idea who you are."

He touched one of the notes and traced its outline. "When did he move into this house?"

"Not sure. I could find out when we get back to Earth Red."

He thumped the wall with the heel of his hand. "We can't wait that long! Once we get back there, time will zoom by here."

Dr. Malenkov withdrew an envelope from his jacket and pulled out a letter. "I keep this note of permission with me if by happenstance someone should ask me why I spend so much time here." His eyes darted back and forth as he read. "Ah! Here it is. 'My family and I will be moving into our new home by the end of the summer.'" He folded the letter and put it away. "That would be next week."

Looking again at Kelly, Nathan pointed at the floor. "Was this your dad's bedroom?"

"Until Grandpa moved into a nursing home. Why?"

"I'm betting a young Tony Clark won't be able to resist solving a mystery." He reached for the letter. "May I see it, Dr. Malenkov?"

"Certainly." He unfolded it and gave it to Nathan. "It is hand-written and difficult to read."

Nathan peered at the messy script. "I can make it out." After reading it for a few seconds, he smiled. "A handwritten letter is just what we need."

Gunther looked over Nathan's shoulder. "I can hear the wheels spinning from here. What are you plotting?"

"A treasure hunt of some kind. We have to show him some-thing that will entice him to make the bow."

"Daddy loves a mystery," Kelly said. "He'll move heaven and earth to solve one."

Nathan pulled his wallet from his back pocket and fished out a twenty-dollar bill. Showing it to everyone, he said, "How about strange-looking money from the future?"

She took the bill and looked it over. "That just might work. Put mystery and money together, and he'll do anything."

"Very interesting," Dr. Malenkov said, "but how will you incorporate constructing the bow?"

"I'll need pen and paper." He glanced at Kelly and smiled. "And duct tape."

9

THE CHROMATIC CIRCLE

With a dramatic swirl of his pen, Nathan signed the bottom of a wrinkled sheet of paper in red ink. He lifted the page and read it out loud. "Tony Clark, I implore you to heed my words. I am from a future time, and I must go back before the window to my world closes. I have heard of your woodworking prowess, and I need a trustworthy young man like you to perform an unusual task. Yet, knowing also of your intelligence, I realize that it will take much persuasion to get you to believe my tale.

"I need a special violin bow. It must be ten feet long, proportional to the dimensions of a normal bow, and light enough for a person to carry without trouble. I realize that this is an odd request, but I cannot reveal its use except for the fact that I need it to save my world.

"Ah, yes! I know you must be doubting. That is why I left proof of my incredible story. You will find attached a twenty-dollar bill. Notice the date and the unusual design. Put it under a magnifying glass and study the details. You will undoubtedly agree that no counterfeiter in the world could create it.

"If you, Mr. Clark, will just construct this bow, a friend of mine in your world will contact me, and I will come back and give you a bill that matches the one I enclosed. With two such bills in your possession, displaying differing serial numbers, dates, and Federal Reserve banks, you will be able to prove that the one you hold now is genuine, for why would a counterfeiter create two different plates if it would be so difficult to make even one? Such a bill could make you rich and famous.

"If, however, fame and fortune are not your desire, I implore you, for the sake of my world, and perhaps yours as well, do me this favor. The task is small, yet the rewards are great. I remain, respectfully yours, Nathan of the Red World."

Gunther clapped his hands. "That was amazing!"

"Sounds like some spam emails I've been getting," Daryl said. "This one is even wilder."

"But every word was true." Kelly grinned as she jerked the page out of his hand. "You're a sly one, you are."

"Thank you, my lady." Nathan gave her a mock bow, then held up a roll of duct tape. "The perfect way to attach a twenty-dollar bill."

"I'll take care of that part," Gunther said. "When they move in, I'll make sure he gets it."

Kelly handed over the letter. "Just remember, even though he has a big head about his talents, he's not stupid, so try to come up with a clever way to deliver it."

"Trust me. I'm already dreaming up something. And I'll get a regular bow for him, too."

Nathan tossed the roll of tape to Gunther. "Okay. I guess that's all we can do for now. We'd better get back to Earth Blue."

Francesca took Dr. Malenkov's arm and leaned against his shoulder. "Hurry back, Son. If Tony gets to work right away, it will probably be only a few days from your perspective, or maybe even less."

"Right. We'll try to figure out a way to stay in touch. Maybe Dr. Gordon's got a handle on those pictures by now. He might have an idea about how to stay safe when we go to the misty world for real."

"It's going to take more than Dr. Gordon to get us past those stalkers," Francesca said.

Kelly leaned close to Francesca and kissed her on the cheek. "I'll miss you."

"And I will miss you, as well." The younger girl averted her eyes. "Goodbyes are always painful."

"Do you remember our last goodbye?" Kelly asked. "I kept my promise."

Francesca's voice quavered. "You've been ... praying for me?"

Kelly nodded, her own voice cracking. "I'm not very good at it, so I don't know if God heard me, but a promise is a promise."

"He heard." Francesca took Kelly's hand and drew it gently toward her. She blew on Kelly's knuckles, then pulled her hand closer, pressing Kelly's palm against her own chest. "Prayer from the heart is like a beautiful melody — God loves the music of the soul."

Kelly backed away, teetering slightly as she caressed her knuckles. Nathan almost jumped over to catch her, but she recovered. She seemed withdrawn, sad, maybe even upset. She swiveled toward him, her eyes glistening. "Uh ... can we go now?"

He took her hand. "Yeah. Sure."

Nathan, Kelly, Daryl, and Gunther returned to the van and drove back to the observatory site. Along the way, they discussed plans for delivering the letter and twenty-dollar bill to Tony. The radio played in the background, filling in the periods of silence. News reports described the latest nightmare-related deaths and gave rule updates straight from Zelda the prophetess. During the five hours of travel, they took turns catching naps. Since Kelly's eyesight stayed clear, she had no trouble driving while the others snoozed.

When they reached the forest and unloaded the motorcycles, Kelly wheeled one of them under the shelter while Gunther held the other upright in front of the mirror and aimed its head-light toward the glass.

Kelly pulled the tarp down to hide her motorcycle. "I think we're ready."

"Good." Nathan handed the camera to Kelly and the mirror to Daryl, then pulled his violin from the van. He tuned the strings, making ready to play the *Carmen* piece that would restore the image of Earth Blue to the tri-fold mirror. For some reason, it had blacked out and returned to a normal reflection, probably because Daryl Blue had changed the channel to Earth Red in order to consult with Dr. Gordon.

As Kelly and Daryl joined Nathan in front of the mirror, Gunther gave them a nod. "I guess I'm a guardian angel for Tony Clark now, too, the angel on his shoulder who keeps prodding him to make that bow."

"Let us know when it's done." Nathan pointed at the ground. "Maybe you could plant a sign right here where we can read it."

Daryl snapped her fingers. "That's it!" She pushed the mirror square into Kelly's hand and backed away from Nathan. "Forget posting a sign. I'll stay here and set up communications!"

Nathan lowered his violin. "How? They don't have the internet, and even if they did, how would you hook up? Interfinity's radio telescope hasn't been constructed."

"It's what, the early eighties?" Daryl spread out her hands. "The rudiments of the internet are already in place. I know how to construct a radio transmitter and receiver, and I know all the protocols. It shouldn't take long."

"But wouldn't it mess up your life?" Nathan asked. "I mean, you'll age twice as fast here compared to Earth Red, maybe faster."

"Hey, we're talking about saving the universe." Daryl smiled and slid her arm around Gunther's waist. "We'll figure it all out. He's got the muscles and wheels, and I've got the brains."

"And a whole thimbleful of humility," Kelly added.

Daryl pointed at her. "At least that much. Maybe more."

Nathan raised his violin again and eyed Daryl with new admiration. She was willing to make a huge sacrifice—leave home and family to embark on a mind-bending project with an almost complete stranger. "I'll tell Daryl Blue to watch for your call."

Taking a deep breath, he began the *Carmen* piece. Kelly pressed closer and crouched to stay out of his way as he stroked the strings. Soon, the mirror darkened, and their images warped into ribbons of color. Nathan pushed through the demanding piece, his arms weakened by the strenuous climb over the void, even though it was nothing but a vision.

Several seconds later, the observatory floor came into focus. Daryl Blue rose from her chair, so slowly it was painful watching her. As Dr. Gordon had said, Earth Yellow's time passage compared to the other Earths fluctuated, so Daryl Blue's motion appeared jerky, almost at a standstill for a moment and maybe at a tenth of her normal speed at other times.

Gunther pushed the motorcycle closer and offered a weak smile. "Be thinking about us. The nightmare situation here is really a ..." Flashing a grin, he shrugged. "A nightmare."

"We will." Nathan nodded at Gunther. "Hit the light."

The headlamp's beam bounced off the three mirror faces and intersected a few feet in front to create an elliptical halo, flat and standing upright, with a rainbow-like perimeter—seven layered stripes that surrounded a glowing yellowish-white oval.

With a nod to Gunther and Daryl, Nathan repacked his violin in the case, took Kelly's hand, and walked into the ellipse. As usual, the scene around them shattered into millions of pieces. As if taken by a fresh breeze, the pieces flew apart and disappeared, revealing the telescope room. At first, the room was distorted in a twisting coil, but it slowly straightened and clarified. Within a few seconds, they were back.

Daryl hurried over to them. "Where's Red?"

Nathan gestured behind him with his thumb. "She stayed

to set up a network so we can communicate with Earth Yellow. Since time's moving a lot faster there, she could try to call you soon."

Jogging to the desk, Daryl shouted back, "I'll bet I know what frequency she'll use. I'll see if I can locate it."

Kelly tightened her grip on Nathan's hand. "Keep me close. My eyesight's messed up again."

He tried to get a look at her eyes, but she kept her head low. Obviously all these changes were getting to her. After several hours of normal eyesight, now she had to view the world through a dirty filter. Home had become a place to dread.

As he led her to the computer desk, he glanced up at the ceiling. Daryl Red and Gunther were no longer there, nor was the motorcycle. The grass waved furiously, rain beat against the ground, and a man sloshed by, far faster than humanly possible. Nathan caught a glimpse of his circular glasses. It had to be Dr. Simon, but was it the Blue or Yellow version? It was impossible to tell.

The ceiling faded to black and then to the familiar chaotic blobs of color. Daryl, staring at the laptop, slid her finger across the touch pad. As a line of numbers ran along the bottom of the screen, she shook her head. "No trace of Red's signal yet. I'll tune Dr. Gordon back in."

Nathan led Kelly to a chair at an adjacent desk and scanned the dim chamber. The telescope cast a long shadow across the tiles, the entry for guided tours stood slightly ajar, and the elevator door was closed. The floor indicator displayed a red numeral one. "Where's Clara?" Nathan asked.

Keeping her gaze locked on the computer screen, Daryl flicked her thumb toward the ceiling. "Clara Red and Dr. Gordon are still up there. Clara Blue went to get some munchies."

Nathan looked up. His faithful tutor stared back at him, her arms crossed over her open trench coat. Dr. Gordon sat next to her, studying an image on his laptop screen.

Clara's voice boomed through the speakers in the wall. "You weren't gone very long. Did you accomplish anything significant?"

Still looking upward, Nathan eased closer to the center of the room. "Quite a bit. We spent at least twelve hours over there."

"Only an hour and a half here," Clara said. "Tell us what happened, and we'll report on the photos."

As Nathan began the story, Clara Blue returned with sub sandwiches, enough for everyone. Daryl only nibbled at hers, while Kelly ate more heartily. Nathan took a big bite at every convenient pause in his tale. His stomach clock told him he hadn't eaten since the sandwich at Burger King, and all the rope climbing in the misty world, real or not, had left him famished.

After he told of Daryl's commitment to stay on Earth Yellow, he settled back in a desk chair. "That's about it."

"Very interesting," Dr. Gordon said. "I trust that you will find our discoveries equally interesting." He swung around in his chair and looked up at them, though it seemed downward from Nathan's viewpoint.

"Daryl," Dr. Gordon continued, "the photographs I selected for examination should now be in your folder. Please display number one on your screen."

"Will do." Daryl pecked at her keyboard for a second, then pointed at her monitor. "Got it!"

Nathan rolled his chair closer and peered at the photo. Tsayad, facing the camera, appeared to be speaking in song, probably a minute or so after he greeted them on the glassy path. Carrying his songbook, his head tilted slightly upward, he seemed normal enough, at least as normal as a vision stalker could look.

"Do you see anything unusual?" Dr. Gordon asked.

"Besides the white hair, the pale face, and the mist all around?" Nathan shrugged. "Not really."

"Daryl, focus on his hands and enlarge the area."

"No problem." Within a couple of seconds, the stalker's hands filled the screen, both grasping the songbook.

"Nathan," Dr. Gordon said, "I want to see if you notice this feature on your own in order to be sure that I am not just imagining it."

As he studied the photo, Nathan drifted closer and closer to the screen. What could Dr. Gordon be seeing? The stalker's right index finger pointed at a note on the right-hand page, and his left thumb held the book open by pressing against the left-hand page. Nothing unusual except ...

"Wait!" he said out loud. "Daryl, can you blow up that line of music, the one his finger's on?"

"Sure thing."

Nathan rose to his feet and drew so close his nose came within inches of the monitor. "It's C Major, but it's kind of strange. There are lots of sharps and flats, no sense of following the key."

"Exactly," Dr. Gordon said. "Did your experience in that world provide any reason for such dissonance?"

Nathan's mind latched on to that word—dissonance. It had cropped up, something Scarlet had said. The stalkers feed on fear and the dissonance fear creates. It wasn't much, but it was something. "I'll think about it," he said. "Go on to the next one."

"Very well. Daryl, display number two."

A new image replaced the first, a photo of the three domes, including the twelve stalkers surrounding Scarlet's dome. Barely visible between the legs of two stalkers, Scarlet sat in her trembling crouch, appearing small and frail.

"This discovery is subtler," Dr. Gordon said. "Concentrate on the positioning of the people surrounding the dome."

Nathan again leaned as close as possible. He and Kelly had heard this ungodly choir singing their dissonant notes. Could their song be related to the musical staff in the book? They had sung while they faced Scarlet, but the notes had come so quickly, and the combination had been so irritating, he hadn't focused on any pattern, either musically or in the way they stood. But now, he could concentrate.

Able to see through the dome to the other side, he counted the genders—seven men and five women. He drew back for a moment. Something else was like this, something in his musical training that echoed this seven-versus-five circular pattern. A phrase popped into his mind—a chromatic circle. If the males stood for the natural notes, and the females the sharps or flats, they could easily represent the complete scale. He lifted a finger toward the closest choir member. "They're musical notes. Each stalker stands for a note in the chromatic circle."

Dr. Gordon nodded. "Good. I was wondering if I was just imagining things."

"Anything else unusual in the pictures?" Nathan asked.

"Just the one of Francesca in the Wal-Mart. That's number three, Daryl. I included this one after you told your story. I am confident that you will quickly discover the inconsistency."

She tapped the laptop pad and brought up the photo. In the image, Francesca appeared to be a little younger than the girl who had accompanied him to the misty world, maybe a year, maybe less. The flash from the camera had illuminated her body and face brilliantly. Wearing a blue smock over a red shirt, she held her violin in the crook of her arm. Nothing unusual about that, yet, the image of Dr. Malenkov startled him. Yes, he had seen her adoptive father at the Wal-Mart, but now the object in his hands became clear, a huge violin bow.

Nathan backed away from the screen. How could that be? If Nikolai and Francesca already had a bow, why didn't either of them mention it while he was plotting to get one constructed? Unless . . .

He looked at Kelly, then at Daryl. They had seen the ghosts, too, but how could Francesca have traveled to the Wal-Mart in Earth Blue from her bedroom in Earth Yellow? It just didn't make sense.

Then, like a soft echo, Scarlet's words came back to him once again. *You*, my love, are one of the gifted, and another is searching for you in her dreams. Perhaps we can guide her to a convenient place to meet you.

"It was a dream," Nathan said out loud. "Scarlet guided Francesca's dream thoughts to me at the Wal-Mart, and somehow the approach of interfinity is breaking down the barrier to the world of dreams. But why wouldn't Francesca have mentioned the bow?"

Dr. Gordon stroked his chin for a moment, then looked up at Nathan again. "How quickly do you forget your dreams, especially the details?"

Nathan responded with a nod. Dreams always faded quickly, usually by the afternoon. That could explain why Francesca hadn't mentioned the bow. Scarlet had probably planned the whole thing—calling him to Earth Yellow to reunite with Francesca and showing him the kind of bow they needed in order to play the celestial violin. Scarlet planted the idea in his mind long before he tried to swing the basket over the strings.

"So what do we do now?" Nathan asked.

Dr. Gordon rose and walked toward the telescope, one hand in his pocket as he assumed a thoughtful pacing mode. "I suggest going back to the four hundred mirrors to search for your parents. Risking unnecessary cross-dimensional jumps isn't wise, but if you locate Solomon, acquiring his aid would be worth the risk. In the meantime, Daryl Blue will try to communicate with Daryl Red. When the bow is finished, we will summon you for another journey to Earth Yellow."

"What effect is interfinity having on Earth Red?" Nathan asked.

Dr. Gordon stopped and looked up. "Confusion and widespread panic, not only from the appearance of long-dead airline crash survivors, but the rift in the cosmos is now visible in the heavens. At night, a black chasm obliterates our view of at least a tenth of the stars. They are simply gone."

"Gone?" Kelly asked as she cast her wandering gaze upward. "How could stars disappear?"

Dr. Gordon shrugged. "That's what the top astronomers on the planet are trying to figure out. But while they're scratching their heads, the world continues to have a sanity meltdown."

"Yeah," Nathan said. "It's kind of like that here on Blue. People are confused, especially older folks who feel like they're living in the past. And the skies are messed up, too. It's been cloudy most of the time, but whenever it clears, I can see a layer of sparkles mixed in with the blue."

Dr. Gordon resumed his slow pacing. "And the weather phenomenon continues to puzzle me. It's as though Earth Yellow's atmosphere has encroached on the other two without a reciprocating effect. Maybe our two universes are materializing within each other somehow, one overlapping the other so that the worlds will merge physically. If so, the danger level has become literally astronomical. The gravitational collapse alone would annihilate both planets. Our peril cannot be overestimated."

"That's not exactly comforting." Nathan slid his Earth Blue cell phone from his pocket and checked the battery indicator. Still plenty of power. "Okay," he said, standing, "I'm off to see the mirrors again. Give me a call if you hear anything from Daryl Red. If you can't get me on the cell, try the landline. If it's out, try smoke signals. I'll get back in touch somehow."

Clara Blue tapped his shoulder. "Shall I go with you?"

"Better not. Daryl might need your help, and if we have to jump dimensions, we want to punch as few holes as possible."

"I won't make a very big hole," Kelly said, rising slowly from her chair. "Besides, you need my ears."

"And your tackling skills. You never know when I'll need someone to pull me out of a dream."

Clara Blue crossed her arms over her chest. "Okay, Mr. Practical, have you thought about where to get fuel, or did you forget that the Toyota is almost empty and operating gas stations are likely to be few and far between?"

Nathan licked his lips. He cringed at the hint of gasoline still coating the surface. Siphoning his way to Iowa wouldn't work, but Clara's smirk revealed that she already had an idea cooking. "Okay," he said. "I give. Whatcha got?"

She pointed in the general direction of the observatory's rear exit, "I checked the outbuilding. If you look behind the lawn mower, you will find two small gas cans. It won't be enough to get all the way to central Iowa, but it's a start."

Daryl Blue gave Kelly a peck on the cheek. Her voice cracked. "Take care of yourself. I don't want to lose another Kelly-kins."

Blinking rapidly, Kelly took her hand. She opened her mouth to speak, but, after a second or two, she closed it again and returned the kiss.

Silence descended on the telescope room. The gravity of countless dangers seemed to weigh on everyone's mind. With interfinity at hand and Mictar lurking in every dark corner, the shadow of death seemed to hover overhead.

Offering only a wave, Nathan and Kelly left quietly, hand in hand.

After gassing up the Toyota and packing the violin, camera, and mirror, they began the long drive back to Newton. The skies, now gray and darkening, spattered cold rain across the windshield and slickened the pavement.

Nathan flipped on the radio and pressed the scan button, searching for a good signal. The digital readout sped through the FM frequencies, topping at 107.9 and starting over again.

Obviously, no stations were nearby. When he pressed the button again to end the search, mild static buzzed through the speakers, and a rhythmic bump sounded every second or so, as if a percussionist struck a drum in time with an inaudible melody.

Nathan reached to turn the radio off, but Kelly grabbed his wrist. "Leave it there. I hear something."

He pulled his hand back. "What?"

"I'm not sure. Just let me listen."

As they passed close to the Burger King they had visited in Earth Yellow, the static increased in volume and pitch. Nathan decelerated and pulled into the parking lot. "Let's change the frequency one notch at a time." He pressed the tuning button. The static altered, pitching higher again.

"Anything?" he asked.

"Try going up a few more."

He hit the button twice. The static separated into several scratchy voices, some bass singers, some sopranos, and a couple in between. As he continued climbing the frequency range, the jumbled sounds clarified until the chorus of voices sang without distortion. Although each singer performed with professional polish, they sang oddly blended notes, without melody, without purpose. The voices seemed to compete with each other, some in one key and some in another, until the combination sounded more like an operatic war than a choir performance.

Kelly winced. "That's awful! It sounds like Pavarotti is having a temper tantrum."

"Can you interpret?" Nathan asked, turning the volume down slightly.

"They're all saying different things, but I'll try to pick up something." She opened the glove box and withdrew a pen. "Got any paper?"

He pulled "Foundation's Key" from his pocket. "Use the back of this."

She retrieved Daryl's puzzle book, scooted her feet up on her seat, and set the paper and book on her knees, drawing them close to her eyes. While she jotted down some words, Nathan pulled slowly out of the parking lot. "Let's see if we can keep moving and still pick it up." As he accelerated, the signal faded but not enough to squelch the voices.

Kelly turned up the volume and continued to transcribe lyrics. "I count at least eight different voices, and they're all saying something different. I'm piecing them together the best I can."

Nathan glanced at her as she worked. At times, she just listened intently, then, with tiny, precise letters, she slowly formed a word, pursing her lips to mouth the syllables as they painstakingly appeared on her paper.

He squeezed the steering wheel and looked up at the darkening sky. It was a good thing they had over four hours in front of them. With so many voices, her transcription could take every minute of it.

Although no other cars competed for road space, Nathan took his time. Every few miles, as the signal wavered, he adjusted the volume. Soon, he noticed a pattern. Whenever the thickness of the clouds overhead decreased, the strength of the signal increased. He gazed up at the thinning blanket overhead. Was the music, if it could be called that, coming through the wounds in space? Could the singers be the twelve white-haired freaks torturing Scarlet from their stance in the chromatic circle?

Nathan pressed down the gas pedal. Scarlet needed help. He had to rescue her from their clutches. Even if it meant wounding the dimensional fabric again, ending her suffering would be worth it.

He leaned through the gap between the seats and grabbed the mirror from the back. Propping it on the dashboard, he stared at it while still accelerating.

Kelly looked up. "What are you doing?"

"I want to see if Scarlet will help us get back to her."

Her glassy eyes blinked twice. "Scarlet? What can she do?"

"She watches me through the Quattro mirror. She said she's the one who rescued us from the plane crash."

"Do you need music?"

"To show a transport destination, I think so. But we have this stuff on the radio."

Kelly laughed. "I wouldn't call that music. I'd call it the opposite of music."

"Maybe we can find a normal station now." He pressed the scan button again and watched the digits climb.

"Nathan!" Kelly pushed his hand away. "I was just getting some important stuff. I think it's about your parents."

"Why didn't you tell me?" He pushed the tuner until the singing returned.

"I wanted to wait until I had it all."

He lowered the mirror and breathed out an exasperated sigh. "Go ahead. Keep translating."

She settled back again and tapped her pen on the page. "It's really strange. Most of the voices are singing about morbid things like death, fear, and war, but there's one female who inserts other words out of the blue. So I started concentrating on her voice. She sings in what sounds like F-sharp Major, and every time she sings an A-sharp, I hear a word that doesn't fit what she's saying overall. That's when I started writing down the A-sharp words that my mind translates."

"Wow! That's amazing. With all that noise, you gotta have perfect pitch to pull out those notes."

She doodled on the page, making a warped quarter note. "It has to be more than that. I've always been good at identifying notes, but ever since you showed up at my house, I've been hearing things I've never heard before. All the sounds separate neatly from each other, almost like I can see them in my mind."

"You're the interpreter. You picked up a sixth sense of some kind."

"I guess so." She tapped her pen on the paper. "Anyway, here's what I have so far. 'Solomon location square music.' "

He glanced at her notes. Whoever was sending them a message had mentioned his father's name! His voice spiked in volume. "Is that it? Isn't there more?"

"Not yet." A hurt expression wrinkled her face. "It's really hard. I'm doing the best I can."

He clenched the steering wheel. Everything was moving too slowly, much too slowly. "I know you're trying, but there has to be more. The words sound important, but they don't make sense."

"You switched the station," she said, pointing at the radio with her pen. "I'll have to keep listening to pick it up again."

Nathan stared at the radio. She was right. It was his fault. He slammed his hand against the dashboard. "I can't believe it! I'm so stupid sometimes!"

"I'm not touching that one." She angled her ear toward the radio and squinted at the paper again, her pen poised. "But it'll help if you turn down *your* volume for a while."

Nathan bit his tongue. That was the sharpest rebuke he had heard from Kelly in a long time. As he glared at the road, a dozen retorts flashed through his mind and begged to burst out, but he pressed his teeth down harder. He deserved the scolding. They had a plan, and he switched gears. And why? Because he wanted to rescue Scarlet. Somehow the maiden in red had captured his will, and he couldn't get his mind off her.

He set the mirror in the back and gazed at Kelly. Her lips once again pursed, she continued to painstakingly transcribe from the midst of the turmoil. In some ways, she mirrored Scarlet—fair of face and form, possessing a fire within that defied description, and, with her vision so brutally wounded, carrying an air of vulnerability that called out for his protection.

Finally, he let out a long sigh. It was time to make up for his blunder. He reached over and laid a gentle hand on her arm. "I was wrong, Kelly. Keep me in line. You're good at that."

Kelly kept her gaze fixed on the paper. A little smile grew on her face, a gentle smile that spread a soothing balm over his aching heart.

Nathan allowed a smile of his own to emerge. It felt good to apologize, very, very good.

The translation process continued. Sometimes the voices would stop for a while, as if giving the singers a few minutes to rest, but they always started back up again, beginning with a ten-second-long burst in which everyone belted out a C-natural at various octaves before crashing into the usual cacophony of horrible dissonance.

After an hour or so, the music came to a halt, another rest. Kelly slid her feet back to the floorboard and held the paper in front of her. "There might be more, but here's what I have so far. 'Solomon location square music key circle sleep interpreter dream bedroom Patar.'"

"Very interesting." Nathan let the words sink in, analyzing them as they passed through his mind. It was just a jumble of words, but his father's name was in there, so it had to be important. And, strangely enough, every word was a noun. The sentence needed verbs, at least a couple to give it meaning.

He turned the volume up one notch. "Can you catch any verbs when she sings a different note, maybe stray verbs that don't fit in with the rest of the stuff she's singing?"

Kelly lifted her feet again. "I'll try, but the music is so obnoxious, it's giving me a headache."

"Let's make a pit stop while they're resting. We need gas anyway." He exited the interstate at Walcott, a few miles west of Davenport. An Iowa 80 truck stop and a Pilot Travel Center faced each other on the secondary highway, but darkness covered every opening except for a faint glow from the window in the Pilot's doorway.

Driving slowly, he pulled up to one of the Pilot's service islands. There was no sign of power — no prices on the pumps or words on the instruction screens. It felt like a disaster scene, a war zone or the aftermath of a plague.

He opened the door and slid outside. "Come on. Might as well see if we can use the restroom." As he approached the entry, he glanced up at the late evening sky. The clouds had raced away, replaced by a purple canvas speckled with hundreds of shimmering lights, much bigger and brighter than stars.

The air had grown hot, very hot. Did that mean it was still summer on Earth Yellow? Or maybe Indian summer? Or could it have already cycled to the next year's summer?

He pushed his sleeves up past his elbows. Although he had long ago shed his sweatshirt and thrown it in the backseat, he had to live with the overly hot shirt. He had nothing but skin underneath.

Kelly, walking slowly next to him, her poorly focused eyes meandering from side to side, had also stripped down to her shirt, but her short-sleeved white tunic, loose and flowing, likely kept her cool.

A crashing sound made him pivot. Kelly clutched his hand and froze. "What was that?" she asked.

Nathan scanned the highway. At the truck stop across the road, a man in a business suit had just broken a door window with the butt of a rifle. He reached through the jagged hole and opened the door from the inside, then disappeared into the darkness.

"Armed robbery," Nathan replied, pointing in that direction. "The upper class has sunk to looting."

She squinted toward the truck stop. "What are we going to do?"

"I don't think it's a good idea to get shot stopping a beer and pretzel heist."

Kelly let out a weak sigh. "No. I guess not."

Still looking back, Nathan pushed the door open and walked inside. When he turned, the twin barrels of a shotgun pressed against his forehead.

10

ABODAH'S MESSAGE

"Store's closed," a woman on the trigger side of the gun announced. "Got a problem with that?"

Nathan backed away a step and pushed Kelly behind him. Swallowing, he tried to keep his voice steady. "Uh ... no problem. I just needed gas, and the door was open, so I—"

"Thought you'd see what you could take," the woman finished. She lowered the gun to her hip. With only an oil lamp on the counter casting light on her stocky body, her features blended in with the dim interior of the store. Yet, her wide eyes communicated more fear than bravado.

"I wasn't going to take anything." Nathan drew in a deep breath, keeping his eye on the shotgun. That lady could pull the trigger at any moment. The thought of Tony Clark getting his guts blown out sent chills across his body. But he had to move on, conquer this fear, and press forward. "I know how to stop what's causing all these weird events," he finally said, "but if I don't get gas, I can't get where I'm going."

The wrinkles in her brow slowly eased. "You got money?"

Nathan flicked his thumb toward the pumps. "Does the credit card thing work?"

She shook her head. "Cash only, but if I can't get the generator running, nothing will work."

He dug out his wallet and rifled through his bills, trying to calculate how much he could buy. "What's the price per gallon?"

Now, instead of fear, her eyes gave away confusion. She set the gun butt on the floor and glanced back and forth as if lost. "Uh ... Three seventy-nine ... I think."

A gust of wind pulled open the door and slammed it shut again, knocking over a stack of newspapers. The room grew suddenly cold, and the smell of burning firewood drifted by. An overhead fluorescent light flickered on, and a hum sounded from the cash register.

"What am I talking about?" the woman finally said. "That's way too high." She leaned the shotgun against the counter and ran her fingers through her short graying hair. "What?" Using both hands now, she grabbed two shocks and pulled. "What happened? My hair is gone!"

Kelly blinked at her. "Was it long and as black as a raven?"

"Yes!" Her whole body quaked as she continued to comb her fingers through her hair. "What's going on? Why aren't there any customers?" Finally, she backed into the counter and stared wide-eyed again. "Is the world coming to an end?"

Kelly stepped slowly forward, her hand out to guide her way. When she reached the woman, she set her hand on her shoulder. "Turn on the pumps, and I'll tell you all about it."

The woman stared at her and nodded stiffly. "Okay. I can do that."

Giving Kelly a smile, Nathan strode toward the door. He picked up one of the spilled newspapers, that day's *Chicago Tribune*. With no sports or entertainment sections, it seemed lightweight ... void of anything frivolous. He quickly thumbed through the few pages. No advertisements appeared anywhere, just long articles and a few black and white photos.

As he made his way to the car, he pushed his sleeves back down and read the front headline. In big, bold letters it spelled out "PANIC!" and underneath, a smaller headline read, "Midwest and Southeast Hardest Hit by Cosmic Terror."

When he shifted his eyes to read the article, a thump and a

loud hum jerked his attention toward the gas pumps. The island lights flashed on, and zeroes appeared on the digital meters. Nathan set the paper on the trunk, pushed the nozzle into the tank, and squeezed the trigger. The gallons meter began counting, but the dollars and cents meter ticked up at a rate so slow, it would easily stay under a dollar by the time he finished.

While the gas flowed, he read the newspaper's lead article. The governments of Earth Blue had determined the cosmic abnormalities were the result of some kind of imminent alien invasion. The long-dead airline disaster victims had to be imposters, brought to earth to create havoc and gain influence. The United States would lead the effort to battle against the encroaching power, apparently another realm invading through some kind of wormhole in space. Details about how they would carry out this battle were sketchy at best. The entire country, of course, operated under a state of emergency. With widespread blackouts and very little fuel available, law enforcement had been relegated to foot patrols in many areas. The National Guard kept order in the cities, but little if any help was available in rural areas. Crime was rampant.

Nathan folded the paper in half. Saving the airline passengers had brought more trouble, proving Patar's warning. The stalker's words, spoken while everyone else on board sat frozen, had penetrated his mind and locked in place. *If these souls are cheated out of death, their escape will create more darkness than light. Take care not to stir darkened pools when you know neither the depth of the water nor the creatures that lurk beneath the surface.*

Nathan shivered. Patar was right again. Maybe it was about time he listened, put away his emotional attachments, and do what someone far wiser and more experienced told him to do. Without his father around to steer him away from a dumb step, he needed a word of wisdom, or maybe a kick in the pants, which Patar seemed more than willing to deliver.

After topping off the tank and grabbing the newspaper again, he hurried back inside. Kelly hadn't come out, and with her eyesight still so blurry, he didn't want to leave her alone for very long.

As soon as he opened the door, the clerk, sitting on a stool behind the counter, greeted him with a big smile. Kelly leaned against the front of the counter, munching on a stick of beef jerky.

"Welcome back, Nathan," the clerk said. "Kelly and I are having a very nice talk."

He laid the paper on the counter. "It looks like you're feeling better."

"I am. This lovely young lady explained everything to me."

He gave Kelly a quizzical look. "Oh. That's good. I guess." Nodding at the paper, he added, "How much for this and the gas? The pump only registered about fifty cents."

The clerk waved a hand at him. "On the house. And more to boot."

"Drinks and snacks," Kelly said, holding up a bulging plastic bag. "We're all set."

After getting back on the road, Nathan reached into the bag and pulled out a Dr Pepper. "What went on back there?"

Furrowing her brow, Kelly swallowed the last bite of jerky before answering. "It was so weird. For a minute, she was all blurry, then I could see her clearly, but she was younger, with long jet-black hair. Then, she went blurry again. The whole time we were talking, everything seemed to fade in and out, even the store itself, like I was seeing two different worlds. But the other world was always clearer."

"Dr. Gordon must be right. The two universes are coming together. You're seeing into Earth Yellow, and it's clear to you, just like it is when you're there."

"I guess so." She flipped the radio back on. The choir had already restarted their ghastly song, so she quickly assumed her translating position and planted her pen on the paper. This time, she squinted more than usual, cocking her head from time to time as if making sure she heard something right.

Nathan drummed his fingers on the wheel. He ached to ask what she heard, but any interruption might ruin her concentration and make her miss something. He had to be patient and let Kelly finish. This was her job, her talent. She could do it.

After about a half hour, Nathan's cell phone rang. While Kelly stayed glued to her task, he flipped open the phone.

"Hello," he whispered.

"Nathan. It's Daryl ... Daryl Blue. I can barely hear you. What's wrong?"

"Nothing. I just have to stay quiet. What's up?"

"Red's got something cooking. No voice yet, but she's going to try to send a text message to you."

"Wow! That was fast."

"Seems like it to us, but it's been months on Earth Yellow. She said she had trouble getting the parts she needed. With the whole world in a nightmare turmoil, it was tough getting anything done."

"Yeah." He glanced at the newspaper in the backseat. "Trouble's popping on this world, too."

"All three dimensions are ready to crack. Dr. Gordon's been monitoring the news on Earth Red. Every nuclear-equipped nation has an itchy finger poised over the doomsday button. If we don't fix this thing soon, it's going to make *Independence Day* look like a friendly picnic with our alien friends."

Nathan heaved a sigh. "We're working on it."

"I know, but there's a new problem. I can't tune in the mirror at the Earth Yellow Interfinity Labs site. Dr. Gordon thinks someone might have moved it to make ready for the construction of the laboratory's first building, back when they were called StarCast. That means we can't go there unless your magic mirror does the trick. Plus, the time difference between us and Earth Yellow makes communicating with Daryl Red a real chore. Basically she has to wait for hours to get a response from me that takes only a few minutes. So, as soon as you get the text message, try to answer her. When she finally gets it, she'll have been waiting a long time."

"Got it. Talk to you soon."

Nathan closed the phone. Kelly looked up expectantly. After he gave her a quick summary of the call, she returned to her painstaking chore, straining to listen while squinting at her paper.

A few seconds later, the phone chimed its text message note. Nathan flipped it up and punched through the menu silently, glancing at the deserted highway as he pulled the car to the shoulder and stopped. When he reached his inbox, he read the initial screen. Three messages.

He began paging through them, starting with the oldest. Since each message had to be short enough to send in the cell phone's text format, he had to piece the three together to complete the entire note.

"Nathan. News update. Tony Clark moved into Francesca's old house, and Gunther delivered the letter. Tony's making the bow and should have it done in a couple of weeks. That might be only a few days for you. Maybe hours. Who can tell? Anyway, I had to modify one of the original IBM PCs and use an asynchronous cable to hook it to my radio transmitter. What a pain! But at least it works. Daryl Blue picks it up and modulates it to a cell signal. Just reply to let me know you received it. She'll pick it up again and send it my way. I'll be waiting."

Nathan typed out a reply with his thumbs. "Good work. Will try to get there soon." He sent the message and clapped the phone shut. After pulling back onto the highway, he squeezed the steering wheel again. The fate of the entire world—no, three worlds—waited for him to get a ten-foot-long bow that was being constructed by a teenager in another realm, take it to a ridiculously dangerous fourth world, and play an impossibly huge violin, all while saving his parents and three color-coded supplicants from death at the hands, or the voices, of the choir from hell. Could it get any more complicated?

When they reached the final exit, just a few miles from the Earth Blue home, Kelly turned off the radio. "Okay, I have all the verbs and a few other words, too, and I had to mix them in with the nouns, but there were a lot of possible combinations. Here is one that makes some sense." She licked her lips and held the paper close to her eyes. "'Solomon lives. Location is square where music harmonizes. Key is circle of fifths. Sleep with interpreter. Follow dream in bedroom where Patar stalks.'"

Nathan ran the sentences through his mind. At least now they had a real message, probably instructions from Abodah, the woman who had helped them in the misty world, but what exactly was she saying? As a rebel who worked secretly as Patar's ally, she was trying to hide her words from the others, but it seemed too cryptic. What could a dream in the bedroom be about? Patar had spoken during a weird dream there, but was it really a dream? And he appeared on the plane, too. He said something about giving a gift that could be used to battle Mictar.

Patar's strange words again echoed in Nathan's mind. Take care not to stir darkened pools when you know neither the depth of the water nor the creatures that lurk beneath the surface.

What creatures could he have been talking about? The supplicants?

As Patar's words faded, Nathan silently formed the new sentence on his lips, repeating one phrase in a whisper. "Key is circle of fifths."

Abodah had to be talking about the musical circle, but how could it relate to the mirrors?

"So," Kelly said. "Got any clue?"

"Maybe. Let's fire up the mirror and check out all the squares again."

When they arrived at the house, Nathan pushed the garage opener, but the door wouldn't budge. Obviously, the power outage continued. He parked in the driveway, helped Kelly out, and the two skulked toward the door. Nathan carried the Quattro mirror and his violin, while Kelly kept the camera on a strap around her neck. Clouds once again blanketed the sky, bringing a new chill to the air. As Daryl had indicated, summer on Earth Yellow had long ago flown by, and winter was at the doorstep. Could another snowfall be far away?

Once inside the bedroom, Nathan restored the mirror squares to their original positions. Kelly held up the "Foundation's Key" music while he played it through. Instantly, the squares flashed with light, and, over the next minute or so, the reflection morphed into four hundred scenes.

"Okay," he said, lowering his bow, "what's the message again?"

Kelly squinted at the back of the page. "Solomon lives. Location is square where music harmonizes. Key is circle of fifths. Sleep with interpreter. Follow dream in bedroom where Patar stalks."

He walked closer to the mirrored wall. "So we need to figure out which squares make a circle of fifths."

"I was supposed to learn about that stuff in music theory," Kelly said, rising to join him. "But it got purged when my mother left."

" 'Foundation's Key' is in C Major. The circle of fifths for that key will start with C-natural." He pointed at one of the squares and shifted his finger from square to square in a circular pattern as he continued. "Then it moves by fifths through twelve notes, G–D–A–E–B–F-sharp, and so on. We have to figure out which square represents C-natural and find the circle in the mirror."

"How can a mirror represent a note?" She angled her ear toward the wall. "I don't hear any music."

Nathan lifted his bow again and played a long middle C. "Did that change anything?"

"Not that I can tell, but I'm half blind. And I didn't hear anything but the violin."

He played every C possible, pausing after each one, but nothing changed. Some of the images showed country landscapes and deserted highways, others provided views of city skylines, and a few gave them glimpses of rooms inside homes with families huddling around fireplaces or storm lanterns. In one sparse living room, four wide-eyed children locked their stares on a father as he read to them in the glow of a single candle.

Kelly moved a finger gently across the family's image. "They're so scared!"

"Can you see them?"

"Barely, but I don't really need to. It's like I can feel what they're feeling."

"Your interpretive skills must be getting stronger," Nathan said.

"I know, but sometimes it's a curse. I don't want to feel what other people are feeling, especially when they're terrified."

Nathan laid his hand over hers. "If we want to help them, we have to figure out what following the dream means."

She drew back and lowered her head, whispering, "It'll have to be your dream. I don't think mine will ever come true."

"Why not?"

She shook her head. "Never mind. Let's concentrate on yours."

He tried to catch her gaze, but she kept her eyes low. What could be getting her down? What dream could be so lofty that it could never come true? Undo something in her past? Her mother coming home? Maybe one of those. But it was probably better not to ask. If she really wanted him to know, she'd tell him.

He tried to infuse a bit more energy into his voice. "My

dream is to get my parents back, but it seems like it won't ever come true, either."

"Maybe Abodah meant a literal dream," she said, looking up at him again. "Maybe you have to go to sleep here, and Patar will stalk your dream. Then he'll tell you what to do."

Nathan's voice spiked sharply. "Sleep? Now? The universe is about to collapse and you want me to take a nap?"

"What choice do you have? You've been awake for what? Thirty hours? And listen to you. Since when do you yell at me like that? You're exhausted."

Her words stung. He had been trying to squash down the tension, but it had just burst through. He took a deep breath and let it out slowly. "You're right, as usual. It *has* been a long day. The Earth Yellow clock really messed things up."

"There's still enough mattress left to lie down on." She pulled the ripped mattress away from the wall and laid it flat on the floor. "Now you have a comfortable place to rest. Why don't you just lie down and see what happens? I've had more sleep than you, so I'll stand guard."

Nathan eyed the mattress. He probably could fall asleep, and maybe Patar would come and pay his dreams a visit. He had done it before. But what if some kind of interpretation was needed and Kelly wasn't there?

Thoughts of Francesca's dream flowed back into his mind. She believed that she and Dr. Malenkov had dreamed together by touching while asleep, but he never remembered it, so didn't that mean her theory might be wrong? On the other hand, one of the photos proved that her teacher stood behind her with a violin bow, but could he have just been a figment of Francesca's dream, not really there in a conscious state?

Still, if Francesca believed it, she must have had a good reason. After all, this was the younger version of his mother. Her gift of insight far surpassed his own. Not only that, the message from Abodah said to sleep with the interpreter.

But how could he do that? Sure, any touching would be innocent, maybe holding hands just to get the job done, but wouldn't even that kind of contact be forbidden in his father's sight? Wouldn't closeness on a mattress raise the temperature of his already simmering hormones? And what would Kelly think? He couldn't just ask her to sleep with him, could he?

He took her hand and drew her closer. "My thoughts are really jumbled. Can you—"

"Read your mind again?" She gave him a sly smile. "As tired as you are, it might put me to sleep."

He nodded at his violin, still in his hand. "Would it help if I played some music?"

"Good idea. Just play like you did for Tsayad, something from your heart."

"Will do." He raised his bow and brushed it softly across the strings. His mood called for something gentle, something that would communicate his innocent fondness for Kelly and his desire to treat her emotions with tenderness.

Tilting her head slightly, she smiled and sighed, her glassy eyes focusing more easily than usual. The music seemed to warm her heart.

For some reason Kelly's comfort and ease annoyed him. He pushed deeper into the strings. As if driven by an uncontrollable inner passion, he made the bow rocket back and forth. A thousand thoughts raced through his mind, so fast he couldn't focus on a single one. They streamed from his frazzled brain directly into his instrument, flying into the air as a string of music, melodic at first, then tortured and dissonant.

Kelly's smile faded. After several seconds, she blinked twice and turned her head.

Nathan stopped playing. His chest heaving through labored breaths, he coughed out his words. "What's wrong?"

She swiveled back. A tear moistened her cheek as she looked him in the eye again. "I ... I'm not a harlot."

Nathan stiffened, but he managed to keep his face calm. "I know you're not. I've never thought that."

"Then your music tells lies."

He let the violin droop at his side. "Mictar said that, not me. Maybe I'm just mad at him."

Kelly shook her head. "You believed him. You think I'm not good enough for you." She sniffed, and her voice cracked. "And maybe ... maybe you're right. You need a sweet little princess who's as white as snow."

"Look." Nathan raised his bow but resisted the urge to point it at her. "I'm not going to lie to you. The stuff I heard bothered me, but it's in the past."

"You'd like to think so, but in your eyes I'm damaged goods."

"Damaged goods? Did you hear that in my music?"

She nodded. "And now ... now you want us to sleep together." Biting her bottom lip, she crossed her arms and turned away. "I promised myself I wasn't ever going to make the same mistakes again. Not for you. Not for anyone."

He touched her arm but thought better of pulling her around. "But it's just so we can dream together. Nothing else is going to happen."

She turned back, her cheeks ablaze. "Nathan Shepherd, don't pretend you know what it's like. You were raised in a protective dome. You've probably never even kissed a girl. You have no idea how it feels when the lights go out and ..." Her cheeks turning redder than ever, she looked away. "Never mind. You wouldn't understand unless you've been there."

He set a gentle finger on her chin. This time he turned her face toward him and looked her in the eye. "You're right. I don't understand. But this much I do know." He paused, hoping the words would come out with all the strength and resolve he felt inside. "You can trust me. No matter what happens, you can trust me."

As new tears welled in her eyes, her lower lip quivered. "I trust you. I ... I just don't trust myself."

Nathan pulled back his hand. "Then I'll have to be strong enough for both of us." He sat on the floor and patted the mattress. "You get the comfy spot, and I'll sleep down here. We can hold hands and stay apart at the same time."

With a doubtful look, she lowered herself to the mattress and lay down. She curled up and faced him, one hand extended. "Okay, Nathan. I'll trust you ... for both of us."

As he lay down, he touched her fingers. The light in the room faded, leaving only her body's silhouette, the bare outline of her facial features, and her shining eyes in view. After a minute or so, her lips puckered slightly as she spoke again.

"*Have* you ever kissed a girl, Nathan?"

Nathan hesitated. The question was a simple one, but he wanted to give more than a simple answer. "No. I want my first kiss to be when the pastor says, 'You may now kiss the bride.'"

She let out a low humming sound. "Actually, that's really romantic." Her voice now came from out of almost total darkness, except for the weak glow in her eyes. "But is that your belief, or your father's?"

This time he didn't hesitate. "Both. I know I was raised in a dome, like you said, but I want my wife to be the only girl I ever kiss, and the only way I'll know for sure is to wait until our wedding day."

As a whispered sigh drifted toward him, her glowing orbs blinked out. "I hope I'm there to see it." Her grip on his hand tightened for a brief second, then loosened, but their index fingers remained curled together.

Nathan lay back and closed his eyes, but Kelly's anguished face remained branded in his mind. Her voice replayed, "I'm not a harlot ... In your eyes, I'm damaged goods ... I promised myself I wasn't ever going to make the same mistakes again. Not for you. Not for anyone."

The words echoed over and over. Did he really think she was damaged goods? She made a promise never to do again whatever it was she had done. Could he treat her as though she were the untouched princess she had talked about? Could he ever stop wondering what she had done? Was Mictar right when he said, *"You want to know every lurid detail. She is your dark shadow, and you will never find your parents while you entertain a harlot at your side."*

He grimaced at the spiteful words. But were they true? Would his parents accept her? Or would his father see her as a harlot, a wicked wench to be despised?

As the stalker's accusations echoed, Nathan replayed a scene from only a few months ago in London. He and his father were walking back from his mother's performance, but she had stayed at the hall for a reception, planning to take a taxi with Clara later.

Fog shrouded his thoughts, the effects of sleep looming close by. His mind drifted, allowing the mist to dress a London street and bordering sidewalk, well-lit but with only a few people tromping over the wet concrete.

His father strode with a lively gait. "Your mother was fabulous, as usual."

Nathan laughed. "Yeah, but the other violinist looked annoyed. He couldn't hold a candle."

"Oh, I don't think so. He was just ... intimidated."

His father stopped suddenly and looked toward an alleyway. Nathan followed his line of sight. A woman had sprawled across the gutter, her legs in the alley and her head and torso on the dirty walkway.

Nathan shrugged. "Probably just a—"

"Be right back!" his father said as he jumped into a trot toward the alley. Stooping, he helped the young woman get up from the pavement. She was filthy, her skimpy clothes were torn, and makeup smeared her face.

As Nathan walked closer, his father used his own jacket to wipe mud from the woman's arms and legs and brushed tears away from her face with his thumbs. Finally, he gave her money, at least three or four bills. One couple paused and stared at them, then walked on, shaking their heads.

After talking to her for a couple of minutes, he hailed a taxi and helped her get in the back, then paid the driver. When he finally returned to Nathan's side, the two again headed toward the hotel.

Nathan stared at him, trying hard to keep his tone in check. "She's a prostitute."

His father stuffed his hands into his pockets. "I know."

"You rubbed her arms and legs, and you gave her money."

He glanced at Nathan, then refocused on the sidewalk ahead. "Yes, I know that, too."

"Everyone else on the street will think you were her last customer."

His father lifted his head higher. "And everyone who knows me will realize that couldn't possibly be true, no matter how it looked."

"But what about propriety? How many times have you told me not to touch a girl if she's not my wife?"

His father stopped and laid a hand on his shoulder. "Propriety can be a wise tutor, Son, but it can also be a cruel taskmaster. The key is to know when to dismiss propriety. It is good not to touch a woman who is not your wife, but to refuse a touch when a life is at stake is cruelty. It is a great sin against God and against humanity."

"But what if a life isn't at stake? You didn't know if that prostitute would have died. Maybe she was just drunk."

His father let out a sigh but kept a gentle smile. "She *was* drunk, Nathan. She is a slave to her body and to those who use her body for their pleasures. She sees no light in her dark prison, so I gave her a glimpse of the light that you and I follow." He laid an arm over Nathan's shoulders, and the two walked on. "Sacrificial love is a light that shines in the darkest places, no matter who is watching."

Nathan opened his eyes. The two glowing orbs had returned. Kelly was looking right at him, close enough for her injured eyes to focus clearly. He didn't dare turn away from her. "What are you doing?" he asked.

"Reading your mind again."

"But I wasn't playing music. I—"

She set two fingers on his lips and let out a quiet, "Shhhhh." Then, interlocking her index finger with his again, she curled up and closed her eyes. "Sweet dreams, Nathan." After letting out a long yawn, she added, "You're the best."

He released a long breath and let his eyelids droop. Kelly's cool, soft hand sent more prickles across his skin. Her closeness felt good, too good, but he had work to do, and his exhaustion would kick in before long. He yawned, then sighed. Sleep would soon come.

After what seemed like a few minutes, he opened his eyes and checked out his surroundings. He lay on the floor, one finger still curled around Kelly's. The room was much darker than before. Had he awakened in the middle of the night, or was he dreaming?

He sat up and looked back at the floor. His body still lay there, breathing rhythmically. Smiling at his own awkward fetal pose, he gave his sleeping body a light pat on the shoulder. So this was a dream, a strikingly realistic one, but definitely a dream.

Something new lay on the floor near the mirror. A body? Nathan jumped up, leaving his sleeping form behind. He rushed to the mirror and knelt. The body appeared to be a man, a rather hefty one lying on his stomach. Craning his neck, Nathan listened. Yes. The man was breathing.

With careful hands, Nathan rolled him over. In the dimness, he could barely make out the man's bearded face, yet, even with dark bruises blotching his skin all around his eyes, his identity was clear—Jack, his friend from the airplane crash.

11

THE FIFTH REALM

Nathan shook the man's shoulder. "Jack! Can you hear me?"

Letting out a groan, Jack fluttered open his eyelids, but it was too dark to see his eyes. "Who's there?" he asked softly.

"It's Nathan. Remember me?"

A weak smile shifted Jack's beard. "Remember you? I've been searching for you. But in my condition that has been a lost cause."

As Nathan leaned closer, a sick feeling boiled in his stomach. Jack's eye sockets were empty. "Did Mictar do that to you?"

Jack reached out a hand. "Help me up, and I'll tell you about it."

He pulled Jack to a sitting position, glancing at Kelly to see that she still slept soundly. The sight of his own snoozing body near hers seemed too strange to be true.

"This is really a weird dream," Nathan said. "I've never had one so vivid ... well, one other. But that was recent, too."

"As well you might expect." Jack sniffed the air. "Ah! Kelly is nearby. I'll never forget her scent, a lovely vanilla mixed with strawberry."

"Yeah, she's here. She's sleeping."

"Then she will have to hear my story another time." Jack pulled a crumpled fedora from underneath his jacket. As he passed the brim through his nervous fingers, his vacant sockets aimed toward Kelly. "When I rode on Mictar's back into the mirror, there was a sudden flash of light."

As if cued by Jack's words, the mirror in the room flashed. The reflection transformed into a movie screen of sorts, showing Jack riding the evil stalker's back. Mictar staggered under the weight in the same bedroom they sat in now, while a funnel-like swirl of mist spun in the center of the room. In the background, Nathan's parents looked on in horror. Although no sound came from the mirror, Jack filled the air with a vibrant storytelling voice.

"A window opened, and a man who looked just like Mictar began to climb in. At the same time, your father tackled the real Mictar and sent us both toppling over a desk, breaking it into pieces. I leaped to my feet and tried to crawl over the bed, but Mictar kicked your father away, pounced on me, and covered my face with his hand. Light as bright as the sun scorched my eyes, so painful I can't describe it. From that point on, I couldn't see, so I can only tell you what I heard."

"Wait a minute," Nathan said. "Maybe you won't have to. I hear something."

Noises erupted from the mirror. The movie's sound kicked in. His father lay on the floor near the bed, holding bloody fingers over the side of his head. Jack, still on the bed, groaned loudly under Mictar's scalding hand. Patar burst through the window and lunged at Mictar.

The two stalkers wrestled on top of Jack, clawing at each other and ripping the mattress.

Nathan's mother leaped to her husband's side. "Solomon! Are you all right?"

He shook his head, and if he said anything, the grunts and strange sounds coming from the combatants drowned him out.

Jack rolled off the bed, and the weight release sent one end of the mattress into the air. Mictar and Patar crashed to the floor, still wrestling savagely. They sang in bursts of harsh notes that sounded more like musical profanity than song.

Nathan's mother helped Jack crawl to safety next to her husband, just a few inches away from the expanding swirl of mist.

Jack blinked. "I can't see!" he cried. "It feels like my eyes are on fire!"

Smoke poured from his eye sockets, creating twin black plumes that drifted toward the ceiling. Nathan's mother swabbed his forehead with her sleeve, but her anguished face proved that she had no idea what to do.

Patar kicked Mictar in the groin, leaped up, and rushed to Jack. He laid his hand over the bearded man's eyes. "You will lose your sight," Patar crooned, "but you will not die."

Mictar climbed to his feet and pointed at Jack. "I tasted his life force!" he shouted. "I must have the rest!"

Scowling at his brother, Patar barked a reply. "A taste that leads to slavish lust should never be taken. You have struck the match, but you will not bask in these flames."

Mictar hurled another musical obscenity. ". . . with your trite moralisms! His life energy seal is broken. He cannot survive."

"Not in this realm." Using his free hand, Patar scooped some mist out of the swirl. He sniffed it, then, after letting some of the mist filter through his fingers, he sniffed it again and applied it to Jack's forehead. He now seemed to be talking to Nathan's parents. "I am sending him to a place where he can survive—the realm of dreams. His only hope will be to find the healer of the broken womb, and when the crack is sealed, perhaps he, too, will be restored."

Patar lifted Jack to his feet and guided him into the swirl.

Mictar pointed a stiff finger at his brother. "Your healer is a fool! A chicken with no head! He is so enamored with selfish infatuations, he will never find his parents or this eyeless rescuer!"

As the mist enveloped Jack, Patar stayed outside the swirl and looked back at Mictar. "Perhaps you are right. The road ahead of the healer is cruel and heartbreaking, far more difficult than he is now able to endure, but I will never give up hope. He is the only one remaining who can complete the duet."

The mist seemed to eat away at Jack's body. Within seconds, he was gone.

"I must have more!" Mictar roared and lunged at Nathan's parents. A scream shot from Patar's mouth, a visible lightning bolt of sound, black and jagged. Just as Mictar reached Nathan's parents, the bolt slammed into his body and covered him with darkness. Mictar grabbed each parent and screamed. "I will take them with me!"

Patar dove headfirst and clutched Mictar's ankle. "Into the mist!" he yelled. "I will keep my brother here!"

Nathan's parents jumped up, breaking away from Mictar's grasp. His father staggered, but his mother held him upright as they hobbled toward the swirl. Both had splotches of black on their arms that dripped like sticky tar down their bodies.

Another musical note sounded from Patar. He followed it with a shout. "Solomon, I set you free from your manacles."

A sizzling crack broke apart the metal bracelets on Solomon's wrists, and they fell to the floor. Nathan's parents leaped into the swirl, and, in a few seconds, they, too, disappeared.

Patar released Mictar and jumped away. He brushed his hands against each other, sending crumbs of black down to the floor.

Slowly rising to his feet, Mictar coughed and wheezed. When he finally straightened, he let out a spiteful laugh. "They have been anointed with dark energy."

"Not enough to harm them," Patar said in a matter-of-fact tone. "They will resist it."

"Perhaps, but they cannot escape from where you have sent them."

Patar laid a hand on the outer perimeter of the swirl. White mist brushed against his fingers. "I sent them where you cannot accost them. You are transforming into material dissonance yourself, so you will be a living specter until you find a way to revive."

Mictar, his face now a mass of black, looked down at his equally black, formless body. "I am able to refuel, and I know just the place to restore myself. There is a certain girl who does not even yet know how gifted she is. I tasted her, and now I must have her."

"She is of no concern to me," Patar said, waving a hand of dismissal. "I will keep this portal open long enough for the healer to find it, but by the time you are reenergized, the path Solomon and Francesca have taken will no longer be available."

"True enough, but I will find another path."

"Not unless there is substantial healing." Patar picked up a clump of mattress padding and squeezed it tightly, letting the crumbs fall to the floor. "The paths are fragile, so the catalyst you desire for your machine is out of your reach."

Mictar laughed again. "This is a delicious irony, indeed. If your healer does his work, he will be the reason I am able to capture his parents."

"True enough. But there is another way, a way that will make your Lucifer engine impotent." A sad frown sank the lines on Patar's face. "You know what that is."

Mictar spat a wad of black goo onto the floor. "The boy would never do it. He is a romantic, too dependent on emotions to perform such a selfless act." He gazed at the dark club that was once his hand. "If I could get to her safely, I would do it myself. Such a source of energy would make me invincible. Lucifer would no longer be necessary."

For a moment it seemed as though a smile was about to break through on Patar's face, but he suppressed it. "Is it not strange that a mere wisp of a girl has chilled your heart and painted a stripe of yellow down your back?"

"Laugh on, my brother. Since you enjoy the human euphemisms, I will counter with, 'he who laughs last, laughs best.'"

Patar nodded. "We shall see. Perhaps the healer's journey will teach him the wisdom he needs to carry out what you and I cannot bear to do ourselves."

"You overestimate his character." Mictar set a dark foot on the windowsill. "He is human, and he will die with all the other 'rodents' that populate the planets."

As soon as Mictar jumped out the window, the mirror dimmed, and the image transformed into a normal reflection of the room.

Now in near darkness once again, Nathan let out his breath. How long had he been holding it? The scene before him had held him so transfixed, he had lost all grip on reality.

He looked back at his sleeping body. Of course, not sensing reality should be no surprise. After all, this was only a dream.

He turned to Jack. He seemed real enough, frumpy clothes stained with blood, thinning hair with a bald spot in the back, and skin reeking of body odor and cologne.

"Did you hear all of that?" Nathan asked.

Jack continued to thread his hat through his fingers. "I did. Much of it for the second time, though the discussion between those stalkers was new to me."

"Okay," Nathan said, holding his hands against his temples, "my brain is officially overloaded. If I'm dreaming, then maybe nothing I saw really happened. But if it did happen, then you were sent to the realm of dreams. Does that mean that the Jack I knew is really here? I mean, you're not just dreaming this?"

A wide smile brightened Jack's blackened face. "I'm not dreaming, but if you are, how can you possibly be sure that I'm telling the truth?"

Nathan lowered his hands. "That's the problem. Dreams aren't real, so I can't count on anything I see or hear."

"And I can't prove I'm real, at least, not until you wake up."

"Why when I wake up?"

Jack blinked his vacant eye sockets. "I could tell you something you don't know. Then you could check on it after you wake up."

"Okay," Nathan said, nodding. "I'm with you on that. What do you have in mind?"

Jack stroked his beard for a moment. "When you passed by me while I was kneeling at a cemetery plot, did you see me?"

"Yeah. I was in a hurry to get to the funeral, but I saw you there."

"If you get a chance to look at the tombstone, you can read my name inscribed there: John Alton Flowers. Or it might be easier to call someone and search the death records. Then you'll know that I'm really here, because you couldn't have dreamed my name."

Nathan nodded again. "Okay. Fair enough. If I can remember. I'm not too good at remembering dreams."

"All I can do is pray that you will." Jack pushed up to his knees. "And pray that you can help me leave this place."

Nathan rose to his feet and helped Jack the rest of the way up. "I'm guessing I'm the healer they talked about, and I have to seal a crack in a womb, or something like that, to get you out of here."

After straightening out his fedora, Jack laid it gingerly on his head. "I can't help you with what all that means, but it sounds like you'll be learning a lot as you go."

"Too much, I think. Maybe I should get Kelly's help. She's always been able to interpret—"

Music played from somewhere nearby, interrupting his thought. The thrumming beat of a bass drum accompanied a sweet composition of strings, the same piece that had bridged the gap between Earths Blue and Yellow at the observatory—Beethoven's Ninth Symphony. This time the fourth movement played on invisible instruments, and soon a host of voices trilled the German lyrics of "Ode to Joy."

Nathan let the mesmerizing beauty wash over him. The last

BRYAN DAVIS

time something like this happened in a dream, Mozart's *Requiem* had painted the air with a Latin hymn of sadness and comfort, words that he could easily translate. But these lyrics were unfamiliar. He had never learned German or studied the poem that had inspired Beethoven to pen this masterpiece.

He glanced at Kelly, still asleep on the mattress. "Excuse me a minute."

"Certainly," Jack said, touching the brim of his hat.

Nathan walked over and gave Kelly a gentle nudge. She yawned, sat up, and stretched her arms, but a copy of her body still lay in bed, unmoved and still clutching his hand.

"Is this a dream?" she asked.

"Pretty sure." He pointed at her sleeping body. "Unless you have a clone."

She grinned. "That's cool. I can talk to you while I'm resting."

"It looks that way, but ..." He paused, not quite sure how to express his doubts.

"But what?"

"I'll buy that a vision stalker can enter someone's thoughts while he's sleeping. But two people dreaming the same dream? It doesn't make sense."

She spoke while stretching into another yawn. "You don't believe Francesca?"

"Her father never remembered the dreams," Nathan said. "She was the gifted one, so they were probably just hers."

"Whatever." She rolled her eyes, but a sweet smile accompanied her gesture. "Just dream on, Nathan."

He nodded toward Jack. "Recognize him?"

"Uh-huh." She blinked several times. "I like this dream. I can see clearly." She waved at Jack.

"He can't see you. Mictar took his eyes."

She squinted to get a better view. "Good thing he's only part of a dream."

"I'm not so sure."

He took her hand, and the two walked toward the mirror where Jack stood, worrying his hat again with his fingers. "I hear the young lady," he said, nodding.

Kelly touched one of the scorch marks on Jack's brow and grimaced. "I know how much it hurts."

"I could tell you the story," Nathan said, "but if this is all a stupid dream of mine, it would be a waste of time."

Kelly frowned. "It's not just your—"

The mirror flashed again. The reflection transformed into a furnished bedroom, brighter and devoid of the broken scatterings left behind by the battle between the stalkers. A fully-dressed bed sat on the far side, and a desk and chair abutted the adjacent wall. Several posters hung on the painted surface, featuring basketball players in graceful stop-action poses. One was obviously Michael Jordan flying through the air in a North Carolina uniform, but the others were unfamiliar.

Kelly rattled off the players' names. "Magic Johnson, Michael Jordan, Kareem Abdul-Jabbar, James Worthy—"

"Okay, okay. I get the picture. You don't have to show off."

"I'm just proving something. If this were your dream, you wouldn't know the players, so I couldn't tell you who they were."

"Maybe I know them in my subconscious mind. I've heard all those names before."

"True, but—" With a sudden thrust, she pointed at the mirror. "Nathan, look at the wall next to the stack of soda cans!"

He searched the image. A violin bow hung from hooks on the wall, stretching across the room from one end to the other. The door in the reflection opened, and a young man stepped in. After adding a Pepsi can to the top of his pyramid, he turned on a television atop a dresser and flopped on the bed.

Kelly gasped. "My father!"

"Are you sure?"

"He's younger, but I've seen pictures. That's him all right."

"But why would we be seeing him?" Nathan asked. "What's the point?"

Kelly hovered her hand over the glass. "If this is Earth Yellow, and he's already made the bow, maybe we should flash a light and go there."

"But it won't work if I'm just dreaming this."

Kelly set her hands on her hips. "What's it going to take to convince you that I'm really dreaming this, too?"

"I didn't mean that. I was just saying if it's only a dream, then how can we—"

Jack tugged on Nathan's sleeve. "If I may offer an opinion?"

"Sure. What do you think?"

"Instead of merely arguing about whose dream this is, perhaps you could do as I have done and offer evidence. When you awaken, you can compare what you have dreamed to what you find in reality."

Nathan rolled his eyes. "My own dream is giving me advice. What next?"

The mirror suddenly darkened. Kelly's father disappeared, along with the bed, cans, and bow. A familiar face and form took shape. With eyes glowing reddish brown and a matching calf-length dress of unadorned cloth coating her body in red, Scarlet set her hands on the inside barrier. "I have been waiting for you, Nathan."

His throat clamped shut. Her startling beauty and haunting voice sent a jolt through his entire body, stiffening his limbs.

Kelly let her arms fall to her side. "Is that Scarlet?"

Scarlet turned and cast her gaze on Kelly. "Nathan, I am glad to see that you have brought the interpreter. There is a brightness in her spirit that will serve you well."

Nathan held back a wince. Kelly might not like the "serve you" part. Then again, if she wasn't dreaming with him, she wouldn't care. She was just a figment. Yet, since Scarlet was able to penetrate dreams, she was probably really there. Why would she mention Kelly if Kelly weren't real?

Scarlet turned back to Nathan. "Ah! I hear the great ode. Do you know the words? They speak now of your oneness with your friend!"

Nathan cocked his head to listen again. "It's in German. I never learned German."

"I hear English," Kelly said. "It's beautiful."

Scarlet's smile seemed to light up the room. "Then speak the ode, interpreter. Let your beloved hear the words of truth."

Kelly nodded with the music's rhythm and translated the German phrases.

Whoever succeeds in the great attempt
To be a friend of a friend,
Whoever has won a lovely woman,
Let him add his jubilation!

"Yes," Scarlet chirped. "It is jubilation to win the heart of a faithful woman. And now I will sing another truth to you, Nathan Paul Shepherd, for you have won my heart, and I will be faithful to you as long as I live." Moving her hand in a wide circle over the mirror, she sang in a lovely alto.

The circle of music, eternal and blessed,
The key to salvation where mortals find rest;
To find the right portal to seek what was lost
And journey to danger, you must count the cost.

For hearts will be humbled and lives will be spent.
A brave one will fall in the endless descent,
And sight will be lost while perception is gained.
The free will be bound and all captives unchained.

The stalker appearing will show you the square,
Then take care to follow, yet heed my sad prayer.
The journey will force you to choose whom you love;
The bright one, the sad one, the creed, or the dove.

As the tune faded away, Scarlet faded with it, her melancholy eyes leaving a residual glow. A wisp of a voice trailed away like a distant echo. "Come for me, Nathan. I will be waiting."

Seconds later, a new form replaced her lovely visage. A tall, pallid stalker approached the mirror from a distance, his ankles surrounded by a white cloud, as if he had just marched out from the misty world.

Kelly grabbed Nathan's arm and pulled him close. "Is that Mictar or Patar?"

"Patar," Nathan replied. Then, lowering his voice, he added, "I hope."

As the white-haired man drew near, he slowed, dragging something behind him. His load resembled a human body, but shadows covered the face.

Patar turned his head, perhaps intentionally, just enough to show that he lacked a ponytail. He stopped and stared at Nathan, his eyes pulsing red. "Son of Solomon!" His voice echoed throughout the room. "When will you learn not to trifle with the power of Quattro?"

Nathan gulped. "What ... what do you mean?"

As the dead body swayed under his tight fist, Patar's voice deepened and rolled into a prophetic cadence. "While worlds hang in the balance, you are toying with emotions. While terrified children seek rescue from death, you are playing house with those fair of face and capturing their fragile hearts."

"But I'm not. I'm just—"

With a lightning fast thrust, Patar jerked the body forward and shoved it close to the mirror.

Kelly covered her eyes with her hands. "Oh, dear God!"

Nathan stared at the macabre sight, a face stretched out and hanging by the hair from Patar's powerful grip. With blackened, vacant eye sockets, a warped reflection of Nathan's own face stared back at him—Nathan Blue, his mouth agape in a silent scream.

Nausea boiled in Nathan's stomach, and his mouth dried out. He couldn't say a word.

Patar lowered Nathan Blue's head but kept a grip on his hair. With his other hand, he pointed directly at Nathan. "If you continue to attend to the trivial and neglect the essential, you will join your counterpart in the agony of the endless void. Your lack of wisdom will not only allow interfinity to come, it will accelerate its arrival."

Fighting back fear, Nathan squared his shoulders. "Why didn't you just give it to me straight before? Maybe I wouldn't have wasted so much time."

"I told you to play the violin. Was my command unclear? You have your own mother's testimony to its existence. The bow is ready, yet you are sleeping with your girlfriend in a world not your own."

Nathan's face grew hot. He felt caught, naked, ashamed. What could he have been thinking? Was Patar right? Should he have waited in Earth Yellow until the bow was ready?

Balling his fists, he tried to rally his defenses, but they seemed weak, even in his own mind. "I had to come back and study the photos, then we came here to look for—"

"Your parents." Patar nodded, and his voice took on a sarcastic tone. "I know. I know your reasoning all too well." A semi-transparent image floated in the background—Nathan and Kelly sleeping hand in hand. Patar scowled. "I can see for myself what you are really doing."

Nathan kicked the wall. It hurt, but he tried to hide the pain. "I wanted to find my parents so I could get some straightforward advice, not the runaround you always give me!"

"Finding and playing the violin was straightforward enough," Patar said. "A thorough explanation would seem foolish to you, and if I were to provide you with the simplest solution, you would ignore my counsel."

Nathan shouted, "Try me!"

Patar laughed. "Your arrogance dresses you in a clown's garb, son of Solomon, if you think you know the crisis or its solution better than I. Trust me. You will despise my counsel."

"Then prove it. Show me that I'm a fool. Better that than for me to run around the dimensions like a chicken with its head cut off ..." He bit his lip. That was exactly what Mictar had called him. After taking a deep breath, he pointed at the body hanging from Patar's grip. "Better than ending up like the other Nathan."

A smile widened the stalker's pale face. "Very well. I will prove it. Here is the simplest solution." He drew closer to the mirror, so close, his eyes took up most of a square. His voice dropped to a low bass. "To heal the wounds and bring the crisis to an end, return to the place you call the misty world and ..." He paused, his smile vanishing. "And slay the supplicants."

Patar's words sucked every ounce of air from Nathan's lungs. He could only gasp his reply. "What? You can't be serious!"

"You heard me. Slay them and cast their bodies into Sarah's Womb, and harmony will be restored. Although we pity their wretched estate, we cannot allow emotions to cloud our thinking. They must die."

Nathan took two steps back. "But I can't ... I can't *kill* them!"

Patar's smile returned. "I have done as you requested and given you a straightforward command. You despised it and played the fool, exactly as I predicted. If you wish to disbelieve me, there is nothing more I can tell you. You are free to follow the other option, to find the violin and play it, but that path is far more treacherous."

His legs now weak, Nathan shuffled back to the mirror. "What about the circle of fifths? Scarlet said you'd let us know how to find the key."

"As I said earlier, you are unwise to trifle with the power of Quattro. I am aware of the song of that doomed supplicant.

Her plaintive cries will not avail her." Patar stroked his narrow chin for a moment. "Yet, I will again do what you ask and give you enough information to locate the key you are seeking ... if you have enough wisdom to find it."

Patar sang a low C for at least five seconds, switched to a short E so high the window pane vibrated, then, touching mirror squares in turn, he sang various notes in rapid succession. Each square flashed with a unique color as he touched it, and the note continued to play from the glass, carrying a vibrato that made it shimmer. When he finished, the entire room blazed with colors that danced on the walls as if celebrating the pulsing music.

Shifting his gaze back to Nathan, Patar bobbed his head as if listening to the song he had created. It certainly was captivating and beautiful, yet, even with the extraordinary flood of musical notes, Beethoven's ode still broke through.

"Interpreter!" Patar said, pointing at Kelly. "Interpret the great song! The son of Solomon must hear the brilliance of the poet's message, the one that enchanted Beethoven himself."

Trembling, Kelly cleared her throat and spoke.

Be embraced, you millions!
This kiss for the whole world!
Brothers, beyond the star canopy
Must a loving Father dwell.

Do you bow down, you millions?
Do you sense the Creator, world?
Seek Him beyond the star canopy!
Beyond the stars must He dwell.

The words ended. Patar's frown deepened as he continued. "Heed what you have heard, son of Solomon. You will find what you seek beyond the stars, but if you wish to save the cosmos that bears them on its shoulders, you must carry out the task

I have set before you. Kill the supplicants, throw their bodies into the womb, and all will be healed. Yet, if you choose the alternative path and reach the fabric beyond the star canopy, I can no longer give you advice. It is fraught with danger, and even I cannot tell what you must do to avoid a fatal step."

Nathan spread out his hands. "But why all the puzzles? Why can't you just tell me where the key is?"

"To protect your life. If you lack the wisdom to find the key, you will surely lack the wisdom to safely follow the alternative path. The wisest of all decisions would be to sacrifice the supplicants, but since you have allowed one to romance your heart, I doubt that you are clear minded enough to make that choice."

With that, Patar vanished, and the mirror darkened, leaving only a reflection of the room, no song, no colors, no music. A glow from a yard lantern outside provided the only light in the room.

Nathan raised his hand and searched for his fingers in the mirror. No sign of his or Kelly's reflections, nor Jack's, who stood staring into nothingness.

Looking deeper into the image, Nathan found two bodies, his own on the floor and Kelly's on the mattress. The sleeping Kelly trembled, clutching Nathan's hand tightly.

He squeezed Jack's shoulder. "I'll try to figure out how to save you, but I'll have to wake up to do it."

Jack fumbled for Nathan's hand and shook it heartily. "I will be waiting."

Nathan guided Kelly back to the bed. "I think I've had enough of this dream."

"You don't know German," she said.

They each sat down, their legs melding with the legs of their sleeping bodies. "Right. What's that got to do with anything?"

"This is my dream," she said. "You couldn't have translated."

"And I never told you my middle name before."

"Paul?"

He lowered his head. "Okay. I was being stubborn, but it will help me believe it for sure if we test the theory. When we wake up, you tell me my middle name, and I'll know you were sentient in my dream, and I'll tell you the names of the basketball players."

She nodded. "Fair enough."

Nathan lay down, blending his two bodies into one. Kelly did the same, and the two dreamers joined hands to mimic their physical forms.

12

FINDING RED IN YELLOW

As the dream ended, Nathan's mind fell into blackness, then a ringing sound stirred his senses. He awoke and sat up. Angled rays of sunshine flowed in from the window. Was it morning?

The ringing sounded again, a telephone. Nathan patted his pocket. His cell was still there, but that wasn't making the noise. He jumped up and bounded out of the room, following the rings. He finally found a wall mounted phone in the kitchen and snatched up the receiver.

"Hello?"

"Nathan. It's Daryl Blue. I couldn't get you on the cell, and it took us forever to find this phone number. It's not in the book, and they must've changed it when Kelly died."

"Sorry. I didn't know that."

"Listen. Red's fit to be tied. Time is flying there, and she's sent me about a thousand messages. I can't keep up. I told her to cool her jets, but she says she's only sending a couple a day. And when you get back into cell range, you might want to put your phone on silent. It'll chirp like a coffee-addicted canary if you don't. She's probably sent you, like, a hundred text messages."

The mention of coffee perked Nathan's nose. He opened a kitchen cabinet, searching for the source of the aroma. "So what's going on in Earth Yellow?"

"That Mictar freak tracked Francesca down, so Gunther took her and her father into hiding. Daryl's living with Kelly's father and grandfather, posing as an exchange student from England. It works out great, because Kelly's dad is handy with tools, so he helped her get her network stuff up and running. They have a pretty cool setup now."

"Can we find Francesca? We'll need her to play the violin."

"Red hasn't heard from her in a while. Gunther knows how to make contact, but I guess the heat's been on, so he doesn't want to risk it. The last time Red talked to him, he said that wherever he goes, people report him to Mictar—something about Gunther not being in their dreams. Any idea what he's talking about?"

"Maybe, but it would take too long to explain." Nathan withdrew a partially open canister of Folgers coffee from the cabinet. A small envelope fell in its wake and settled on the counter.

"Anyway," Daryl continued, "the bow is ready. Red wants to come home before she graduates from high school."

"Let me think a minute." Nathan read the front of the envelope. The script said, "Daddy" in Kelly's handwriting.

He glanced down the hall at the bedroom door. He could use her help in deciding what to do, but the phone was attached to the wall by a cord. He'd have to come up with an idea on his own.

He and Kelly could go back to Earth Yellow. Maybe Gunther and Francesca would see them in their dreams and come out of hiding. But he really couldn't decide until he and Kelly solved the mirror puzzle and found the key to locating his parents.

"I'll have to get back to you," he finally said. "Tell Daryl Red to hang tough. We'll get her back home before she's an old lady."

"She's going to be ticked, but I'll tell her."

Nathan hung up and ran down the hallway. When he careened into the bedroom, Kelly stood close to the mirror, her gaze fixed on the reflection.

"Paul," she said softly. "Your middle name is Paul."

He eased close to her side and watched her eyes in the mirror. "Michael Jordan, Magic Johnson, Kareem Abdul-Jabbar, and . . . uh . . . James something."

"Close enough." She slid her foot over the spot where Jack had stood. "Do you think he was real?"

"Hard to tell. He gave me something to check, though. I'll do it as soon as we get a chance."

She pointed at the mirror. "The colors faded."

"Faded? I don't see anything."

"Do you hear the notes? They're a lot softer now."

He shook his head. "Nothing."

"How does the circle of fifths work?"

Nathan drew a circle in the air and pointed at the top. "In C Major, we need to find a C natural and work around from there. Since you have perfect pitch, you should be able to pick it up."

"But I hear more than one C-natural."

He forked three fingers. "The C-natural we need," he said, using his other hand to point at his middle finger as he wiggled the other two fingers in turn, "must have G-natural on one side and F-natural on the other."

"Okay. I get it." She took the envelope from his hand. "What's this?"

"Something I found in the kitchen by the coffee."

"The coffee?" She opened the envelope and slid out a folded card. "It's my handwriting."

"I noticed." He leaned over to get a look, but she kept the card folded, reading the Hallmark poem on the front. "Is it to your father?"

She nodded. "When I was little I used to write notes to him and put them next to the coffee. I knew he'd see them first thing in the morning."

"Are you going to read it?"

"But I didn't write it. Kelly Blue did."

"Must have been right before she died. Her father never got a chance to read it before he got murdered."

"I guess it will be all right." She flipped open the card and held it close to her eyes, blinking as she tried to focus. Nathan drew back while she read out loud.

Dear Daddy,

This is very hard for me to write, for a lot of reasons, but I have to say this in case something happens to me. You see, Nathan and I are about to do something very dangerous, and if I don't come back, I want to make sure you know what's on my mind.

I always knew that Mom was the one who broke up your marriage, but when she left, I treated you like dirt. For some reason, I punished you for what she did. Now, I know you're not perfect, and you drove her crazy with all the sports you were into, but you didn't deserve how either one of us treated you. Mom broke your heart, and I should have been there to mend it. Instead, I stomped on it and smashed it to bits. I'm so sorry!

Without Mom around, you had such a hard time! You always wanted a son, but you were stuck with a daughter, and you didn't know how to raise me, so you did it the only way you knew how. So, instead of being an expert in makeup and girly gossip, I know how to do a pick and roll, clean spark plugs, and shoot a can off the top of the last fencepost.

Kelly, her fingers now trembling, turned the card over and read the back. Her voice rattled.

I love you, Daddy, and I'm so sorry for how I've treated you. I take back all the terrible things I said about hating basketball, fixing cars, and hunting. In fact, I'm even wearing that safari outfit you bought for me, and I let Nathan use the one you bought for Uncle Bill so we would match. I'm sorry for saying it was ugly and didn't fit. It feels really good right now, like you're giving me a warm hug. If this is my last day on earth, I will die wearing your gift of love.

Remember what Nathan told us about forgiveness. If I don't see you again on earth, I hope I see you in heaven.

Kelly pressed the card against her chest. Her face twisted. Tears streamed down her cheeks as she lowered her head and wept.

Nathan laid his hand behind her head and pulled her close. As she cried on his shoulder, the room seemed to grow cold as if haunted by the father and daughter who once lived there. It was a sad home, indeed. He could almost feel the aching hearts. After years of turmoil—a broken marriage, misplaced expectations, and too many unspoken words of love—Kelly Blue's father died without knowing what his daughter wanted to tell him. Yet, he died a hero. He blocked a shotgun blast to save a life.

Nathan gave the imaginary ghost of Tony Clark a nod. *You died to save me.*

One of the note's sentences repeated in his mind. *Remember what Nathan told us about forgiveness.* Apparently Nathan Blue had been bold enough to tell Kelly and Tony about what mattered most. He firmed his chin and nodded again. He would do the same. As soon as the time seemed right.

After a minute or so, Kelly drew back, sniffing. "Can't ... can't dwell on this. We have to ... to move on." She stuffed the envelope into her back pocket and shuffled to the mirror. Leaning close to the squares, she slid sideways along the carpet, listening to each one. As she eyed the mirrors above her head, her voice strengthened. "I'm too short to reach the higher squares."

Nathan pushed the trunk close to Kelly's feet. She stooped to listen to the lower squares and straightened as she moved from row to row, then climbed on the trunk when she reached the third row from the top. Finally, she paused just to the left of the center of the mirror and pointed at one of the squares. "I think I got it. This orange square is the C note we want."

He stood on tiptoes and touched the square to the left and just below the one she indicated. "Is this the F?"

She nodded and pointed at the square to the right of the C and one row down. "And this green one is the G."

"I don't see the colors." Nathan picked up his violin and bow. "Okay, listen for these notes. They should make a circle that goes down from the G and then around to meet the F. Since they're squares, it won't be a perfect circle, but it should be close."

He played a note. "That's a D-natural."

She pointed at the square one row down and to the right of the G. "Got it."

He played another note. "A-natural."

"Right here." Again she moved down a row and one to the right. "Just play the note. You don't need to tell me what it is."

As he played through E – B – F-sharp – D-flat – A-flat – E-flat – B-flat, Kelly moved her finger from square to square, making as perfect a circle as the squares would allow. When he finished, Nathan set the violin down and studied the mirror, mentally drawing the circle Kelly had outlined.

The twelve squares enclosed thirteen others, but one lay in the geometric center. He pointed at it. "What note is coming from that one?"

Still on the trunk, Kelly bent slightly to set her ear close. "Another C-natural. Middle C."

"That's gotta be it."

When Kelly dismounted the trunk, Nathan slid it to the side and picked up his violin and bow again.

" 'Foundation's Key'?" she asked.

"Yep. Let's see what's there." With the tune now memorized, Nathan played it through. Within seconds, the squares again showed their four-hundred different destinations.

Together, Nathan and Kelly moved close to the mirror and studied the chosen square. It held a night scene, a cemetery with dozens of tombstones of various shapes and sizes dotting a hillside and casting long shadows in the light of a rising moon.

In the midst of the purplish canopy above, a dark gash of emptiness stretched from one horizon to the other, taking up about a fifth of the sky.

Nathan touched the glass where a tombstone rose, the very same marker Jack had knelt beside, but the inscription was far too small to make out.

As if summoned by his desire to read the letters, the scene rocketed toward them, like a camera zooming in on a target. Could Scarlet know what he wanted to see? Was she the cross-dimensional camerawoman? When it stopped, the tombstone spanned the entire mirror.

Nathan moved his finger away from the name and read it out loud. "John Alton Flowers." As he stepped back, his hand trembled. "It's Jack. He's really alive in the dream world."

"How do we get him out?"

"I'm not sure, but I can't worry about that right now." He touched the image of the tombstone again. The view eased back until the dark gash in the heavens draped the square reflection. "It must be Earth Red. Gordon mentioned a rift in the sky."

"So, do we go there?" Kelly asked. "Flash a light and take off?"

"I don't think so." He nodded toward the hallway. "That call was from Daryl Blue. It's already been a couple of years on Earth Yellow, and the bow's finished, so Daryl Red wants us to come back and get her before she dies of old age."

"I don't blame her. Two years away from home! I can't imagine!"

"But do we give her a break, or follow what we learned in the dream?"

"Learned from the dream? You mean to kill the supplicants?"

Nathan wagged his head. "Not that part. I could never kill Scarlet, or anyone else."

"Of course you wouldn't want to kill her, but your father

said Patar would guide you in the right way, and Patar didn't exactly mince words."

Nathan stared at her. She was dead right. The other Nathan's empty eye sockets were a pretty good clue that Patar wasn't messing around. But if he could find his parents, he could explain to his father what was going on. Maybe Dad didn't know everything about Patar. He'd never condone killing the supplicants, even if it meant saving the universe ... Or would he?

"I meant the part about the key," he finally said. "We know where it is now."

Kelly pointed at the square in the lower left corner. "Look! It's Daryl Red! And she's with my father ... I mean, Tony Yellow."

Nathan crouched to get a good view. Daryl sat at a desk in front of a green-screen computer monitor, typing madly while Kelly's father stood next to her holding an umbrella over her head. A strange gadget was poised at the edge of the desk's surface. It looked like an old radio with a miniature satellite dish spinning slowly around. A drizzle of rain clouded the background of trees and shrubs, and droplets fell from the sides of the umbrella. Two orange extension cords trailed away beyond the mirror's edge.

Her mouth hanging open, Kelly touched the glass. "She does look older. But what did she do to her hair?"

Nathan took a closer look. Kelly's vision improved whenever she viewed Earth Yellow, so it made sense that she could notice details. Daryl's red hair had been pulled back and fastened tightly by a banana clip that left the rest of it in a mess of glitter-sprinkled ringlets blown about by the moist breeze. Her serious stare at the monitor gave her the aspect of a college student conducting research for a major project. She did, indeed, look at least two years older.

"Maybe we should go there," Kelly said. "We can get the bow and play that violin."

Nathan touched the square they had singled out earlier. "But this has to be the key. We can't ignore everything we learned in the dream, especially since Scarlet said we needed to use it."

Kelly nodded. "I guess you're right."

After finding a screwdriver and a flashlight in the garage, Nathan pried the key square loose and pulled it away. The other squares dimmed and slowly reconstructed the reflection, but the image of the dark cemetery in the square in Nathan's hands remained steady. Using the screwdriver again, he removed the square that had shown Daryl on Earth Yellow and placed it on top of the other one.

He draped the camera strap around Kelly's neck and held up the flashlight. "We'll use this for our flash. It could come in handy in that dark place we're going."

"I have a better idea." She picked up the violin and headed for the bedroom door. "Let's pack everything we might need and flash the mirror from inside the car. If Scarlet doesn't mind transporting everything, a stocked vehicle would come in even handier."

After stuffing the trunk and backseat with pillows, blankets, boxes of nutrition bars, and bottles of water, as well as the violin, the camera, and the two mirrors, Nathan tossed his empty backpack into the rear and slid behind the steering wheel. Kelly sat in the passenger's seat and propped the central key mirror on the dashboard. Since the car sat on the driveway in the same cold drizzle that apparently still plagued Daryl Red on Earth Yellow, the air within carried a moist chill.

"Let's drive out to cell range," Kelly said. "We can get an update from the two Daryls."

Nathan started the engine. "Gotta hurry, though. No telling how long the mirror will keep showing that cemetery."

While he drove, the rain eased up, allowing sunshine to peek around the fast-moving clouds. The holes in the dark blue sky seemed closer, bigger, even brighter. He kept glancing at his open cell phone. When the signal bars rose to an adequate height, he slid his finger toward one of the numbers. The phone suddenly trilled. Nathan read the screen. "Text messages. A bunch of them."

Kelly blinked at the display. "Can you go to the most recent?"

"I think so." Slowing down to pull onto the shoulder, he worked the phone's keys with his thumb. "I'll read the ones that came in this morning, starting with the earliest."

After shifting the car into park and cutting the engine, he read the tiny text.

"Nathan, if you don't get your butt back to Earth Yellow pronto, I'm going to strangle you with a violin string. Love and kisses, Daryl."

"Nathan, I can't wait until doomsday. Then again, maybe doomsday is almost here. Signed, A Candle in the Wind."

"Nathan, Kelly's dad keeps asking me out, and he's getting more aggressive. I told him to buzz off and get interested in Kelly's mom. Signed, The Other Woman."

"Nathan, if I don't hear from you today, I'll strangle Tony with a violin string, then myself. Well, I would if I wasn't so yellow. Signed, Daryl Red Singing the Blues."

He turned to Kelly. "That's the latest."

"How long ago did it come in?"

Nathan checked the time stamp. "Just a few seconds."

"Then you can probably send her a message before her day is over."

"It'll be faster if I just tell Daryl Blue what to say." He turned on the phone's speaker and pressed a speed dial. "You can listen in."

After half a ring, Daryl answered. "Nathan! Finally!"

"Is something wrong?"

"Everything's wrong. Your land line doesn't work anymore, so I couldn't call you. Daryl Red's ready to kill Tony, and—"

"Yeah, I picked up on that."

"But that's not the worst of it. We lost power at the observatory overnight, and we're almost out of generator power. In a few minutes, we won't be able to communicate with Daryl Red at all. She knows about it, and she's ready to jump off a cliff ... if she could find a cliff in Iowa. And who knows how long cell service will hold out?"

"Can you send one message for me?"

"I'll try. We might only have a few seconds left."

He glanced at the mirror in the backseat, the square that would open a portal to Earth Yellow. What should he do? Go to the nightscape scene in the circle of fifths square and hope that Daryl somehow survives the ordeal? But even if she could cope, what if Tony kept his eye on her and not on Kelly's mother? That would mean no Kelly Yellow. Not only that, if he and Kelly traveled to the place Patar indicated, what might happen? If he succeeded in healing the interdimensional wounds and repelled interfinity, how could he ever risk allowing interdimensional travel again? Daryl Red would never be able to get home. He would save the universe but ruin her life and maybe a lot of other lives on Earth Yellow. Sure, that would be a reasonable trade-off, but who was he to make a decision like that?

"Nathan?"

The voice from the cell phone shook him out of his thoughts. "Yeah. Sorry. I was just thinking. Where was I?"

Her voice faded to a whisper. "What do you want me to tell Daryl Red?"

He gazed at Kelly's glistening eyes and let out a sigh. "Tell her I'm on my way." He clapped the phone shut and banged on the steering wheel with his fist. "I can't believe this!"

"It'll be okay," Kelly said, touching his elbow. "We'll go to the other place as soon as we get Daryl out of her jam. Don't forget, what we do there only takes a little while here and on Earth Red."

"I know, but I keep getting the feeling that I'm putting on the clown suit Patar talked about."

"Don't worry about that freak of nature." She rubbed his upper arm. "Just keep telling yourself that he wanted you to kill Scarlet. You're not the clown. He is."

He cut off the engine and reached for the other mirror on the backseat. "I'd better see if I can fire this thing up without going home. Every second we talk could be an hour for Daryl. We don't want her strangling your father."

After playing "Foundation's Key" on the violin, the mirror's image morphed from a reflection of the car's interior to Daryl, still sitting at the desk, now with her head resting on her folded arms. As expected, the rain had stopped, removing the need for an umbrella and for a doting, younger Tony to shelter her from getting wet. The computer monitor cast a green glow across her red hair, painting it with a light brown hue. Her head moved up and down slightly, yet not with a breathing rhythm.

"I think she's crying." Kelly pointed the flashlight at the mirror. "Can we go?"

Nathan gave her a nod. "Let's do it."

She flashed the light. Instantly, the world surrounding the car melted like candle wax and dripped away, revealing the familiar house. They still sat in the car, now parked between Daryl's table and the cottonwood tree in the front yard.

Since the engine wasn't running, they hadn't made a sound. Nathan pressed his finger to his lips and opened the door quietly. Kelly slid out through the driver's side, and the two skulked toward Daryl on tiptoes.

The old-fashioned radio hummed, and the tiny satellite dish rotated, making a slight squeak with every turn. Daryl's head bobbed, and her quiet weeping blended with the other sounds.

Nathan gritted his teeth. He wanted to say the right thing, something funny to break the tension, like, "Don't shoot me,

I'm only the violin player," but her pitiful cries squelched any thought of using her as the butt of a joke.

He reached forward and laid a gentle hand on her shoulder. "I'm here, Daryl. I'm sorry it took so long."

A MOTHER'S LAMENT

Daryl's head popped up. She stared at Nathan with red eyes, tears following well-marked tracks down her cheeks. At first, a hint of a smile turned her lips upward, but a furrowed brow took over and twisted her face into a ferocious scowl. She rose slowly from her chair, her shoulders raised. As she rounded the corner of the desk, she lifted her hand and pushed a finger into Nathan's chest. "Do you have any idea how long I've been waiting for you, Mister Nathan Shepherd?"

She pressed him hard with her finger. He backpedaled, but she closed the gap. "I'll tell you how long! Two years, eight months, fourteen days, three hours, seven minutes, and . . ." She glanced at a watch on her wrist. "And forty-five seconds!"

Nathan halted, and Daryl kept poking his chest, her cheeks now flaming. "I finished high school, started college, rejected three marriage proposals, started my own computer consulting business, and moved into an apartment to get away from Romeo, a.k.a. Tony Clark, who is ignoring Kelly's mom in order to deliver a single red rose to me every day. I've been trying to push him away, but I still have to come to his house to use the transmitter, because I can't get a signal from inside my apartment, and I can't run an extension cord from my kitchen to the park across the street. So he says I'm coming here because I can't stay away from him."

Daryl drew in a long breath. As she raised her finger to make another point, she stared at Kelly and Nathan in turn. Her brow loosened, and her bottom lip began to tremble. She lunged forward, grabbed Nathan around his waist, and leaned her head against his chest. "Oh, Nathan! I'm so glad you came to get me! I waited and waited and sent so many messages, and I only got one answer over two years ago. I thought I'd never get out of this place! Never!"

As she sobbed, Kelly rubbed her back. "I'm sorry it took so long," Kelly said. "It was only overnight and part of a day for us."

Nathan added his own hand to Kelly's comforting rub. "Didn't you get another message? I just sent it telling you I was on my way."

Daryl just shook her head. Her tears seeped through Nathan's shirt, but he didn't dare pull away.

"That must mean power's out at Interfinity Blue," he said. "Daryl Blue couldn't relay it."

Squeaking hinges sounded from the front door, followed by a booming male voice. "Hey! What's going on here? Who are you two?"

Nathan turned his head. A gangly young man, at least six foot three, ambled out of the house. A younger Tony Clark strode toward them, his eyes bugging out as he approached. "Why is Daryl crying?"

Nathan pushed Daryl away gently and cleared his throat. "We're old friends from high school. Daryl's just really glad to see us." He extended his hand. "I'm Nathan."

As Tony took Nathan's hand, he leaned over slightly and peered at Nathan's face. "You look just like Flash, a friend of mine. You're a little younger, but I swear you're his twin. You wouldn't happen to be related to Solomon Shepherd, would you?"

"My father's name is Solomon, but he's a lot older." Trying not to grimace at Tony's crushing grip, Nathan gestured toward the computer and transmitter with his thumb. "That's quite a setup you've got there."

"You bet it is." Tony released Nathan and took three long strides toward the desk. "We're getting signals from outer space, and Daryl's trying to translate them. Maybe we can 'phone home,' like in *E.T.*" He slapped his thigh and let out a roaring belly laugh. "Pretty funny, huh?"

Kelly clutched Nathan's arm and whispered, barely moving her lips. "My father was a real comic, wasn't he?"

Daryl wiped her eyes. "Tony, why don't you go inside and get them something to drink? They came a long way to get here."

"Will do." Tony glanced at the car in the middle of the yard. "Must've been too tired to stay on the road." He grinned. "Get it? Too tired? The car has tires?" Now chuckling, he strode back into the house, repeating the joke to himself.

Daryl grabbed Nathan's shirt and jerked him close. "Get me outta here before he comes back! I've been listening to those lame jokes for over two years."

"Wait!" Kelly raised her hand. "Shouldn't we make sure he switches his affections to my future mother? If he's heartbroken over you, maybe they won't get together."

"Don't worry, Kelly-kins. Your mother will make sure she catches the rebound. She's chasing Tony like a hound hunting a fox. She's not likely to lose his trail."

"We can't just leave," Nathan said. "We have to get the bow."

Daryl sighed. "Right. The bow. I forgot."

Tony pushed the door open with his foot, two long-necked bottles dangling from each hand. "Got a game tonight," he said as he passed the cold, wet bottles of Pepsi around. "Coach would kill me if I had a beer."

Nathan took a long drink and nodded his appreciation. "So, uh, Tony, Daryl tells me you constructed a big violin bow."

"Yeah. I found this letter that promised me a rare twenty-dollar bill if I followed all the instructions. But when I finished the bow, no one showed up to give me the money. So, I just hung it up on my wall." He took a long drink and let out a quiet belch. "It looks pretty good there, actually. I decided to—"

Tony's jaw dropped open. "What did you say your name is?"

"Nathan. The same guy who signed the letter." He pulled out his wallet and withdrew a twenty. "Sorry it took me so long to bring it."

Tony snatched the bill and examined it closely. "It's just like the other one. Andrew Jackson's head is a lot bigger."

"Yeah. Check out the date. It's from the future, too."

Tony's eyes bugged out twice as far as usual. "That's like the new movie!" He looked at Daryl. "What's it called?"

Daryl rolled her eyes. "*Back to the Future*, Tony."

"That's it!" He shifted his wild stare back to the twenty. "I have to see that again!"

After taking another drink, Nathan eased toward the front door. "All right if I get the bow?"

"Sure." Using his long legs, Tony strode ahead of him and held the door. "You paid for it. Besides, what am I going to do with a ten-foot-long bow?"

Nathan went inside and headed straight for the bedroom. He could hear Tony's voice as he followed. "You know where to go?"

"Yep!" He entered the bedroom and reached for the bow, suspended by metal hooks, but it was too high up on the wall.

Before Nathan could grab the desk chair, Tony marched in and pulled the bow from its perch. "Here you go."

Nathan took it and gestured for Tony to sit. "Let's talk for a minute."

Tony set his drink on the desk and pulled up the chair while Nathan settled on the bed with the bow at his side. "Listen," Nathan said, "I can tell that you like Daryl. Am I right?"

"Yeah." Tony grinned. "She's something else! Smart, cute, funny, and she loves movies."

"But she hasn't been responsive, has she?"

"No. Playing hard to get, I think." Tony took a quick swig from his bottle. "She keeps coming around here, though. Almost every day, really, so she must like me a little. I've been sending her roses, but I'm not sure it's working. You got any ideas?"

Nathan took in Tony's earnest expression. His sincerity and frankness were refreshing. Maybe it wasn't right to keep the truth from this poor guy. "You ever wonder why Daryl knows so much?" he asked. "I mean, she's not just smart, she probably upgraded that computer like she knew every bit of technology that was ready to hit the market."

"Yeah. She's on top of things all right. Kind of spooky sometimes."

Nathan pulled the twenty-dollar bill from Tony's fingers and showed it to him. "This isn't the only thing from the future."

Again, Tony's eyes seemed to pop out from his skull. "Daryl is?"

Nathan smiled and nodded. "And so is the girl who came with me. We have to take Daryl back to the future."

As Tony stared at Nathan, his smile slowly weakened, and a deep line traced across his brow. He shook his head and chuckled under his breath. "You had me going for a while. Who put you up to this? Flash? You're really his brother, right?" He looked around the room. "That old camera hound's probably already got a hundred shots of me acting like a fool. He'll probably show them to the whole team, and they'll get a kick—"

"It's not a joke." Nathan laid the twenty back in Tony's hand. "You saw the car in the yard. Did you see any tire tracks?"

"I already figured that out. If everyone on the team chipped in, they could carry it. They couldn't afford a Delorean, so they brought a Toyota. I've never seen that model, though. I guess it's new."

"You could say that." Nathan leaned closer to Tony. "Listen. I'll prove we're from a future world, but you gotta help us out. First, did Daryl teach you how to use that computer and transmitter?"

Tony shook his head. "She wouldn't let me touch it, but I watched her enough times to figure it out."

"Good. When we get back, I'll try to contact you through it. Second, when you go to see *Back to the Future* again, I think you should ask that other girl who's been trying to get your attention."

"Molly? The law school student?"

"Yeah. I think ..." Nathan bit his lip. He was about to say, "you'll have a wonderful life together," but that would be a lie. Taking a breath, he finished with, "you and she should get married."

Tony's brow bent down a notch. "Molly's cool most of the time, but she's got a nasty temper if you cross her, you know, typical Irish. But if you can prove what you say, I'll keep her in mind. I mean, if you know the future, I'm not going to argue with you."

"One more thing. Can I get Flash's phone number? I have a message from the future for him, too."

"Sure." Tony jotted down the number on a pad and ripped off the top sheet. "Here you go."

Nathan stuffed the sheet into his pocket. Considering all the information he had just spilled, would Tony be able to keep it to himself? He was probably a prime target for Mictar's dream-stalking, so he might not be able to hide what he knew.

Rising from the bed, Nathan looked Tony in the eye. "Are you a next-day dreamer or a traveler?"

"Neither. I don't dream at all. Makes life easier. I pity those folks who are getting harassed even when they're trying to sleep."

"Yeah. It's like the Gestapo." Cradling the huge bow in both hands, Nathan headed for the door. "Let's go."

By the time they reached the car, Kelly was already in the front seat with the mirror in her lap, and Daryl had made room for herself in the back among the snacks and bedding.

Nathan eyed the car and the bow. It would never fit. He laid the bow on top and looked at it doubtfully. Could they take the chance that it might not come along for the cross-dimensional ride?

"I'll get some duct tape," Tony said. "That ought to—"

Tires squealed as a van turned from the highway onto the narrow road, whipping the dying brown corn stalks as it passed between the fields.

Nathan whispered, "All right!" The familiar "Stoneman Enterprises" lettering and the slender feminine arm waving through the passenger-side window meant that his celestial duet partner had arrived.

"Friends of yours?" Tony asked.

"Yeah. I'll introduce you in a minute."

When Gunther pulled to a stop in the driveway, Francesca jumped out and ran to Nathan. Wearing jeans and a long-sleeved gray T-shirt, she seemed dressed for manual labor. Her raven curls bounced in a bushy ponytail behind a baseball cap as she sidled up to him. "I'm ready to go!"

He gazed at her sparkling eyes, now at the same level as his own. "Tracked us down in a dream?" he asked.

She gave him a sly wink. "Gunther and I are better than a pair of bloodhounds."

Gunther, his bulging flannel shirt showing a bit more muscle as well as a few extra pounds around the waist, lumbered up the driveway. Dangling a set of keys, he gestured with his head toward the van. "I'll trade you. That bow'll fit easily in the back."

Nathan traded keys. "Help me move all our stuff?"

"No problem." Gunther headed straight for the Toyota.

Dr. Malenkov stepped out of the van and walked slowly toward Nathan, his face solemn under his slightly grayer head.

Giving the teacher a smile, Nathan reached for his hand. "We'll take good care of her."

"Yes, yes," Dr. Malenkov replied, accepting the handshake. "Your mission's purpose cannot be delayed by my concerns for one precious life. With what is at stake, perhaps many sacrificial souls will be willing to risk everything. What is one life, or two or three for that matter, if billions are saved? I only wish I were young and gifted so I could take her place."

Nathan felt his smile shrivel. As usual, Dr. Malenkov's words were saturated with wisdom. He wore the sad countenance of a father sending a daughter to the front lines of war, not knowing if she would ever return to his arms.

After Nathan introduced Tony to the newcomers, it took only a couple of minutes for everyone to move the food, drinks, bedding, and other items from the Toyota to the van. Soon, with Nathan behind the wheel, Kelly in the front passenger's seat, and Daryl and Francesca in the back, they were ready to go. Kelly held the key mirror in front of the radio while Francesca studied Nathan's copy of "Foundation's Key." After a few seconds, she lifted his violin. "Let's get this show on the road, Son!"

Nathan set his elbow on the window frame and leaned his head out. "Here comes your proof, Tony. Don't blink."

While Tony backed away from the van, his eyes as large as ever, Francesca played "Foundation's Key," giving the simple melody an exquisite rendering. The mirror darkened and again showed the field and sky, but now, with one horizon brightening to soft purple and orange, it seemed as though morning was about to break.

Holding the flashlight with both hands, Daryl pointed it at

the mirror. "Fasten your seat belts! We're getting out of here!" She clicked the switch, sending a beam at the mirror. The reflected glow filled the van's interior, so bright it shimmered across the surrounding glass.

Nathan shielded his eyes from the blinding light. A heavy, static-filled bass rhythm pounded from the radio speakers. It banged against his eardrums and pulsed through his heart—throbbing, aching, pressing in from all sides.

As the glow slowly dimmed, the static eased. Music blended in, a violin playing a lovely, yet depressing piece. The windows cleared, but dark sky surrounded them, as if they were wrapped in a blanket of black. Not a single star interrupted the inky canopy.

Nathan rolled down his window. The music grew louder. With low tones that sang of loneliness and sorrow, it seeped into his mind and weighed down his heart. It was the music of the melancholy, a mournful dirge that swept away every joyful thought.

"The words are so sad!" Kelly said. "Someone's in a lot of pain."

"You hear words? Can you tell us?"

"Let's see if I can find a good place to start." After a few seconds, she sang the words quietly, keeping very close to the violinist's tune.

Weep, O my soul. Weep and lament.
Weep for the loss of my heart.
Weep for the solitude, weep for the past,
Weep as my soul tears apart.

I have lost my beloved, my shelter, my rock.
I have lost the fruit of my womb.
I have lost the light that shines in the night.
I have lost my heart in this tomb.

Kelly let out a long breath. "It's repeating the first part."
A surge of heat pulsed into Nathan's cheeks. The music

seemed familiar, but he couldn't quite place it. He leaned around the seat and eyed Francesca. The flashlight's glow revealed two pensive faces in the back. "Recognize the music?" he whispered.

She nodded, speaking with a faint tremor in her voice. "I wrote it as something to play when I'm thinking about my parents. It helps me grieve, sort of like a musical way to cry."

His voice spiked louder, and it seemed amplified in the darkness. "Did you ever record it?"

"Never. It's not even finished, and the part that's playing now is new to me."

"Someone else finished your work?" Kelly asked. "Who could do that?"

Nathan flung open the door. "My mother could!" He pushed his foot out and felt for a place to set it. With everything so black, he couldn't tell if the van was suspended in the middle of space or trapped in a coal mine. The toe of his shoe pressed against something firm, giving him enough confidence to get out and scan the area, but neither streetlamp, nor headlight, nor star shone through the murky blackness.

From somewhere close by, the music played on. Nathan drank in its beauty. Only one person could play with such perfection, such passion. Only one. She had to be around somewhere.

He spun back to the van. "Daryl, hand me the flashlight."

She reached the long tube through the open door. The glow spilled over her trembling hands. "What ... what's out there?"

"Don't know yet." When he took the flashlight, he laid a hand over hers. "What's wrong?"

"I'm terrified of the dark." She gulped and took a deep breath. "But it's okay. Just leave that on, and I'll be fine."

He aimed the light toward the apparent source of the music, but the beam disappeared only a foot or so away from the bulb, as if swallowed by the darkness. "Mom?" he shouted. "Are you out there?"

His voice sounded like he had yelled into a saturated towel, stopped cold and absorbed.

The music continued unabated. If anything, it seemed louder, even sadder than before. He took a step toward it, but the floor under his leading foot crumbled away. He jumped back to solid ground just in time.

Breathing heavily, Nathan leaned into the van. "Francesca, can you come out and play an echo?"

"Sure. Most of it, anyway." She joined him near the driver's door. Kelly, too, got out of the van and leaned against the panel on the same side, while Daryl stayed put in the backseat.

"Okay," Nathan said. "It sounds like she's starting over. Play right behind her and echo each measure. Play it fortissimo."

Francesca echoed the first measure. Her own notes carried into the black air, pure and true.

The other violin halted in mid-measure. Francesca played the notes and stopped at the same place.

After a few seconds, the music began again, this time playing another piece, fast and furious.

Kelly jerked on Nathan's elbow. "She's yelling. She's calling your name. She says, 'Where are you?'"

Nathan tossed the flashlight to the seat, took the violin from Francesca, and played a reply, pouring his thoughts into the music, just as he did in the misty world. He hoped to shout, "I'm here. How can I find you?" But he wasn't sure the message was getting across.

He lowered the violin and waited, trying not to breathe. His legs trembled, aching to dash ahead as he strained to hear the slightest noise.

The music hummed again, this time calmer, long strokes that caressed his mind with loving hands.

"Nathan!" Kelly interpreted. "My son! My love! I am enraptured to hear your song. God has granted you passage to my prison, but the path to where I sit is fraught with danger."

He played a quick response. "What is this place?"

Her music deepened to the lower registers of the violin. "Your father believes that this is a cosmic storage warehouse for dark energy," Kelly said. "It has a fabric network that erodes as energy is added, paralleling the erosion of the dimensional barriers. Falling through the fabric could take you to one of many dimensions, perhaps one that has not yet even been discovered. The danger is great, for the fabric of space crumbles even as we speak. After nearly falling into the void several times, we found a sturdy place. Yet, I sense that the foundational cracks are closing in."

Nathan pressed his toes down. Still solid, solid enough to support a van, yet a plunge into the void lay only two steps in front of him. He played again. "So we're not in outer space? Is that why we can breathe here?"

"That is our guess. It seems that we are in a web structure that has trapped an oxygen-rich gaseous pocket within. Perhaps it was created artificially for the purpose of holding prisoners, but who can solve such mysteries when trapped within a realm of darkness? Your father ventured out to seek answers, or at least food and water, but he never returned. I fear that he has fallen into the depths below."

Nathan poised the bow above the strings but hesitated. Dad would definitely try to figure out what was going on, but he would never leave Mom for very long, not intentionally. Now stroking the strings more slowly, he tried to explain the recent events. "Mom, Patar told us to find what I'm looking for here, so I guess that was supposed to be you and Dad. Then he said if we wanted to go on, we would have to take the most dangerous step of all."

His mother's violin replied again, Kelly still giving the strings a voice. "Perhaps that is the step your father has taken, a step into one of the fabric's wounds. Where that will lead you, I do not know."

Nathan played a burst of notes—"I was afraid you'd say that."—then lowered his bow. He looked at Kelly and Francesca in turn. "What do you think?"

"What are our options?" Kelly asked. "Will the mirror take us anywhere?"

From the backseat, Daryl leaned over the front and extended the mirror toward the open driver's door. The glass showed only darkness, not even a reflection. "Give it a whirl," she said.

Nathan played "Foundation's Key" through, but the mirror stayed dark. After trying three more times, he shook his head. "Quattro must not work here."

His mother's violin replied. "Son, I heard you play the song that calls for Quattro's aid. Although it opens a window to a sacrificial supplicant, the mirror is little more than a polished piece of glass. It was given as a tool for times of trouble when you are unable to escape on your own or when you need to find your way on a journey. It will not serve you well when it is time to turn and face the danger head-on or when you have already found your destination."

Nathan stared at the blank mirror. She was right. Whenever he used the Quattro to get out of danger, he turned his back and let someone else do the work. That was great when he was getting shot at in the river and about to crash in a doomed airplane, but what about now? Maybe it was time he stepped up and took charge.

He played one more question. "Mom, are you hungry and thirsty?"

"Yes, Son," Kelly said. "It has been quite some time since I have had food or water."

"Keep playing, Mom. I'm coming."

After a few seconds, his mother's initial lament began again, though with a noticeable change in tone, just a shade more lively. Nathan set the violin on the front seat and handed Daryl the flashlight. "Put the mirror away, and fill my backpack with a few bottles of water and some of those nutrition bars." He paused for a second, leaned farther into the van, and smiled. "Please?"

She flashed the light at his face and then at her own wide smile. "Sure thing, boss." Within seconds, she had filled the pack and passed it forward.

Kelly tapped him on the back. "What are you going to do?"

As he withdrew from the van, he slid his arms through the straps. "I'm going to rescue my mother."

She hooked her fingers around his elbow. "I'm coming with you, and don't try to talk me out of it."

"And me," Francesca chimed in.

Daryl groaned. "I guess I'm supposed to make it a brave and cheery foursome, aren't I?" She let out a huff, opened the back door, and slammed it again. She circled around the van, holding the flashlight and propping Tony's bow against her shoulder. "You were going to forget this, weren't you?" she said, tipping the bow toward Nathan.

He caught it with one hand and balanced it in his grip. "You sure you're okay?"

"As long as I have this," she said, aiming the flashlight downward, "I'm fine."

After passing the bow to Francesca, Nathan studied the spot where the beam spread across the ground. Weak and failing, the glow seemed to spill from the bulb as if it were shimmering water, and it disappeared into tiny cracks in the black floor. He stooped and traced one of the cracks with his fingernail, but, as he tried to scratch through it, he couldn't make a dent. The light had somehow liquefied, so it had to go somewhere ... but where?

And their voices had also changed. The vocal sound waves traveled a few feet, enough to talk to each other, but they either dispersed or became absorbed. Yet, somehow, music pierced every obstacle.

He stared into the darkness. His father could be wandering in this black mosaic of impossibly dangerous ground, unable to call for help or for guidance. No wonder his mother played the dirge on her violin, hoping her lament would draw him back to her arms.

He straightened and pointed toward the sound. "The music's coming from that way, but the ground's too brittle. We'll have to make a wide circle and go single file."

Daryl extended the flashlight toward him "Want to lead the way?"

"Sure." Stooping low again, he swept the beam slowly from side to side and crept forward. As before, the light splashed and then spread out and filtered into the fabric, leaving a residual glow that painted a shimmering path. When he reached the point where the floor fell out from under him, he halted. The light poured straight down and disappeared as if swallowed by a greedy dark monster below. He searched for a safer route to the right and followed a meandering path toward the sounds of the sad violin.

When it seemed that he had to be within a few yards of his goal, the floor in front of him dropped away into nothingness with no obvious path to the left or the right. He stopped and pointed the beam forward. The light spread out and then fell downward, like water shooting from a hose, but the faint glow carried far enough to paint a portrait of a dark female form standing with a violin raised to her chin. Her eyes reflected the failing light, two brownish-orange circles only fifteen feet away.

He took in a deep breath and shouted as loud as he could. "Mom!"

The music stopped. A voice, as quiet as gentle rain, replied. "Nathan?"

He shouted again. "I can't see how to get to you!"

The shadow's arm pointed. "There is one brittle path to your right, perhaps eight to ten feet away. Your father took it when he left on his journey, but I fear it could be far weaker than before."

"I'm probably the lightest," Kelly said. "I'll take the backpack to her."

"She's my older double," Francesca countered. "And I probably weigh only a couple of pounds more than you do."

Daryl raised a finger. "I volunteer to stay. Someone has to survive to tell your parents about your untimely deaths."

"If anyone goes, it'll be me." Nathan slid the backpack off. "Mom! Put down the violin!"

The shadow crouched for a moment, then rose again.

"Catch!" Nathan slung the pack her way. His mother braced her feet and extended her arms. The pack hit her in the chest, but she managed to hang on to it and stay upright.

"It's food and water, Mom! I hope it's enough."

Her shadowed arms lowered the pack and then drooped at her side. Her cry seemed barely able to stretch across the gap between them. "You are a blessed young man, Nathan, a true son of your father."

The words draped across his mind—*a true son of your father.* Was he really? Would his father have made the same choices he had made? With all of Patar's stinging accusations, he felt more like a bumbling fool than a chip off the faultless block. Yet, if it were within his power, there was one thing his father would never do—leave his mother to sit alone in a prison of darkness.

He inched his way to the right. "I'm coming over there!"

As he searched for the path, a slight tug on the back of his shirt told him Kelly was close behind, as usual. Nothing seemed to scare that girl anymore. And her presence probably meant that the other two girls were tagging along as well.

When he found a spot where the beam stopped pouring unhindered into the void, he held his torch steady. No doubt about it. With the liquid light scrambling into much wider cracks, that part of the floor had to be fragile, but it was the only way to his mother's island. He had to risk it.

He set a foot lightly on the path. It seemed firm enough.

"How are you going to get her back?" Kelly asked.

"I was thinking if I found a safe route, we could just use it again."

He pressed his weight down. So far so good. Only about eight more steps. He pushed his other foot forward. Again, no problem.

She let go of his shirt. "I'll stay two steps behind you."

"Crawl on your hands and knees," Daryl said. "You'll distribute your weight."

"Good thinking." Nathan pointed the flashlight ahead. His mother's shadowy form reached out, now only about ten feet away. The glow washed over her face, revealing her anguished expression—a deeply furrowed brow above eyes filled with alarm. He tossed the light to Daryl and eased his body down to his hands and knees.

Now blind, he inched forward, sliding over the tactile blackness. He felt like a trapped miner trying to escape from a deep tunnel—no light, no map, and no idea if he was about to tumble into an air shaft.

"You can do it, Nathan," Kelly said. "You're almost there!"

"Maybe. If I could see."

"I'll try to blaze the trail." Daryl aimed the light at the floor where Nathan's hand would slide next. "Is that better?"

The beam poured through the widest cracks yet. "Only if seeing impending doom is better." He glared at the fragile floor. Should he chance it? Maybe he could just jump and latch onto his mother's arm. But would she be able to hold on? He chided himself with a nervous laugh. Of course she would. That's what mothers do.

Nathan gritted his teeth. He rose to a crouch and lunged,

but the floor crumbled beneath him. He flailed for his mother's hand, but he swiped through empty air. Yet, for some reason, he wasn't falling. Something held him suspended over the blackness, while another force pressed against his throat, choking him.

"I've got you," Kelly grunted. "I won't let you go."

He looked up. Kelly's fists clutched his shirt, and his collar was strangling him, but if he lifted his chin to let it slide up, he'd probably slip right out of the very thing that kept him from a one-way ticket to nowhere.

Her knees bending, she pulled, but her arms quaked violently. "Swing your leg up!" she yelled. "Francesca will catch it."

The younger Francesca dropped to her knees and reached down. "Aim for my hand!"

He couldn't answer. He couldn't even breathe. When he tried to swing, a faint ripping sound jolted his senses. His shirt was tearing! He had only seconds before he would plummet.

Grunting, Kelly swung his body from side to side to add to his momentum, each movement causing a new tearing sound. She cried out with a guttural scream.

Nathan grimaced. The pain in Kelly's wounded shoulder had to be ripping through her body. How long could she hold on? Finally, he thrust his leg up as high as he could.

Francesca grabbed his ankle. "I've got him!" she yelled. "Pull!"

With the pressure on his throat loosening, Nathan sucked in precious air. As they slowly eased him upward, a new sound grated in his ears, a faint cracking from beneath his rescuers' shoes. "It's collapsing!" he shouted. "Let me go, and run for it!"

"Never!" Pushing with her legs, Kelly lunged backwards. Nathan shot up over the edge and sprawled on top of her with a heavy thump. More cracking sounded from beneath their bodies. They scrambled to their feet, but the floor gave way.

MENDING NIGHTMARES

As they fell, Nathan grabbed Kelly's arm, then Francesca's. He looked up. Daryl stood at the rim, gazing down, the flashlight still in her hand. The glow illuminated her terrified face as she shrank in Nathan's view, and a stream of liquid light followed them into the depths like dripping, phosphorescent wax. Seconds later, she disappeared in the upper reaches, and blackness swallowed her puny torch.

Now with complete darkness surrounding them, there seemed to be no sensation of falling, not even a rush of air. Yet, since they could breathe, they would have to feel air breezing upward, wouldn't they? Unless, of course, the air pocket was falling with them, or the ceiling had actually zoomed upward, or . . .

Nathan shook his head hard. Every option seemed impossible. This place didn't follow any rules — physics, gravity, or logic.

Francesca compressed his arm. "Is everyone okay?"

"I'm fine, except I can't see anything." Nathan blinked at the darkness. "Did we stop falling?"

"We stopped," Kelly said. "My vision is working again, so I guess we moved to another dimension. I can see that we're standing on solid ground, but I don't feel pressure under my feet."

Nathan turned toward her. White beams once again shot

from her eyes, sweeping the area like car headlights. The beams passed over vertical stone slabs near his feet, but the light didn't linger long enough for him to figure out what the slabs were. He reached for one of the stones and ran his finger along the top—smooth marble, about three feet wide and four feet tall. "We need the violin to turn on the lights."

"I put it down," Francesca said. "I needed both hands to haul you up."

Kelly jerked on Nathan's sleeve. "I hear something. A scream. And it's getting louder."

"I hear it, too."

A high-pitched wail grew in volume, coming from somewhere above. Kelly's eyebeams aimed toward the sky. A large, rectangular object fell through the shafts of light and landed with a rattling, squeaking thump a mere five feet away.

Kelly shifted her beams to the point of impact. A van labeled "Stoneman Enterprises" sat in front of them, still shaking and shifting on its shock absorbers.

A light flashed on at the driver's window. A girl leaned out into the glow, her face veiled by shadows. "Wow! What a trip!"

Nathan squinted at her. "Daryl?"

"In the flesh ... At least, I think so ... Actually, now that I mention it, I'm not really sure."

"Did the floor collapse?" he asked.

"No. I figured, do I want to be stuck in a cosmic web for all eternity chatting with your mom? I mean, she's really nice and all, but I came here for adventure. So, I said, 'What the heck? Might as well go out in style.' So instead of just jumping after you, I drove the van into the hole."

Kelly's eyebeams shifted back and forth as she shook her head. "Crazy as ever."

"Did you pick up my violin?" Nathan asked. "We need some light."

"Yep." Daryl extended the violin and bow through the window. "I'm all for fiddling away the darkness."

Nathan set the violin under his chin and raised the bow. Just as he was about to play, Kelly grabbed his wrist.

"No!" she whispered. "Wait!"

Nathan lowered his voice to match hers. "What's up?"

"I hear singing. It's getting closer."

Nathan ducked behind the stone slab and pulled Kelly down. Daryl jumped out of the driver's door, and she and Francesca joined the huddle.

"Is the van in plain sight?" Nathan asked. "I can't see it."

Daryl aimed the flashlight at the letters on the side panel. "As plain as a zit on the Mona Lisa."

He pushed the light toward the ground. "Douse it!"

Daryl flicked it off. "As if that's going to help."

"The singing's getting closer," Kelly said. "It's a male voice."

"I hear it now." Nathan passed his hand in front of Kelly's eyes. "What about your eyebeams? Won't he see them?"

"If it's daylight to him like it is to me, he probably won't." Kelly aimed her eyes at a winding path. With the beams steady now, the residual glow washed over the surrounding slabs, clarifying them.

"Tombstones," Nathan whispered.

"Shh! I see him now."

A youthful male shuffled into the light, his head down and shoulders sloped. As he drew slowly closer, Kelly's beams followed, painting twin circles on his torso, but he didn't seem to notice.

Appearing to be about fifteen and dressed in a dark, form-fitting shirt and loose, equally dark trousers, he sang a mournful tune, using the vowel sounds they had heard from the stalkers.

Kelly translated in soft whispers.

To wander home,
To rest, to roam,
'Tis peace entombed
And mortal gloom.
Awaiting dark,
Forlorn and stark,
I weep for days gone by.

The young man lifted his head and gazed above, tears streaming as he lamented.

To see my Scarlet's rosy face,
To hear my Amber's golden song,
To feel again our hued embrace,
Apart we're weak, together strong.

He stopped suddenly and stared straight ahead. Passing by their hiding place, he strode to the van and touched the side panel with his fingertips. He pivoted on his heels. Kelly's beams struck his eyes, raising a splash of blue.

The boy sang a short burst of notes.

"I see you." Kelly translated. "Stand and show yourselves."

She stood and stepped toward the boy, but Nathan rose quickly and moved in front of her. "I'm Nathan Shepherd," he said, extending his hand. "Who are you?"

The boy stared at Nathan's hand. "I am Cerulean."

Nathan stepped back. "You speak English. I thought you would answer in song."

"If you thought this, then why did you address me in English? I merely responded in kind."

"I . . . I'm not sure. Habit, I guess."

A sympathetic smile bent Cerulean's lips. "I am familiar with your facial expression, Nathan of the Red World. You are flustered and confused."

Nathan pointed at himself. "How do you know me?"

"I have seen Nathan of the Blue World many times through his mirror. I learned to love him dearly, though I am no longer his supplicant. He has gone to be with the Everlasting One."

As Kelly's beams moved across Cerulean from his torso to the top of his head, Nathan studied his boyish features—smooth skin, bright sapphire eyes, and dark blue spiked hair. With his top shirt button unfastened, the upper portion of his chest was exposed, revealing darkness just under his neckline, a stark contrast to his pale skin.

"How did you get out of your prison?" Nathan asked.

"I am still in my dome, if that is your meaning. This is the realm of dreams, and I am doing what I can to prevent a stalker from frightening someone you know quite well. Daryl of the Blue World is dozing under a dimensional mirror, making her vulnerable to a dream attack. Since she is terrified of great heights and graveyards, a stalker has manipulated her night vision and created this cemetery. I entered her dream to cancel the stalker's efforts and bring her peace."

"That wasn't a song of peace you were singing a few minutes ago," Nathan said.

"That was my own lament, for I have not been able to be near my sisters in a very long time." Cerulean gave him a weak smile. "Daryl would not be able to understand it, anyway. In fact, she likely did not hear it at all." He nodded in the direction he entered the graveyard. "She is just now phasing into her dream world, believing herself to be in the eighth grade and reliving a night when she was lost in the woods and came out in a church cemetery."

"I remember that night," Daryl said as she rose to her feet. "I'll talk to her."

Cerulean pulled her back. "You will only add to her confusion. Watch quietly, and you will learn a great deal."

In the distance, a glow appeared, revealing Daryl wearing a blue nightgown. With her hair tied into pigtails and tears streaming down her cheeks, she seemed much younger. As she drew closer, the glow spread, illuminating the graveyard. A bat fluttered up from behind a tombstone and dove at Daryl's face. With a pitiful cry, she flailed her arms wildly. When the bat angled away, she hunched down and walked on, still sobbing, but instead of tears, a black mist emanated from her eyes and rose into the air.

"What's that black smoke?" Daryl Red asked.

Cerulean touched his face near his eye. "Dark energy, a product of her fear. The stalker who created this vision will collect it for the interfinity engine."

"Interfinity?" Nathan repeated. "That's what my father called the merging of dimensions."

"Because your father learned it from us. Mictar's engine is also called Lucifer, but the reason would take too long to explain."

"That means my father must have gone to the misty—"

"Shhh!" Cerulean set a finger over Nathan's lips. "It is time to supplicate for this dear child. I feel the stalker is ready to cultivate this garden of terror."

A ghostly apparition arose from one of the graves, a semi-transparent man in a torn pilot's uniform. Pus oozed from open facial sores and dripped to the ground, raising a sizzling splash. A putrid stench permeated the graveyard as he limped toward Daryl Blue. He reached out with long, gnarled fingers and moaned through his words, stretching out the syllables in a lamenting tone. "Soon you will join me. You will fall from the heavens and perish."

"My uncle," Daryl Red whispered. "He was a pilot, like my father, but he died in a plane crash before I was born."

Daryl Blue turned to run, but the ground behind her collapsed, creating a deep chasm. Flailing her arms again, she stood on tiptoes to keep from falling. A rush of black mist flowed, nearly veiling her head.

The man continued his slow approach, repeating his ghostly mantra as he came closer and closer, his trembling hands still reaching. "Soon you will join me. You will fall from the heavens and perish."

Cerulean leaped into the open and sang with a powerful, vibrant voice.

Begone you ghost of fear and gloom
And hearken now to Daryl's choir.
They cast aside your phantom hands
And rescue her with freedom's fire.

Suddenly a thousand voices joined together to sing. The tune seemed familiar, something Nathan was sure he had heard a hundred times, but the lyrics sounded foreign, like an old, forgotten language.

Rop tú mo baile,
a Choimdiu cride:
ní ní nech aile
acht Rí secht nime.

Kelly quickly translated from the beginning. "You be my vision, lord of my heart. None other is anything but the king of—"

"I know the song," Nathan interrupted. "The modern version goes like this." He sang the melody, though he lagged far behind the voices.

Be thou my vision, O Lord of my heart;
Naught be all else to me, save that thou art.
Thou my best thought, by day or by night,
Waking or sleeping, thy presence my light.

As the voices continued, a stream of sparkling light flowed through the air, pulsating with the rise and fall of the tune. The stream wrapped around Daryl's torso and pulled her away from the precipice. Now more perplexed than frightened, she stared at the apparition. As the stream released her, the black mist around her head thinned out, and the sparkling light flowed into the air, seemingly taking the angelic voices with it.

Cerulean continued his song.

Go back to shadows all ye ghosts;
Restore the ground from whence it came.
Begone ye graves and stones of death;
Restore the light to Daryl's flame.

The ghostly man faded away. With a loud rumble, the floor of the chasm behind young Daryl rose back to the surface, snapping in place as if it had never collapsed. The weak glow around her body brightened, and as it flowed across the graveyard, the tombstones sank into the ground and lush grass sprouted over the patches of bare earth that had marked the resting places of the departed.

Soon, the cemetery looked like a lovely meadow. Orange and blue wildflowers sprouted at Daryl's feet. She plucked one after another, twisted the stems together, and pushed the bouquet into her hair. Now smiling brightly, she skipped away in the direction she had come. As she did, the brightness faded, leaving the onlookers in a slowly dimming world.

"She will awaken soon," Cerulean said. "You will have to find an escape."

A new sound emanated from somewhere above, a cacophonous mixture of notes, sung in an array of vowel sounds.

Nathan covered his ears. The music, if the horrible noise could be called that, sounded familiar. "The stalkers?" he asked.

Cerulean aimed his blue eyes toward the dimness above. "They are standing around my dome and capturing the energy of supplication. They use their foul song to transform my prayers and Daryl's deliverance into dark energy." He dipped his head and sighed. "Even my rescues are being used for evil purposes."

"Is there anything we can do?" Kelly asked.

"Nothing. You must go. When her dream ends, this dreamscape will collapse and you will fall into another reality, or perhaps a nonreality. I cannot predict where you will go. Because of Scarlet's sacrifice, it is impossible to tell how long the opening will remain."

Nathan gave him a nod. "Better to use the mirror."

Cerulean caressed the glass with a gentle finger. "Scarlet will guide you to safety."

As the light continued to dim, Nathan and the others hurried to the van. While Nathan settled into the driver's seat with the violin, Kelly mounted the mirror on the dashboard. Daryl and Francesca watched from the back, leaning forward between the headrests.

Nathan began playing "Foundation's Key" again, hurrying through the notes. The mirror darkened. A faint image of a face appeared in the midst of the black reflection, a feminine face with shining red eyes. A voice, soft and gentle, emanated from the glass — Scarlet's voice. "I heard you calling for me earlier, my beloved, but I could not find you."

"I was in a place of blackness, where my mother is."

Her auburn eyebrows dipped. "It seems that my vision cannot penetrate there, but since you are in the realm of dreams now, I can speak to you."

Nathan lowered the violin. "Where should we go?"

"Although I long for your presence with me, the mirror you have can only return you to one of the earthly realms. Yet, I can send you to someone who can give you help."

"My father?"

Scarlet's eyes dimmed. "I have been unable to locate him. Even his dreams are out of my reach."

"Then, who?"

"Illuminate the path, and you will see." The face in the mirror clarified. Scarlet, her lips trembling, spoke in a near lament. "Don't forget to come for me, Nathan. I cannot escape, and the stalkers will never let me go. You are my only hope."

"But how? How can I get back to you?"

Her voice faded. "Look for me in the mirror that sings my song. I know not the title, but it strums the sorrows of my heart and eases my pain." Seconds later, she disappeared. A construction site replaced her image, a building with no roof and a man on a ladder adding bricks to the top of a wall.

As the light in the dreamscape dimmed to blackness, a loud crack sounded from underneath the van. The left rear wheel sank. The frame of the van thumped against the ground, angling their bodies toward the depression.

Nathan grabbed the steering wheel. "Daryl Blue's waking up!"

More cracks erupted. The van sank again. The entire world around them faded to black.

Daryl aimed the flashlight. "Say the word, Captain!"

"Hit it!"

The beam shot out and bounced off the mirror. Instantly, the surrounding blackness began to fizzle. By the thousands, dark pinpoints sparkled with colorful light until the image in the mirror materialized all around them.

With the entire landscape now in view, Nathan scanned the area to get his bearings. The van sat on a bare foundation, facing a tri-fold mirror that had been bolted into the concrete floor. A curved, plaster wall stood behind the mirror, making a semicircle and leaving the area behind them open to the trees. Only a few stacked cinder blocks marked where the rest of the observatory's domed wall would be built.

Nathan leaned his head out the window. "They're building Interfinity Labs here."

"You mean StarCast," a man with a British accent said. "It is not Interfinity yet."

Nathan looked at the outside rearview mirror. A man walked toward him on the driver's side, a short, bald man with owl-like glasses. "Dr. Simon? Simon Blue?"

Dr. Simon opened the van door and motioned for Nathan to get out. "We have much to do and little time to do it."

Nathan hopped down to the foundation and hugged himself to fight the cold breeze. "Interfinity's almost here. We have to figure out how to get back to the misty world and play the violin."

"Yes, yes," Dr. Simon said, waving his hand. "I know all about that. But first we have another disaster to try to avert."

"No! We'll just create more holes in the dimensional fabric."

Dr. Simon pointed at the sky. "There are many holes, and the wounds we inflict on the dimensional fabric are miniscule compared to the greater danger the stalkers are creating."

"Exactly! We have to stop them. That's why we can't afford to get distracted. I have to find the violin as soon as possible."

"Nathan Shepherd," Dr. Simon said, giving him a fatherly glare, "are you a true son of Solomon? If you are, then where is your compassion? If you knew someone was about to die, would you try to save his life? Or would you skip away to do what you perceived to be your duty, saying 'Have a nice day,' while he dies in flames and his widow and children are doomed to suffer for years to come?"

Nathan stepped back. Dr. Simon's words shot through his heart like a heated poker. What would his father do? Would he risk the lives of billions, hoping he had time to rescue them later, in order to save one soul he was certain would die? He took a deep breath and looked Dr. Simon in the eye. "What do you have in mind?"

Dr. Simon pulled a small three-ring notebook from his

pocket and leafed through the pages, stopping somewhere near the middle. "The space shuttle Challenger will launch tomorrow, and it will explode moments later because of a flaw in the O-ring seal in one of its solid rocket boosters. Apparently, extreme cold exposed the flaw and created a disastrous chain reaction."

"So now you want me to be an astronaut?" Shaking his head, Nathan stepped back again. "You're out of your mind! They would never let me on board to—"

"Don't take me for a fool," Dr. Simon snapped. "I know you can't buy a ticket and stroll aboard a space shuttle. But you can use the Quattro mirror to send the seven astronauts elsewhere before they ever set foot in the craft. That should give us time to convince them to inspect the O-rings. At the very least, we could delay the launch and hope for warmer weather."

"But won't the astronauts dream about the explosion? And the launch workers? At least some of them have to be next-day dreamers, right?"

"If only it were that simple. It seems that many major disasters are hidden from dreamers. Just a few months ago, a Midwest Airlines flight crashed after taking off from Milwaukee. In order to test a theory I have, I went to the gate shortly before takeoff and interviewed some of the passengers about their most recent dreams, and they all reported that they slept without dreaming the previous night."

"No dreams at all?"

Dr. Simon shook his head. "My theory is that Mictar has access to disaster lists, and his stalkers suppress the dreams of the victims. Zelda has already explained and taken advantage of this phenomenon in quite theatrical ways. The day before a disaster, she announces that one is coming. She writes the details down on a parchment, seals it in a black envelope, and locks it in a vault. The stalkers plant false dreams about disasters that never occur, making people believe that such dreams are unreliable.

Then, after the real disaster occurs, amid much fanfare, she opens the vault and reads the exact account of what happened. She explains that these events will occur from time to time as a means of warning the people that their dreams are not to be relied upon and for proving her position as prophetess."

"But how do the people stand for that?" Nathan asked. "Why don't they rise up and demand to see the parchment?"

"Many have protested. Now they are dead, the victims of dream stalking. The entire world lives in fear, and since each individual assumes that he is likely not a disaster victim, self-preservation becomes the weightiest factor in his decision-making process. Apathy becomes a life-saving choice." Dr. Simon's voice deepened. "The question for you, Nathan Shepherd, is whether or not you will join in their apathy."

Nathan lowered his gaze and replayed the video footage of the Challenger disaster in his mind. How many times had he wished he could travel to the past and stop the tragedy? Now he had the chance to do it, an impossible dream come true. But what about the billions of others in the three color-coded earths?

As if reading his mind, Dr. Simon spoke in a soothing tone. "Who can tell when the worlds will merge or how much time we have? The hours you spend on this assignment will take only moments in the other worlds. I have been traveling back and forth between Earths Blue and Yellow for several Yellow years now, and the ultimate collision still has not arrived."

Nathan stared at the sincere eyes behind the circular lenses. Dr. Simon had a good point. Interfinity seemed like a doomsday prophecy that would never arrive — lots of ominous signs but nothing that proved it would result in the end of the cosmos. Maybe it was a big, barking Doberman without any teeth.

He looked at his female companions. Three more pairs of eyes stared at him. Kelly leaned against the van's side panel, rubbing her arms in the cold breeze as she seemed to search his mind with her gaze. Daryl stood next to her, shifting uneasily from foot to foot. Francesca crossed her arms and glanced between him and the other girls. With her lips parted, she seemed ready to offer advice, but she stayed silent.

He sighed. If only one of them would help him make this awful decision.

Kelly pushed away from the van, shivering. A splotch of red blemished the shoulder of her sweatshirt as she shuffled toward him, giving evidence that some of her stitches had broken loose. "Don't go, Nathan." She stopped and grimaced before looking him in the eye. "We can't afford to get sidetracked for a whole day. Besides, we couldn't stop the jet from crashing."

"Right," Daryl offered. "Crashing the government's space party and convincing the Feds to postpone the flight would make your airliner mission look like a game of Pin the Tail on the Donkey."

Nathan shifted his gaze to Francesca. She glided toward him, her eyes sorrowful, yet piercing. Leaning close, she whispered, "You must do what you believe to be right. Not what Solomon Shepherd would do; what Nathan Shepherd would do. Your father has been your guide, your rock, but the wisdom he instilled in you is not a spreadsheet of formulas that yields an unmistakable result in the bottom cell. Wisdom is a jewel with many faces. Looking at it from all angles gives you a variety of perspectives, and each face tells a different story, some lovely and some tragic. Often more than one will present an option that seems right, yet, since their paths diverge, only one can be chosen." She kissed him on the cheek and backed away. "Wisdom provides a glimpse of the face of God, Nathan Shepherd, but not always his whole counsel."

Barely able to breathe, Nathan watched the lovely young lady rejoin the other girls. With her long dark locks flowing in the breeze, she looked more like his mother than ever, and her breathtaking words proved that the heart of his mom beat within her breast.

He turned toward Dr. Simon and tried to show in his expression the pain of his decision. "I can't go. I have to save the cosmos."

Dr. Simon firmed his chin, but he seemed more resigned than angry. "Very well. I will not beg you to have pity, but I can offer another option that will take far less time and effort." He glanced at his wristwatch, then returned his gaze to Nathan. "In just over two hours a pilot will take off from a Chicago area airport and crash due to mechanical failure. Saving his life should be a simple task."

Nathan shook his head. "I can't do it. Regardless of what you think, interfinity is almost here. I saw how everything is crumbling. You know how the nightmares are enslaving everyone. We need to—"

"What's the pilot's name?" Daryl asked.

Dr. Simon raised his eyebrows, then flipped to another page in his notebook and pointed at a line near the top. "Harold. Harold Markey. Twenty-eight years old, father of two."

Daryl fell back against the van. "My uncle!"

"I see," Dr. Simon said. "Your father's brother, I assume."

Her eyes wide and pleading, she grabbed Nathan's arm. "We have to rescue him!"

"We?" Nathan pointed at Dr. Simon. "If it's so easy, why not him? And where's Simon Yellow, anyway? Can't he help?"

Dr. Simon adjusted his glasses and looked at his watch again. "My Earth Yellow counterpart is already at Cape Canaveral. Since Scarlet desires rescue, and since we know how to open the portal to the misty world, we assumed she would send you to find one of us."

Nathan balled up his fist. "How do we get to her? Tell me!"

"I have the appropriate musical piece right here." Dr. Simon withdrew an iPod from his pocket. "I will give it to you if you acquiesce."

Nathan glared at the white rectangular iPod. "You mean I have to go to Florida and save the shuttle before you'll give me the tune?"

"Or to the local airport to save the pilot." Dr. Simon took yet another look at his watch. "Make your choice, one pilot or seven astronauts. Either option presents you with a noble task. Our primary goal is to save lives, of course, but we also want to harness the power of Quattro. As long as Scarlet and the other supplicants are imprisoned, they might as well be useful, and perhaps we can learn how to use their power of deliverance on a wider scale at a later time."

Nathan looked again at his three female partners in turn. Daryl folded her hands in a begging posture, her clenched fingers trembling. Francesca stood stoically, but shivers made her arms and legs shake. Kelly bit one side of her bottom lip and met his stare. She seemed to have an idea, yet remained unsure whether or not to reveal it. Did she know another way to get to the misty world?

Nathan turned back to Dr. Simon and half closed one eye. Would this self-proclaimed deliverer really hold back information that could save the universe? He tried to read his expression, but he showed no signs of bluffing, not a hint of fear or doubt.

Finally, Nathan shook his head. "I have to stick to my mission."

Daryl spun around and slammed her palm against the van, but she said nothing.

"Don't be a fool!" Dr. Simon shouted. "You won't be able to accomplish your mission without passage to the stalkers' world. You can dream your way to the violin, but you can't play it as a ghost."

Nathan held back a grimace. Simon wasn't bluffing. He was

in control, and he knew it. Turning toward Kelly, Nathan silently searched for help. She edged closer and slipped her hand into his, giving it a gentle squeeze. Apparently she knew something, but she didn't want to give it away to Dr. Simon.

Nathan pulled in a long breath. "If you want to save them, then go for it. I'll find another way to get to the violin."

"Very well." Dr. Simon pushed the iPod back into his pocket. "I will work with my counterpart to prevent the space shuttle disaster. Then we will get another musician to play the violin in the stalkers' world. I doubt that such a stubborn, insensitive boy would be able to play the piece properly anyway."

Nathan tightened his fist again. "Stubborn? Insensitive? Just because I won't—"

Daryl jumped in front of Nathan. "Let *me* try to save my uncle."

SCARLET'S SONG

Dr. Simon stared at Daryl. "You? Why?"

"Because I'm here. Because I can. And because I can't help them play a violin. I can't even play 'Chopsticks' on a piano." She looked at Nathan. "I'm sorry. I understand why you can't save him, but I have to try. My father has been depressed ever since his brother died. That's why he got fired by two big airline companies. Maybe I can save Daryl Yellow from going through what I had to suffer."

She turned back to Dr. Simon. "Will you take me to that airport?"

Dr. Simon glared at Nathan. "Of course I will. If you rescue him, I won't be able to experiment with Quattro, but I'm glad to see that someone has a heart."

Nathan's cheeks flamed. He was ready to shout one of a dozen protests that boiled in his mind, but when Kelly's thumb caressed his knuckles, the rage settled to a simmer. He set his jaw and nodded at Daryl. "I understand. Do what you have to do. We'll figure out how to get to the misty world somehow."

His scowl deepening, Dr. Simon waved toward a car sitting in a field beyond the unfinished wall. "We should go now. I will try to reunite you with the others after you save your uncle." He marched away, not looking back.

Daryl followed, her anguished gaze locked on Nathan. With her red tresses billowing across her sad eyes, she blew him a kiss, then turned and ran to catch up with Dr. Simon.

As soon as they were out of earshot, Nathan motioned for Kelly and Francesca to huddle with him. "Any ideas?"

"Not from me," Francesca said. "Even if we could drive back to Iowa and use the portal in my old bedroom, it would take too long."

Nathan shook his head. "Right. Too slow. We have a mirror here. We should be able to use it."

"Let's dial up Daryl Blue," Kelly said. "You know that tune, and we can ask Gordon Red about the iPod."

"Do you think he would know the right music to get to the misty world?"

"Maybe he won't have to know. Remember Scarlet said to use *her* tune. It might be labeled in the iPod's directory in a way we can recognize."

Nathan pointed at her. "Brilliant. The van's already facing the mirror, so we can use the headlights."

"But we can't drive it into the observatory."

"We're not going to. We'll stand at the transportation point with the van behind us."

Kelly turned toward the mirror. "Why don't we just talk to Daryl and Dr. Gordon? That'll save us from causing another wound."

"Sure." Nathan shrugged his shoulders. "We can try that."

Francesca hurried to the van and returned with the violin. "What do you play to summon Earth Blue?"

"Waxman's 'Carmen Fantasy.'"

Nathan reached for the violin, but she held it back. "Really?" she asked. "I love that piece."

"I know. You taught it to me."

She raised the violin. "Shall I?"

"Mother," he said with a formal nod, "I would be honored."

Furrowing her brow, Francesca played the opening notes, keeping her eyes on the mirror. As her hand danced across the fingerboard, beautiful music flowed through the snow-laden saplings and drifted toward the unfinished wall to their right. The man on the ladder, maybe a couple of hundred feet away, turned, his trowel frozen in place as he paused to listen.

Nathan watched himself, Francesca, and Kelly in the reflection. The image faded, first as if a cloudbank had drifted in front of the sun, then as if late evening had spread a blanket of darkness across the field. Soon, a hint of light shone through—the lamp on the computer desk in the observatory. The glow strengthened, revealing Daryl tilting her head toward them, but her movements seemed slow, painfully slow. A smile emerged, but it took several seconds for it to spread across her face.

Francesca lowered the violin. "She's in slow motion."

"Earth Yellow is still speeding along," Nathan said. "To her, we probably look like we drank a gallon of coffee."

Kelly stepped closer to the mirror. "Makes it tough to communicate. How do we tell her to ask Dr. Gordon what's on the iPod?"

Nathan joined her and watched the Earth Blue scene. Daryl had raised her hand to wave, but she looked like an old movie advancing one frame every five seconds. "The Challenger disaster is tomorrow. Do you know what year that happened?"

"That was before I was born," Kelly said. "I saw a replay, and it gave me nightmares, but I don't remember when it happened."

Francesca counted on her fingers. "It's nineteen eighty-six. I've missed some time here, but I've been keeping track of the years since you first showed up at my house."

"Did we have mobile phones back then?" Nathan asked.

"Yes. I've seen them for a while, but my father says they're too expensive."

He looked at the bricklayer. As the muscular man went back to work on the wall, a bulky device swung at his waist. Nathan nodded toward him. "Want to bet he's got one?"

"Looks like it," Kelly said. "Who're you going to call?"

"Tony Clark. He can use the computer and transmitter to send a note to Daryl Blue telling her exactly what we need. Then she can send back a list of the songs on the iPod."

"How long will that take?"

"Probably a lot less time than driving back to Iowa." Nathan took a step toward the bricklayer, but Kelly pulled him back.

"Let me do it," she said.

"Uh ... okay." He squinted at her. "But why?"

"Trust me on this, Nathan. He'll respond better to me."

As Kelly jogged toward the office part of the StarCast building, Nathan leaned against the van and watched. Even with loose-fitting jeans and a baggy sweatshirt, as she pumped her arms and swayed with her gait, her feminine form was obvious.

He let out a sigh. No doubt she was right. Once Kelly turned on the charm, what guy could resist helping her? Especially with blood oozing from her shoulder.

Within a minute, Kelly was talking on the worker's mobile phone, the bricklayer standing at her side ... too close to her side in Nathan's estimation. Soon, she jogged back, huffing white mist.

Nathan stepped between her and the bricklayer. "Get it done?"

She nodded. "My father's sending the message now, and Eddie will tell us when he calls back with the list of songs."

"Eddie?"

She cast a glance toward the worker. "I had to give him my phone number to get him to agree to help."

"Your phone number? But that'll just get him your father here on Earth Yellow."

"I know. But it wasn't a lie. I gave him my real phone number."

"Look," Francesca said, pointing at the mirror. "Something changed."

Nathan and Kelly turned. Daryl was now reading a paragraph of text in an instant messaging window on the computer screen, but the characters were far too small to decipher. Her hand inched toward the touch pad, traveling at a fraction of normal speed.

"Is she going to send a note to Gordon Red?" Kelly asked.

Nathan crossed his arms. "Probably, but this is like a marathon race between two snails."

As he watched the unbearably tedious action in the mirror, Kelly picked out a spot a foot or so away from him and leaned against the van. She copied his pose, crossing her arms and adding a shiver.

He glanced at her. From time to time she looked over at the bricklayer, but her lips stayed tight, showing no signs of emotion. As warmth again crawled along his skin, he slid an inch or so away. Was Kelly interested in that guy? What was he, about twenty-four? And what if she was interested? Should that be making him feel like his heart had just plunged into his stomach? Yeah, probably. He'd be a fool to think he hadn't grown attached to her. Any hint that her heart might search for another guy made him feel lonely and cold inside.

Heaving a sigh, he slid back, regaining the space he had given up. Daryl was now eyeing a new message on the screen, a list of some kind, maybe the songs they were waiting for. He leaned close to Kelly, almost brushing her cheek as he whispered. "Cold?"

Shivering harder, she nodded. "Very!"

He draped his arm over her shoulders, careful to avoid her wound, and pulled her close. As she snuggled into his embrace, a smile trembled on her lips, but she said nothing. Still nearly cheek to cheek, he whispered again. "Keep me in mind, okay?"

She turned her head and met his gaze, a look of confusion in her eyes at first, but her face slowly relaxed. Tears welled, and her lips trembled harder. "You're already there, Nathan. I thought you knew that."

New warmth flashed across his skin. He wanted to break the eye-lock, but he didn't dare. Not now. Not when her heart was so vulnerable.

He cleared his throat and tried to speak with enough passion to truly express the fire kindling inside. "I did know it. I just want to stay there." He wanted to add "forever," but it wouldn't pass through his lips.

She turned back to the mirror, a tear running down her cheek. "I'll never ask you to leave."

Daryl slowly tapped her keyboard, her movements jerky now as the speed changed sporadically. A few seconds later, a masculine voice sounded from beyond the curved wall.

"Kelly! Your phone call!"

She pushed upright and looked at Nathan. "Want to come?"

He shook his head and winked. "You can handle it. I'll stay with Mom."

Flashing a bright smile, she brushed away her tear and jogged toward the building.

Francesca buried her hands in her sweatshirt pockets and slid through a thin layer of snow on the foundation. She stopped at Nathan's side, blowing vapor for a moment as she watched Kelly. After a few seconds, she looked at Nathan. "She's a lovely girl, you know."

He didn't answer at first. He didn't know how. Once again it seemed like his mother, his real mother, had spoken. He knew he had to answer truthfully. Mom would never settle for anything else. He pushed his toe across the snow. "Yeah. I know."

Francesca grinned and took Kelly's place at his side. She snuggled even closer than Kelly had. "It's so strange to have a son my age. I can be affectionate without fear of misunderstanding."

He looked into her eyes, soft and walnut brown. There was

no doubt about it. The spirit of his mother lived inside this beautiful teenager. And he loved her—completely, devotedly, with pure passion. New warmth yet again flooded his body, but he just let it flow. The joy of innocent love should never be squelched.

Soon, Kelly jogged back and hopped up to the foundation, a sheet of paper in her grip. Smiling, she showed it to Nathan while Francesca looked on. "Eddie wrote them down while I called them out. He was fast."

Nathan scanned the list. "Looks like about forty pieces. We can't just try them all. I don't even recognize some of the titles."

Francesca shook her head. "Same here. You probably learned the ones I taught you ... or will teach you, I suppose."

"But what would be Scarlet's song?" Kelly asked. "Is there anything you recognize that relates to her?"

Francesca ran her finger down the page. "Something with *red* in the title or something *close* to red?"

"Not likely," Nathan said. "Scarlet said it strums the sorrows of her heart. The clue would be in the content, not the title. It would probably be emotive, something that makes you feel lonely or lost."

Francesca pointed at each title in turn. "'Brahms' Lullaby'? No. 'Rhapsody in Blue'? No. The 'Hallelujah Chorus'? No. Never heard of this one. Never heard of this one, either."

Kelly set her finger on a line near the bottom. "Here it is. I'm sure of it."

Nathan read the title. "'Moonlight Sonata'?"

"I used to play it on our piano whenever my parents ..." She bit her lip, then blinked rapidly as her voice pitched higher. "Whenever they weren't getting along. It always made me feel kind of lonely, but after a while, I would always feel better."

"It's worth a try." Nathan looked at Francesca. "Do you know it?"

"Not memorized, but I can hear some of it in my head. Maybe I could improvise. It could come back to me while I play."

"Yeah, I've heard the first movement enough times. We could work it out together."

"But it's a piano piece," Kelly said. "A violin could never get the sound right. It needs to be melancholy, with lots of forlorn echoing."

"Maybe that won't matter." He nodded at Francesca. "Let's give it a try."

Francesca raised the violin once more and played the first notes of the sonata, soft and solemn. She closed her eyes, apparently concentrating on the music flowing through her mind. With her wavy raven locks dancing across her shoulders in the freshening breeze, she looked like a goddess; her perfect posture against a snowy backdrop painted a portrait of strange contrasts—black over white, a lively nightingale against a backdrop of decay and death.

Goose bumps swept across Nathan's body, but not because of the cold. This goddess was his mother in the making, a virgin virtuoso who would one day lay her pristine gifts on the altar and give birth to a new generation of talent.

As she played on, Nathan shook his head. She was so good, so very, very good. Even though she was still so young, her playing carried a sweet perfection he had never been able to reach. Try as he might, something was missing, something elusive, a heart and passion that resonated with every stroke of her bow.

Why, then, had she, as his mother on Earth Red, told him otherwise? At least once a month for the last three years she had looked him in the eye and said, *"You are an heir, the recipient of a musical inheritance. You have more talent than I could ever hope for. You just have to learn to reach into your heart and let it bleed through your fingers."*

He sighed and turned to the mirror. It seemed to darken at times, but the slow-motion scene of Daryl in the observatory always came back. She had typed something on the screen, but, again, it was too far away to read. Could she have figured out the tune? Maybe she was telling Dr. Gordon which one they had selected.

Finally, Kelly leaned close to Nathan and whispered, "I don't think it's working. She's playing the notes perfectly, but it's just not the same."

"I don't think there's any chance of finding a piano around here."

"I have an idea." She opened the van door. "See if you can find a classical station."

Nathan hopped into the driver's seat and flipped on the radio. "What are the chances they'll play the 'Moonlight Sonata'?"

"Probably zero, unless we exert some influence." Kelly leaned in through the door. "If you find one, try to catch the station's call letters."

Nathan twirled the tuning dial, mumbling as he paused at each strong signal. "Country ... commercial ... sounds like jazz ... classic rock ... country again ... another commercial ..." He halted at a station. A woman read a series of orchestral concert announcements, each one enunciated perfectly and with a formal air. "This could be classical, and it's a clear signal."

After a few moments, the woman gave the station's call letters, WNIU, then a Listz concerto began.

"WNIU?" Kelly repeated. "I can get the number from directory assistance."

"Eddie's phone again?"

"Yep. I just have to dream up a song request they can't resist." Kelly headed toward Eddie's ladder once again, calling back as she ran, "Get ready to crank up the volume."

Nathan turned up the radio's volume to max and stepped around to the rear of the van. He pulled out the mammoth violin bow and stood in front of the mirror at the point where the light beams had created a dimensional window before.

As the Listz concerto reached its ending crescendo, he set the bow on the floor and gestured with his head for Francesca to join him. "You and Kelly should stand here while I turn on the headlights."

Still holding the violin, Francesca took her place. "Assuming her efforts are successful."

"Trust me. She'll come through. She always has before."

When the final note faded, the voice of the station's female announcer returned. "I received a most unusual request."

Nathan grinned at Francesca. "Here it comes."

"A girl named Kelly wishes to dedicate a special piece to the astronauts of the space shuttle Challenger who are scheduled to launch tomorrow morning. She claimed that she had a terrible vision about the shuttle exploding shortly after takeoff. I know what you're thinking. Travelers are forbidden to speak about their long-distance prophecies, and reliance on dreams that forecast disasters is dangerous, but I cannot ignore her courage. My own cousin will be aboard that shuttle, and I will pass along the technical information she has given me. In the meantime, to express my gratitude, I will interrupt our scheduled programming and play her request, Beethoven's magnificent 'Moonlight Sonata.'"

Vibrant piano notes played from the radio speakers and reverberated in the semicircular structure. Wearing a broad smile, Kelly hopped back onto the observatory foundation and bowed dramatically. While Nathan clapped, she straightened and winked. "You should be proud. I did it all without a single lie."

"I am proud," he said, reaching for her hand. "You're the best." He pulled her and Francesca together, positioned them in front of the mirror, and dashed back to the van. With his hand on the headlight switch, he waited for the mirror to do its magic. It had already darkened, and the Earth Blue observatory floor vanished. Seconds later, the now-familiar crystal walkway appeared, swirling mist still bordering each side.

He searched the scene for any sign of stalkers. The walkway seemed clear. But would it be clear when they landed there? Would they be able to see this time? No doubt Kelly's vision would be fine, but what about his and Francesca's? She had the violin, but would he be able to play light into existence again?

He tightened his grip on the headlight's knob. There was only one way to find out. With a quick pull, the headlamps flashed on. The beams bounced off the reflective glass and created the familiar rainbow halo in front of the mirror. Multicolored light bathed Kelly and Francesca.

"Hurry up!" Kelly yelled, cradling the huge bow in her arms. "I can feel it taking us!"

Nathan reached across to the passenger seat and felt for his mirror square. It was gone! But where? He couldn't go without it. And what about the second one? It was probably in the back somewhere, hidden under the bags of food they had transferred from the car.

"Nathan! Hurry!"

He jerked out the keys, silencing the radio, then slapped the lights off. Just as the two girls began to fade within the halo, he leaped into the halo and grabbed Kelly's shoulder. Color splashed into his eyes, and the construction scene crumbled away, leaving behind a canopy of darkness.

A hint of moisture brushed across his face. "Kelly. Do you see anything?"

"Not yet." A slight groan stretched out her reply as she pulled away from him.

"Nor I," Francesca said. "But I know I've been here in my dreams. It feels the same."

Nathan rubbed his finger and thumb together. Wetness. He cringed. He had grabbed Kelly's wounded shoulder. No wonder she groaned. Obviously the bleeding was getting worse.

A glow appeared in the distance. Then, second by second, the darkness faded, revealing the seemingly endless walkway of the misty world. As before, music played in the air, the same sweet melody, and the harmony he had played to brighten the world was still intact.

"That's better," Nathan said. "Time to find the biggest violin in the universe."

"Wait!" Francesca pulled on Nathan's arm. "I can't see anything except beams of light coming from your eyes. Kelly's eyes, too."

Nathan peered at Francesca's pupils. They dilated and contracted as his gaze crossed hers. He listened again to the music. "Do you hear anything?"

"Yes. A voice singing a simple melody. Just notes. No words."

"Do you hear a harmony blending in? A second voice?"

She shook her head. "Only one voice."

"What key?"

She closed her eyes for a moment. "C Major."

He grasped her wrist and pushed the violin toward her chin. "The song asks a question. You have to play an answer."

She set the bow over the strings. "I think I understand."

Closing her eyes again, Francesca played. At first, her notes seemed out of key, certainly nothing close to C Major, but as she continued, her tune blended in, duplicating the harmonizing voice Nathan could already hear.

She opened her eyes, blinking, but said nothing as she increased to forte. Her eyes shifted back and forth as if following the path of a butterfly. Finally, she lowered the violin and winked. "You're a good teacher, Son."

He reached for the bow in Kelly's arms. "I'll lead the way, but you two stay close."

As he strode down the smooth walkway toward the fogbank in the distance, mist from the bordering rivers rose in columns and swirled at his side. Carrying the long bow made for an awkward march, but concentrating on keeping the two ends balanced helped distract him from the dangers that lay ahead. Still, questions lurked. Would the guards be at the doorway? What would he do when he arrived? The guards carried those sound-generating rods that really packed a wallop. Might there be a way to neutralize them?

Soon, he plunged into the fogbank. Now blinded by the soupy veil, he slowed his pace. The entry door to the chamber of domes would be too narrow for the bow, so he turned it ninety degrees and pressed on. The mist stayed thick, and as the path widened and the floor transformed to the rougher terrazzo, he slowed further and listened. Only the anxious breathing from the girls behind him reached his ears. Although his shoes stayed in plain sight, little else crossed his field of vision, only mist rising slowly in silent clouds of white. Under his shoes, the gemstones now seemed dull, unable to sparkle in the haze.

He stopped and stared in the direction he thought the supplicants had been before. Would there be any obstacles? Where had the stalkers gone? Could this be their night hours, and everyone had gone to bed? Still, wouldn't they post guards, knowing he had come before and might try to return?

Creeping slowly forward, he watched for the triad of domes. The outline of the closest one slowly came into view as well as the back of a lone male stalker who stood facing the glass, holding one of those sonic stun rods.

Nathan paused and set down the bow. Would he have to fight this guy? Why was he watching the dome? To call the others to form the circle, should Scarlet sing a prayer? Was he guarding all three domes, or was there another stationed at each of the other two, out of sight beyond the misty veil?

He pulled the girls into a huddle and whispered as softly as he could. "I'm going to try to take this guy out. If there are others, we'll take them on one at a time."

Still facing the dome, the stalker began to sing, a series of low vowel sounds that alternated between a long *A* and a long

O. It sounded more like a chant than a song, a report that weakened as it tried to pierce the soupy air.

Kelly whispered the translation. "The second hour ends. The third begins. All is well. All is well."

Another voice rang out, echoing the song of the first. Then a third crier repeated the call, but he added a different ending, and Kelly again provided the words. "The supplicants have opened the dream gates. Let us follow and discern their purpose."

Nathan pulled the girls close again. "Okay. There are three, but if they report every hour, maybe I can take out this one without a sound, and we'll have almost an hour to get to the violin and play it. With all the mist, the other two will never know what happened."

Francesca shook her head. "It won't work. You have to play the violin to open the stairway door."

"True." Nathan looked past the guard. Barely visible inside the dome, Scarlet sat upright with her head low and her arms wrapped around her knees.

He crept a few steps closer. If he could get her attention, maybe she could help. He waved a hand over his head, but she stayed perfectly still. The guard had mentioned that the supplicants had "opened the dream gates," so she must have been asleep, shutting out the surrounding prison that had left her in an eternal state of slavery.

Nathan rose to tiptoes and eased forward. It was time to act, now or never. When he came within reach, he paused. A strange sound emanated from the stalker, a slight wheeze accompanied by slow, rhythmic breaths. Was he asleep, too?

The final words of the third guard reentered his mind. Let us follow and discern their purpose.

He pumped his fist. Scarlet was helping after all. She and the other two supplicants were distracting the guards in the world of dreams.

Gesturing for the others to follow, Nathan sneaked past

the stalker and gazed into the dome. Scarlet, now easily visible, kept her face buried between her knees, her reddish locks draped over her arms. She trembled. Her head twitched. Yet, she stayed asleep.

Nathan waited for the girls to catch up, Kelly carrying the oversized bow and Francesca holding the violin. The threesome circled the dome and stepped into the enclosed triangle.

As before, the floor panel displayed a row of seven lights in the glass. With a misty cloud hovering over them, it reflected only their tired, anxious faces. "We don't have a tune playing in the air," Nathan said. "How are we going to figure out the code?"

Francesca readied the violin. "We'll just have to try every octave. Maybe we can figure out the code without waking them up."

She leaned close to the glass and played A through G, watching for a flashing light. When she hit the lowest D, the fourth light flashed red. With every rise in octave, a different light gave an identical signal.

Nathan glanced at the stalkers in turn. With eyes closed, they seemed mesmerized, as if lost in deep thought. The other two supplicants copied Scarlet's pose. They, too, displayed noticeable twitches, shaking off an occasional shiver as they dreamed on.

After playing the highest notes, Francesca ran through the pattern she had learned, using the proper octave for A, then for B, and so on. When the lights had returned to their white state, she played the notes again, turning the lights blue, then a third time to complete the unlocking procedure. As soon as the lights faded to black, the panel's reflection disappeared, revealing the dark stairwell.

Francesca stepped into the liquid glass and waved at Kelly. "Let Nathan take one end of the bow while you follow with the other end. We'll have to hurry to get the whole thing in before the door closes." She descended into the darkness.

Nathan grabbed the bow and backed down the stairs, keeping an eye on the surroundings. As Kelly shuffled forward, he pushed his way down. The glass seemed thicker with every step. When his head submerged, he broke into the clear, but as soon as Kelly's feet pushed through, she slowed to a trudge as if she were wading through tar.

Nathan pulled, threading the bow through his hands as Kelly descended. When she submerged up to her neck, she halted, apparently unable to go another inch. He laid the bow down, grabbed her around the waist, and kicked her feet out from under her. Then, pulling himself up, he hung on, hoping his own weight would be enough to draw her through. Slowly, very slowly, she descended. Her chest heaved, then froze as her face lowered into thickening glass, cutting off her air supply.

Francesca joined in, tugging on both bodies with all her might. Kelly popped through, and the three tumbled down the stony staircase. Nathan grabbed both girls and braced his feet and back against the sides of the corridor, stopping their fall.

Suppressing a groan, he struggled to his feet and helped Francesca up, then Kelly. He rubbed a scraped elbow through the sleeve. "Are you two okay?"

Kelly took in several deep breaths and nodded without a word, but she grimaced as she held a hand over her shoulder. Francesca extended the violin. One of the strings dangled, a curl of wire bouncing up and down underneath. She pulled it out and tossed it away. "The key will be tougher to play without that string."

"You'll adjust." Nathan picked up one end of the bow. "At least this isn't broken."

"Thank God for that," Francesca said.

He looked up through the glass door. No sign of stalkers. "We'd better get moving."

Francesca led the way, padding softly on the uneven steps. When she reached the dead end, she applied the key again, adjusting her fingers to play each note on the three remaining strings.

As before, a glow ate away the door. A light from the other side cast a dim wash over their bodies, allowing Nathan to set a hand on Kelly's good shoulder. "Watch your step. The next one's a real doozy."

16

HEALING MUSIC

Kelly peered down into the dark chasm, looking past a rope dangling from a pulley in front of her. "Whew! Good thing Daryl Blue isn't here to see this."

"Exactly why I wanted her to stay at the observatory." Nathan bit his lip. That came out more harshly than he had intended.

Francesca used the smaller bow to draw the rope into the corridor. "We have to be extra careful. It isn't a vision this time. No waking up if we fall."

Nathan shivered at the thought of plunging helplessly into the void. "Let's get going. Leave the big bow here for now." He pulled the basket to the top, got inside, and copied the lowering procedure he had used in the vision. It seemed odd that every sensation felt the same, the heavy weight of the loaded basket and the warming friction as the rope slid through his hands. Yet this time the lingering fear made his arms quiver.

Gritting his teeth, he focused on his father's words, a lesson that now seemed a century old. If you really believe you have an immovable foundation, even if you plunge through a thousand evils, you know you will eventually land in a place of safety. Courage isn't the absence of fear. It's the ability to control fear and do what you have to do in spite of it. If you have faith in the one who calls you to a task, you just do it and trust that he'll get you out of a jam.

After swinging over to the side of the chasm, he pulled the rope to send the basket back to the top.

Francesca's voice filtered to his level. "I'll go first," she said to Kelly. "Watch what I do." She climbed into the basket, waited for Nathan to lower her, and then worked with him to swing to the side. He glanced back at the iron hook in the wall, his anchor in case he couldn't hold the weight. If the rope slipped, at least they wouldn't fall forever.

After using the hooked rod to haul her in, he reeled the basket up again. Moving stiffly, Kelly copied Francesca's actions, and when all three stood safely on the ledge, Nathan let out a long breath and pointed at the violin strings spanning the chasm. "Can't play them without the bow."

Nathan climbed into the basket and, with the girls' help, hauled himself up. When he finally reached the stairwell he found the bow hanging over the doorway threshold. He fastened the rope around his waist, grabbed the bow, and balanced it on the top edge of the basket. Then, after loosening the rope again, he and the girls reeled him down. As soon as the basket reached a point just above the strings, he stopped its descent. "Okay," he called. "As soon as I tie myself in place, you two go to the fingerboard."

He looped the rope around his chest and fastened a double knot. Then, as if a child again on a playground swing set, he pushed his body against the basket and forced it into a slow swing, making the arc bigger and bigger as he continued to heave back and forth. Once he started playing the strings, he wouldn't be able to keep the momentum going, so he had to get as much amplitude as he possibly could.

As the basket swayed over the strings, he looked at the oversized fingerboard. Kelly sat in Francesca's lap. Their combined weights held down the string in the proper place to play the first note.

Taking a deep breath, Nathan grasped the bow with both hands and leaned heavily against the side of the basket, making it tip over. He pressed his feet against the sides to keep the basket in place and lowered the bow toward the string. Letting it rub gently, it played the first note of "Foundation's Key." A loud tone erupted from the string and reverberated through the chasm. The chamber's faint light strengthened. The walls shook. Rocks broke away and tumbled into the void.

As he swung back for the next note, he glanced at the girls. Fighting the quakes, they staggered to the proper string and pounced on it.

Now approaching the string, he pushed the bow down and stroked it smoothly. Again, the note echoed through the chamber and shook the walls, and again the girls rocked back and forth. With the chamber still brightening, the fear in their faces clarified. Francesca barked out their next position as they hurried to the third string.

The torturous process continued through the fourth, fifth, and sixth notes, until a shrill voice sang from above. Nathan glanced up. A stalker glared down at him, apparently cursing him in his strange musical tongue.

"No time to sing with you," Nathan mumbled. "I'm kind of busy."

As he swung back for a seventh note, a tug on the rope jerked him out of line, but he managed to adjust the bow's position enough to play the note. He looked up. Two stalkers pulled violently on the rope while a third looked on from behind. With a mighty heave, the two yanked again. The basket slipped away from Nathan's feet and shot toward the ceiling.

Still clutching the bow, he plunged feet first into the void. When the basket snagged on the pulley, the rope tightened with a twang, and the knot he had fashioned punched him in the solar plexus, knocking his breath away. The loop slid up his sides, ripping his skin before stopping at his underarms.

Trying to catch his breath, he looked all around. Above, the stalkers worked feverishly to jerk the basket loose and send

Nathan plummeting. Below, the dark reaches seemed just a bit brighter, a vague grayness.

Up at the ledge, Kelly held the loose rope that led to the anchor hook in one direction and down to Nathan in the other. She leaned over the chasm as far as she could. "Hang on! Francesca will talk to those idiots!"

Francesca played the smaller violin with a raging flare, scolding the stalkers with rapid-fire shots of squealing notes.

One of the stalkers sang in reply, an equally blistering volley of shrieks.

Kelly yelled the translation. "You fools are destroying our world! You will kill us all and ruin our escape plans!"

The knot that fastened the rope to Nathan's body slipped, loosening the loop around his chest. Still clutching the bow, he grabbed the line with his free hand. "Tell him their plans will kill billions of people!"

Francesca played the reply. The stalker spat out a quick retort and continued working on freeing the basket. Nathan held on tighter. If that crazy shrieker succeeded, the anchor hook would be the only thing keeping him from a final plunge.

Kelly cupped her hands around her mouth and shouted again. "He says, 'Who cares about your world?' He added a couple of other words, but I won't repeat them."

The knot unraveled. Just before the loop slipped away, Nathan dropped the bow and wrapped both hands in the rope. As the stalkers jostled his lifeline, he began to swing again. The rope slid through his fingers with every pass through the arc.

Above, Kelly kept her grip on the line that led from him to the loose coil on the ledge and then to the anchor. There was no way she would be able to haul him up, and, if the basket ripped away, he definitely didn't want to jerk her down with him. "Kelly! Let go of that rope! The hook should hold me if I fall."

Even as his words echoed around him, he wondered if he

could hold on if he fell far enough to reel out the slack between him and the anchor.

Kelly let go and stood next to Francesca, who continued assaulting the stalkers with frenetic notes. They ignored her and tore at the basket's wicker until it looked like shredded wheat. Suddenly, one of the stalkers tumbled into the void, then the other two followed. Flailing their arms, they plunged into darkness.

As Nathan swung to the side, one white-haired body zoomed past him, then another. The third one thrust out his hand and clawed Nathan's back, digging five sharp nails deeply before snagging his belt. The rope slid at least a foot in Nathan's grip. Blood seeped between his fingers, but the loop around his knuckles drew tight, halting his fall.

The stalker, now hanging on by one hand, flapped an arm, reaching for the rope with his other hand, but it kept jerking away as the two fought for position.

Nathan kicked savagely at the stalker's body, then tried to plant a foot on his shoulder. As they struggled, Nathan caught a glimpse of his face—Tsayad, the same stalker who had greeted them on their first visit. At that time, he had seemed like a friendly host, but now he was the grim reaper. The result of this meeting would be "kill or be killed."

Finally, Nathan shoved his heel into Tsayad's neck and pushed with all his might. The stalker's gripping fingers stretched out, and he slipped away, screaming a cacophonous song as he vanished into the grayness below.

Nathan regripped the rope and looked up. Daryl stood at the edge of the doorway, frantically trying to pull the basket down as it continued to rip against the pulley.

"Daryl! How did you—"

"Never mind that!" she shouted. "Can Kelly and Francesca pull you up? I won't be heavy enough to counter your weight!"

Nathan looked at his torn hands. Blood streamed down his

forearms as he called back. "They're at the other end of the rope. I would have to change my grip, and I'm not sure I can without falling."

"Should I try to find a winch of some kind?"

"No time!" Kelly screamed. "Swing him toward me!"

Daryl grasped the rope and worked it back and forth. Nathan timed her efforts and helped from his end. Soon, he could touch the sheer walls on each side, still far below Kelly's level.

Kelly picked up the hooking pole and fished for the rope but couldn't quite reach it. She dropped to her stomach and extended as far as she could. As he swung to the opposite side, Nathan could see Francesca sitting between Kelly's legs, gripping one with each arm. As she pushed Kelly farther out, she yelled. "Don't worry! I've got you!"

Finally, Kelly snagged the rope. "Pull me back!"

Nathan tried to watch their efforts, but as Kelly eased back up on the ledge, all he could see was the rope hooked in the pole and Kelly's and Francesca's fingers wrapped around the end. As they pulled, Nathan tried to push his shoes against the wall and climb, but his toes couldn't catch hold of any crevices. With rivulets of blood now pouring into his sleeves, he couldn't hold out much longer.

With Francesca still holding on to the rope, Kelly leaped out, grabbed it, and began to climb toward the top. Gripping with hands and crossed legs, she slowly inched upward, the sounds of gentle grunts making their way down to Nathan's ears as she huffed and puffed.

Nathan held his breath. With her shoulder so badly wounded, how could she possibly make that climb? The pain had to be pure torture.

Daryl, now on her knees, reached out a hand, but Kelly was still far below ... struggling, grunting ... gaining a foot or two, then sliding down a few inches before battling again to regain lost ground.

"Come on, Kelly-kins!" Daryl yelled. "You can do it!"

The mystery of Daryl's presence rushed back into Nathan's brain. Had she already rescued her uncle? With time racing so quickly on Earth Yellow, that made sense. Apparently Dr. Simon had kept his word and allowed her to join them. It was a good thing! Without her kicking the three stalkers over the edge, he would have been done for.

The seconds dragged on. Kelly inched upward, slowing as she neared the top. Finally, Daryl thrust a hand down and jerked her to safety in the stairwell. Kelly struggled to her feet, whirled back toward the rope, and, with Daryl hanging on to her waist, leaned back over the void. She grabbed the remnants of the basket and jumped out over the chasm. Their combined weights lifted Nathan upward. At the ledge down below, Francesca reeled the line through her hands, guiding him to her, while Kelly and Daryl sank toward the violin strings.

Even from where he dangled, Nathan could see Daryl's terrified eyes, but she managed to keep her body relatively calm, just a few weak kicks with her feet as she struggled to hang on to Kelly's waist.

When he came within reach, Francesca clutched his shirt with one hand and hoisted him to safe footing. Still holding on to the rope, he spun around and helped Francesca pull. They stopped Kelly and Daryl's slow descent. The two girls hung over the void, their bodies twisting as they swung back and forth. With each pass, their feet swept just inches over the violin strings. The basket, now torn to shreds, fell away piece by piece until it was gone.

With Francesca standing in front of him, Nathan pulled the rope, but it slid through his bloody hands. They were too wet and pain-racked to hang on.

Francesca kept a firm grip. "We can do this!" she yelled. Inch by inch they managed to haul Daryl and Kelly a foot higher.

"Hang on!" Kelly yelled. "We'll swing toward you!"

Nathan tried to ignore the blood still dripping from his throbbing hands. "When they get close to this side, we'll have to let out line to lower them to the ledge."

Francesca nodded, grunting. Sweat streamed down her cheeks and dampened her collar. As she and Nathan pulled and released, Kelly and Daryl swung precariously, coming closer and closer to the ledge with each cycle. Twenty feet away. Fifteen feet away. Ten.

"Almost here!" Francesca yelled. "A couple more times ought to do it!"

Nathan glanced at the hooked pole. That would help, but could he grab it without letting go of the rope? He shook his head. It wasn't worth the risk.

As the two girls swung away again, Daryl stared wild-eyed at the void below. When they passed over the center, her dangling feet brushed one of the strings, playing a loud, vibrating note. Again, the echoes bounced off the walls. The floor shook and buckled beneath their feet.

Francesca dropped to her knees and lost her hold on the rope. Nathan tightened his grip and looped his legs around Francesca's torso, anchoring him in place. He had to elevate them! Fast!

Flexing his muscles, he pulled with all his might. Pain shot through his torn hands. Once again, the rope slipped through the blood. Daryl smacked into the strings, tearing her loose from Kelly. As Kelly continued on her arc toward the ledge, Daryl clutched a violin string with one hand, her legs kicking wildly over the void. "Kelly! Help me!"

Francesca climbed to her feet and held the rope again. With the pressure lessened, Nathan snatched up the hook and reached for Kelly. She swiped it away and, after sliding down to a knot, she held on with one hand and swung back toward Daryl. She reached down and grabbed a string. It stretched for a second, then pulled her back to the center. Still holding on to the rope, Kelly released the string and snagged a fistful of Daryl's shirt.

"I've got you!" Kelly yelled. "Let go!"

"I can't! I'll fall!"

"You won't fall! I won't let you fall!"

"You can't hold my weight with one hand! Your shoulder's hurt!"

Kelly grunted so loud, her voice seemed to shake the floor. "You just ... have to ... trust me!"

"I can't!" Daryl stared down at the void again and shook her head frantically. "I just can't!"

Kelly looked at Nathan, her eyes wild. "Pull us up! I'll have to jerk her loose!"

Nathan strained against the rope. "How about if we set you down on the strings?"

"No! This one's about to break! I don't think it will hold us."

Nathan and Francesca pulled. Kelly rose, still clutching Daryl's shirt. For a moment, the shirt slipped up over her head, exposing a thin camisole underneath as well as her waist, but when it caught under her arms, she began to rise. As her waist elevated to the string's level, she hung on, halting her progress and stretching the string upward.

"Let go!" Kelly screamed. "You're slipping!"

Daryl said nothing. Her face as taut as the string, she just hung on.

Kelly turned again to Nathan. "Give us a hard pull!"

"No!" Daryl shouted. "I'll let go!" She closed her eyes, then, after taking a deep breath, released the string. Kelly shot up, Daryl still in her grip. The string let out a thunderous twang. The walls and floor responded with a jolt that rocked the entire foundation.

Nathan and Francesca fell on their backsides. The rope reeled through their fingers, but Nathan twisted his hand and caught the line, jerking the girls to a stop.

Daryl's shirt slipped over her head, leaving it flapping in Kelly's hand. Daryl plummeted into the darkness, screaming, "Kelly!"

"Oh my God!" Kelly's call stretched out, loud and wailing. "Daryl!"

Francesca struggled to her feet and buried her face in her hands. "Oh, Lord! Have mercy!"

Nathan, now holding Kelly's weight by himself, called out, his voice shaking as the ground settled. "Swing back, before you fall, too!"

Sobbing, Kelly began swinging the rope, her gaze fixed on the void. As she neared the ledge, Nathan pulled her into a final swing. She let go of the rope and landed gracefully. She fell to her knees and banged her fists on the ground, one hand still hanging on to Daryl's shirt. "Why did you let this happen?" she screamed. "Why?"

Francesca stooped and rubbed Kelly's back, but she said nothing.

Nathan looped the rope around the pole and fell to the ground next to Kelly. He reached out to touch her head, but drew his hand back as blood dripped to the rocky floor. She, too, dripped blood from one hand. A path of dark red dampened her sweatshirt at the shoulder and stretched down her arm.

Nathan tightened his jaw. They couldn't wait. No matter how terrible it was to lose Daryl, they had to go on. As bile rushed into his throat, he tried to spit out his thoughts. "We have to get back," he whispered. "There's no telling when more stalkers might show up."

Francesca laid a hand on his knee. "Give her a minute. She just lost her best friend."

"She wasn't my friend!" Kelly threw the shirt at Nathan. "That was Daryl Blue!"

Nathan picked up the shirt, sky blue and spattered with Kelly's blood. As he lifted it closer to his eyes, he choked up.

How could that be? When she stood up on that stairwell and tried to pull the rope, she must have been out of her mind with fear. Then she grabbed Kelly's waist, jumped over the pit, and helped pull him to safety. It must have been like a thousand nightmares at once. A tear welled in his eye and spilled down to his cheek. He whispered to himself, "But she did it anyway."

Kelly continued, spasms rocking her voice. "She knew ... the 'Moonlight Sonata' ... would bring her ... to this place. She must have ... followed the stalkers ... through the door."

Francesca looked up at Nathan. "Maybe she found out Daryl Red had to leave, so she decided to take her place."

He nodded, a grim heaviness weighing down his shoulders. He wanted to kick himself in the teeth. For a moment, finding out the victim was Daryl Blue instead of Daryl Red had been a relief. But what kind of idiot would have a thought like that? He had brushed her away because of her phobia, and now she was gone. She had battled her fears, only to fall prey to the very phantom that had stalked her. And was she still falling now? Was this a bottomless chasm that would keep her plunging, trapping her in a nightmare that would never, ever end?

Nathan bit his lip hard. He had been such a jerk! Daryl lost her life saving an insensitive moron.

After taking a deep breath, he shook his head hard. No time for this. Jerk or no jerk, they had to move. He pulled on Kelly's arm. "I'm sorry. We have to go. I don't know why we don't already have a bunch of stalkers screaming their fool heads off from those stairs."

Kelly didn't resist. She rose and looked up at the stairwell, her eyes red as she wiped tears from her cheeks. "Who goes first?"

Francesca grasped Nathan's forearms and turned his palms up. "You can't pull anyone with these."

"Loop the rope around my wrists, and you can tie it around your waist. I can walk away from the ledge and haul you up one at a time. While the first one goes up, the other can help me while down here, then the first one can pull from the top to help with the other one."

Kelly sniffed and wiped her nose. "And then we'll pull you up together."

After successfully completing their plan, the three tiptoed up the stairs, Nathan in the lead, followed by Kelly, then Francesca, the violin once again in her grasp. When he reached the transparent door, he peered out. With heavy mist still draping the world above, the outer walls of the domes were barely visible, and no one was in sight.

Francesca replayed the key. Nathan climbed the remaining steps, pushing through the glass until he emerged at the surface. While Kelly and Francesca exited, he looked around. Everything seemed exactly the same. Scarlet and her supplicant counterparts slept, still twitching from time to time, while the rest of the world likely slumbered.

Nathan laid a hand on Scarlet's dome. Could the supplicants be keeping the entire population asleep somehow? Should he try to wake her up to ask, or would that ruin everything?

Kelly tugged on his shirt and pointed at the wall. "Check it out."

He glanced up. Earth Red, now barely visible through the mist, had changed. Fewer orange and purple stains blemished the surface. Many of the cracks between it and Earths Blue and Yellow had thinned out, and only fine streams of mixed colors ran through the channels.

"I guess we did some good," Francesca said. "But was it worth it?"

"And that choir from hell will just undo what we did." Nathan stooped and tried to push his fingers under the dome but couldn't find a gap. He heaved an exasperated sigh. It was too risky to wake Scarlet, but how else could they rescue her?

Kelly crouched at his side. "Let's just ask Scarlet what to do ... the safe way."

"The safe way?"

She lay down on the hard floor. "Let's enter the dream world and see if she'll talk to us there."

He spread out his hands. "Sleep? Here? You gotta be kidding!"

"Aren't you exhausted? You can probably go to sleep if you try."

"Go ahead, Nathan," Francesca said. "I'll keep watch. If anything happens, I'll wake you up."

As he lay next to Kelly, she took his hand. Her grip hurt his wounded palm, but he didn't pull away. "My mind's racing so fast, I don't see how—"

"Shhhh ..." Francesca raised the violin. "Just close your eyes and relax."

Nathan clenched his eyelids shut. As Francesca began playing, he tried to erase his thoughts, but his mind swam through a dizzying swirl of primary colors, oversized violins, and dark chasms. The sight of Daryl's terrified face shattered the swirl and smoldered across his memory like a sizzling hot brand.

Francesca's tune shifted to the first measures of "Brahms' Lullaby," the same piece his real mother had used to settle his mind on so many nights. She hummed along, adding words to her soothing voice, now deepening into his mother's lovely contralto. "Nathan, my darling, you are brave and worthy. You are a valiant warrior, and you have fought with all your might, but now you need to rest. Shut out the failures, for they are in the past and cannot be changed. Let the worries of the next battle slip away, for it is in the misty future, a time unknown."

The sound of Kelly's heavy breathing blended in with the lovely tones and his mother's gentle voice.

"Go now to be with Kelly. She waits for you in the land of dreams. She calls for you there, an entreaty from her heart that someday you will answer in the fullness of love. Yet, for now, take her hand and travel to that world. Your wounds will not suffer at her touch, and the journey of rest will make you strong."

Francesca's voice faded. The swirling colors again appeared in his mind. They slowed and took shape, creating the form of Kelly reaching for him. He extended his hand. She grabbed it and pulled. Letting himself fall toward the colors, he splashed into the painting and felt himself blending in with the artwork in a seated position.

As his eyes adjusted, he scanned the area. Kelly sat next to him, her arms wrapped around her upright knees. Sitting across from them, Scarlet took the same pose, her bare feet touching Nathan's shoes. The mirrored walls of the supplicant's dome reflected their seated forms.

Scarlet smiled. "Welcome, my love. You were wise to visit me in this manner."

17

A SCARLET DREAM

Nathan glanced at Kelly, then cleared his throat and met Scarlet's wide-eyed gaze. "Are you and the other supplicants keeping the stalkers busy?"

"Yes. Cerulean, Amber, and I have engaged them in a more direct battle than usual. Even though many of them know that they are really asleep, they will not soon back down from the challenges we have delivered. When it comes to dream stalking, they are a proud people."

Nathan set his finger on the terrazzo floor. "So, if you're in a battle, how are you here?"

"It is part of the strategy. The stalkers lost three of their warriors, so I excused myself to make it a fair fight, a battle of song taking place in another part of this realm. I hoped all along you would join me, so it works out perfectly." She rose to her knees and, laying her hands on Nathan's shoulders, kissed him on the cheek. "I know what you have done. Repairing the cosmic fabric is a violent affair, and you took great risks. If not for the ongoing battle in the land of dreams, a cadre of stalkers would have awakened to join the three guards, and they would have killed you all."

She settled back to her seat. "I also know what you have lost. We realize that the suffering of the few is often necessary to end the suffering of the many, but that does little to ease your pain. Even as I heard Kelly's cries from the heart of Sarah's Womb, I felt remorse for asking my beloved to rescue me."

"Your beloved?" Kelly said. "You mean, Nathan?"

"Yes, and even using these words of endearment seems so selfish to me now. He is my beloved, because I have become his supplicant, his prayer mistress, the one who would give her life for him if need be. Yet, you, Kelly Clark, might well see my words as romantic advances, mere flirtations or tokens of superficial lust. If I have caused you any emotional turmoil, I beg your forgiveness. There is no such intention in my mind."

Lowering her head, Kelly nodded. For a moment, she said nothing, but she finally whispered, "I forgive you."

Scarlet scooted closer and leaned her head against Kelly's. "Alas! Even my confession has brought you grief. I sit as a prisoner in a crystal, and even in my sleep I have inflicted pain. I have asked for forgiveness, and I have aroused guilt. I am called to be a rescuer, but I have begged for rescue and have thereby heightened my beloved's danger. Instead of seeking deliverance at his peril, I should rather be content to suffer at his hands."

Nathan glanced at his blood-smeared palms. "Suffer at my hands? Why?" Even as he spoke, the words of Patar drifted back into his mind. *To heal the wounds and bring the crisis to an end, return to the misty world and slay the supplicants. Cast their bodies into the widening abyss, and harmony will be restored.* Did Scarlet know?

She pulled back from Kelly. "You have healed many wounds today, Nathan, but until the breach is sealed, the stalkers will be able to continue their assault with their machine." Her countenance turned grim. "I take it that you have not seen Lucifer yet."

"Mictar said something about it, and so did Cerulean. Is that the name of the machine?"

She nodded. "It transforms energy into a force that degrades the dark matter in the cosmos and tears apart the fabric that separates the dimensions. The stalkers use me and my fellow supplicants to transform our harmonic prayers into dissonance, dark energy that will feed their destructive machine. Yet, how can I cease praying for my beloved just because someone uses my good for his evil purposes?"

"How long has this been going on?" Kelly asked.

"Mictar has been feeding and testing Lucifer for centuries, always looking for a breach in the barrier between this world and the three earths. He finally was able to penetrate a small rift and complete his plan."

Kelly's face turned pale. "Why hasn't he used the machine already?"

"He needs a catalyst, the purest of energies, the gift of light and life."

As memories of Mictar's electrified hand returned, Nathan shuddered. "People's eyes?"

"Not the eyes themselves. They are but a spiritual channel to the soul. He absorbs the essence of light and life through the eyes, but the process destroys them. When he returns to this realm, he will feed Lucifer with the stolen energy, but he needs a special catalyst to create the final chain reaction that could very well complete the process we call interfinity."

"But he had a chance to steal my mother's life essence, and he didn't. He kept her alive to learn the secret of Quattro."

A loving smile emerged on Scarlet's face. "A demonstration of his one weakness, my darling—hunger for power. He doesn't know that I help you through the mirror. He only knows that it has power that has thwarted his efforts, and he wants it. It hasn't occurred to him that the supplicants would aid people with no thought of reward. He has no concept of a selfless act, so he likely believes the mirror you have been carrying has power in and of itself. Still, I wonder if he yet had a plan for your mother. With his lust for life energy, I cannot understand how he resisted taking such a powerful force as hers."

"What would happen if he got hold of one of the mirrors?" Kelly asked.

Scarlet's smile wilted. "If he were to handle one of the mirrors a gifted one has used, he would be able to see a supplicant through it and learn the power behind Quattro. If Nathan of Earth Red was the last to use it, the mirror would maintain an energy channel directly to me. Mictar would be able to use his own power to reach into it and kill me. I would not be able to defend myself."

"If he wanted to kill you," Nathan said, "why hasn't he done it already? You're just sitting here under this dome. Couldn't he reach you whenever he wanted?"

"If he were to physically attack me, he knows that I would be more than his match. You see, the stalkers did not put me here to keep me from escaping the misty world." Scarlet gave him a sly wink. "They put me here to protect themselves."

Nathan raised his eyebrows. "To protect themselves?"

"Yes, my love. Listen and learn." Scarlet lifted her gaze toward the ceiling and hummed. Then, as her hum grew louder, she formed soft words that blended into her tune as perfectly as a fragrance in a gentle breeze.

> To supplicate, meditate, ruminate,
> 'Tis a cut by knife, a lonely life, filled with strife.
> I can never be a mother; I can never be a wife.
> I can only be a servant whose heart with love is rife.
> But in my supplications, in songs for precious few,
> I bare Shekhinah glory, and pass it on to you.

At that point, a sudden radiance flashed. Scarlet's body brightened, the purest white light pouring from her skin, eyes, and hair. As she raised her hands, the light spread throughout the dome and covered Nathan with sparkles that tickled his skin.

Scarlet continued her song, beginning the tune again.

> To activate, animate, initiate,
> A kingly heir, the faith you wear, a life of prayer,

You must never fear the darkness, you must never breed despair.
You must lift your hand toward heaven and give up all your care.
And in your supplications to the king in whom you trust,
You take this glory in your hands and rise up from the dust.

The radiance began to fade. Scarlet's song reverted to humming with a few soft words sprinkled in.

"Never doubt ... Never fear ... Never give in ... I am always near."

When the light finally dimmed, Scarlet's lips formed a gentle smile. "The stalkers know that we are more powerful than they, so they used deception to lure us into a trap. The dome contains my energy and prevents me from harming them and them from harming me. But if Mictar learns about the mirror's path to my heart, he can absorb my power and kill me."

"And feed Lucifer," Nathan said.

"And that is a purpose we must stop at all costs. As I said before, the suffering of the few is often necessary to stop the suffering of the many, so it would be better for all if you were to kill us and end the madness of the stalkers. Yet, if Mictar is the one who takes my heart, he will gain so much energy, he will likely become so powerful that no one can stop him."

She unfastened the top button on the front of her dress. "Here. Let me show you."

"Wait." Nathan held up his hand. "Don't do that. I don't need to see—"

"See what, Nathan?" She moved her fingers to the second button but left it fastened. "Surely you don't think I am making romantic advances, do you?"

"Uh ... well ... I'm not sure what I was thinking. It's just that I shouldn't look at—"

"My heart?" Sadness wilted her expression. "Nathan, if you are to defeat the stalkers, you must recognize that you are in a prison of your own making. Just as surely as I sit in a dome of glass, you have constructed walls round about you. You think you are heeding your father's will, yet you are following edicts chiseled in stone rather than the love written on his heart. If you will defeat the stalkers, you must learn this soon, for a time will come when you will face a far more daunting obstacle than your sense of propriety regarding what lies behind my buttons, and you will need my heart to overcome it." She pulled her lapels apart, popping the buttons loose. Underneath, a void appeared—no skin, bones, or arteries, just a red heart floating in the midst of darkness, throbbing faster every second. "You see, Nathan, there is nothing impure in my actions, for a heart of love is all I really am."

As if powered by her inner light, a red glow pulsed from her skin with every beat of her heart. "I am called to die, Nathan. I should never have tempted you to think otherwise."

Nathan could barely breathe. His own heart beat exactly in time with hers, and so hard it seemed to be pushing up into his throat. He glanced at Kelly. She also seemed transfixed by the sight. After forcing in some air, he managed to talk without squeaking. "There has to be a way to save the world and you with it."

"There is." She pulled his hand into the void. "Take hold of my heart, Nathan, for it is the only way to absorb the energy you will need."

Nathan gasped. Again, he could barely breathe. His entire body shaking, he spat out, "You ... you mean ... grab it?"

She kept a firm grip on his wrist. "Yes, Nathan. Feel the rhythm that drives the music within and fuels the eternal song that lifts psalms for deliverance for your sake and for the sake of those you love."

As he wrapped his fingers around her heart, hot flashes stormed through his body. Yet, the heat didn't come from within his own body; it streamed directly from hers. While the warm organ throbbed in his grip, music flowed as well. Hundreds, maybe even thousands of songs permeated his mind all at once, arias with words he couldn't understand, yet so lovely they brought tears to his eyes.

One recognizable phrase burned in his mind, "Bound forever, God I feel it, sealed with fire to the one I love. Now even in the darkest of places, I will be ready to hear your call."

Still keeping her hand on his wrist, she drew to within inches of his face and whispered, "This is only a dream, but you will remember this touch forever. When we finally meet in reality, you will know what to do." She touched her lips to his, then exhaled her sweet-smelling breath into his lungs.

An electric jolt threw him back. Kelly caught him in her arms and set him upright. Panting, he looked again at Scarlet. Within the void, her heart, now imprinted with blood from his hand, slowed its beating until it stopped. Then, with her head bowed to rebutton her dress, her eyes shifted toward him, a gentle smile again growing on her face. "You have no reason to feel guilt, my love, for this is only a dream, and my real heart has not stopped beating."

Nathan looked at his bloody palm, but he couldn't tell if the touch had added any marks that weren't already there. "Why did you do that? What does it all mean?"

"Just remember that my heart is available should you need it." Scarlet looked up at her low ceiling as if trying to pierce the mirrors with her gaze. "I sense a great danger, like a fleeting shadow that disappears when you look for its source. Although you have not seen him recently, Mictar has not been resting. I fear that he has prepared an evil surprise for you, and you may well apply what you have learned sooner than you wish."

Kelly, too, looked at their reflections above. "What should we do now?"

"Cerulean, Amber, and I will keep the stalkers occupied long enough for you to escape. Daryl Blue left the portal open to the Earth Blue observatory, and you will find that passage at the point where you arrived earlier." Scarlet's voice dropped to a whisper. "But use it with care. If the observatory is empty, then it is safe to pass through. Otherwise, you must seek another route."

Nathan drew an image of the observatory in his mind. With Daryl Blue gone, no one was there to watch for intruders.

"Once you awaken," Scarlet continued, "you must hurry. You have slowed interfinity's approach, but when the stalkers awaken, they will be sure to redouble their tortures in the dreams of mankind and use the supplicants to once again scourge the interstitial fabric. Although they fear Sarah's Womb, they will likely station guards there to abort any new attempt to play the birthing song. I suggest that you do whatever is in your power and imagination to locate Nathan's father."

Nathan swallowed hard, his voice agitated. "But how? And what could my father do?"

She touched her chest, now covered by her buttoned dress. "He knows what must be done. If you are unwilling, then perhaps he will find the courage to complete the task."

Nathan clenched his fist, but the pain in his palm forced him to relax. He soothed his tone. "I'll be back, but it won't be to kill you. If I can't figure out how to save the three of you and the universe at the same time, maybe this universe really isn't worth saving."

Scarlet's eyebrows lifted. "Is that so? We are merely supplicants who live to serve others. Would you risk the universe to save three insignificant souls?"

Nathan swallowed again. He wanted to say he would, but something in her voice told him it would be stupid to answer right away.

She returned her gaze to the ceiling. Nathan followed her stare. The mirror above now showed a launch pad and a space shuttle blasting off in an explosion of fire and plumes of vapor.

Nathan felt his breath being sucked away again. Although he

had watched this scene a dozen times on various documentaries, he couldn't break free from its hold. Kelly gripped his arm, her nails digging in, but he ignored the pain.

The shuttle turned slowly, arcing upward and leaving behind a trail of frozen cotton. As the sun reflected off its pristine white shell, the hypersonic craft soared across a blue canopy, carrying seven intrepid souls into the great beyond. Then, in an enormous billowing cloud of white, the craft blew into pieces. The smoke trail split into twin columns, and dozens of white streamers rained upon the earth.

Nathan jerked his head down and closed his eyes. Dr. Simon had failed. Even with all his intelligence and planning, he couldn't prevent the tragedy.

Kelly massaged his arm, soothing the slight abrasions she had inflicted, but they were nothing compared to the lacerations in his heart. He glared at Scarlet, anger scalding his senses, but he couldn't speak the rage in his gut. It wasn't hers to bear. It was his alone. He was the one who had decided to forsake the seven souls.

He exhaled heavily and shook his head. "I see your point."

Scarlet gazed at him stoically, a tear streaming down her cheek. "If you still want me to watch over you, you will have to retrieve one of the mirrors." Her body seemed to slowly vaporize. The sound of "Brahms' Lullaby" filtered in. "My dearest one, my beloved, I desire always to be at your side." Her body slowly faded. "But that is up to you."

He reached for her, but his hand passed through hers. "Yes," he called. "Stay beside me. Always."

A thin smile appeared on her transparent face, but then, alarm. "He is coming! Wake up!" She disappeared, and everything turned black.

Nathan flinched. Something touched his head. As he blinked, the violin grew louder.

"When will they wake up?" someone asked—a female voice, anxious and familiar.

The violin stopped. "I hear something. We'd better get going."

As the distant sounds of stalkers' songs seeped into his consciousness, Nathan opened his eyes. Daryl knelt over him, a worried look on her face. He glanced at her collar, a pink collar at the top of her reddish shirt. "How'd you get here?" he asked.

"Film at eleven." She grabbed his elbow and hoisted him to his feet, the mirror square in her hand.

Nathan stared at it. It had to be the one he wasn't able to find on the seat of the van. Why had she taken it without asking? He shook his head to scatter the cobwebs from his mind. That question could wait.

"We'd better scoot before the paparazzi show up," Daryl said.

Francesca helped Kelly to her feet, and as they turned toward the mist that shrouded the exit door, Nathan stared at Scarlet's dome. She stood at the glass and gazed at him, her eyes wide. He turned slowly around. Cerulean, now on his feet, watched from the edge of his dome. Amber, too, had awakened. With blonde hair draping her arms, she pressed her palms on the glass and stared.

As Nathan crept close to Scarlet's dome, she mouthed, "I love you."

She touched the top button of her dress but left it fastened and drew as close to the glass as the curved dome would allow. She pressed her hand against her chest in the same place he had seen her beating heart.

He laid his hand on the glass, then removed it, leaving a red imprint. Tears welled as he replied, "I love you, too."

"Nathan!" Kelly hissed. "Someone's coming!"

With the chaotic songs drawing closer, Nathan backed away

slowly. Scarlet, too, backed away, sliding her feet toward the center of her prison.

"Nathan!"

After a final nod, he whirled around and grabbed Kelly's hand. "Let's go!"

The four plunged into the mist. Nathan strained to see through the cloud, but it was too thick. He bent over and stared at the floor, allowing the now familiar patterns in the terrazzo to guide him toward the exit. When they finally burst into the clear, they sprinted down the glassy walkway, Nathan and Kelly in front, Daryl and Francesca behind, Francesca still carrying the violin and bow.

"Can you tell where we came in?" Kelly asked, puffing as she ran.

"If Daryl Blue left it open, like Scarlet said, maybe it will be obvious."

Something tugged Nathan's shirt from behind. "Daryl Blue was here?"

Nathan slowed to a halt and turned around. Daryl Red's curious gaze demanded an answer. "Yeah." He hesitated for a moment, his throat tightening. "She was here."

"Where is she now?"

Nathan looked over Daryl's shoulder. No one was coming. He could barely spit out the words. "She fell into the void. She's gone."

Daryl covered her mouth. Her face twisted, and she leaned her forehead on Nathan's chest. "No, no, no! It can't be! Now everyone we know on Earth Blue is dead!" She wailed something unintelligible, then wept uncontrollably.

He patted her on the back of the head. His hand trembled so hard, he wondered if he was offering any comfort at all. With all the tragedies, how could he say anything that would bring solace? Yet, there was one possibility. Her lament was partially true—Nathan, Kelly, Tony, and Daryl of Earth Blue were dead, but one remained. Maybe that reminder would help. "Clara Blue's still alive," he said softly.

Daryl cried harder. Her voice squeaked as she wagged her head. "She's dead, too. Mictar showed up at the Earth Blue observatory. That must be why Daryl Blue came here. She had to escape Mictar."

Kelly took Daryl's hand. "How did you find out?" she asked.

Daryl sniffed, wiped her nose with her sleeve, and forced a steady voice. "When we got back to the mirror at Interfinity Labs, we called up Earth Red first. Dr. Gordon had seen the attack and told us that Daryl Blue escaped. But she couldn't stop Mictar from killing Clara."

Nathan shook his head. Too much death. Way too much. And no time to cry. "Were you able to save your uncle?"

"Actually, he dreamed about the crash, so it was easy to convince him not to fly. He said he would risk facing the consequences in tonight's dream." She held up the mirror. "I wanted to try to use this so Dr. Simon would be satisfied and let me come and find you, but since I was willing to save my uncle, and he felt so bad about Clara, he let me come."

"I guess Mictar didn't consider one death a big disaster, so he didn't bother to stop the dream." Nathan looked at his face in the mirror—dirty and worn out. But this was no time to rest. They had to find the portal and get moving before the stalkers figured out where they went. Scarlet probably couldn't hold them off for long. He marched forward. "Let's go. It can't be much farther."

When he reached a point where the mist cleared on one side, he nodded at the exposed chasm. "This must be it."

Kelly lowered herself to her hands and knees. "I can see the observatory floor. No sign of Mictar. I don't see any movement at all."

Nathan took her hand and hoisted her up. Her keen eyesight

in this world had helped once again. "I guess that means it's safe," he said.

"So what do we do?" Daryl asked, setting her toes on the edge. "Jump in?"

"Right. Just like before."

She looked at him. "Like before?"

"Don't worry. It was painless, remember? We—" He stopped and shook his head. That was Daryl Blue before. Of course this Daryl wouldn't remember, and she wouldn't be afraid of heights either. He let out a silent sigh. The thought of Daryl Blue's sacrifice again tore at his heart. It was at this very spot that he had given her such a hard time for being scared, and what had she given him in exchange? Her life.

Swallowing back a sob, he embraced Daryl and kissed her on the cheek. She returned the hug, rubbing his back, then scratching it gently. When he pulled away, she tilted her head, her green eyes sparkling. "Not that I didn't get a kick out of the hug, but what was it for?"

Nathan could barely speak. "Because you're just like Daryl Blue."

Francesca turned toward the chamber of domes. "I hear something. A stalker's song. Coming this way."

Nathan waved for everyone to gather together. "Let's do it."

Without another word, the four joined hands, lined up at the edge of the walkway, and leaped into the void. Blackness engulfed their bodies, yet only a slight breeze wafted upward as they fell, far softer than a normal plunge would have brought. When the darkness melted away, replaced by the observatory's telescope room, Nathan swung his head back and forth. With every light off except for a single desk lamp, his eyes couldn't pick up much more than shadows. "See anything, Kelly?"

"This is Earth Blue," she replied. "I'm sort of blind again."

Nathan shuffled toward the computer desk. "C'mon, Daryl. First things first."

Her voice trailed behind him. "What's first?"

"Contact Gunther. We have to send Francesca back. He can pick up her and the van at the observatory."

"You mean if the van's still there. Who knows how much time has passed on Earth Yellow?" Daryl sat at the desk and pecked at the laptop keyboard, speaking her message as she typed. "Hey, Tony! It's Daryl. How're those biceps doing? Listen, if Gunther hasn't already dreamed what I'm typing, tell him to get his butt to the observatory. His van might still be there." She looked up at Nathan. "Anything else?"

Nathan reached into his pocket and jingled the keys. "We'll send the keys with Francesca."

Daryl typed the final words and clicked the send button. Almost instantly a new message popped into her inbox.

While Kelly and Francesca gathered around, Nathan leaned over Daryl's shoulder and read out loud. "This is Gunther at Tony's place. I already retrieved my van, but I will start toward the observatory right away. I have been in touch with Dr. Simon, so I have learned more about the interfinity crisis. It's strange, though, ever since the Challenger disaster, the dream problem has faded considerably, so life is starting to get back to normal. Now everyone's arguing about why a space shuttle explosion could make a difference. No need to write back. I'll probably be an hour down the road by the time you finish reading this. I'll pick up Dr. Malenkov on the way. He misses Francesca terribly. By the way, Tony's already engaged to Kelly's mother, so that's worth celebrating. Now we just have to get Francesca and Solomon together. I tracked him down at Tony's college and had lunch with him. Wow! What a cool guy! But he's so smart, I feel like a jackass around him. See you soon, I hope. By the way, you left the camera in the van. I'll take good care of it."

Nathan grinned. Just hearing about Solomon Shepherd in college gave him a warm feeling inside, even if it wasn't his real father. That meant they might meet on Earth Yellow someday. That would be cool.

"So," Francesca said, leaning closer to read the text. "You're uprooting me from this great adventure and sending me to marry a man I have never met?" She pointed at herself. "Don't forget that I have lost two years in Earth Yellow time. I'm not old enough to get married."

"What are you now?" Nathan asked. "Sixteen?"

"Last I checked, but when you miss so many months, birthdays get tough to figure out."

"I think that means you're scheduled to get married pretty soon." He looked up at the mirrored ceiling, now showing only blackness. "My parents' wedding was in December of nineteen-eighty-six. That's probably not very far in Earth Yellow's future."

She poked his side with the violin bow. "Listen, I want to work this out as much as you do, but I'm not getting married at sixteen years old."

"Shades of *Fiddler on the Roof*!" Daryl brushed the bow away as she rose from her chair. "Whatcha gonna do, Mr. Matchmaker?"

Kelly, her eyes now glassy again, reached for Francesca and patted her arm until her hand rested on her shoulder. "Come with me. We'll have a talk."

Nathan let his gaze follow the two girls into the darkness. What could Kelly be telling her? One of those girl-to-girl secrets men never get to hear about? He turned to Daryl. With her bright eyes and wide smile, her face beamed, as usual, but her slightly older visage gave her an air of wisdom. "Don't worry, Nathan, dear. You can trust Kelly."

"Yeah. I know. I'm just wondering if I could learn something, too."

Daryl swung the chair around to the computer. "I'm going to check with Dr. Gordon real quick—see if there's a bad-guy forecast. You know, partly cloudy with a chance of Mictar floating over the horizon."

"Can you bring them up on the ceiling? We should close the portal so the stalkers can't find us. Besides, I'd like to see Clara." He scanned the room again. If Mictar killed Clara Blue, her body was probably around somewhere. It wouldn't be like him to drag it along. Of course, he had to search for her, just in case. "I'll look for Clara's body while you switch the telescope settings."

"Coming right up!" As Daryl reached for the laptop, a deep voice boomed from above.

"If you touch that setting, I will slaughter you where you sit."

Daryl jerked her hand back and looked up. "Uh-oh."

Nathan squinted at the dark scene above. Near the apex of the curved ceiling, a man stood at the edge of the misty world walkway, too distant to recognize. Still, his acidic voice gave away his identity.

"If you seek your tutor, Nathan Shepherd, you will find what's left of her in the elevator." Mictar made a slurping sound, then laughed. "Her life energy was a bit old but invigorating nonetheless."

His cheeks as hot as fire, Nathan shook his fist. "Coward! You attack old ladies and sneak up on your victims from behind." He pointed at the floor, spewing his words. "Why don't you jump down here and face me man to man?"

"Your bravado is quite humorous when you are surrounded by three protective females." A chuckle drifted down. "The rooster crows while the hens shelter him under their wings."

Nathan clenched his teeth. A dozen retorts stormed through his brain, but they all seemed like the rants of a child. As he stared at Mictar, something new came into focus. The stalker clutched a handful of black strings. Was it hair? Was he dragging a body?

Nathan hissed at Daryl. "Is there a way to magnify him?"

"Yep." She eased her hand toward the touch pad. "Here goes."

Nathan glanced at Kelly and Francesca standing hand in hand near the telescope. With their heads angled upward and their eyes wide, they seemed almost hypnotized.

He looked up again. Mictar's image zoomed toward him until his body nearly filled the curved ceiling. A woman hung from a tangle of black hair in his tight fist, her face suspended a few inches off the walkway surface while her body lay prone behind him. Even though most of her features were veiled, there was no mistaking her identity.

"Mom!" Nathan shook his fist again, spitting as he screamed. "What are you doing with her? Give her back to me or I'll ..." He let his voice trail off. He had no idea what to say.

"Or you'll what?" Mictar's evil grin spread across the top of the dome. "If you see fit to match your actions with your bold words, go back to where you found your mother earlier. Follow the sounds of my choir, and you will eventually find me. If you hand over the Quattro mirror, I will restore your mother to you alive."

Mictar walked away, dragging Nathan's mother's limp body behind him.

Still clenching his pain-racked fist, Nathan spun to Daryl. "Get Dr. Gordon!"

"You got it!" Daryl tapped on the keyboard and made the adjustments—switching the radio telescope, playing the music to arrest the chaotic sounds, and opening the audio channel to the other dimension. Within seconds, a mirror image of the observatory floor appeared on the ceiling, except that the two people watching the computer screen had become Dr. Gordon and Clara. They looked up, and the four sets of eyes met.

Clara spoke up first. "We heard every word, Nathan. What are you going to do?"

"What choice do I have?" He looked at the mirror on the desk where Daryl sat. "I have to save my mother."

A hand touched his back. "We'd better send Francesca to Earth Yellow first."

Nathan turned. Kelly and Francesca stood in front of him, still hand in hand. "We don't have to wait for that. The mirror will take us to my mother. Daryl can send Francesca home."

"Too early to ship her, anyway." Daryl pointed at the laptop screen. "I'm watching the clock. It's been two hours and seven minutes, Gunther Standard Time, since his email time stamp. He has a ways to go."

"Then Kelly and I'll go now. You can get Dr. Gordon and Clara up to speed while you're waiting."

"But I don't know the whole story. I walked in on the show when the credits started rolling."

Nathan let out a huff. "Okay. Here's the super short version." Taking in a deep breath, he told the story rapid-fire, giving all the details he thought important.

Daryl looked on in wonder, even gasping when he described Daryl Blue's fall. Dr. Gordon and Clara listened in silence, Gordon pacing slowly with his hand on his chin and Clara staring from her chair.

Finally, Nathan spread out his hands. "That's it. Kelly and I had better run."

"I agree," Dr. Gordon said, now looking up at Nathan. "Since Earth Yellow and Red have stabilized, travel should be safe, but that might not last long."

Nathan picked up the mirror and gave it to Kelly. "Will you hold it while I play?"

"Wait!" Francesca drew close to Nathan, almost toe to toe. "Kelly convinced me. I'll do what I have to do, even if it means getting married so young." Raising hesitant fingers to his cheek, she whispered. "Earth Yellow needs its version of Nathan Shepherd as soon as possible."

As Francesca handed him the violin and bow, Nathan's insides quaked. He replied, matching her whisper. "That's an amazing sacrifice. I'm sure it will all work out."

She kissed his cheek. "If your father is anything like you, I'm sure it will."

Again flushing hot, he stared at her gleaming eyes. "I ... I don't know what to say."

"Just be sure to tell Kelly why Nathan Shepherd is who he is." She touched the violin bow. "Remember, your talents are a gift, not a birthright."

He watched her finger rub the bow's polished wood. "I'll remember."

She backed away, tears now streaming. He couldn't keep eye contact, at least not without breaking down. Forcing a smile, he turned to Daryl. "Are you going back to Earth Red after you send Francesca home?"

She shook her head hard. "You guys can keep world hopping if you want, but someone needs to run the Earth Blue observatory."

"What about Mictar?" Kelly asked. "If he shows up again, he won't hesitate to kill you."

Daryl grinned. "I dealt with Tony nearly every day for over two years. I have a sixth sense now about when tall, bug-eyed guys who want to suck my life energy are coming around."

"Let's get serious," Nathan said. "It's really dangerous. You shouldn't stay."

"Well, if it isn't Mr. Dangerous himself telling me what to do!" She gave him a light punch on the arm. "Go get 'em, tiger. I'll be a phone call away if you need me."

Nathan shook her hand, interlocking their thumbs. "I couldn't do it without you."

She pulled her hand away and stared at her palm. "Then take my advice. You wash up and let Kelly-kins change her bandage. Otherwise you'll leave a trail even a hound with a sinus infection could follow."

18

PHYSICAL DARKNESS

After changing her bandage, Kelly walked into the telescope's shadow with the mirror in both hands. She pointed the reflective surface at Nathan, who stood ready to play the violin. Even though he had washed, his wounds burned like fire. Still, his hands felt nimble enough to manage a tune.

Above, Clara and Dr. Gordon watched from their upside-down perspective while Daryl looked on from the Earth Blue computer desk.

Once again playing "Foundation's Key," Nathan kept an eye on the dark reflection. Although his fingers and palms ached, he pushed through the performance. As before, though it seemed so long ago, the mirror showed the Earth Red graveyard, but the rift in the dark sky was much smaller.

He stopped playing and reached to the floor for a small flashlight he had found in the desk. Pointing it at the mirror, he nodded at Kelly. "Here we go."

The glass bounced the beam, enhancing it with supercharged energy. Static pounded once again, this time from the speakers in the observatory wall. Spinning darkness enveloped them in an ebony cocoon, slowly decelerating until it came to a stop.

Nathan reached out his hand. The inky blackness felt solid, a thin fibrous netting like black spider webs, yet not sticky. The noise died away. The last time they arrived in this dark realm, his mother's sweet violin replaced the static, but now no sad melody would signal that she sat in the midst of a fragile floor, waiting for deliverance.

Pressing his feet down, he tested the dark floor. Solid. Not a hint of crumbling. At least now they probably wouldn't plunge into the realm of dreams.

He tucked the violin under his arm and aimed the flashlight into the darkness. It was time to push ahead and find the hideous monster that dared to drag his mother around like a discarded mannequin.

The beam washed over a fibrous mass, a stringy substance that looked like the thickest cobwebs in the cosmos. He half expected a Shelob-sized spider to skitter down and wrap both of them up for a midnight snack.

Although the flashlight beam started out strong, when it struck the webbing, the light energy poured down the strands. As it trickled toward the floor, a slight crackling noise sounded from the material, and the liquid light thinned out the net as if burning it away.

Nathan clicked off the flashlight. Better to save the batteries. Although cutting the strings away might help, the process was way too slow. Using the light as a blowtorch would take hours, and the beam didn't shoot out more than a few inches.

Kelly's voice came from behind him, muffled by the matrix. "I hear something. It sounds like stalkers doing their shrieking circle around Scarlet's dome."

He turned, but only blackness met his eyes. Still, the warmth of her body radiated over his, and her gentle breaths caressed his cheek. She was definitely close. "That's what we're looking for. Mictar must be nearby."

She turned his body ninety degrees to the right. "They're coming from that way. I'll correct as we go."

Taking a careful step, he pushed a mass of webbing to the side and plowed through. With every touch, the strands popped and crackled, emanating tiny multi-colored sparks that sprang across his field of vision and died away. With thick outcrops of tangled netting obstructing their path, they high-stepped, sometimes planting their feet in soft, crackling piles. As they pressed down, the surface felt like spongy moss but looked like glittering obsidian.

Nathan halted. The popping sounds continued for a moment, then stopped. Could the extra noise have been an echo? Not likely. The stringy mass snuffed out nearly every sound, so the noise had to be pretty loud to make it to their ears.

"What is it?" Kelly asked.

"Shh!" He touched her arm. "Hear anything?"

"Besides the horrible singing?" She paused for a second. "No."

He lifted a foot and pressed down again, raising another shower of crackling sparks. "I mean that noise. When I stop walking, I hear it again."

"The singing pretty much drowns everything out for me."

Nathan strained his ears. Only Kelly's breaths interrupted the dead silence. Could Mictar be lurking? Maybe he lied about trading for the mirror and really planned to ambush them and steal what he had been trying to get ever since this ordeal began. Could the other stalkers provide a clue?

"Can you translate their song?" he asked.

"Some of it." She drummed her fingers on Nathan's arm. "They're going on and on about a final merging of the three earths, something about a great sacrifice that will turn on the Lucifer machine."

"That can't be good."

"Tell me about it. Now they're saying only Earth Yellow will survive, and they will inhabit it once the rodents are eliminated."

"Rodents? Must be their pet name for humans."

"I don't think they're singing about field mice."

Nathan pressed on, but the popping sounds continued. Whoever stalked from behind always waited for them to start moving again before taking his own steps. Maybe Mictar didn't want to attack two people at once, but he had seemed adept at handling that many before. Then again, Kelly didn't hear it, so maybe it was in his imagination.

After a minute or so, Kelly turned him a few degrees to the left. He paused and craned his neck. Dissonant song, a series of long vowel sounds, finally reached his ears, warped and distant. The stalkers were somewhere out there.

He turned and listened again, but the shrieks allowed for no other sounds. Mictar apparently didn't have the guts to show himself. Nathan suppressed a sigh. Even if they were being stalked, what could he do? Just wait around? He lowered his head and trudged on.

Kelly grabbed the back of his shirt. "Don't leave me. If we're getting close to those white-haired freaks, I'm sticking to you like glue."

As they struggled forward, the song grew louder. In his mind, he labeled the noise the "foul vowels," but the moniker sounded too corny to say out loud. Besides, it was probably better not to talk. If they could hear the stalkers, maybe the stalkers could hear them. "If you hear anything important," he whispered, "let me know. Otherwise, we'd better keep quiet."

She replied with another quick tug on his shirt, enough to let him know she understood.

After a minute or two, he reached a thick wall of webbing, too thick to swipe away with his hand. He turned on the flashlight and set the beam on the black barrier. The light poured down the surface, sizzling all the way to the floor.

He flicked the light off again and felt the spot with his fingers. Although the beam had left an indentation, it couldn't have been more than a millimeter deep. It might take hours to burn through it.

He set down the flashlight, violin, and bow, then tried to tear at the wall with both hands. Although it seemed soft enough, like cotton or terrycloth, his nails couldn't penetrate.

After a few seconds of futile scratching, he picked up his things and whispered to Kelly. "The wall's too tough. Let's see if there's a crack in it somewhere." He slid the flashlight into his pocket and pushed the violin into her hand.

"I heard it," she whispered.

"Heard what?"

"The popping noise behind us. Someone's back there."

"If Mictar was going to attack, I think he'd have done it by now."

"Maybe not. He could be waiting for a more convenient place. It feels kind of stupid to march right into his lair."

"I know. But I don't think we have much choice." Laying his left hand on the wall, he pushed forward through thick webbing, trying to forge a path parallel to the barrier. Still clutching his shirt, Kelly followed.

The foul vowels continued to emanate from beyond the flexible wall. As Nathan trudged, it seemed that the wall curved, as if it were a circular shield protecting whatever was inside. He halted and slid his hand upward on the barrier, standing on tiptoes to reach as high as he could. The shield curved slightly away. The barrier was a dome, a much bigger, darker dome than the prisons that held Scarlet and the other supplicants.

He knelt and pushed his fingertips into the intersection between the shield and the floor. The wall bent inward, allowing his fingers to slide through. With a quiet grunt, he lifted. His wounded hands ached, but the thick cottony material budged. Now able to curl his fingers up on the other side, he pulled harder. The material spilled slowly around his hands, like viscous gelatin warmed by his touch. As he held the curtain a foot or so off the floor, cacophonous vowels poured through the gap, now much louder than before.

He let the wall down and rose to his feet. "It's heavy, but I'm sure you can handle it. If you hold it up, I'll squeeze through. Then I'll hold it up for you from the inside."

She pulled harder on his shirt. "I don't want to be separated, not even for a second. The minute you get inside, who knows what might happen? Mictar might grab you, or you might fall into someone's nightmare."

"Do you have another idea?"

"Remember what your father said?" She pulled his wrist and dragged his knuckles over the mirror's surface. "When you get in trouble, look at the mirror. I'd say that being stuck in a cosmic spider web with that creep lugging your mother around fits the definition of trouble."

He stared at where the mirror had to be, but blackness veiled everything. "How can I use it? I can't even see it."

"Scarlet has a light of her own. I think she'll shine it for you, but you probably have to ask."

"No music?"

Kelly pressed his palm flat on the glass. "Just talk to her and see what happens."

Nathan stared at the spot where his hand met the mirror. The image of Scarlet came to mind, her pleading eyes as she leaned close, his fingers wrapped around her pulsing heart, and finally, as he drew his hand away, the imprint emblazoned on the heart's surface. His need for rescue grasped her sacrificial provision. Now he finally understood. She was his supplicant in more ways than one.

"Scarlet?" he said softly. "I could use some help here. Can you give us a little light?"

Warmth surged through his body. His chest tightened, forcing him to gasp for breath. Finally catching air, he heaved it in and out. Light seeped from around his hand, outlining it in red. The glass grew so hot, he jerked away. The glow spread over Kelly's face, her expression solemn, yet filled with wonder. She seemed to have no trouble handling the heated mirror.

As if sketched on the surface by an animated light pen, Scarlet's image appeared in the reflection, the same pose she had struck when he saw her in the dream, her dress open, her heart pulsing bright red. Crimson light burst forth in a broad ray, melting the strands of black webbing.

Nathan took the mirror, now merely warm at the edges, and pointed it at the dome wall. The red light sizzled against the barrier and streamed down to the floor, like blood flowing from a wounded beast. The beam narrowed into a slender shaft and cut into the thick material, raising splashes of reddish sparks that arced to the floor and jumped around in a frenzied dance before dying in a puff of smoke.

Moving the mirror in a tight circle, he burned a wide swath, cutting deeper and deeper as he edged toward the wall. Finally, the light broke through.

The horrible song exploded from within. The mirror's light dimmed, and its cutting power diminished. The dripping red sparks solidified and dropped to the ground as black beads that rolled across the floor.

Nathan swept the beads out of the way with his foot. Obviously the foul vowels were neutralizing Scarlet's light, somehow transforming it into dark energy. He took three steps closer and stood within a few inches of the wall as he continued to cut. Maybe that would intensify the beam's effect.

The breach in the wall grew. Since the material was so soft and pliable, anyone could probably slide through the gap. He nodded at Kelly, who was already edging close to the hole, the red glow covering her entire frame in its bloody mask. "Try to go in," he called. "I'll be right behind you."

She pushed the dripping curtain to the side and stepped into the dome. Grabbing the violin, Nathan rushed in. As soon as he broke through, Kelly grabbed his arm. Her shivering body sent tremors into his own. "It's so cold in here!"

The stalkers' wails pierced his eardrums. "And loud!"

She pressed her hands over her ears and shouted. "They're cheering. Like someone scored a touchdown."

"That can't be good." Using the mirror's waning beam, he scanned the area. Dozens of dark streams, like thick rivers of smoke, passed horizontally through the red light, each one emanating from a central point. As one of the streams brushed Nathan's cheek, a burst of song blasted into his ears, and a cold chill plunged through his skin. The cloud of black passed by and splattered against the wall, combining with other streams to seal the breach Scarlet had cut.

"Looks like the door closed behind us," Kelly said.

Nathan pulled her to his side. "Let's find where those black things are coming from. Mictar has to be behind this."

Angling his body toward the source of the streams, he pointed the mirror, still glowing with enough red light to guide their steps. With the violin tucked under his arm, he skulked forward. In the absence of black webbing, he and Kelly moved easily across the dark floor, though the flowing air grew colder and the horrendous singing grew louder with every step.

After a few seconds, they reached a dark hole, an eight-foot-wide circle in the floor from which cold, song-soaked air poured forth, gusting and spewing new black streams with every dissonant phrase.

Now shivering violently, Kelly hugged Nathan with both arms. Her teeth chattered. "Any ... any idea where we are?"

Nathan, warmth still radiating from within as a result of his touch on the mirror, gazed into the hole. "Right over the three domes, I think. This must be where they create dark energy with their songs." He gazed up. Some of the streams escaped through a hole in the cap of the dome. "I guess the energy absorbs light and heat and solidifies in the wall and in that tangled web outside."

Kelly thrust her finger upward. "What's that?"

A dark form hovered above the hole in the floor, several feet higher than their heads, almost invisible in the crimson-coated darkness. Nathan gave the violin to Kelly and aimed the mirror at the vague shape. The residual glow swept across the form, a woman suspended in mid-air. As the song ebbed and flowed, she rode the current, rising and falling with the sounds. Her long dress flapped around her legs, but her dangling feet never came within reach.

Nathan gulped. Could she really be who he thought she was? He pressed his hand against the mirror. "Scarlet! Can I have a little more light?"

A gasping reply wheezed from the surface. "Nathan ... Dearest one ... The stalkers are weakening me ... but I will do what I can."

As the red glow strengthened and illuminated the area, the woman's face clarified. Long dark locks brushed across her face and flew above her head as the cold breeze buffeted her body. Her skin seemed polished, reflective, almost like a Barbie doll's plastic coating, but her identity was clear.

Nathan shivered in spite of the mirror's warmth. "It's my mother!"

"Nathan!" Kelly shouted. "Behind you!"

He jerked around. A tall specter lunged toward him, a long black arm reaching out. Nathan ducked, dropped to the ground, and swept his leg under the attacker. His foot struck something solid. The shadow lurched forward and toppled over him, but Nathan, still clutching the mirror, rolled out of the way and leaped up. Then, guided by the mirror's dimming light, he rushed over to Kelly.

As the shadow climbed to its feet, Nathan pulled Kelly to the opposite side of the hole in the floor. Kelly's teeth chattered. "Mictar?"

"It's got to be." Nathan's chill heightened. He huddled close to Kelly and pointed the mirror at the slowly approaching phantom.

Had Mictar followed them through the web? If so, why hadn't he attacked earlier?

The tall shadow stalked into the red glow. With a smirk on his pale, narrow face, he stopped at the edge of the hole, holding something in his hand that was too dark to identify. "I must admit that I'm impressed with your courage. I didn't think you would come."

Fighting off the shivers, Nathan squared his shoulders. "What do you know about courage?"

"Impudent brat!" Mictar took two long strides around the hole, but Nathan and Kelly matched his movements, keeping the stalker directly opposite them. Mictar pointed a long, bony finger. "Either give me the mirror, or begone! This place is beyond your understanding."

As he spoke, the song died down, and a light, dim and pale blue, shone from an invisible source within the hole. The cold wind eased, allowing Nathan's mother to float down to eye level. With her skin white and her body stiff, she seemed more like an embalmed corpse than a living human. Still, light glimmered in her eyes, a sign that maybe she was alive.

Nathan reached for her, but her hand dangled a few inches too far away. Should he jump? If he caught hold of her, would they fall into the hole? Who could tell where they would fall? Maybe the middle of the three domes where the supplicants lived, but maybe not.

He glared at Mictar. He couldn't give up the mirror. Mictar would just use it to kill Scarlet and take so much energy, all would be lost. But what else could he do? Stall? If so, for what? No one was coming to help.

Nathan held up the mirror. "Give her to me first!"

"Oh, I see. You lack trust." Mictar gazed at Nathan's mother, his eyes wide as if admiring his prisoner. "If you look closely, you can see that I have kept her alive. She would be no use to me dead. That's why I never took her eyes when I had the opportunity. I needed at least one gifted human to finish my work."

"So," Nathan said. "You want the mirror, and I want my mother. We're at a stalemate."

"Not necessarily." Mictar pointed into the darkness. "Leave the mirror wherever you wish and walk away from it. While I go to retrieve it, you are welcome to collect your mother and leave."

A whisper drifted into Nathan's ear. "My beloved, I see where you are now. You are inside the Lucifer machine. According to the stalkers' songs, Mictar has poured the life energy into your mother and plans to use her as a catalyst to activate the energy and spread it throughout the machine."

Nathan glanced at the mirror. A hint of Scarlet's lovely eyes appeared in the reflection. He couldn't just hand her over to that beast. There had to be another way.

Turning back to Mictar, he flexed his exhausted muscles. Now that he knew what was going on, how could he use Scarlet's information?

Backing away a few steps, he pulled Kelly along. "So if we decide to keep the mirror, would you let Kelly and me go?"

Mictar raised the object in his hand into the light—a jet-black violin. "I have no use for you, and I likely will not be able to capture you in an expeditious manner. When I am done here, you will die, so it matters little to me what you do now." He lifted a white bow to the strings. "If, however, you wish to stay, by all means do so. You might learn a thing or two from a real violinist."

As Mictar's thin hands gripped the violin and bow like a seasoned master, the words he spoke at the hospital came back to Nathan. *Your base use of that instrument proves that you have no respect for its true power.* At the time, the statement seemed little more than a verbal slap, but now it echoed as a dark prophecy.

The sight of the black violin and white bow made Nathan ill. Something terrible was about to happen.

Mictar stroked a string, then adjusted its tension. As he continued tuning, Kelly whispered, "I have a bad feeling about this."

"No kidding. It's like waiting for your own funeral to begin. Got any ideas?"

"Dissonance creates the dark energy." She pushed the violin into his hands. "Here's your weapon to counter it. Go to war."

"Shouldn't I use the mirror? Won't Scarlet be able to help?"

"Maybe. You hold the violin." She took the mirror. "I'll hold Scarlet."

Nathan scanned the dark floor. "Where's my bow?"

"You didn't give it to me." Kelly pointed at a spot near Mictar's feet and whispered, "Wait. There it is."

Nathan eyed his bow, maybe two steps to the stalker's right at the ten o'clock position as they viewed the hole, themselves at the six o'clock point and Mictar at high noon.

Mictar began playing. The notes, although perfectly rendered, gave no hint of structure or form. Light flashed from his hands and arced along the bow and over the strings. The same sparkling light that had sucked the life out of so many victims now made the black violin seem to blaze as it poured out measure after measure of dissonance. He shouted into the hole "Sing, my people! Let every Earth hear the sounds that will finally bring them together!"

The voices burst into song again, this time louder and fouler than ever. Cold air blasted from the hole, pushing Nathan's mother higher in the blue light. The dark streams collided with her body and bounced off, seemingly energized and animated as they rushed away.

Gasping for breath, Nathan raised the violin and looked at the mirror, still glowing but only enough to illuminate Kelly as she held the square with both hands. Plucking the strings, he played the opening measure of Beethoven's "Moonlight Sonata," but with one of the strings missing, he had to figure out a new fingering for the remaining ones. And with his raw, bleeding hands feeling like they were on fire, how could he possibly win a battle of violins?

As he played, the notes seemed feeble against the onslaught of the stalkers' song and Mictar's resonating instrument. The stalker glared at Nathan and played more vigorously. Black vapor poured from his violin and streamed toward the feminine body floating above their heads. As if echoing the notes, sparks of white sizzled through the streams and covered her with an electrostatic aura. Her body twitched, shocked by every twinkling light that surged between her and Mictar.

"Louder, Nathan!" Kelly said. "I feel the mirror getting warmer. Give it all you've got!"

Nathan pulled the strings harder. A rush of white light rose from each one, but as it lifted into the air, one of the dark streams zipped by and swept the light away, like a crow snatching a morsel.

As he moved his hand up and down the fingerboard, he played on. More light erupted from the violin. More dark clouds, screaming as they passed, gobbled up the sounds. The mirror's glow strengthened. Scarlet's eyes grew brighter. Red light washed over his violin, and as the next flash of light erupted from his strings, the dark streams veered away as if forced out of their flight by the new fountain of red.

Pain surging through his fingers, Nathan nodded toward the hole. It was time to get as close as possible to his mother. Maybe somehow he could counteract whatever Mictar was doing to her. While he continued the sonata, he and Kelly sidestepped toward the edge. The blast of frigid air pummeled them, but as Scarlet's light strengthened, warmth from the mirror radiated across their bodies and pushed the cold back. Nathan's mother floated lower in the column of air, but her face stayed quiet, expressionless as the stalker's electrified onslaught continued.

Scowling, Mictar eased around the circle, but Nathan kept watch out of the corner of his eye and shuffled in the same direction to match the stalker's movements. Kelly backed up, keeping pace. Nathan spotted the bow again. Only a few more steps and they would be within reach.

Mictar shouted into the hole. "We are almost there, my people! This fool with a fiddle is no match for me and eleven of you!"

The cold gale freshened, amplifying the noise and lifting Nathan's mother higher. Her body convulsed. Black streams shot out of her hands and feet and zoomed into the far reaches of the Lucifer machine. A loud crack sounded from below.

Nathan glanced into the pale blue light. Were the glass walls that displayed the earths cracking? Was the machine working to break down the barriers? Shuffling to stay on the opposite side of the hole from Mictar, Nathan looked at his bow, still not quite within reach. He could probably make a leap for it, but what could he play that would counteract this apocalyptic sound? And how many did Mictar say were fighting against him? Eleven? Didn't twelve stalkers surround Scarlet before?

He refocused on the strings and continued his pizzicato performance, adding as much vibrato as he could. His hands ached more horribly than ever, but he couldn't give up. He had to fight harder—pour more energy into the music, fill it with the passion he felt inside for his mother. He had to save her life. He had to battle this monster and rescue the entire universe. Yet, he had only a violin and a plucking finger. How could that possibly be enough to overcome the flood of dissonance? But what else could he do?

A sweet voice drifted from the mirror, soft and indistinct. Scarlet's face clarified in the reflection, somber, unflustered, glowing with crimson light. As her lips moved, her song energized, and the lyrics formed in red clusters of radiance, each one reflecting the character of the word in power, resilience, and emotion.

> *The strength of pure evil, the darkness, desire,*
> *The greedy, the grabber, the lustful, the liar,*
> *The music of takers can never withstand*
> *The song of the giver, the bloody red hand.*

Nathan snatched up the bow and began playing the tune that Scarlet sang. Although the notes were foreign, somehow they came to him just in time to move from mind, to hand, to the strings of his crippled violin.

> *He plays for his maker, his mother, his bride;*
> *He takes no account of his pain or his pride.*
> *His weapon, his music that calls for a song,*
> *The lyrics of old that bring right to a wrong.*

As Nathan played, Mictar locked his gaze on him. The black vapors from the stalker's violin collided with the white that rose from Nathan's, meeting in a striped swirl around his mother's body. Pain scorched his hands. Blood oozed over the bow, but, as Scarlet's song strengthened, he played on.

> *With fingers of scarlet he reaches for life;*
> *Through boundaries forbidden he plunges a knife.*
> *The heart I laid bare is the flesh on the cross;*
> *The kiss is the wine that sets flames to the dross.*

The circular clusters of crimson light emanating from the mirror expanded and ate away at the dark streams that brushed against them. Then, after drifting toward Nathan's mother, the clusters joined in the battle of black and white vapors, lengthening and blending into the swirl. A splash of sparks burned away the blackness in the cyclone, leaving only a spin of red and white. The blue light from the hole faded, and the wind died down, allowing his mother to slowly sink.

Again, Mictar screamed into the hole. "It is time! Sing the death march, and I will activate Lucifer's fist!"

A new song lifted into the air—frenzied, chaotic, screeching. Mictar stroked his black violin furiously, lifting the thickest black clouds yet into the air. The dark streams began to curve. They encircled the hole in dozens of orbits, ranging from lightning-fast rivers of black near the center to slower, more distinct streams as the orbits fanned out near the outer walls of their dome.

The streams congealed, making a single thick cloud of black that spun around Nathan's mother and sucked away the red and white swirl. The new cloud sparkled with purple light, illuminating the chamber with a violet hue. The force of their orbit burst open the outer walls, and the cloud spread out into the webbing. Like a swarm of bees, the sparks buzzed through the strands, eating through them like cotton candy.

More cracking noises erupted from beneath their feet. Nathan grimaced at the sound. The channels between the earths had to be multiplying. He played harder. They were losing the battle, but what choice did he have? The cosmic fabric was being eaten away by the swarm of dark energy, and the universe lay in his hands—his aching, bleeding hands.

Now crying as his mother spun slowly in the swirling wind, he swayed in time with Scarlet's song, a new song, a louder and more plaintive cry.

O light of dawn! O sound of spring!
O freedom bells! Arise and sing!
Without your voice, without your song,
All light is dark, all right is wrong.

Reveal your aid, your shepherd's staff
That kept my life from being chaff,
That stayed the stalkers' bleeding verse,
That eased my supplicating curse.

As Scarlet's voice faded, a new song arose in the swirling wind, the familiar vowel sounds of the stalkers, yet carrying a strangely beautiful melody.

Kelly set her feet as the wind whipped her hair wildly. "Nathan!" she shouted. "It's Abodah!"

Nathan searched for the source. A tall figure emerged from the torn webbing, leaning into the tornadic flow of dark streams as she sang.

"Abodah!" Mictar shouted as he continued playing his violin. "Begone, you traitor! You have no business here."

Still fighting the wind, she staggered up to the edge of the circle and scowled. With a series of short notes, she sang her answer.

"I am not your slave," Kelly translated, her shouts beaten back by the cyclone. "Nor am I a traitor. I have come to set these captives free."

Mictar sneered, but he seemed out of breath as his fingers continued to fly up and down the violin's neck. "It is too late. Lucifer has the catalyst in its grip, and the dark energy is ripping apart the barriers. It would take much more than a singing supplicant and a boy on a three-stringed fiddle to stop me now."

Abodah set a hand on Nathan's shoulder and sang a soft tune.

"Stop playing," Kelly said. "You are only delaying the inevitable, and you must be strong enough to follow my counsel."

Nathan lowered the violin and shook out his stinging hand. "What do I do?"

A deep crease spread across Abodah's forehead as she sang again.

Kelly had to lean close to Nathan to battle the wind as she translated. "Sacrifice. When we stop this machine, the supplicants will be the only way to create dark energy." She pointed at the hole. "For the sake of billions on the three earths, you must go down there and kill all three."

19

TO SLAY A SUPPLICANT

As the wind blasted his face, Nathan looked at his mother, now vertical and spinning faster and faster. Heeding Abodah's advice had already accelerated Lucifer's destructive force. "What about my mother?" he asked.

"Leave her where she is," Kelly said, still translating for Abodah. "If you are going to accomplish your mission, she will be a hindrance to you. You cannot drag her with you and effectively carry out this plan."

"How do I get into the supplicants' domes?"

She pressed her lips close to his ear and sang seven high notes. When she straightened, she continued her song, and Kelly gave it words. "That is the key to Scarlet's dome. Lower each note by one octave to open Cerulean's, then another octave to open Amber's."

Abodah paused, shifted her gaze toward Mictar, and sang a final few notes.

"Go now," Kelly translated. "This stalker of souls is mine."

As Abodah walked slowly around the circle, Mictar stayed put, his face defiant as he continued playing his violin. Still, a hint of concern crept across his eyes. With her head erect and her stare fixed, Abodah closed in slowly, raising her hands, palms out, as if creating a shield in front of her.

Nathan backed away from the edge of the hole, fighting the blistering torrent. Kelly did the same. Still shouting to compete with the riotous noise, she tucked the mirror and took Nathan's hand. "Are you really going to do what she said?"

"I'm not sure yet, but I know one thing I'm going to do."

"What?"

"I'm going to get my mother." Taking a deep breath, he nodded toward the hole. "When I get to the bottom, I'll try to signal if it's safe." He let go of her hand and ran toward the hole. When he reached the edge, he leaped up and out toward his mother's spinning body. With a grunt, he collided with her and, still clutching his violin and bow, wrapped his arms around her shoulders, then locked her waist between his legs.

Now spinning with her, he sank slowly ... too slowly. With every revolution, Mictar and Abodah flashed across his vision on one side and Kelly on the other. The two stalkers fought hand to hand, while Kelly dashed toward the hole. When he spun to the other side, a sudden weight thumped against his back, and a slender arm joined his around his mother's shoulders. Soft lips and a whisper tickled his ear. "Not for one minute, Nathan Shepherd, will I let you leave my side."

The two descended, now much more quickly. The spinning slowed, allowing a view of Mictar and Abodah as they wrestled on the floor. With Mictar no longer playing the violin, the cyclone slowed as well, but the wind from below continued to blast cold air upward through the bluish light.

With Kelly's cheek pressed against his, Nathan couldn't see her eyes to gauge her fear, but, as they descended below the edge of the hole, her shivering arms sent tremors through his body. The edge of the mirror bit into his side, but the pain was worth it. Scarlet had come along for the ride. Yet, the touch seemed cold. Had she used all her energy? Would she be able to help them once they arrived?

The blue glow faded to purple, then to black. After a few more seconds, a faint light emanated from far below, a circle of white that grew rapidly as their rate of descent increased.

Finally, the three domes came into view. A group of stalkers encircling Scarlet's dome continued to sing their horrible verses, apparently not yet noticing the three bodies floating into their domain.

From Nathan's perspective it seemed that Scarlet lay motionless on the floor under the center of her dome. Cerulean looked on, his hands pressed against the wall of his prison. Amber, too, stood near her wall, her eyes fixed on Nathan and company.

The three earths came into view on the matrix of glass squares. Hundreds of channels now etched the regions between the planets, each one with mist of blended colors running through it. The mist collected in a blanket of clouds hovering over the contact points at the surface of the earths.

As they came within twenty feet of the floor, a male voice rose with the upward draft, a lovely tenor, sweet and pure. A soprano blended in, as clear as carillon bells. Cerulean and Amber lifted their heads and sang the most beautiful vowel song Nathan had ever heard, filled with passion, yet flowing with peace.

One of the stalkers pointed at Cerulean and shrieked four loud notes. The others stopped singing, and some hurried to the boy's dome while the others split off toward Amber's. Shouting and arguing, the stalkers seemed unable to decide which supplicant to surround with their dissonant song.

The wind eased, further increasing Nathan's rate of descent. At this speed, he would have to hit feet first and roll, and hope the two supplicants kept the stalkers occupied. He couldn't possibly fight that many, especially if they had those sonic paralyzers.

As they descended toward the door to Sarah's Womb, Nathan slid down his mother's body to make sure his feet would strike the floor first. At the last minute, he swung to the right. His foot landed a few inches away from the glass door, and he lunged with a spin, trying to keep his mother's stiff body from hitting the ground.

Holding his violin and bow aloft, he rolled over Kelly, raising a loud "oof," and came to a stop on his side. He jumped to his feet, helped Kelly to hers, and straddled his mother as he raised the violin to his chin. Kelly pressed the mirror against her stomach and rolled her free hand into a fist. With new blood streaming down the front of her sweatshirt, she looked like a warrior princess, ready to pounce.

As Nathan played the notes Abodah had whispered, one of the female stalkers turned and shrieked three horrible vowels. Several others spun around. Two of the males withdrew sonic rods and marched toward Nathan and Kelly.

When Nathan played the final note, Scarlet's dome let out a loud hum. The two stalkers halted and exchanged glances, fear widening their eyes. Nathan played the notes at a lower octave. Cerulean's dome hummed a note, one step up from Scarlet's. Then, after Nathan played another seven notes at the next octave down, Amber's dome joined the other two in a harmonic trio of resonating hums. While the nine other stalkers backed toward the side door that led to the glassy walkway, the two holding paralyzers ran to join them.

Scarlet's dome evaporated, leaving only a circular swatch of dirty terrazzo. Nathan gave the violin and bow to Kelly and, picking up his mother, staggered to the circle. Scarlet lay curled in a fetal position, her arms crossed and her body shaking.

After setting his mother down gently, Nathan dropped to his knees beside the quivering supplicant.

"Scarlet?" He laid a hand on her sweat-drenched red hair. "Can you hear me?"

Her eyes fluttered. She turned her head and blinked at Nathan. With barely a whisper, she said, "My beloved?"

Kelly knelt beside Nathan and handed him the mirror, but, with a gentle push, Scarlet brushed it to the side. "There is no need for that," she said, her voice fragile, yet sweet. "We have seen each other through glass, mirrors, and dreams, but now, at last, face-to-face." She raised her hand and laid it on his cheek. "And touching you is my dream come true."

Her fingers, warm and soft, melted his fighting spirit and reached into his heart, wringing it out like an old sponge. Tears crawled down his cheeks. His throat clamped so tight, he could barely squeak. "Are you ... going to live?"

Cerulean and Amber lowered themselves to their knees, completing a circle around the fallen supplicant. "It depends," Scarlet whispered. She unfastened her dress's uppermost button, exposing the top of the void. "Will you take my life and give it to another?"

Nathan glanced at his mother. With her skin pale and slick, she hardly resembled the vibrant woman he once knew, the warm, loving Francesca Shepherd. She lay there cold and stiff, staring upward with unblinking eyes.

Kelly laid her hand on Francesca's chest. "I'm not getting much. Maybe a flutter. I don't think she'll last long."

Nathan clutched Scarlet's hand. "Isn't there another way? Can't I take your place? I would die for my mother if I could."

"Not you, my love, for you are not a supplicant. Nor Cerulean, for he can die only for a soul in Earth Blue. And Amber's life is reserved for someone in Earth Yellow. Only I can do this, but you must transfer my life to hers. The power is in your hands." Scarlet pulled apart her lapels, popping open three buttons. "You know what you have to do."

Nathan lifted his hand and stared at his wounded palm. Blood still oozed from the lacerations. He shifted his gaze to the heart floating in the midst of the black hole, beating erratically as she labored to breathe. So far, he had touched her only in a dream, a grip on her heart that never happened and a caress of lips that was a mere thought. Now she begged him not only to shatter his ideas of chivalry and self-sacrifice, but also to steal away her life.

He turned toward Kelly. As he gazed into her eyes, he silently begged for help. She would understand his turmoil. Even without a word, she could interpret his cry. He needed her to speak the words that would release him from his dome.

Kelly laid a hand on his cheek. "It's the only way, Nathan. You have to do it. You can't die for your mother yourself."

As Kelly pulled her hand away, a sob erupted from the pit of Nathan's stomach. Weeping, he reached into Scarlet's body and wrapped his fingers around her heart. She grabbed his wrist and heaved in a breath. Then, letting it out slowly, she smiled and whispered, her voice just a breathy sigh. "I give my life energy to you now, my beloved. Taste the freshness of a life reborn, drink the nectar of love renewed, feel my presence in your soul. Then, when the fullness of my power embraces you, use it to awaken your mother." She clutched his shirt and pulled him so close, her lips brushed his earlobe. Her voice spiked with urgency. "But don't ever ... ever forget me."

Feeling her heart throbbing in his grasp, Nathan gasped in shallow breaths. "I'll never forget you. Never."

Scarlet's smile widened. She blinked rapidly. Then, she heaved in another breath and sang in a whisper, each word labored and failing.

To give! To give! My spirit cries out.
I have no gift but life.
Into thy hand I pour it out
And finally end my strife.

Her lips trembled. "Now, Nathan. You know what to do."

He touched his own quivering lips to hers. Her chest expanded once more, and she let out a long sigh. Her hot breath poured in and filtered into his lungs, fresh and soothing. As he lifted away, her head lolled to one side. A weak smile graced her lips, and her eyes closed. Her heart fluttered once, then fell still.

Nathan pulled back his hand, his skin now hot and throbbing. Had he really absorbed her life energy? Trembling, he fastened her lowest button and reached for the next.

"Nathan," Kelly said. "I'll do that. You have to wake up your mother."

With tears dripping onto Scarlet's dress, Nathan shook his head. "I have to do it. Don't ask me why. I just have to." Yet, he knew why. Scarlet had given everything she had, even life itself, for him. He had to be the one to seal her shroud.

As he worked, the aroma of roses freshened his nostrils, and a bittersweet film coated his tongue. A sense of cool wetness slaked his parched throat and eased the constricting muscles.

When he fastened the top button, he shifted on his knees toward his mother. He looked at Cerulean and Amber in turn. "What do I do?"

Amber, her lips straight and somber, grasped his wrist and moved his hand over his mother's mouth. "Lay your anointed palm here and call upon the interpreter to push on her chest three times. Have her say, 'In the name of the Father, the Son, and the Holy Ghost, restore the breath of life and renew the spirit within this fragile shell.'"

Nathan rested the heel of his hand on his mother's chin, laid his hot, bloody palm over her lips, and spread his fingers across her cheeks and nose. He nodded at Kelly. "Go ahead and push."

Placing the heels of both hands on his mother's sternum, Kelly pressed her weight down. "In the name of the Father ..."

Dry air cooled Nathan's palm. Then, as Kelly lifted her weight, suction from his mother's nose and mouth pulled his hand closer. His skin tingled, but nothing more.

Kelly pressed down again. "The Son ..."

This time the air blowing out felt drier and colder.

She lifted her weight. Suction again pulled Nathan's hand. This time, stinging pain crawled across his skin and radiated up his arm.

Kelly rose to her feet and pushed down with her full weight. "And the Holy Ghost, restore the breath of life and renew the spirit within this fragile shell."

Air poured from his mother's mouth, this time blistering cold, but Nathan kept his hand in place. Icy currents injected his bones with numbing pain that shot through his skeleton. His arms and legs stiffened. His knees and elbows locked. His fingers as rigid as icicles, he pressed his hand over her mouth and moaned.

Kelly pulled back. The rush of cold air reversed. Then, like lava rising from a volcano, heat boiled deep within Nathan's chest and spread out into his limbs, loosening his joints. As warmth pushed into his face, the smell of roses again brushed his senses, and bittersweetness coated his tongue.

Nathan licked his lips. Scarlet was ready to sing her final song, a song of new life.

The volcano erupted. A flood of superheated energy surged through his arm and gushed into his hand. Red light flashed from his fingers and coated his mother's face with a scarlet glow. As sheer agony ripped through his brain, Nathan lifted his head and let out a guttural scream, a high piercing note that seemed to shake the floor.

His mother's body jerked. She coughed, then sneezed. As her eyes blinked open, Nathan pulled back his scalded hand, peeling away loose, melted skin that had adhered to her face.

Her brow arched, and her eyes darted all around. "Nathan?" Her voice sounded like a tinkling bell, quiet and clear. "Are we in heaven?"

"Mom!" He threw his arms around her and pulled her against his chest, rocking her back and forth as he cradled her body.

Sobs choked his words. "No ... Mom ... we're not in heaven. But ... but you're alive ... That's all that matters."

She hugged him so tightly, she nearly squeezed his breath away. "Oh, my son, my son! It is paradise to see you again!"

Kelly's voice quaked. "Hello, Mrs. Shepherd. I'm Kelly Clark."

As Nathan pushed away, his mother smiled. "Yes, Kelly. I met your counterpart on Earth Blue. You ... I mean, she ... saved my life there."

"She did? How?"

"I hope to tell you the story later." She glanced around the room. "I see now that we are in the stalkers' lair. Where are they?"

"Gone," Nathan said. "At least for now. I think they're afraid of the supplicants." He rose and reached to help his mother. "Can you stand?"

She gave him a weak nod. "I think so."

Using his less bloody hand, he hoisted her up, then nodded toward the supplicants. "This is Cerulean and Amber, the supplicants for Earths Blue and Yellow."

Cerulean bowed, shaking his stark blue hair, while Amber spread out her yellow dress and dipped into a formal curtsy. Cerulean gazed at Nathan's mother with his stunning eyes. "I am not of your world, but I am at your service."

Amber stepped forward and touched Nathan's hand. "Alas! Your bow hand is in need of repair. You cannot play to open the portals."

He looked at the torn, melted skin. Puffy redness swelled his fingers. "True. At least for now. But Francesca Shepherd is here. She can take over." He looped his elbow around his mother's. "Do you know where Dad is? Did he ever come back to that place where I found you?"

She shook her head. "Soon after you and the others fell into the void, the floors all around me became solid. When I tried to search for your father, Mictar found me and put me in his machine. Since he enjoys boasting about his accomplishments, I picked up some clues about the structure of all these realms. We need to get back to the Earth Blue mirrors and look for your father there."

"I hear something," Kelly said. "Sounds like the stalkers, but I don't see them anywhere."

Nathan pulled Cerulean closer. "Are the stalkers scared of you?"

The slightest of grins bent the young man's face. "Of that you can be sure, yet I do not know if Amber and I can repel them all. Scarlet was our leader, and her courage and wisdom exceeded ours."

"But they probably don't know that," Nathan said. A deafening crack rifled through the room. He jerked his head toward the source, the Earth Red side of the chamber. Two huge rifts shot out from the surface of the mist-shrouded planet and slowly crawled across the wall toward the other two earths. Glass squares exploded in their paths and rained sparkling shards to the floor. Earth Red itself expanded, pulsing and throbbing as if ready to burst. At the rate the cracks were moving, they would reach the other earths in mere moments.

Kelly whispered, "What does it mean?"

"The end of the worlds." Nathan looked at Scarlet's motionless body, still lovely, even in death. She had said one obstacle remained in defeating the stalkers, and now that he knew what it was, the very thought of it made him sick to his stomach. "Can you open the door to Sarah's Womb?" he asked Cerulean.

"Yes. What do you plan to do?"

"I can't say it. Just open it, and keep the stalkers at bay." He stooped and slid his hands under Scarlet. "I'll be back as soon as I can."

Kelly picked up Nathan's violin and the mirror. "I'm coming with you."

With a grunt, he rose to his feet, lifting Scarlet's limp body. "Of course you are."

"And I, as well," his mother said. "You will need a violinist to open the lower door."

As he shuffled toward the floor panel, he nodded at them. "Fine, but let's hurry."

Cerulean ran ahead of him, his slender body seeming to glide as he approached the door. He knelt at the side of the glass panel and sang. Rapid-fire notes burst forth from low to high on the musical scale as if someone had run a finger along the piano keys. The lights in the panel flashed so quickly, it seemed impossible to match them with the notes. When Cerulean finished, he took a breath and sang a series of seven notes, then repeated them twice to unlock the door.

He looked up at Nathan. "It is open, my friend. Do what you must."

Nathan looked back at Earth Red. Still throbbing like a heart, more surrounding glass squares popped as its twin jagged tentacles reached toward the other worlds. He set one foot in the viscous liquid and turned to sidestep down the stairs. As he descended, Cerulean and Amber turned their backs and stood hand in hand, guarding the entry. A few white-haired heads appeared in the misty distance, but they ventured no closer.

Without a word, his mother and Kelly followed, his mother now carrying the violin. Soon, he walked in darkness, but having traveled this path a few times, he could easily navigate its rocky floor even without a light. Still, sidestepping with a dead girl's body in his arms made for slow going in this steep stairway. He didn't want to scrape her extremities on the walls. Even in death, every hair on her head seemed sacred.

"Mom," he called. "We'll be at the next door in a few seconds. Did you get the notes?"

"Yes, Son. A string on your violin is missing, but I can manage with three."

Nathan slowed his pace. Although the dark corridor revealed nothing, he sensed the door's looming presence. "We're here. Go ahead and play it."

He felt her body squeeze between him and the wall. Seconds later, seven lovely notes lilted in front of him, then repeated twice to complete the key. As before, a glow appeared around the rectangular doorway and ate away at the edges. Soon, light from the chasm shone into the corridor and washed over the statuesque violinist, still poised in playing position, the very same pose her younger twin had taken not long ago.

She looked down into the void. Rumbling thunder erupted from below, making the corridor shake. As Nathan leaned against one of the walls to keep his balance, his mother hummed a tune. "I hear a song," she said. "It is as if Sarah is singing to us in the midst of her groanings."

"Sarah?" Nathan slid close to the precipice. "Is she a real person?"

"I don't know. I call her Sarah only because others have. There are many mysteries yet to solve."

He leaned out. As another rumble of thunder sounded, a dim red glow arose from the yawning chasm, mixing in with the varied light rays coming from the outer walls. As he pictured himself throwing Scarlet into the void and watching her helpless body plunge into darkness, nausea curdled his stomach. He looked into his mother's eyes. She seemed ready to speak, but he quickly looked away. He wanted to cry out to her for help, but that time had passed. He had to do this himself.

As if reading his mind once again, Kelly drew close and whispered. "You need to hear what Sarah has to say."

She cleared her throat and sang, her words flowing in a rhythmic cadence, strong and clear.

The womb of Sarah sings a prayer;
She begs for children in her care.

For now 'tis time to pay the price,
A daughter born to sacrifice.

Beloved son of gifted birth,
A scarlet child of scarlet earth,
You hold her body in your grasp,
Another dome, another clasp.

O man of sorrows, gallant knight,
Whose heart doth quake at such a plight;
Release this child of sorrows nigh,
Then "free at last" will be her cry.

When she finished, she sniffed and wiped her nose, but spoke no more. Nathan's mother, too, stayed silent. In the wash of Sarah's glow, they just looked at him with sad faces.

He lifted Scarlet's body closer. The red light rained over her lovely face and painted her lips and cheeks with a crimson blush. Even in death she emanated youthful innocence, pure love, and the radiance that only the passion of sacrifice can generate.

Sarah's Womb rumbled once again. Nathan kissed Scarlet's cheek, then, rocking her body back once, threw her into the chasm.

He dropped to his knees and watched. As her tiny form shrank, her arms and legs flew about, and her dress flapped in the breeze. Her hand brushed one of the violin strings as she plummeted past. A loud note thrummed in response. Then, as Scarlet's body melded with the red glow and disappeared, the note deepened and grew louder.

The corridor shook once again. Nathan lost his balance and tipped over the ledge. A hand grabbed each arm and yanked him to safety. He toppled back to the stairs, smacking his elbows. As the two hands, his mother's and Kelly's, reached for him again, he shook his head. "I'm okay." The trembling stopped. The tension in the air eased. Apparently, Scarlet's sacrifice worked. He took a deep breath, closing his eyes for a moment to hold back a surge of tears. "Let's just get out of here."

He turned over, pushed up with his arms, and leaped to his feet. Climbing backwards for a moment, he watched the ladies follow, their tired bodies struggling up the stairs as the faint red glow framed them in scarlet. He turned and walked forward. Even the color was now painful. For the rest of his life the color red would remind him of this tragic day.

As the thrumming note continued to sound, Kelly interpreted, trying to keep the rhythm in spite of her heavy breathing.

> *I'm free at last! Let all rejoice!*
> *O raise your head! O lift your voice!*
> *Let angels sing, let earth agree,*
> *Imprisoned billions now set free!*

The ground trembled again but this time as if settling rather than breaking apart. Nathan maintained a steady pace, not wanting the song to end too soon. Kelly continued.

> *Beloved Nathan, son of song,*
> *You broke my chains, made right the wrong.*
> *I asked for rescue, begged for air.*
> *You saved my soul from Mictar's lair.*
>
> *So now I leave a gift sublime,*
> *The poet's flair for words and rhyme;*
> *A smell, a taste, you'll know I'm near;*
> *Unbidden words will soon appear.*

Kelly's voice had weakened. Nathan turned back and signaled a rest. Kelly nodded, leaned against the trembling walls, and sang on. Now able to concentrate, her voice strengthened again.

> *And then another gift I'll bring*
> *To add to hymns your heart will sing;*

For songs of love deserve reply,
A dance that lasts until you die.

A day will come when love mature
Will take the hand of one made pure
In everlasting song and dance,
A knight, a lady, sweet romance.

A hint of a smile graced Kelly's lips. Tears flowed. Gazing at Nathan, she reached out her hand. He took it and drew close, listening carefully as her voice waned.

What once was scarlet ... now is white,
A dove redeemed ... her plumage bright,
With feathers spotless ... fresh, renewed,
Restored, untouched, no stain imbued.

Kelly shook so hard she could barely speak. With tears flowing, she closed her eyes as the dying tone of the strummed violin breezed past. Her voice warped, and she sang like a wounded songbird, faltering at almost every word.

And ne'er ... forget ... my love, my life,
As you caress ... your lovely wife,
While you enjoy ... her lasting bliss,

She opened her eyes and looked at Nathan again. Pure love flowed from her beautiful brown eyes as she finished.

Remember Scarlet's dying kiss.

Nathan took in a deep breath, savoring every word. He licked his lips, tasting the familiar flavor of Scarlet's lasting presence and enjoying the aroma of fresh roses as it tickled his nostrils. A thousand words sprang to his mind, a song that begged to be sung, but it would have to wait for the right time, the right place. For now, they had to hurry back to the upper floor. The other two supplicants were waiting.

He pulled Kelly to his side, and the two climbed the rest of the way, arm in arm. When they reached the top, they crouched together under the glass door. Nathan looked back at his mother. What would she think of his closeness to this girl she barely knew?

His mother smiled. "Your eyes reveal your thoughts, my son." As she lifted the violin and bow, she added, "We will talk later. For now, enjoy every pure touch of friendship that God grants to us. We need the strength it provides."

She played the seven notes three times. Nathan pushed through the glass and began rising to his feet until his head emerged into the upper chamber. When he stepped to solid ground, he looked back. His mother had taken Kelly's hand, and the two of them pushed up through the doorway together. Kelly's face, though flushed and tear-streaked, beamed like the sun itself.

Cerulean twisted in their direction, still in a guardian stance with Amber. "It seems that the stalkers are assembling deep within the mist," he said. "I fear that they are preparing for an attack."

20

A KNIGHT AND A LADY

With Cerulean and Amber following, Nathan led his mother and Kelly out of the floor panel area and toward the exit to the misty hall. "Think we can sneak past them and make it to the exit?" Nathan asked.

Cerulean peered through the mist. "It is not likely. They are adept at —"

A loud thump sounded from behind them. Dragging Abodah's by her hair, Mictar shuffled across the circle where Scarlet's dome once stood. Dozens of deep scratches marred his face. Blood dripped from his chin down to his shirt.

He jerked Abodah's body forward and slid her toward them. She came to a stop next to Amber's bare feet, her loose limbs flopping like a rag doll's. Gasping for breath, Mictar pointed at Nathan. "I will not be beaten so easily, fiddle boy. Lucifer merely needs refueling. You have done nothing to destroy its potential."

Cerulean took a step toward Mictar and pointed at the glass squares behind Scarlet's circle. "You fool! You are already beaten. One of the worlds you wanted to enslave has been set free."

Nathan looked at the wall. He had forgotten to check on what Scarlet's entry into Sarah's Womb had accomplished. As if slung away by a catapult, the image of Earth Red shrank, now the size of a baseball and getting smaller. The jagged channels leading to the other two earths had shriveled and were drawing back.

"Who is the fool?" Mictar countered. "You have pronounced your own death sentence. Now the Earth Red refugees can see what must be done to save the other worlds. It seems that the deaths of the supplicants will free the other earths."

Cerulean ripped open his shirt, revealing a pulsing heart within a dark void. With every beat, a blue glow radiated from his chest. "I am ready to die. Are you?"

When Amber began unbuttoning her dress, Mictar waved his hand at her. "Oh, stop the dramatics! You supplicants always think you're actors on a stage."

Amber refastened her top button and took Cerulean's hand. "We project the reality within us," she said, "without shadow, without shield. There is no guile in our words."

"While you," Cerulean added, pointing at Mictar, "brew deception in every word you speak. My offer to die is unmixed truth, and I make no apologies for my dramatic flair."

With a flippant wave of his hand, Mictar gestured toward the image of Earth Blue, now covered with clouds of green haze and bombarded with channels streaking across from Earth Yellow. "For whom will you die? The gifted ones on your planet are all dead. What hand will draw out your healing energy and transfer it to a new host? Who will cast your body into Sarah's Womb?"

Cerulean glanced at Amber, then at Nathan and the others. He seemed unable to reply.

Flexing his hand in and out of a fist, Nathan also felt at a loss for an answer. Finally, he stared at Mictar again and sharpened his tone. "The abode of the lambs is not for the wolves to know. We will keep our own counsel." He closed his mouth abruptly. Where did those words come from? Licking his lips, he again tasted Scarlet's presence. Obviously, the girl with the rose-petal scent had risen to speak in his stead.

"Bah!" Mictar waved a hand at him. "You don't fool me for a second. You have no idea how to save the other two worlds." He nodded at the exit door. "Or yourselves."

Looking that way, Nathan spied two of the white-haired singers, one at each side of the door. With sonic paralyzers drawn, they locked their stares straight ahead. At least fifteen others appeared out of the mist and marched toward them, spreading out into a horizontal line as they approached, each one with a paralyzer in hand.

When they came within twenty feet, they straightened their line and formed a semicircle that blocked the way to the exit door. Once in place, they stopped and held out their rods, like soldiers waiting for a command. Although their erect bodies seemed disciplined and ready, fear streaked their faces as their gazes locked on the two surviving supplicants.

"Now," Mictar said, waving his hand at his soldiers, "we shall see who is ready to die."

As if turned on by a single switch, the sonic paralyzers flashed light from their ends, some red, some yellow, some blue. A squealing note erupted from each one, loud and piercing.

Nathan slapped his hands over his ears. Agony throttled his brain. Dropping to her knees, Kelly did the same, arching her body over the mirror square, now on the floor. Nathan's mother bent at the waist and groaned, also covering her ears.

Cerulean and Amber spread out their arms. Cerulean took in a deep breath and sang a long bass note. Amber blended in a higher pitch, an alto that trilled more beautifully than any songbird. The supplicants' music seemed to repel the paralyzing noise, but how long could they keep it up?

The stalkers' line fractured. At least five backed away a step. Some held their rods with jittery arms while others placed a hand over one ear.

"Cowards!" Mictar screamed. "Two supplicants cannot overcome eighteen stalkers!" Yet Mictar came no closer. He circled around Nathan, keeping plenty of space between himself and the supplicants. Shouting to overcome the battling tones, he pointed at Nathan. "We are at an impasse again, son of Solomon. Your father would be proud. If you could find him, I'm sure he would tell you so."

Nathan lowered his arms and clenched the fingers of his less-injured hand into a fist. "What do you want now? Scarlet's dead."

"I still want the mirror." He shifted his finger toward the spot where Scarlet once sat imprisoned. "And now that she is gone, I will be able to use it without restriction."

As Kelly rose to her feet, she handed Nathan the mirror. "Does it still have power?" she whispered.

"I don't know, and I'm not sure if he knows, either."

"He's no idiot," Kelly said. "We shouldn't let him have it."

"If you give it to me," Mictar continued, "I will not only tell you where your father is, I will release all of you, including the two supplicants. Your father is alive and quite well, but he won't be for long." He waved a hand at the stalkers. They turned off their sonic rods and drew back a few paces.

Cerulean and Amber stopped singing, both breathless. Amber coughed, while Cerulean clutched his chest, still keeping an eye on Mictar.

As complete silence descended on the room, Mictar eased closer to Nathan. "What do you say? Will you accept freedom and full restoration of your family, all for the price of a square of glass?"

Nathan looked at the mirror. The surface reflected nothing. Perfectly transparent, it showed blackness tinged with a vague red glow. Shifting to his mother, he searched her eyes for an answer. "Any advice?"

She squeezed his shoulder. "If we could be sure he is telling the truth, we could give him what he wants. Regaining your father is worth far more than losing the mirror. No matter what he is able to do with it, I trust that your father will be able to counter it."

"If he's telling the truth?" Nathan laughed under his breath. "The lambs should never trust the wolf when he speaks." As verses of lyrical beauty rushed through his mind, an idea formulated. Was Scarlet helping him decide? If so, the idea was certainly in keeping with her sacrificial character.

Watching Mictar out of the corner of his eye, he turned to Kelly. "If I can clear the way to the exit door, do you think you can get Mom and the supplicants to Earth Blue?"

She nodded. "But I told you, I'm not leaving your side, not for a minute."

He lowered his voice to a soft whisper. "Kelly, you have to. We're all making sacrifices, right?"

She returned a shallow nod.

"Then trust me. If this works, it might take quite a bit more than a minute."

"I trust you," she said as she gazed into his eyes. "More than ever."

With the mirror tucked under his arm, he walked toward Mictar. "Tell us where my father is, and let them go. And you have to let them take Abodah's body, too. I'll stay here with the mirror as a pledge until they're safely on their way."

Mictar stared at him for a moment, raising one eyebrow. "You make a solemn promise to give me the mirror?"

"I do."

Mictar laughed. "It is so easy dealing with humans who choose to bind themselves with codes of honor. They are fools to give up the arsenal of deception."

"Stop babbling, Mictar." Nathan lifted the mirror high. "Are you going to take my offer, or not?"

"I accept. You will find your father in the dreamlands of Earth Yellow. Amber knows how to get there."

Nathan turned to Amber. "Is that true?"

She knitted her brow. "I have seen a man there who resembles you, but he was unresponsive. Alive, to be sure, but I could not revive him. I had no way to pull him out of the dreamlands, so I left him there. We would have to go there physically to make a bridge of escape."

"And can you do that?" Nathan asked.

She gave him a firm nod. "I can."

He looked at Cerulean. "Can you take us to the dreamlands of Earth Blue?"

"Certainly. Why do you ask?"

"A friend of mine named Jack is there. After I find my father, we have to rescue him, too." Nathan kissed his mother on the cheek. "Go. Kelly will show you the way."

She raised a finger, apparently ready to protest, but she lowered it and nodded. "I trust that you know what you're doing, Nathan."

Cerulean scooped up Abodah's body and led Kelly, Amber, and Nathan's mother toward the door. The stalkers parted down the middle, giving them plenty of room to pass. Kelly turned for a moment, pressed her hand against her chest, and then trailed the others as they hurried through the exit at a fast trot.

Nathan couldn't hold back a smile. Kelly's gesture meant, "You're still in my heart. I'll never ask you to leave."

Extending the mirror toward Mictar, he closed the gap between them. "Here it is. I'm keeping my word."

"Of course you are." As soon as Mictar jerked the glass from Nathan's grip, he nodded toward the stalkers. They closed ranks and blocked the path toward the exit. Mictar laughed, making his ponytail sway behind his head. "You're a bigger fool than I ever imagined."

Nathan backed away. "I'll use your own question. Who is the fool? The one who sacrifices all he has for the ones he loves, or the power-greedy monster who craves mysteries beyond his understanding?" He nodded at the square. "Go ahead and try to use the mirror. I want to be here to see what happens."

Two stalkers grabbed his arms, one on each side. Nathan struggled, but when one showed him a sonic paralyzer, he settled down. "What's the matter?" Nathan shouted. "Scared of a kid who's smarter than you?"

Mictar waved a hand. "Release him. He is not a threat." Narrowing his eyes, he took a step closer. "Is this a battle of wits, son of Solomon? Are you baiting me to use the mirror because you think it will bring me harm, or are you bluffing, hoping that I will now be fearful of it and not use it?"

"Like I said . . ." Nathan folded his arms across his chest. "We will soon learn who the fool is."

"I see." Mictar set the mirror on the floor and backed away, matching Nathan's distance from its edge. "Let the battle begin."

As Mictar glared at him, Nathan tried to hide a nervous swallow. He had no idea what the mirror would do, so he really wasn't bluffing at all. He just trusted that the plan came to his mind because of Scarlet, so maybe she had something up her sleeve. Then again, maybe not. She was dead and gone. His idea might be nothing but vain hope in a phantom. Still, no matter what the mirror did, at least his mom and the others were getting more time to escape. He cleared his throat and tried to summon an icy stare. "What are the rules?"

"Very simple. I believe the mirror is a window that is energized by spiritual power, and the catalyst is music. The dark energy I can create will make the mirror into a portal through which I can reach and gather all the life energy I want. I will feed on hundreds of eyes and build the Lucifer machine without the need of transforming the supplicants' energy or even traveling to your worlds. It is now clear to me that the power called Quattro was actually Scarlet using her sorcery through that dimensional corridor." He pointed at the mirror. "The danger is that if Scarlet's spirit still resides within, and I cannot reach her body, her power would likely kill me. But if I shattered the mirror, I would destroy her soul and lose a powerful device for my future plans.

"Now, the choice is up to you. If you pick it up, my people will attack you. If Scarlet is in the mirror, she will come to your defense, and you can easily defeat them and escape. If she is not there, my people will kill you. On the other hand, if you leave the mirror with me, I will let you walk out of here to join your friends. If Scarlet is not within, I will kill hundreds, perhaps thousands of people with it. If she is, then she will destroy me, my brother will help you heal the wounds, and all your problems will be over."

Nathan stared at the mirror. What should he do? Scarlet was within him now, wasn't she? So if he took the mirror, the stalkers would kill him, and if he left it behind, Mictar would use it to murder countless people. So there really wasn't any choice. He would just have to trust Scarlet. "Let me get this straight. You're saying I can do whatever I want with the mirror, right?"

"Correct. Make your choice now. I don't have time for dawdling."

Nathan walked straight to the mirror, picked it up, and charged toward Mictar. He reared back and swung it at the stalker's face as hard as he could. The edge caught Mictar square in the cheek, cut through his nose, and came out the other side. With a return swing, Nathan bashed Mictar in the head with the flat of the mirror, smashing the glass into hundreds of sparkling shards.

He kicked some of the shards at Mictar. "How's that for a battle of wits?"

Bleeding profusely, Mictar toppled over and landed face first on the floor. Instantly, the ear-crushing sound of sonic paralyzers filled the air.

Nathan cringed. He had to fight the ear-splitting pain, but how? Could Scarlet help him?

A stream of words ran through his mind, song lyrics. Then a shout punctuated the final line. *Run!* Nathan tensed his muscles and sprinted toward the line of stalkers. He sang the lyrics, but Scarlet's voice burst from his throat.

Begone you stalkers of the night!
And flee the wrath that gives you flight.

The white-haired soldiers scattered, some dropping their rods as they dashed into the mist. Nathan zoomed out the exit door, cut through the cloudbank, and burst into the open on the glassy walkway between rising columns of mist.

Puffing as he ran, he smiled. Even without the mirror in his grasp, Scarlet had again been his supplicant.

Well ahead, something came into sight, four human shapes, fuzzy in the vapor-rich air. One carried a load, obviously Cerulean with Abodah draped over his arms. Soon, Kelly's frame came into view, staring at a watch on her wrist.

"I'm late," he said, breathing heavily as he came to a stop. "I'm sorry."

She took his hand. "I'm just glad you made it." A sad smile emerged as she added, "My beloved."

He gazed at their hands. She held only the ends of his fingers, keeping her grip away from the worst part of his wounds. Now it seemed as if he could read *her* mind. The touch communicated more than a mere welcome; she was sad about Scarlet's death, too. The "beloved" comment wasn't a romantic overture at all; Kelly was telling him that she would be his supplicant if she were able. She would do whatever it took to save his life, even at the cost of her own.

"Did you give him the mirror?" his mother asked.

He tried to smile, but the effort was just too much. "I gave it to him. I don't think he'll be bothering us anytime soon."

The expressions on his mother's and Kelly's faces told him that they understood well enough.

Cerulean shifted Abodah higher. "What do we do with our friend?"

"Is she dead?" Nathan asked.

The blue-eyed supplicant nodded sadly. "A traitor to her people, yet a savior for worlds she has never seen."

"I will take her," a new voice said.

Nathan spun toward the sound. It came from behind the misty wall in the direction opposite the stalkers' chamber. A tall white-haired man strode out from the cloud—Patar, his face grimmer than usual. As he approached, he extended his arms, making a cradle. "I can see my brother's handiwork," he said, his eyes fiery red. "Yet it seems that you have escaped his wrath."

As Cerulean passed Abodah's body to Patar, a dozen conflicting thoughts rushed through Nathan's brain—anger, sadness, revenge, bitterness, sympathy—all pushing through to be spoken, but, although this was the same man who insisted that he kill Scarlet, he couldn't bear to say anything harsh. As the scent of roses again invigorated his mind, he nodded at Patar. "You have lost a mate. I have lost a beloved friend. I pray that their sacrifices will never be forgotten by the worlds they died to rescue."

"Well spoken, son of Solomon." A hint of wetness glinted in Patar's eyes. "You likely have little time to spare. Since the portal window is not set to a specific destination, you will need to be anointed. Then, you must go at once."

Cerulean leaned over the edge of the walkway on the opposite side of the portal chasm and scooped mist into his cupped hands. He straightened and extended his arms toward Nathan. "This will mark you for travel to Earth Blue," Cerulean said.

Nathan dipped his finger into the mist and dabbed his forehead with the wetness. When everyone had been anointed, he grasped his mother's hand, then Kelly's, ignoring the pain. Turning back to Patar, he said, "Will I see you again?"

"It depends. You have seen for yourself the results of my counsel. You know what I expect you to do."

Nathan looked at the two remaining supplicants. Amber, every bit as lovely and mysterious as Scarlet, caught his gaze. She folded her hands in front of her waist and gave him a smile that could melt the coldest heart. Cerulean's sapphire eyes sparkled. Somehow they revealed his spirit—as deep as Sarah's Womb, as honest as Scarlet's songs, and as selfless as Abodah's life-giving sacrifice.

Turning back to Patar, Nathan gave him a nod. "Yeah. I know what you expect. But I'm going to do everything I can to find another way."

"Then you will likely see me again, son of Solomon." Without another word, Patar turned and walked away in the direction he had come.

As the tall stalker blended into the mist, a gentle pull turned Nathan toward his mother. She raised his hand to her lips. Then, with a gentle kiss, she bathed his knuckles with her warm, moist breath. "There is a new song in your heart, my son. I'm looking forward to seeing it lived out in our next journey."

Holding a crippled violin and a bow with several hairs flying loose, she gazed at him, her raven locks a frizzy mop, her skin pale and smudged, and her eyes sparkling with love. She no longer looked like the greatest violinist in the world. For now, the virtuoso performer had left the stage, and his loving mother had joined him in the audience.

He shifted his gaze to Kelly. With blood staining most of the front of her sweatshirt, obscuring the fierce cardinal logo across her chest, she was the image of the ultimate sacrificial lamb, and at the same time, a lion with a ferocious bite. Yet she was even more than that. In the beauty of undying, unquestioned love, she was like Scarlet in so many ways. Even better.

Now trembling, he edged toward the precipice, still holding his mother's and Kelly's hands. "Let's go."

The trio leaped into the void. As Nathan looked back, Cerulean and Amber followed. Darkness swallowed his vision, but soon a blue path formed, a ribbon of light that guided their fall. The light split into hundreds of colors and painted a familiar scene, his bedroom on Earth Blue, still strewn with mattress padding and pieces of the broken desk. His mother and Kelly materialized at his side, then Cerulean and Amber.

Cerulean's body carried a thin, blue aura, as though he were coated with phosphorescent paint. Amber's complexion, however, seemed normal for a fair-skinned blonde, though her hair and eyes glowed as if bathed in golden sunlight.

The matrix of mirrors still covered the wall, reflecting everyone in the room. Kelly shuffled toward it. Her injured shoulder drooped as she blinked at the images of three weary interdimensional travelers and two radiant supplicants. "What now?" she asked.

Nathan looked at Amber. "How do we get to the Earth Yellow dreamlands?"

The petite girl glided forward. Her smooth steps carried her body like a princess, though her simple garments labeled her a pauper. "First we must get to the people for whom I supplicate. Then we will have to locate a portal viewer there, one that belongs to the Earth Yellow realm."

"A portal viewer?" Kelly repeated.

Amber touched one of the mirror squares on the wall. "The device you call a Quattro mirror. When we obtain it, I will tell you what we must do, but we will have to find the gifted one born on Earth Yellow. The one for whom I supplicate is accustomed to exploring dreams, so she is ready and able to help us."

"Do you mean Francesca?" Nathan asked.

Amber glided back to him, smiling as she caressed his mother's cheek. "Yes, my beloved Francesca, the Earth Yellow counterpart of this beautiful lady, is the gifted one."

Nathan smiled. "We spent quite a bit of time with her, Mom. I didn't know you had so much spunk when you were younger."

"Spunk?" She laughed. "Maybe I've grown old too fast. I think I need to show my son a little more of my old self." She delivered a mock punch to his cheek. "If it's spunk you want, it's spunk you'll get, especially since we might have to move heaven and two or three earths to find my husband."

Nathan winked and pulled out Nathan Blue's cell phone. "We'd better get going."

"Calling Daryl?" Kelly asked.

"If she's still there." He read the display. The phone had service, but just barely. With Earth Blue in chaos, they were lucky to get anything, and with Earth Red getting set free from interfinity's grasp, who could tell if they'd ever be able to find a portal that led home? Maybe Daryl would know what had happened while they were gone.

He pushed a speed dial and waited. After two rings a stressed-out voice answered. "Nathan! Where have you been? Do you have any idea what's been going on here?"

"Uh ... not really. But we managed to save the world."

"Not this one, honey. It's snowing in the Congo, a hurricane struck Antarctica, and the Mississippi River is jammed with ice from Minneapolis to New Orleans. We might be getting Earth Yellow's weather, but we're getting it in all the wrong places. And Tony says Earth Yellow is in chaos, too. He—"

"Tell me later. Listen, are you still in touch with Earth Red?"

Daryl groaned. "That's another problem. We have radio telescope contact, but no visual. The frequency has been changing, but it was slow enough for Dr. Gordon and me to keep up with it. Everything's peachy now on Earth Red, but I think we're drifting apart."

"Is it still possible to get home? Earth Yellow is our first stop, but we have to be sure we can make the jump when we get done."

Daryl's voice crackled. The connection was fading. "Maybe, but we might need to click Dorothy's ruby slippers together to make it work. Dr. Gordon and I will experiment. We'll try to come up with something by the time you get here."

"Well, you don't have to worry about Mictar for a while. Scarlet and I kicked his tail back in the misty world, so the local brain trust should have clear sailing. At least you can be glad of that."

"Glad? Great! Just what I need, Pollyanna, high on testosterone. If you could beam up Mr. Spock instead, I'd appreciate it."

Nathan grinned. "We don't need a Vulcan to solve the problem. If anyone can figure it out, you can."

"Thanks, Captain Kirk. Don't forget your buddies back home."

"You should hear from us soon. Everything happens so fast on Earth Yellow, maybe it'll only be a few minutes for you."

Nathan slapped the phone closed and looked at his traveling companions. Light from the window shrouded all four in the failing glow of sunset. His mother sat on the mattress with Kelly, stretching back her sweatshirt and peeling away her blood-soaked bandage. The violin and bow lay near their feet, another casualty of their many skirmishes. Cerulean and Amber whispered to one another, their eyes shining brighter than ever before.

Kelly looked up at Nathan, smiling through her wincing face. With her hair in disarray, a gash still marking her brow, and blood splattered from her chin down to her hands, she was a mess . . . a beautiful mess.

Nathan's lips trembled, but he managed to return her smile.

As he stooped to pick up the violin, the scent of roses again washed over his senses. He leaned close to Kelly, close enough to hear her pain-filled, shallow breaths, and whisper-sang Scarlet's prophetic good-bye.

> *A day will come when love mature*
> *Will take the hand of one made pure*
> *In everlasting song and dance,*
> *A knight, a lady, sweet romance.*

When he finished the song, he touched her bloodstained cheek, still whispering. "How long can your lonely heart wait?"

Kelly laid her hand over his, tears sparkling in her glazed eyes. "As long as it takes, Nathan Shepherd. As long as it takes."

Read chapter 1 of *Nightmare's Edge*,
Book 3 in the
Echoes from the Edge series.

1

WAKING UP THE DEAD

Nathan ducked under a low-hanging branch and pushed a dangling python out of the way with his bandaged hand. The snake hissed, startling him for a moment. With its beady eyes and flicking tongue, it seemed so real, as did everything else in this dim jungle.

Yet, Cerulean, the blue-haired, blue-skinned, blue-everything young man who marched ahead on the narrow path, paid no attention. After all, if this place was a realm of dreams, even the forest was imaginary. Still, with the thick green foliage of overarching trees darkening their steps in deep shadows, and high humidity dampening Nathan's armpits, every detail painted a three-dimensional portrait that felt as real as it looked.

He pulled off his sweatshirt and tied the sleeves around his waist, looking from side to side. With just a slender candle in Cerulean's grip lighting their way, how could two awake people know how to find another one of their kind in this dark land, especially since the images conjured by frightened sleepers seemed as real as their own skin and clothing?

Nathan wiped his brow and hurried to catch up with Cerulean, Earth Blue's supplicant from the misty world. Keeping his eyes focused straight ahead and the white candle out in front, Cerulean stayed quiet. Nothing seemed to faze him. Earlier, he had ignored the twelve talking chipmunks dressed in purple tuxedos. Nathan thought they had been funny at first, chattering about their political ambitions and the proper way to shave an elephant, but when a six-foot-tall electric razor buzzed into the forest, Nathan dove out of the way. The razor flew past, chasing a three-headed elephant into the forest. Cerulean merely helped him back to his feet and pressed on.

"So," Nathan said as they marched past an old man wrapped in golden chains floundering in a quicksand bog, "this dream world really isn't all that dangerous once you get used to it. Why did you insist on just the two of us going? What's the risk?"

Cerulean didn't even blink. "Not everything is a dream. Jack is here somewhere, is he not?"

"True. But what other real things could enter this world? No one else knows how to get here in real life. Even you had to get Kelly to go to sleep to create a portal. "

"When there are no wounds in the cosmic fabric, the dream world can be penetrated only by a supplicant or through a person's sleeping mind. With interfinity at hand, however, and many holes throughout the cross-dimensional plane, I suspect that passages abound."

"How can you tell the difference?" Nathan asked. "I mean, if that poor guy in the quicksand was real, shouldn't we try to rescue him?"

Cerulean smiled, finally breaking his stoic countenance. "As the elephant has taught you, dreams are as real as you allow them to be. Once you train your mind, you will see through them. The imagined elements in the dreamscape are transparent, and whatever is left is reality." He nodded at the path. "Come. Kelly's dream has now formed in her mind. Since she sleeps at the edge of a cosmic wound, that will be the best place to look for Jack."

Nathan followed Cerulean's lively pace. "Whose dream are we in now?" Nathan asked.

"A mixture of several." As Cerulean passed by a leafy vine that hung from a branch, he gave it a shove, making it swing. "This jungle is a dream setting for all souls who feel lost. They struggle through vines, snakes, quicksand, and many other obstacles of their own making, thus illustrating their lives of desperation. I thought perhaps it would make sense to search here while we waited for Kelly to dream. Even though he is blind, Jack might have found his way here."

"Sounds reasonable," Nathan said, "at least as dreams go."

While following a meandering path for several minutes, they entered a suburban neighborhood, shaded by thundering storm clouds overhead. Now walking on rubberized streets, they passed a headless woman on a bicycle who was trying to find a place to insert her iPod earbuds. In front of a mansion-like house on a perfectly manicured lawn, a man in a clown costume juggled a woman, three children, and a briefcase. As if on a treadmill, he ran in place, huffing and puffing, but getting nowhere.

Nathan stared at them, knowing they couldn't possibly be real. When they faded into ghostlike images, he shuddered. This was just too weird.

With each change of scenery, they passed through a soft membrane, a dry, gelatin-like substance, about ten feet thick, that sent a buzzing sensation across Nathan's skin. The transparent wall raised a tickle for a few moments, but it seemed harmless. During each passage, a precipice appeared on his left, and a vague pull forced him to lean to the right to keep from walking over the side and into a dark void. It obviously marked a boundary of some kind. Could it be the wall between different dreams? Alternate realities that a dreamer could visit?

After a brief walk through a desert, they penetrated a membrane for the third time. He slowed his pace for a moment, allowing his eyes to adjust. It seemed that ribbons of light swirled into the void from every direction, as if it were a drain. The pull seemed harder than ever, but not unbearable. Yet, Cerulean seemed oblivious to it. A strange sound emanated from the depths, like a song—a soft, familiar song. Nathan craned his neck, listening. Could it be? Yes, it sounded like someone humming "Be Thou My Vision."

"What's that dark place?" he asked.

Cerulean paused and looked that way. "The void. This world of visions surrounds it. Every dream eventually crumbles and is pulled in there."

"Why is it pulling me? I'm not part of a dream."

Cerulean jerked his head toward Nathan. "The void affects you?"

Nathan gave him a half nod, unsure if he should be admitting it. "Is that bad?"

"I am not sure." Cerulean stared for a long moment, then marched on.

Nathan followed. Should he ask about the humming? Cerulean seemed to be worried about something, and in a hurry. It would be better not to slow him down.

Soon, they entered the darkest place yet, a cemetery with old tombstones rising at odd angles from grave plots. Bones littered the weed-infested grounds. Gnarled oak trees with hanging moss painted twisted shadows on the winding path that coursed through the abandoned yard. A large raven perched atop one of the burial markers, staring at Nathan as he passed by.

"Inscription," it croaked. "Read. Read."

Nathan paused and leaned closer. "You mean on the tombstone?"

"Yes! Read! Read!"

Cerulean grabbed his arm. "No. It is not wise to heed the words of the dream creatures."

"But if they're not real, what could it hurt?"

His bright blues eyes sparkling in the candle's glow, Cerulean inhaled deeply. "A vision stalker is close. I fear that he has manipulated the environment, and our safety may very well be compromised."

"Just reading the tombstone won't hurt." Nathan took the candle and shuffled to the side of the grave. With the raven still leering at him, he held the flame close to the stone. The inscription, spelled out in deeply etched block letters, read, "Here lies Kelly Clark, murdered in her sleep by Nathan Shepherd. Even now she is unable to rest in peace as her killer shines a light over her bed."

"What?" Nathan slid back. "How could a tombstone know I'm here?"

Cerulean stared at the raven. "Three possibilities. Kelly sees us in her dream, so she created the inscription even as you drew close. Yet, I think that is unlikely since she doesn't see you as a threat to her life. Still, stranger things do happen in dreams. Second, a stalker could have manipulated this place, and he is trying to intimidate you to keep you from proceeding. Third, and perhaps the most dangerous of all, is the possibility that you are becoming part of the dreamscape."

"How is that possible?"

"Amber spoke of this when she heard about Jack's entry. If Patar sent Jack here to keep him alive, then he likely expected the poor man to become part of the dream world, a living phantom who wanders in people's nightmares. He would be alive, yes, but only Patar would know how to extract him without killing him."

Nathan pointed at himself. "Then can I leave safely? I mean, I'm not becoming part of this place yet, am I?"

Fixing his gaze on Nathan, Cerulean shook his head. "You

appear solid, so one of the other two options is more likely. I suspect that a vision stalker is present."

Nathan peered behind the tombstone, but nothing was there. "Who? Mictar?"

"He would be powerful enough." Cerulean took a quick step and grabbed the raven by the throat. It choked out a squawk and flailed its wings under the supplicant's grip, vainly trying to claw his arm. "Where is your master?"

"New inscription," it croaked again. "Read!"

Cerulean shook its body. "You have a voice. Tell me who sent you."

"Read! Read!" The raven broke free and in a scattering of feathers flew into the darkness above.

As a black pinion floated to the ground, Cerulean took the candle back from Nathan. "Come. We must hurry. The longer we stay here, the greater the danger."

"Shouldn't we read the inscription again?"

Cerulean held the flame high and wrapped a hand around Nathan's arm. "It is of no consequence. If the message has been written by the stalker, it is likely a lie. If it is a product of Kelly's nightmarish fears, it will only work to heighten your own. And if you are becoming part of this world, deep emotions will only hasten the process."

"Not knowing will drive me crazy." Nathan squinted at the tombstone, but it was too dark to read. "Taking a second won't hurt."

Cerulean held fast. "The risk is too high. Your uncharacteristic insistence demonstrates that the effect this place is having on you is escalating rapidly. You are losing your ability to reason."

"But I have to know." As Nathan pulled against Cerulean's grip, the supplicant's blue hair grew fuzzy, looking like reeds waving under restless waters. "Let me go."

"Nathan!"

The shout sounded like a thunderclap. Nathan spun toward it. Ahead on the path, a man stood with his fists set against his hips. Tall and lean, he appeared to be dangling a plastic bag from his fingers.

Nathan blinked. "Is it Mictar?"

"No," Cerulean said, loosening his grip. "It is Patar."

Patar walked three steps closer and halted. Now about five paces away, his face bent into a deep scowl. "You should not have come here. It is far too dangerous."

Nathan glanced between Patar and the tombstone. He pointed at the inscription. "I have to know what is says. Kelly might be communicating with me."

"As you can see, Cerulean ..." Patar's voice grew distant, warped, as if he were speaking from the midst of a cave. "He is already being absorbed." The stalker's slender form now seemed foggy, distorted, more like a dream than reality.

Cerulean nodded. "I can see that now. He is showing signs of fading."

"I'm fading?" Nathan pointed at Cerulean, then at Patar. "You two are the ghostly looking ones."

"It's only going to get worse," Patar said. "His mental defenses are withering, and Kelly's nightmare is reaching a climax."

A sudden gust of wind blew away a blanket of clouds. A full moon, at least five times its usual size, hovered in a purple sky. Its glow illuminated the cemetery, allowing a clearer view of the dozens of tombstones.

"Shall I take him out immediately," Cerulean asked, "or should I find Jack first?"

A low rumble sounded at Nathan's side. At the gravesite where the raven once perched, a hand pushed out of the earth, then a second hand and a head. Finally, an entire body, short and feminine, climbed up and shook dirt from her shoulder-length hair. She looked straight ahead and called, "Nathan? Are you here?"

"Kelly?" Nathan stared at her. "It really *is* you!"

Wearing a knee-length nightshirt, she brushed off the soil, revealing letters on the front, Sanity Is Overrated. Then, extending her arms, she staggered toward him, feeling for obstacles in her way. "Nathan? Where are you? I hear your voice."

As she drew closer, he stiffened. Kelly had no eyes, only vacant sockets. Could she be the Earth Blue Kelly, somehow resurrected? Or was she Kelly Red, a recent victim of Mictar's cruel electrified hand? Yet, wasn't she just part of a dream? She looked real enough.

Kelly stopped and touched Nathan's cheeks with her cold fingers. "There you are. Why didn't you answer me?" She shivered and rubbed her arms. "I'm cold and scared. Will you get me out of this dark place? I can't see a thing."

Nathan reached for her hand but then jerked back. "You're just a mirage. I can't take you anywhere."

"You are correct." Cerulean lifted his candle higher. "Stay in the light, Nathan. Do not be deceived."

"This is no time for joking around," Kelly said. Bouncing on the toes of her sock-covered feet, she shook harder. "You can't leave me in this horrible place. It's so cold, so terribly cold. Please take me home." She reached out and groped for him. With missing eyes and dirty face, she seemed like a pitiful waif as her voice broke into a lament. "Nathan ... please ... I'm scared."

"I'll get you out." He grabbed her hand. "Just hang on."

Her chilled fingers wrapped around his bandaged palm. She was solid, real, not a hint of fading.

"Oh, thank you." She leaned her head against his shoulder. "I told you never to leave me, not even for a minute. I felt so alone. So scared. I have no idea how all that dirt got on me. It was like I was buried in a grave."

For a moment, dizziness flooded Nathan's mind, but he

shook it off. "Just stay with me. Cerulean will get us out of here."

"Nathan!" Cerulean warned again. "If you continue—"

"Let him go for a moment." His voice fading even further, Patar poured out the contents of his bag into Cerulean's hand. "When I wrestled with my brother, I recovered Jack's eyes from his energy reserves. You will find him approximately one hundred paces ahead. Restore these and get him and Nathan out of here with all speed."

Nathan stared at Cerulean's transparent palm. Two eyeballs lay there, perfectly formed, with nerves and moist tissue attached. Nathan nearly gagged, but he stayed quiet.

"Because Nathan broke the portal mirror," Patar continued, "you will not be able to travel to my world to play the violin at Sarah's Womb, at least not right now. You can, however, travel to Earth Yellow to gather other options."

"Yes," Cerulean replied. "Nathan's mother is playing 'Foundation's Key' as we speak to see which mirror is the correct portal. While we were waiting, we decided to try to find Jack, since he entered the dream world from Earth Blue. I was unsure of how the dreamscape would affect Nathan, so this was a test."

"And he failed, as usual. His desire for revenge against my brother outweighed his wisdom. He had the power to escape with the mirror intact."

"Nathan," Kelly said, her fingers growing warmer within his hand. "Don't let him talk about you like that. You did the best you could. You were under a lot of pressure."

"You're right. I don't know why they're saying those things."

"Then don't listen. We'll find our own way out."

"Go now," Patar said, "before that rotting cadaver becomes more real to him than life itself. He will soon bond with it beyond all hope of reason." With that, Patar faded out of sight.

Cerulean put the eyeballs back into the bag and stuffed

the open edges into his waistband. Then, lifting the candle, he pulled Nathan's arm. "Jack's up ahead. Let's get him and flee this place."

Leading Kelly by the hand, Nathan went along with the pull. He followed Cerulean, now a blue ghost in his sight. "Did you hear that, Kelly? We can follow him. We'll be out of here soon."

"Thank you, Nathan." She staggered along, her empty sockets still wide. "I knew you wouldn't leave me here."

With the moon shining brightly, the going was easier. It took only a few seconds to find Jack sitting on the ground, leaning against a tombstone. Although Cerulean was now as transparent as thinning fog, Jack seemed solid enough.

Running his fingers through his thick beard, Jack looked around with his empty eyes. "Who is here?" he asked.

"He is losing his grip on reality as well," Cerulean said as he crouched next to the tombstone. "I will have to work quickly."

"He looks fine. He's not fading at all." Nathan turned to Kelly. He almost said, "Right, Kelly?" forgetting for a moment that she couldn't see anything. Still, even without her lovely brown eyes, she looked—

"Take this." Cerulean handed Nathan the candle. "Watch me through the flame."

"Oh. Okay." Feeling dizzy again, Nathan held the flame close to his nose and peered around both sides. Cerulean pulled the eyeballs from the bag. Then, singing unintelligible words at a high pitch, he laid his palm over Jack's empty sockets and pushed the eyeballs into place. Keeping his hand there for a moment, he continued singing while blue light seeped around the edges.

With every second, Cerulean grew more solid while Jack stayed the same. Nathan looked back at Kelly. Her face seemed fuzzier, distant. Still holding his bandaged hand, she angled her head as if listening.

"What's happening?" she asked.

"Everything's okay." As he spoke, her features clarified again. "Cerulean is repairing Jack's eyes. We'll leave in a minute."

Nathan turned back to Cerulean, lowering the candle to see him better. Now ghostly blue again, Cerulean helped Jack to his feet.

"Can you see?" Cerulean asked.

"Very well, thank you." Jack pulled a rumpled fedora from beneath his jacket and straightened it out. "I can see everything well, except for you." He put on his hat and turned toward Nathan, his restored eyes glistening. "Nathan! I'm so glad to see you."

"Same here." Nathan gave the candle back to Cerulean and shook Jack's hand with his relatively uninjured left. "Now let's all get out of this place. I have to figure out what happened to Kelly and get some eyes for her, too."

"Nathan." Cerulean pushed the candle closer. "You and Jack will come with me. You must leave Kelly behind."

"What?" Nathan shook his head hard. "I can't leave her here."

Kelly's arm locked around his. "No, Nathan! No!"

Cerulean pulled Jack and Nathan together and held the candle's flame near their eyes. His voice mellowed to a soothing chant. "Stare at the flame. It is the light of reality. The images around you are mere phantoms. Bring what is real back into focus, or you will not return to the ones you love. Nathan, think of your mother. Listen to her music. It is riding the breeze. She waits for you in the Earth Blue bedroom. You must go back and search for your father. The real Kelly is there as well. We must awaken her from this nightmare, so the two of you can go to Earth Yellow and save two world populations from annihilation."

The flame's glow spread over Cerulean's face, making his features clearer by the second. He compressed Nathan's chin with his hand, forcing him to keep his stare locked on the flame. "You must let Kelly go, Nathan. She is not real. Night is over, and dawn is breaking."

"No, Nathan!" Her voice spiked into a wail. "You promised to stay with me. This place is cold and dark, and I'm scared."

Ever so gently, Cerulean pulled on Nathan's chin, drawing him forward, his voice now hypnotizing. "Release her, Nathan. All will be well. You will see the real Kelly in mere moments. We will awaken her, and she will escape this torture."

Heaving and exhaling shallow breaths, Nathan pried Kelly's fingers loose and pulled away.

"Nathan!" she cried. "What are you doing?"

He turned. Kelly, now ghostly and floating backwards, pressed her hands against her cheeks. "I'll be alone again. All alone in this cold, dark place."

"I ... I can't leave her. She's—"

Cerulean twisted him back. His voice sharpened again. "She's ... not ... real!"

His mind now swimming, Nathan repeated the words in a breathy whisper. "She's not real."

Cerulean blew out the candle. As the light faded, Kelly's voice faded with it. "I'm so cold ... so cold."

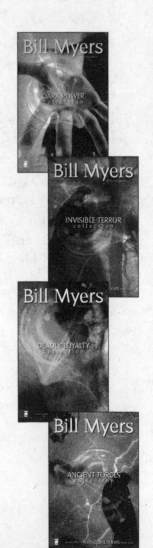

The Shadowside Trilogy by Robert Elmer!

Those who live in lush comfort on the bright side of the small planet Corista have plundered the water resources of Shadowside for centuries, ignoring the existence of Shadowside's inhabitants, who are nothing more than animals. Or so the Brightsiders have been taught. It will take a special young woman to expose the truth—and to help avert the war that is sure to follow—in the exciting Shadowside Trilogy, the latest sci-fi adventure from Robert Elmer.

Trion Rising

Book One

Softcover • ISBN: 978-0-310-71421-7

When the mysterious Jesmet, whom the authorities brand as a Magician of the Old Order, begins to connect with Oriannon, he is banished forever to the shadow side of their planet Corista.

The Owling

Book Two

Softcover • ISBN: 978-0-310-71422-4

Life is turned upside down on Corista for 15-year-old Oriannon and her friends. The planet's axis has shifted, bringing chaos to Brightside and Shadowside. And Jesmet, the music mentor who was executed for saving their lives, is alive and promises them a special power called the Numa—if they'll just wait.

Book 3 coming soon!

Pick up a copy today at your favorite bookstore!

Visit www.zondervan.com/teen